All The Stars In Heaven

A Klondike's Circus Novel

By Nathan Woolford

ISBN: 978-1-917778-53-4

About Nathan

Nathan Woolford is a newspaper journalist, sub-editor and author.

Born and raised in Swindon, Wiltshire, his journalism career began while he was still at school with a weekend job at BBC Wiltshire Sound.

He also wrote articles and features for various local papers and magazines.

Nathan graduated from University College Falmouth with an honours degree in journalism and has worked as a writer and copy editor for more than 20 years.

He is the author of the Klondike's Circus novels, which began in 2022 with Trail Dust.

IS THIS THE END FOR AMERICA'S FAVOURITE CIRCUS?

By Helen Harris, New York Enquirer

The circus world has been in shock this week after the devastating sinking of the Floating Top ocean liner in New York Harbour last Monday.

The vessel was carrying the hugely successful Klondike's Circus back home after a triumphant, all-conquering tour of Europe.

It is still unknown what exactly caused the great freighter to go down in the Atlantic, some three miles off the Staten Island waterfront.

Eyewitnesses say an internal explosion caused the sinking. Others speculate the crew had 'cut corners' for the voyage home, resulting in engine deficiencies that were overlooked.

Whatever caused the colossal collapse, there can be no doubting the magnitude of its significance.

Klondike's Circus, based out of Rio Cristo, northern California, had just completed a whirlwind tour of Europe, playing in London, Paris, Antwerp, Berlin, Geneva and Rome. The final show in Italy made domestic front pages, such was its prestige.

The circus troupe – staff, performers, equipment, stalls, even the tent – were all onboard the Floating Top, a designated 'circus ship'.

Now, owner and manager Kal Klondike has lost the lot, all the kit used in every show, buried at the bottom of the Atlantic, unsalvageable and lost forever.

The catastrophe was not a human tragedy, for miraculously there were no drownings or fatalities of any kind, everybody managing to escape the sinking ship before it was fully submerged.

But for the show's team of horses, there was no such luck. Incredibly, four of the animals managed to free themselves from the ship's stable block thanks to the circus cowboys' quick thinking. But seven horses – in many ways some of the stars of that tour of Europe – all met with the same grisly fate. A watery grave, and a sad, unforgivable end.

The deaths of the horses, the loss of all of the circus equipment and, most emphatically, the destruction of the ship – which had been leased at great expense – have all contributed to the seemingly immediate demise of Klondike's Circus.

New York Harbourmaster Mark Giancarlo was tasked with investigating the devastation. He said last night: "The vessel was a 700-footer. It sunk in just minutes. The mess was horrendous, and my team and others are still retrieving bits of debris from the ocean.

"The cause of the sinking is still unknown. Our investigation will not be concluded for another week or so. Until then, we can only speculate. Multiple sources on the scene have said they heard an explosion. So, we may be dealing with an engine malfunction – or worse. Either way, there is a long way to go until we get any real answers.

"Until then, I am not at liberty to discuss this matter any further. All of our findings will appear in our report."

Just two years ago, Klondike's performers had led the way in the Superstars and Stripes TV spectacular, often hailed as one of the greatest big top productions ever put together. Their tour of Europe was supposed to be the next crowning glory of this entertainment juggernaut.

But now, the whole world has come crashing down for Klondike and co. Indeed, it is hard to see where the famous troupe heads from here.

The accumulated costs from this mess will be enormous, and the publicity after such a horrendous disaster surely unfavourable.

Klondike's Circus had just established itself at the very top of the tree for American travelling shows as the 1960s got under way.

But, alas, Kal Klondike was the captain of a sinking ship. Now, he is under water. And the route to salvation is going to be full of strong currents and angry sharks.

For, right now, that man is in some very deep water,

CHAPTER ONE

They called it Rio Cristo.

A magnificent hidden gem of wondrous natural beauty, hidden among the endless hills and prairies of Marin County.

It sat within a tiny, virtually imperceptible valley, covered almost entirely by grassy peaks and rocky outcroppings. A world within itself, almost entirely hidden from outsiders.

Rio Cristo had been discovered by Oregon Trail pioneers in the 1820s, who had used the site as a temporary shelter, before others who followed in later years built a holding camp, used for supplies and livestock, maintained by western trailblazers for those who followed them to the new states.

The site was later bought out by the US Army, who used it as a garrison and fort. Northern union soldiers trained recruits at the valley before the Civil War, and the garrison was still used as a military base well into the First World War.

Later, the old fort, with its range of support buildings and open land, was purchased by a Napa Valley wine magnate, who used Rio Cristo as a summer vacation spot and getaway snug.

But for the past three years, the hidden valley had been the site of the winter headquarters and holding camp of Klondike's Circus.

The main whitestone building that had stood since the Great War was known as the pavilion, and served as the general headquarters of the circus operation. The supporting log cabins and bungalows provided general lodgings for the staff and performers. And the many other huts and sheds that had once housed military hardware acted as holding bays for midway stalls, ticket booths, confectionary stands and a variety of trucks and assorted machinery used in the everyday operation of running a circus.

Across the grounds, which were covered in oak shavings and gravelled pathways, there was a motorcycle garage, a large stable block and horse corral, miniature performance stages and a seemingly endless colony of trailers.

Ordinarily, at this time of year, the camp would be a vacuum of activity and colour. Many who visited often considered the circus headquarters a portal into another world – where magic and enchantment are commonplace, and where superstars roam. A world of clowns, acrobats, dancers, cowboys and all manner of colourful characters. Those who live only to entertain, their very being a spectacle in itself.

But now, there was only silence and a deep depression across the beloved grounds. The magic was gone.

Where once roustabouts would excitedly roam down the pathways, where clowns would juggle and perform tricks, there was no one. Most poignantly of all, the horse stables and corral were empty.

From a first floor window within the whitestone pavilion, based at the very head of the camp, like a castle overlooking a fortress, a solitary figure surveyed the sombre scene.

Kal Klondike looked down at his empire, one hand on the window pane.

His expression was one of regret, like a farmer looking over a failed crop field.

He was a tall man, with thick, wavy black hair and sideburns. Dark, large eyes sat in a craggy and tanned face, while the lips looked like they had forgotten how to smile. He wore his standard attire of brown leather jacket and dark slacks. His trademark brown fedora sat on a chair beside him.

Klondike merely studied the grounds, seemingly in disgust. He felt like he had aged several years in the past five days. Ever since the disaster in New York.

He closed his eyes. He could still see the panic and hear the screams of fright as his people struggled in the freezing water, fighting to stay alive and afloat. The unfathomable nightmare that had struck his outfit. The screams pierced his dreams in what little sleep he had managed. His legs suddenly went numb as he felt the cold Atlantic water lock his floating body in place.

Then, he saw her in his mind. That haunting wave goodbye. Heard himself scream: "Oh my god…it's Jenny Cross!"

Klondike's eyes snapped open. He shook his head and pulled himself away from the window.

Ruefully, he glanced down at his desk in his sparse office. It was covered in billing sheets. The figures hurt his eyes.

His team had been rescued from the cold waters of the Atlantic by New York harbour staff five days ago. Fished out of the liquid and tossed onto the waterfront. There were various injuries and cases of mild hypothermia.

But everything was gone. The big top itself. Every midway stall, confectionary stand, scaffolding pole… every last piece of equipment used by his circus now sat at the bottom of the ocean.

After the disaster, the entire team had been ferried back across country by the circus's Barrowman Express train. And now, all had returned to their respective quarters at Rio Cristo. Waiting… to hear just what the future would hold.

Klondike suddenly looked up as the door opened quietly, and viewed the welcome sight of Lacey Tanner. With flaming red hair, cinnamon skin and extraordinary violet eyes, she could have passed for a fashion model or movie actress. But Lacey was actually the Klondike's Circus publicity manager, and a vital cog in the running of the operation. Her electrifying press releases and media management were responsible for much of Klondike's success down the years.

Now, dressed in a plain black dress, a far cry from her usual glamorous offerings, she crept in and stood by Klondike, resting a consolatory hand on his shoulder.

"It's almost time, tiger," she whispered.

Klondike shook his head. "What do I tell them? How do I tell them? Where do I even start?"

Lacey glanced down at the raft of bills on the desk. The office was bare of any decoration. Nothing offered any cheer.

"You know," she mused, "it's not all over yet, Kalvin."

He grimaced. "Aw come off it, Lacey. Who you kidding? We can't sugarcoat any of this." He moved back towards the window, glaring out at the camp grounds. "I've got to go out and face them all. And let them crucify me, if that's what they want. I don't deserve anything less."

She frowned. "None of this is your fault, Kalvin."

"That's where you're wrong, smart lady. It's all my fault. All of it. It's me. All me."

She brushed a hand through her hair. "It's so hard to comprehend any of this. Like living through a nightmare."

"I know. I just can't understand… how something so great could become so bad."

Then, she threw herself into him and hugged him tight. He held her back.

"Oh, Kalvin," she whimpered, "how, oh how, did it all come to this?"

She nuzzled her face into his shoulder. He looked up as another figure emerged at the open doorway. A true giant, brawny and dominant-looking, with receding hair and a strangely cherubic face. Henry 'Heavy' Brown. Ringmaster and de facto right-hand man for Klondike, a trusted lieutenant since their childhood together in Hell's Kitchen, New York.

Heavy's face was solemn, as he watched the pair embrace by the window.

Klondike acknowledged him. "It's alright, Heavy."

Lacey pulled back and smiled at the newcomer. There were tears in her eyes.

"I thought I better let you know," Heavy said quietly. "All the guys are gathering by the practice stage at the top. It's almost noon."

"Yeah," Klondike muttered acidly. "I'm just figuring how I'm gunna break this to them."

Heavy looked down. "I think everybody knows."

"Any deserters?"

"I'm afraid so. Some of the roustabouts are gone. The camp staff. I guess they are worried about making their next buck after what happened. So, instead of waiting for an update, they scrammed."

It was silent. The three of them all stared at each other dumbly.

Heavy cleared his throat. "Well…"

Klondike grabbed his hat. His next words were said with a quiet angst.

"Like we just said. It's time."

He led the way out.

They all came out of their lodgings and made their way to the practice stage, in the very centre of the grounds.

A platform made of thick acrylic plastic, the stage was little more than a glorified band stand, with a seating block placed before it for audiences.

But no one was sitting today.

The various performers and staff all slowly made their way down the assorted pathways and gardens to the stage, to await Klondike's big address.

There was no fanfare or excitement this time. Everybody moved like mourners at a state funeral.

At the head of the line was Gino Shapiro. One of the country's premier acrobats and the star of Klondike's Circus, the trapeze artist was known as a flamboyant performer, as charismatic as he was electrifying in the big top's summit. Alongside him was Penny Fortune, his catcher and co-star, a beautiful and talented flyer who had proven to be the great Gino's equal.

Also there was Roddy Olsen, the Puppet Master. The super-talented ventriloquist had been the rising star of the operation, and had become a teen idol and media superstar in the years since his circus debut.

Corky the Clown had walked to the mini-stage with Olsen. A staple of Klondike's Circus since day one, the beloved showman had captivated crowds for years with his juggling and unicycling skills. He led his team of five fellow clowns across the grounds. None wore facepaint or bright clothing. Today, they were just six ordinary guys, bereft of showmanship or humour.

Next came Tip Enqvist and the Daredevils, a team of motorcycle stunt riders whose outrageous Globe of Death routine had become the talk of American circus.

The Range Riders were the circus's cowboy crew, who performed bareback riding and roping tricks to the delight of younger fans.

Then there were the Hightops, a team of female gymnasts who performed daring acrobatic skills, and the Flying Batistas, a family of Mexican acrobats whose speciality act was the human pole.

The Hightops approached the mini-stage along with the Rockin Robins, the circus's team of showgirls. The groups were usually dressed in bright leotards and dazzling dresses. Today, all wore trench coats and slacks, trudging through the camp with dread and disbelief.

Various other performers of all shapes and sizes joined the ensemble. Among them were Gargantua, the human blob, a 500lb behemoth who did handstands and cartwheels.

And Goliath, the 7ft 3in giant who made a living from lifting people above his head. Rumpy Stiltskin, who performed somersaults while walking on six-foot stilts, was unrecognisable as he moved along… on foot.

As they all gathered in the middle of the grounds, an air of disconsolate despair was tangible amidst the group.

At the very back of the ensemble, as if scared to emerge from the trailers and cabins, stood Suzi Dando, the circus songstress. Childlike and elfin in appearance, the youngster looked a picture of pure innocence as she held back, fearful and unstable.

Between them, this almighty team had graced some of the finest stages in America, starred in big-budget extravaganzas and appeared in televised specials and Las Vegas spectaculars. They represented the golden elite in terms of American circus.

But today, here and now, in their home camp of Rio Cristo, collectively they felt like anything but stars.

Their past had been glorious. Their present horrendous. But, worst of all, their future was shrouded in uncertainty.

Now, all stood around that mini-stage at noon. As had been arranged.

And they waited. For the one man responsible for bringing them all together. They did not have to wait long.

"There's no easy way to say any of this. What happened out in New York. What's going to happen to us now. I can't expect any of you guys to understand it. Hell, I don't even understand it myself."

Klondike stood there on the stage like a preacher hosting a memorial service. His hands flapped nervously at his sides as he addressed his team. Lacey and Heavy stood just behind him on the small platform.

The performers all stood in little clusters, mini-groups, all spaced out across the seating area. Still, no one at all had sat down.

Klondike watched them all in rapt fascination. The sea of faces before him looked sad, weary and, most of all, defeated. It was a terrible look, especially when locked on to the faces of so many.

"I promised myself I would tell you this straight up," he continued, trying to acknowledge each and every one of the group. "No messing, no curveballs. No window dressing. Just the truth. Cos, after the week we've all had, there is nothing left to say…so here goes."

He paused, looking straight down at his shoes. He gulped heavily. Behind him, Lacey shuddered, wanting nothing more than to grab him, pat his back, anything. Then, it came.

"Klondike's Circus is finished."

The words struck them all like a bolt of lightning. Many could not believe what the boss was saying. It seemed inconceivable. Impossible.

Klondike continued. "That's right. We are… sadly, all finished. Never in my worst nightmares did I think such a day would arrive. Especially after all the odds we have managed to overcome down the years. But this… what happened back there on the ship… well, it was a mortal blow. To me, and my company."

He paused again, and managed to look up. Now, he looked angry. The tide of faces before him all wore masks of alarm.

"The damage is just simply insurmountable, folks. We had all of our gear on that ship. Everything! From the big top itself, to the grandstands, the stalls, the groundhole punchers, the cotton candy makers, the shooting galleries…" His face took on a grave, grisly look. "And our beautiful horses." He allowed a moment of silence. "Our trapeze rigs, the Globe of Death, the firehouse, hell even Roddy's puppets. It's all gone, god damn it! It's all gone.

"Then there's the cost of the Floating Top itself. The insurance we took out doesn't cover anything like this, a freak occurrence. I've got to pay for the whole liner now… I'm buying a ship that's sunk. There's not a damn thing I can do about it. And, as if all that was not enough, I'm being sued by the New York Harbour Exchange for the mess we caused. It… it just never ends."

Klondike stood there dumbly, as if waiting to be blown away by some great gust of wind, on to brighter realms.

"So, the upshot of all this is, I have to…" he pulled at his collar, feeling choked. "I have to close the circus. For good. There just isn't any choice in the matter. The bills are piling up. Our first show of the domestic season was scheduled to be next month and… dammit all to hell, we don't have anything left."

Finally, after a seemingly endless deathly silence, members of the assembled group let out grunts and groans of despair. A little chatter filtered up from the gathering.

Klondike held up a hand. "I, and I alone, am responsible. And, for that, I want each and every one of you to know… I am sorry. Sorry for putting you all through that back there on the ship. Sorry for the trauma of it all. And… and sorry for now leaving you all out of work, after giving you my word on so many promises."

He finished, looking deflated and forlorn up there. Lacey and Heavy joined him on either side, in a fierce show of unity.

The performers all stared up at them, many in horror. Then came the questions.

Predictably, the volatile Enqvist was first. "We all have contracts with your outfit, Klondike! You have to pay us what you owe us."

Klondike grimaced down at him. Lacey answered, somewhat insincerely. "Of all the things to think of, Tip!" she snapped. "Listen, you'll be paid what you are owed. We have lawyers going through the small print for what happens if an entire season is cancelled due to unforeseen events."

The stunt rider was unrepentant. "Our bikes, our garage, our god damn Globe of Death… all is stuck on the seabed. You owe me and my boys a fortune, Klondike!"

The circus boss lost his composure and stared down at the stunt rider with murderous eyes. "We were all almost killed out there, damn it! And all you're worried about is your stinking money…"

"There's more than that, Kal," Rumpy Stiltskin called out. "The publicity after the boat explosion has been awful. It's been all over the papers. People's even saying we killed those horses."

"I know, I know," Klondike breathed. He looked out and saw the Range Rider cowboys, all stood solemnly, a brethren. He squinted into the midday haze and made out Duster Williams, the veteran horse master who had been one of the unquestioned stars of the European tour. He nodded at the older man, who doffed his stetson at him.

"What happened back there," said Williams slowly, "was unprecedented in circus history. No one could have foreseen that. You can't blame yourself, Kal."

"The hell with that!" Enqvist roared, as his team of riders all puffed their chests out. "That damn ship was old, faulty! A cheap option. I say we were screwed over!"

Many of the group seemed to vent their anger at Enqvist at that moment, seemingly tired of his antics.

Then, Marion Rose, the Robins' dance trainer, spoke up. "What exactly did happen to that boat?"

Klondike snarled to himself. He caught Lacey's pleading eyes beside him. In his mind, he saw Jenny Cross waving goodbye again. "It's still being investigated by the harbour authorities," he said quickly. "It looks like foul play. One of the ship crew may have, er, have been at fault."

"Kal."

It was Roddy Olsen, right at the front, directly below him.

"Yes, Roddy."

"Where… where do we go from here?"

Klondike pulled off his hat and rubbed a hand through his thick black hair. "Well, that's just it, Roddy. We don't. There is nowhere to go from here. It's all over. Everything. The circus is finished. Closed." He studied the young man's soft, tanned face. He still looked like a teenager, fresh out of schooling. "I'm so god damn sorry. But there's nothing else to say on it, folks."

Olsen looked utterly crestfallen. The circus had been his life for four years. It had turned him from a penniless drifter into a superstar. He loved it more than life itself.

"Alright," Olsen said quietly, gazing up at his boss. "So, where do *we* go from here? We… we go our separate ways, huh?"

Klondike just stared back at him. An unspoken, unseen understanding seemed to pass between them. The others felt it.

Corky placed an arm around young Olsen sadly. "We're all feeling it, Rod." The clown looked about him. Without his make-up or costume, Corky looked old, haggard and grey. A middle-aged man struggling to stay relevant. A far cry from his persona as a clown, beloved by children nationwide. "We're a family," he continued, "broken apart by this. It just ain't right."

They all stood in an eerie silence for several moments.

Then, finally, a development many had been waiting for.

Klondike looked down at Shapiro, his star flyer. They had been together for years, since the very beginning. When Klondike had broken away from Ribbeck World Circus back in 1952, the great Gino had come with him… and had become a superstar.

"Well, Gino," Klondike said softly. "I'm sure you must have something to add."

For the first time anyone present could remember, Shapiro appeared lost for words. The ever-present confidence and bravado had evaporated, replaced by a serious, downbeat demeanour.

"Chairman," he finally called out, as if addressing an auditorium full of spectators, "this is indeed a sad day. A sad, unthinkable day. For me and you, chairman, to say we go our separate ways. It is so completely impossible." He held up his hands in a theatrical gesture. "I am heartbroken, people. Your Gino is beyond depressed. All I can truly say is… it has been a pleasure to ride with you all, in this… the greatest circus America ever saw."

There were no cheers, no whoops, just more dreaded silence.

Penny Fortune grabbed Shapiro's arm and looked up at Klondike on the stage. "I want to thank you, Kal Klondike. For giving me this chance… this chance to perform with some of the greatest performers in the world." She glanced sideways at Shapiro, who seemed to sway slightly. "And for bringing me together with Gino Shapiro. The greatest of all time. It has been an utter privilege. Thank you all."

This time, several of the group backed her up with calls of support.

But the surreal, otherworldly meeting had come to an end.

Klondike and Shapiro were just staring at each other, both standing rigidly, nodding, as if in memory. The circus boss whispered to the flyer. "You're the greatest, Gino."

But Shapiro shook his head. "No. You are, chairman. The greatest circus promoter in America. This changes nothing."

Klondike nodded silently. Then, his eyes took in the bigger picture, and widened.

There was no mass exodus, or sudden withdrawal. Everybody just curiously wandered around, aimlessly. Many were taking one last look around camp, their on and off home of the past four years. Several didn't know what to do. Others followed the ones who didn't know where they were going. All in all, it was a chaotic, silent mess – an almost perfect summary of the circus's present.

A half hour later, Klondike ducked into the bar room inside the Rio Cristo pavilion. Heavy and Lacey were already in there, nursing a scotch each. As they had done, Klondike merely waltzed behind the big mahogany bar and poured himself a glass. He reached inside his breast pocket for a cigar… then realised he had run out.

He looked dourly at the half-filled bottles sat around him.

"Even the booze has run out," he muttered dryly. He came around the bar and joined the other two on high stools, leaning against the bar top.

"I can't believe this place is up for sale," Heavy mumbled as he held his glass before him, staring at the deep brown liquid.

Klondike took a long sip of his scotch. "It's the only thing that's gunna save me. Without that dough, I can't pay off the ship, the legal costs… hell, everything."

Lacey had been strangely quiet. She lit a cigarette coyly and leaned forward on her stool. "Kal, why haven't you told any of them about Jenny? What you said after the explosion? That you saw her? On that launch. That she is somehow responsible."

Klondike shook slightly. He saw that wave goodbye yet again, that vision that seemed to plague his conscience. "It's my problem. I've got to worry about it. No sense in tormenting the others with it. Making them have nightmares. They've all got lives to get on with. They need to focus." He downed the contents of his glass. "I'll handle Jenny Cross."

The last words were uttered with chilling finality. Lacey and Heavy looked at each other with concern.

"Er, what exactly are you going to do about her, Kal?" Lacey whispered.

"I'll think of something."

Heavy was lost in thought. "Jesus. What are we all going to do now? There's no home, no circus... no tomorrow!"

Klondike felt exasperated. "I know, Heav. I know. It's like Roddy said. Now, we all go our separate ways. And try to salvage our lives. And our livelihoods."

Lacey wiped away a tear. "Your circus has changed my life, Kal baby. I... I don't think I can just walk away."

There was more to it than that and they both knew it. The two had shared a mutual, but largely unspoken, attraction for years, as well as an almost telepathic understanding of how to run the operation together. They were a partnership. They were one.

Klondike looked downwards yet again. "I can't imagine living my day to day life without either of you in it."

Heavy tried to remain upbeat. "Maybe... maybe we'll all be back together again, one day."

Klondike nodded vaguely, then stood and disappeared behind the bar. He filled three fresh glasses with cognac, an old favourite of the circus management team. Then, he handed them out and raised his one aloft.

"Here's to the circus. The wonderful world of the circus. Which has brought us so many magical memories down the years... more than we could ever have imagined. And here's to our future endeavours. Each of us. May they bring us good fortune... in one way or another."

They all touched glasses. Then, they simply sat there in silence.

The three of them sat there for quite some time.

CHAPTER TWO

The following morning, Klondike awoke in his bungalow at the far end of Rio Cristo. His head was pounding.

Stumbling from his bed, he padded across into the living room. The whole place was a shambles, a swathe of empty whiskey bottles strewn across the floor and overfilled ashtrays covering every surface. His dresser was filled with billing sheets and newspaper clippings.

Ignoring the lot, he headed for the bathroom. After a shower and a shave, he left the bungalow and made his way across the camp.

It was a depressing scene. He was all alone at Rio Cristo now. Of that he was sure. Not a soul appeared as he walked briskly across to the pavilion.

No sooner had he entered the large building when the buzzer for the front gate sounded. Bemused, Klondike grabbed at the intercom handset by the front desk. "Yeah?" he grunted.

"Good morning, this is Goldstone and Sons Real Estate," the high-pitched tone echoed through the building over the speaker. "We were told we can have access to the grounds today for a full survey. We need to complete pictures, assessments and-"

"Go right ahead," Klondike rasped, cutting the man off. "I'll open the gate for ya. Do what you gotta do."

He pressed a large red button at the edge of the desk that opened up the main gate at the front of the complex.

He heard a car rumble past, then shook his head. With a grunt, he mounted the stairway and headed for his office.

Inside, he could not help but stare at the desk and the mass of billing sheets that covered it. The whole stinking mess was hard to digest.

His eyes floated to the window. Outside, he saw a station wagon pull to a stop beside the trailers. Two men in blue suits got out, carrying clipboards. The surveyors, planning the sale of the grounds. The last act.

Klondike rubbed wearily at his eyes. First thing's first, he thought. For the past few days, he had desperately been trying to contact Daryl Addison, his former principal investor who had become a partner in the circus after the hugely successful 1958 season.

Addison had turned his profitable bank and investment firm into a hugely successful conglomerate that had diversified into movies, theatre, pop music and real estate. He ran his empire, Addison Incorporated, from a monolithic skyscraper in San Francisco, and now carried influence in multiple business spheres.

More than that, he had been a father figure to Klondike in recent years, often finding a solution to the circus's most pressing problems.

However, every time Klondike had called his office since they had landed in New York, the man's secretary had informed him the boss was out of town or unavailable. He needed to hear Kal's report into what had happened.

Now, he grabbed at the telephone and dialled the familiar San Francisco number. It was answered on the first ring.

"Daryl Addison, please. This is Kal Klondike calling."

A long, unusual silence followed.

Klondike frowned. "Hello? Can you hear me?"

"Yes, I can hear you…" a woman's voice whispered.

"OK. Mr Addison, please."

Again, the silence. "I'm sorry…"

Klondike stared at the handset. "What? What is this?"

This time, the woman spoke clearly. "I'm sorry, but that will not be possible. You see… you see Mr Addison died yesterday morning…"

She said more, but Klondike didn't hear it. He dropped the handset and stared, as if hypnotised, at the telephone. He felt like he was slipping into a deep abyss, a world of pain and horror, that was tugging at him, drawing him in, like quicksand.

Suddenly, he fell to his knees and wailed aloud. He said only one word, but repeated it insanely.

"No. No. No. No. No…"

Daryl Addison's funeral was a gargantuan affair.

The great and the good within San Francisco all turned up to pay their respects to one of the Bay City's most respected businessmen. The mayor even read a eulogy at the service, held at the opulent St Francis Church in Marine Bay.

The old man had been working late in his office one night before suffering a heart attack, it was said. He had been taken to hospital, but had died two days later.

At the funeral, his casket was buried in the magnificent grounds of the great church on an unusually cold spring day.

Klondike stood among the second row of mourners during the interment. He was surrounded by men in expensive dark suits and hats, all looking downwards.

As a chilling wind blew across the cemetery, the expensive silver coffin was lowered into the ground.

A VIP ring of Addison Incorporated executives stood at the very front, alongside the mayor and several other dignitaries.

The mourning party all slowly disassembled at the conclusion of the interment.

Klondike wandered slowly back through the immaculate lawns, feeling sick all over. He was beginning to feel like he'd lost everything. His partner, his circus, his camp. It was like his very existence was slowly being erased.

He reached the main gate of the church, and turned, taking one last look at the graves and trying to remember the many good times he'd shared with Daryl Addison.

"Mr Klondike?"

He turned abruptly at the voice. A small, middle-aged man in the obligatory black suit, hat and trenchcoat was standing at the gate.

Klondike nodded. "Right."

"Brian Horton, Addison Incorporated." The two shook hands. "May I offer my sincere condolences, sir. Mr Addison often spoke warmly of you and your circus."

"Thank you, Mr Horton. My condolences to you too. I am sure he meant a lot to everybody at AI."

"He sure did," Horton said wistfully. His face took on an awkward expression. "I wonder if I may offer you a ride back into town? Or anywhere you need to be, for that matter." He held out an arm, and Klondike saw he was indicating a limousine sat on the roadside beyond, its rear doors all open. Horton added: "We have some, ah, business to discuss with you, Mr Klondike."

"Who's we?"

"Let me explain. Addison Incorporated was governed by Mr Addison, along with a select board of directors. I was appointed chairman of the board and, now that the owner is no longer alive, it is my unfortunate responsibility to carry the business forward until a vote is made on a new chief executive."

Klondike stared at him.

"What I am saying," Horton continued, "is that I have to address each of the company's many concerns. In place of Mr Addison. Now…" he indicated the limousine again. "Won't you please join us?"

Klondike merely nodded and was led to the huge black automobile. Inside were two elder men, both in trench coats, while a youthful driver sat in a separate enclosure up front, a glass partition blocking out the front seats completely.

"Kal, this is Vincent Mettasina, one of our lawyers, and Arnold Scanlon, a board member and consultant. Please, make yourself comfortable."

Klondike fell into the plush leather seat, facing forwards – and the other two men. Horton climbed in beside him, and the limousine pulled away from the kerb and began its journey back towards the sprawling metropolis of downtown Frisco.

"Can I offer you scotch?" Horton said eagerly.

Klondike nodded, and watched in awe as Horton reached into a tiny drinks cabinet hidden inside the bottom section of the leather backseat. Within seconds, he produced two glasses. A third was then offered to Scanlon. Mettasina refused the invitation.

"Kal…" Horton began, "your circus has been bankrolled and assisted by Addison Incorporated for years. Yes, we got a share of the profits and an impressive catalogue of ads. And you guys were always in the black. But, well, you see…"

Klondike had been about to take a sip of his drink, but now paused, the glass inches from his lips. "Yeah, I see alright. A moneymaking golden goose has just become a dead duck."

Horton quivered. "Something like that."

Klondike took his drink. "So, what are you trying to tell me?"

The limousine rumbled on for several moments. It suddenly felt very claustrophobic in the back. Klondike looked up at the two men sat opposite. Both stared at him like he was a zoo animal.

One of them, Scanlon, finally spoke up. "Look, the fact of the matter is, Daryl made a lot of business decisions single-handedly. He went out on his own an awful lot. Several of our investment platforms were moves made purely down to his interests and relationships. Your circus was one such venture."

Klondike stared at him. He took another sip.

Now Mettasina spoke. "Daryl helped finance your circus due to an old relationship between the two of you. From back when he was a merchant banker, down on Mason Street. Before AI took off and became an international chain."

"That's right," Klondike rasped, "me and Daryl were in business together before he was this financial god. Back when things were tight. He took me at my word. And we helped each other out."

"That's right," the cagey Mettasina said thinly. "Now, after Tuesday's sad news, we as a board have to make a number of decisions about the way forward. About keeping AI on track, and paying off our investors and board members."

Horton took over again. "The long and the short of it is… we have to decide what interests we are keeping on. And what we have to move on from."

Mettasina resumed: "The board has decided unanimously to cut AI's ties with all entertainment outlets. Everything. The shows we support, the music acts… and, sadly, with Klondike's Circus."

Klondike rolled his eyes. It was like a never-ending nightmare. Would the world ever stop spinning?

The others studied him curiously, nervously. He found his voice. "So, that's it, huh? Just like that? Nine years of success, of a partnership that made real money. All thrown to the garbage."

"I'm very sorry, Kal," Horton said quickly. "But the partnership with your circus… it was all Daryl's doing. It was like his side project. None of the board had ever vetoed it, even had anything to do with it. It was just Daryl and Daryl alone."

"And now he's gone, you're washing your hands of everything he worked for?" Klondike barked.

Mettasina answered. "It's not like that. We're restructuring the whole business. And our new focus is on finance and real estate. No more show business ventures. At all. They represent too much of a risk, and generate all kinds of unforeseen issues." He glared at Klondike. "You of all people should understand that."

Klondike took a deep breath, exhaling slowly. He finished his drink and simply placed the glass on the car floor. "Let me out."

The trio in trenchcoats seemed to brace themselves.

"But, but..." Horton rambled, "we're not downtown yet. We're still on the Pacific Pathway. Where are you going to-"

"I don't give a damn. Just let me out." He looked at each of the others slowly. "I don't like the air in here. You boys are talking about green. But all I see is yellow."

They all glared at him in astonishment. Nobody said anything. The limousine rolled to a stop close to the ocean near Golden Gate Bridge. Klondike simply opened his door and stepped out into the sea breeze, slamming it behind him.

As the big black automobile rumbled off slowly, Klondike looked out to sea, then cursed to himself. With another heavy sigh, he looked up at the great, domineering skyscrapers of Frisco ahead of him.

Then, head down, he started walking.

More than 2,000 miles away, a crowd of thousands was making its way into a giant, yellow and pink circus tent.

The legendary Sherman Brothers Circus was playing in Chicago, all pitched up at the Elstree Grounds. The troupe was conducting a full nationwide tour over six months. The Windy City was the latest stop in a long and gruelling schedule.

Beyond the big top, spread in a vague semi-circle, rested a shanty town of trailers, all long, white and pristine, as if they had all come off the assembly line together just hours before.

In one of the larger trailers at the head of the gathering, a man sat at his dresser holding a newspaper.

He was small, barely over five feet in height, with a wiry, agile look. He had a bald, shiny head, and his face looked like it was made of wet rubber. Half man, half elf in appearance, the figure still looked like a celebrity thanks to his stunning stars and stripes tracksuit, which looked befitting of a Las Vegas showman.

Jonathan 'Doc' Irwin was 52 years old. Despite his advancing years, he was considered one of America's greatest living acrobats. Yet, he was also one of its most respected, his years of experience making him one of the nation's foremost experts on the art of trapeze.

Now, he sat silently at the dresser, lost in thought. His grey eyes darted down to the newspaper before him.

IS THIS THE END FOR AMERICA'S FAVOURITE CIRCUS?

He re-read the headline again. Then, he shook his head sadly.

There was a light knock at the trailer door, and a young steward wandered in.

"The show's just getting started, Doc," the young man said. "You've got one hour till you're on."

Irwin nodded. "Thank you, Jimmy."

The steward looked around the trailer excitedly. The walls were full of posters of Doc in the various circuses he had performed in down the years. The All-American, as he was known, had been a mainstay in major promotions for decades. The pictures showed him in his famous stars and stripes singlet as he performed trapeze acts. One poster showed him riding a bicycle along a high wire.

The youngster grinned, excited. Then, he eyed the newspaper the older man gripped.

"What's that? America's favourite circus? Huh?"

Irwin finally released the paper and turned in his chair.

"Klondike's Circus. Northern California," he said quietly. "They've been number one in the country for three years. Along with Ribbeck's outfit." He shook his head. "A terrible tragedy. They were on their way back to the States after a tour of Europe. Their ship… it sunk in New York harbour."

"Ah, yeah," Jimmy said, leaning against the wall, "I heard about that."

Irwin looked downwards. "Now, they're disbanding. The show has been closed down."

"You look, ah, upset, Doc."

Irwin eyed the youngster ruefully. "You know, we worked together once."

"Who?"

"Me and Kal Klondike. Back when I was with Ribbeck's outfit in '48. Yeah, he was a knife thrower back then. The following year he became a booker, then a manager. Then, well, then he began his own circus."

"How long were you with Ribbeck?"

"Just one season," Irwin muttered, lost in thought. "But I never forgot it. It was the first time I'd seen such immense crowds. Thousands… all under one big top. People screaming with joy. It was the beginning of the new era."

Jimmy's eyes were wide. "Were you freelance back then, Doc?"

"Hell, I've been freelance my whole life, son. Ever since I started out. Best way to work, you ask me. You can take on projects you believe in. Choose your path."

Jimmy wandered over to the dresser, and looked again at the newspaper story. He read the opening paragraphs. "What a disaster," he said.

Irwin stroked at his rubbery face. "Yeah… but Klondike will think of something. I guarantee it."

Jimmy smiled and patted his shoulder. He made for the door. "I'll come and get you when it's time," he called as he left the trailer.

Doc Irwin just sat there, his eyes going from the newspaper page to the dazzling circus posters on his wall. He reached for a bottle of garrish, green liquid that looked like it had been pulled from a swamp. Taking a long pull, he tried to smile. Then, he quietly whispered to himself.

"Yeah, he'll think of something."

CHAPTER THREE

"And here's your desk, Miss Tanner. Welcome to Montpellier and Cavani."

The woman in the red blazer made a theatrical gesture and pointed to a large, square table filled with a typewriter, in and out trays, a giant roll-a-dial and several piles of magazines.

Lacey Tanner walked forward, studying her allocated grotto. She noticed her desk was next to the floor to ceiling window that formed the far wall of the building. It was sat on its own, while the other desks were all huddled together in two long lines. Her desk was also twice the size of the others. Its accompanying chair was leather-backed and brand new.

She smiled warmly and nodded at the woman in red, and the secretary who had accompanied them up the stairs and into the bullpen.

"Thank you, Miss Cavani," she said in her dry, airy tone. "This is all so nice. What a beautiful spot to work in."

Edna Cavani rushed across to the desk and pointed at the all-encompassing window. "You can almost see Sunset Boulevard from up here. Look, the whole of Hollywood, right on your doorstep."

Lacey continued to smile. "Like heaven."

She was wearing an immaculate arctic silver trouser suit that seemed to sparkle. She had come for a job interview that morning, and had now been offered her pick of accounts at the leading Los Angeles PR firm. Just like that. In a matter of days, her whole world had been turned upside down, and then realigned in a whole new vortex. She felt like she was navigating a kaleidoscope.

"OK, make yourself comfortable," her new boss was saying, "get to know the girls. And guys. Ask anyone anything about the accounts. But, why, I imagine everyone will be asking you before long, Miss Tanner!" She laughed enthusiastically at her own quip. Then, she made to leave. Turning, she gushed: "And, on behalf of Montpellier and Cavani… good luck!"

Lacey nodded, somewhat bemused. All work had come to a standstill in the open plan office as she was led to her desk. Faces looked up from typewriters, everyone seemed alarmed.

Now, she walked around the giant desk and threw herself into the high-backed leather chair. With a great sigh, she looked down at the movie magazines that seemed to be everywhere. Absently, her hand moved towards the roll-a-dial. A world of contacts and studio insiders was now literally at her fingertips.

Suddenly, she became aware of others. She looked up… and gasped.

About a dozen staff were gathered round her desk at the far end, all smiling happily and looking down at her with wanting in their eyes.

A woman at the front spoke out. "Sorry, Miss Tanner. It's just that… well, it's you. Lacey Tanner! The publicist from Klondike's Circus. We… we've all heard so much about you!"

"Yeah!" another lady blurted. "The media campaigns you put together for Circus of the Stars, and Superstars and Stripes. They were just out of sight!"

Another chipped in: "We're very excited to have you here, working with us."

Lacey found herself backing away into the plush leather seating. "Er, thank you," she stammered. "I never expected such a warm welcome."

The group all seemed to speak at once.

"Miss Cavani told us to listen to everything you say…"

"We heard you've just come back from Europe!"

"Is it true you are friends with the heads of ATV?"

Lacey's eyes darted from speaker to speaker. "My," she gushed, "it feels like I should be giving a press conference, let alone organising them!"

They all roared with laughter.

Then, the first woman who'd spoken calmed the group and addressed Lacey coolly. "We're sorry, Miss Tanner. The truth is, Montpellier and Cavani has been under-performing for some time now. Even Miss Cavani will tell you. We're struggling to attract new clients. Real stars, you know? And also keeping our big whales happy… well, it's hard. But now…" she raised her arms out toward Lacey, as if heralding the arrival of the next messiah. "Now, we have you on board. One of the very best in the business!"

"Oh, come on," Lacey mused, wafting a hand through the air. Then, she eyed the speaker seriously. "What exactly have they told you guys about me?"

The lead woman's eyes enlarged, as if seeing an epiphany. "That you took a West Coast circus, and turned it from a regional promotion into the greatest show in America today. You made the press love Klondike's Circus."

Lacey raised her eyebrows and fell back into her chair again. Idly, without thinking, she reached for a cigarette. Three people leapt forward with lighters. She lit up from the one nearest to her, and shifted uncomfortably. Her mind seemed to drift, through the many mists of time.

"Well, that's not all true," she whispered, exhaling smoke. "I had help. Lots and lots of help."

"Full house!"

Heavy Brown laid his cards face up on the pine table, as the other three players all stared, dumbfounded, at his hand. Each pair of eyes studied the cards, then arched upwards towards their owner, almost in perfect unison.

They saw a cherubic, childlike grin, on a fleshy, meaty face.

Heavy tried not to laugh. It was like taking candy from a baby. With glee, he spread his arms and gathered in the giant pile of multi-coloured poker chips scattered in small piles in front of each player. His own mound of chips was now at least four times bigger than any of his rivals' winnings.

"Well, that's me out," one of the card sharps said, in disgust.

"Me too," said the man to his left. Both got up and stood over the great round table for several moments, as if in shock.

They were in a private, back room located behind The Rhinestone saloon in Fisherman's Wharf, San Francisco Bay. Some of the highest rollers in the city played here, out back at the Stone. But, as yet, over the past week, no one had bettered the prolific run of Heavy Brown. The big man had cleaned up in every match he had taken a hand in. So far.

The only man left seated at the table besides Heavy shook his head in admiration. "God damn, boy," he mused in a southern accent. "That's more than a grand you've taken in today. What you gunna do with all that green?"

Heavy looked at him. "Buy you a new suit, Barney."

The man cackled. "Seriously, Brown, you've got talent. And I mean talent, man. I've been coming to this place for 30 years. I seen all kinds of sharps, intellectuals, rounders… you name it. But you've got a knack, a niche. Like all great players… you find a way to win. That's special."

Heavy began counting his chips, the game evidently now over. "Yeah, well, I had me a lot of practice."

The southerner looked him over, seriously this time. "You know, with your talent, you could win big, my friend. I'm talking Bradshaw's Spur big."

"Bradshaw?"

"In Las Vegas. Where they have the world series of poker. Private rooms there. Big games. Hundreds of thousands up for grabs."

Heavy eyed him silently. He nodded. "Thanks, buddy. I'll bear it in mind."

The southerner cackled again, slapped him on the back and slowly lurched away from the card table.

Heavy sat there, neatly piling his chips. He grabbed at the tall glass of beer sat beside him and drained the lot.

He had been here for a week. Clearing gamblers of their dough. There were worse ways to make a living, he thought idly. Worse ways to live at that. Yet still, he felt empty.

"Get you another, Heavy?" a passing kid in a dungarees asked.

Heavy held the glass before him. "Why not?"

High in the Hollywood hills, brownstone bungalows were scattered among the valleys and boulders like boats in a yachting contest. Every hundred yards or so, another one sprouted up. And all were neatly nestled into the surrounding woodland and shrubbery, their privacy from the outside world all but guaranteed by the vast foliage.

One such bungalow, high in the woods, with what looked like an old rock quarry behind it, looked somewhat rustic and forgotten, as if decades had passed since it had been subject to renovations.

Not that any of this bothered its owner, Andros Murphy, who sat sprawled in a huge outdoor bathtub placed directly in front of the house. Chomping on a giant cigar and reading the latest copy of Racing Forecast while nestled in a cocoon of bubbles, Murphy could not have been more content.

A genial, musclebound African-American with huge shoulders and biceps, he looked like an athlete or professional wrestler, his physique flawless, and his looks appealing.

Murphy suddenly looked up from his paper at the sound of approaching footsteps in the soft gravel pathway that led to the bungalow. Then, his face erupted into a wide smile.

Coming up the sandy trail was a man who could have passed for one of the many Hollywood movie stars roaming the hills. Outrageously handsome, with slicked-back black hair and deeply tanned skin, the figure was tall and athletic, lithe and agile. Dressed in an orange tracksuit, he carried a giant duffel bag over one shoulder.

Murphy led back in his tub, the bubbles rising up to his neck.

"Well, well," he called out. "I am in the presence of royalty. The debonair king of the air, no less. Charmed, your majesty!"

Gino Shapiro chuckled softly as he approached the giant, oblong bathtub in the driveway. It looked like it had been dumped there one day by a lazy removal man, and never taken inside.

"Murph," Shapiro said, laughing at the scene before him. "I'd say stand up and salute but, well…"

Murphy kept smiling. "It wouldn't do either of us any good."

Shapiro looked around at the woodland, the sandy driveway and, finally, the old brownstone bungalow before him. Nothing had changed at all since his last visit, several years earlier.

"How have you been?" Murphy's question brought him back to the present.

"The truth is… terrible, old friend. Just terrible."

Murphy finally got serious, staring up at him from the tub. "Yeah. I sure was sorry to hear about the ship disaster, Gino. Klondike's Circus. I know how much it meant to you."

Shapiro nodded. "You would not believe what I have been through these past few months, amigo."

"I can only imagine, man." Murphy puffed on his cigar thoughtfully as he sprawled in the tub. "I've heard plenty. About Europe. That fancy broad you partnered with in Italy." He held the cigar before him, his hand soaking wet as he led in the bubbles. "God damn… it's good to see ya, Gino."

Shapiro smiled at him. A renowned trapeze flyer in his own right, Murph had been his catcher and assistant for several years, first on the independent scene with various outfits, then with Ribbeck World Circus in the early 1950s. They had eventually gone their separate ways, to the deep disappointment of both. But Gino had always hoped a reunion would occur. Now, he was counting on it.

Murphy continued. "Well, listen, I read your telegram and got straight on the case."

"You've got a gaff lined up?"

"Right. But it's movie work. That's the only kind they know out here. You're gunna be working with me, pal. On the new Feldman picture. Big Top Showdown. Starts shooting next week."

Shapiro's eyes widened. "A circus film?"

"Right. They are still all the rage, ever since The Show of Shows back in '54. That was the highest grossing movie of the year. Now, every producer in Hollywood wants a piece. All the studios do one circus movie every two years or so." He chuckled, looking up. "And they always want real-life flyers on board. For stunts. Technical advice. Credibility, in a way."

"And you, Murph?" Shapiro wandered idly around the bathtub. "You're still in demand? They want a piece of you, eh?"

"You bet!" he cried, cigar clamped in his mouth. "I'm one of the most sought-after movie flyers out here, man. Even after all these years." He eyed Shapiro admiringly. "And bringing you on board, Gino. You! The great Gino, with all your experience in these kinds of matters. Well, that's made the pie all the sweeter, my man."

Again, Shapiro chuckled. Murph had worked the trapeze for years, but had become well-known among film crews and production teams as a safe bet stuntman for circus films.

"Bravo, amigo. Listen, I will be staying at the Magnum Hotel. Downtown. If I can leave some of my kit here, Murph, I would appreciate it."

"Sure, sure, knock yourself out." Murphy narrowed his eyes as Shapiro made to walk across to the house. "There's just one thing, Gino. One tiny question."

Shapiro turned. "Shoot."

Murphy turned in the tub to face him. "Why haven't you hooked up with another circus, man? Any big top in the country would die to have you on board. Especially after last season. They'd pay over the odds to have you. You could take your pick of promotions. Yet… you come to me, asking for work. Why, dammit?"

Shapiro stood there quietly, fiddling with his tote bag. "Is good question," he murmured.

He sighed heavily. The pain of that last meeting at Rio Cristo was still fresh, unnerving. He could not get it out of his mind.

Finally, he looked up sternly. "The answer? Simple. I could not work for any other circus… other than Klondike. Could not sign with a competitor, a rival. No! After what I have been through with that outfit… it would be impossible."

A deathly silence fell over the enclosure. Murphy just sat in his tub, thinking it over. Shapiro stood in the shadow of the house. He looked up at the all-consuming hills that enclosed them.

"So, here I am," he said quietly.

The sprawling Gothic Tudor mansion looked like something from another world entirely. With its endless battlements and arches, stone balconies before crystal glass windows and smooth granite sides, the building looked like a medieval castle, somehow transported to Sacramento, California.

As the vintage, chauffeur-driven Rolls-Royce approached, its backseat passenger sat open-mouthed at the opulent surroundings.

Roddy Olsen had never seen a home quite like it. The mansion overlooked finely manicured gardens, with stone fountains and iron-clad gazebos sitting idly among the luscious greenery.

As the classic motor glided across the sandy lane leading to the monolithic structure beyond, Olsen sat there brooding, struggling to take in the significance of what was happening to him.

Do you believe in destiny, Roddy?

That was what the telegram had said. Delivered to his hotel room in Frisco yesterday morning. He was still in shock after all that had happened. The trauma of the ship sinking. Seeing Suzi so disconsolate. Lost. Knowing his beloved puppets were gone, buried at the bottom of the Atlantic Ocean. And then Kal's announcement that the circus was finished.

He glanced up at the giant mansion now dwarfing the car. And now what lies ahead in this otherworldly castle, he thought. Its owner had invited him here, with that mysterious telegram…

The chauffeur, clad in a grey suit with cap, pulled up at the giant stone steps that led to the entrance to the huge house. He leapt out and opened the rear door. Olsen thanked him and walked shyly up the steps and through the open glass doors.

He came to a reception desk, as if the monolithic building was a hotel, not the home of a single occupant. The front hall seemed impossibly large, with a ceiling some 10 yards above his head. Announcing himself, he was led to the 'Autumn Room' on the south side of the complex.

Inside, he arrived in a grand space that reeked of wealth and privilege. Fine, Oriental rugs covered the polished mahogany floors. Oil paintings and ancient antiques adorned the walls, and ivory bookcases sat in each of the room's corners. A huge writing desk and piano were at the far end, in front of a glass door that led to a balcony.

Taking a deep breath, Olsen crept towards the desk.

"There he is!" a voice boomed from behind him. "Roddy Olsen! The Puppet Master himself!"

A cheerful-looking man with bright red skin and curly brown hair was rushing over to him. He wore a short blazer and waistcoat, like an orchestra conductor.

Miles Courtland. Music impresario and record producer. He had managed some of the hottest teen idols of the 1950s rock n roll explosion, and had recently sold his record label Phantom for more than a million dollars. It was said he was branching out into new avenues, including a rumoured plan to organise a country and western music festival.

Courtland shook Olsen's hand heavily, grabbing his arm in delight. Olsen tried to share his enthusiasm, smiling wanly.

"Roddy, my boy," the tycoon was saying, grinning widely, "I can't tell you what an honour it is to finally meet you. In person! Like this! Thank you so much for coming to my humble abode."

Olsen nodded, still in shock somewhat. "Well, thank you for inviting me, Mr Courtland. I was, er, intrigued by your telegram and, well, had to find out more."

Courtland erupted into laughter, jabbing him playfully in the gut. "That's what I like to hear, daddio!"

He placed a hand behind Olsen and drew him deftly towards a drinks cabinet behind the piano. "What can I get ya?"

"Sodawater will be fine. Thank you."

If Courtland was shocked, he didn't show it, pouring a tall glass full of sparkling water from a large bottle and handing it over, before dousing a snifter with brandy. He offered a silent toast and downed half his glass.

"Mr Courtland, your home is truly spectacular."

"Thank you, Roddy. I had the stones brought in from Nantucket."

They both moved towards the glass doors, which offered a stunning view of the multi-toned gardens that seemed to spread to infinity.

"So," Olsen muttered awkwardly, "you mentioned in your telegram something about a plan, a lifelong dream…"

Courtland smiled at him mesmerically. His host was every inch the showman, seemingly relishing the attention and suspense.

"Ever since I was a child," he began, "I have run shows. Rock shows. Country and western shows. County fairs. Pop nights, getting four different acts to a stage somewhere upstate, splitting the proceeds equally. Booking bands for clubs, saloons. I've done it all, Roddy. When I started producing records, it was a natural step. I turned my acts, my guys, into chart stars. My record label was my roster. My all-star roster."

He finished his brandy and, absently, while barely looking, refilled his glass. He looked at Roddy with warm, somewhat overbearing eyes. "But all my life, I have wanted to run a circus. I have been a fan for as long as I can remember. Why, when my daddy used to take me to a big top as a kid, it was the most beautiful moment. The highlight of growing up. I couldn't wait to get into the tent, with a stick of cotton candy, and be blown away by all the action." He smiled knowingly. "Like so many millions of others, Rod. Magic time. That's what we all call it, right?"

Olsen smiled simply. "It's like a bug. Get's hold of ya. Won't ever let go. The magic of the circus."

Courtland held his glass close to him, enjoying his memories. Then, curiously, his eyes levelled and he studied Olsen, as if eyeing a mysterious entity. "I've watched you from the start, Rod."

The youngster baulked. "What?"

"That's right. That first season with Klondike. Circus of the Stars. Then Superstars and Stripes in Washington last July 4th. Your appearances on ATV and the Late Night Show. You're a diamond, Roddy. A true diamond. What you do is unfathomable. Hard to believe…"

Olsen nodded vaguely. "Er, is there something I can do for you, Mr Courtland?"

His host seemed to smile to himself. Finally, he revealed his hand. "I am starting up my own circus, Roddy. From scratch. It will be called Courtland and Co. The circus camp is right here, in my grounds. We have all the equipment ready." His eyes locked onto Olsen's. "Now, we are assembling the talent."

The young ventriloquist nodded, as if finally understanding a riddle. "Aha. I see. And you want me to star in your circus?"

Courtland stared at him with a queer, superior look. "No, Roddy. I want you to run it."

Olsen shuddered. "What?" he almost yelped. "Run it? You can't be serious?"

"Oh, I am serious, Rod." The smile was ever-present. The skin seemed to get redder with each passing minute. "Courtland and Co is going to be a new kind of circus, my man. Big on magicians, comedy, illusions, singing… and puppets!" He laughed out loud yet again. "And you, Roddy Olsen, can lead this team of magic makers, inspire them to greatness. You can do it,

Rod. I believe in you. You've been to the top in this industry, and you started at the bottom. There's nothing about big tops you don't know."

Olsen was beginning to wonder if Courtland was just eccentric, or actually mentally unstable. However, he knew that everything the music magnate had touched so far in his life had turned to gold.

"Let me get this right, Mr Courtland. You want me to be, what? A manager?"

"Absolutely. The manager of Courtland and Co!"

Olsen frowned. "Would I be a player-manager? I'd perform in your circus?"

Courtland beamed at him. "Listen to your heart…" then, he burst out laughing yet again. "But, of course, we'd very much like you to perform for us. As you see fit."

"Urm, ok. Listen, Mr Courtland, I'm very honoured… by all of this. But, the fact of the matter is… I don't know anything about running a circus. Not a damn thing!" Courtland seemed obsessed. "You'd have help. Bookers. Accountants. Road managers. Crew. The best money can buy."

Olsen held out his hands. "I'm 23 years old. You realise that?"

"So what? You're circus goldust, Rod. People will want to come and work for us because of your name alone."

The youngster was incredulous. "My puppets are sitting on the bottom of the ocean! Rusty Fox doesn't even exist right now."

But Courtland's eyes took on a misty look. "We can arrange anything you want, daddy. We'll get you new puppets, man. All you have to do is join us."

Olsen shifted about nervously. He put his soda water on the writing desk and paced about.

Courtland brought out his trump cards. "I have a vision. A great billboard, above the entrance to our big top. It says…Roddy Olsen Presents – Courtland and Co Circus."

"But why," Olsen mumbled, "why do you want me to manage it so bad?"

"Because you're the greatest, Rod. In my opinion, the biggest name in American circus today. Everyone in the country will want to see YOUR show."

Olsen waved a hand through his thick blond hair. He looked innocent and naive, feeling out of his depth. In every way.

Courtland seized his moment, like a powerbroker eyeing closure.

"You want to know the terms, of course," he said conversationally. "You'll get a one thousand dollars signing on fee. Right now. Today. Then, another thousand for each show, in a 16-city tour."

Now, he moved across to Olsen slowly, cautiously. He placed a hand on the young man's shoulder. "Now, tell me, what do you say to that, my boy?" He moved his right hand outwards, encouraging Olsen to shake it.

Olsen stood still. The whole encounter had felt like a surreal dream. Much like most of the past three months. 1961 had been by far the most dramatic year of his young life. It seemed the madness was far from over.

He thought earnestly. His contract with Klondike's Circus had died with that shipwreck. His beloved puppets were down there too, condemned to a watery grave. He was at his lowest ebb. And yet, amidst the horror, there now came the offer of a lifetime, from one of the most successful men in American showbusiness. All in all, the whole thing was almost impossible to comprehend.

Yet, here they were.

Olsen looked into Courtland's wild, maddening eyes. He forced a smile. Then, he took the man's hand and they shook on it.

Courtland roared like an ox. "Welcome aboard!"

CHAPTER FOUR

"So, you stop the punch right before the kisser. You'll soon get used to it. The sound guys in the studio will make it come across as real. Just get it on target. Then, watch how I make it work. OK, let's go."

The man in the cowboy outfit nodded at his teacher. Then, the two of them raised their fists and started circling each other, as if in a stand-off. Then, the cowboy threw a right hook, with great care. The speaker threw himself backwards, as if sent sprawling by the blow, splattering on to the sandy bank beyond them.

A man was standing behind a camera set up on a tripod nearby. "Looked terrific," he said, disinterested.

Mike Blakelock pulled himself up, dusting the sand from his cowboy attire. He smiled widely. "That was good, Pat. Now, we'll work on your throwing and your kicks. Before long, you'll be a perfect movie fighter."

They both laughed. Blakelock patted him on the back as he climbed the grassy knoll that led down to the sandbank.

They were in a far corner of the vast Anvil Pictures lot. Among the four square miles of movie sets were jungles, deserts, a makeshift beach, a cattle ranch and this, a sealed-off area of man-made prairie land used for showdowns with both guns and fists. At the present time, the spot was being used as a practice area.

Blakelock removed his stetson and wandered across to a simple table sat next to the camera and its operator. He picked up a copy of the script and read through several scenes again.

He was of average height, with broad shoulders and a tough-looking physique. He had short brown hair and serious dark eyes, but his most striking feature was his broken nose, which made him look ruggedly handsome.

As Blakelock read over the scenes, he looked out across the set. And froze.

Walking towards them, not 20 yards away, was a figure from his past. He had not seen the newcomer in years. But it didn't matter. He hadn't changed a bit. Blakelock would have recognised his clothes alone. Brown leather jacket, dark fedora. There was no mistake.

"Kal…" he said breathlessly as the figure approached across the makeshift prairie.

"Mike Blakelock," the newcomer said in a hoarse voice. "We meet again."

Blakelock walked quickly around the desk and the two men shook hands.

"Great to see you. What… what are you doing here? And how did you find me?"

Klondike grinned, looking at the camera and the two others. "I heard you were working in the movies now. I never had you down as a… er, stunt fighter."

"The correct term is action supervisor."

"Well, whatever. Showing pretty boy actors how to hold punches and fall properly… sounds like stunt fighting to me."

Blakelock had to smile. "But how did you find me?"

Klondike eyed him shrewdly. "Well, I've got contacts everywhere. My man at Spotlight found out what movie you were working on. And, well, I know the studio head at Anvil. He once broadcast one of my shows back in the day."

Blakelock rolled his eyes. "Of course. Everybody has worked with Klondike's Circus at some point or another." He stopped abruptly, and looked serious suddenly. "Listen, Kal. I heard about what happened on that ship. I sure am sorry. It just… just doesn't seem fair."

Klondike looked around, pained. "Can we talk somewhere, Mike?"

Blakelock eyed the actor and camera operator. Then, he glanced at the script. Then, back at Klondike. "Sure."

"The broad is crazy, man. I can't imagine what was going through her mind. Just some kind of desperate, demented attempt at revenge."

Blakelock studied his old friend. Klondike's eyes were wide in horror as he described what happened. He seemed tired and weary, but spoke with conviction when it came to the ship incident.

They were sat in the staff canteen in the Anvil Pictures backlot. Both drank black coffee from plastic cups in the nearly deserted hall.

Blakelock could not stop staring at his visitor. He had barely changed in two decades.

They had served together in 13 Regiment, third infantry division during World War Two. The retaking of France, the invasion of Sicily and, most brutal of all, the fall of Berlin in 1945. They fought together, side by side, through the most inhospitable environments imaginable. And now, here they were, chatting on a Hollywood movie backlot.

"I don't really know how she even came to be on that boat. Or anywhere, to be honest. She was locked up in a mental hospital in Seattle. Or, that was what they told me."

"Are you sure it was really her?"

"No question. Hell, we were lovers once. She was a flyer on my show for three years. I recognised her immediately."

Blakelock sipped his coffee. "So, you're saying she was somehow responsible for a bomb being planted on that ship of yours? And she came along on that fake harbour launch... what, to see your demise first hand?"

"That's exactly what I'm saying, god damn it! She wanted to see me, see my face! As everything I hold dear – my circus, my people – as all of it sunk beneath the waves."

Blakelock shook his head. "And all this after she tried to kill Shapiro and sabotage your circus back in '58?"

"Right. That was her first attempt at revenge, for me calling time on our relationship. Now... hell, god knows. She probably blames me for whatever horrors she went through in that hospital."

"Or... she still hasn't got over you. Still feels angry at being dumped."

Klondike leant forward. He squinted, his craggy face looking mean and angst-ridden. "There is no doubt in my mind," he whispered savagely. "She wants to finish me... by killing my circus."

Blakelock leant back in the thin plastic canteen chair, and slowly lit a cigarette. He was struggling to think. "Hard to believe all of this could actually just happen."

"Well, it happened alright, Mike."

Blakelock shifted uneasily. "And so you want me to… what, dig her out? Put all the pieces together?"

"Find her, Mike. And find out what the hell she is up to… and how the hell any of this was even possible."

"Kal, this isn't the way to do this, old buddy. Go to the police. Explain it all. Tell them what you just told me. There's probably a warrant out for her capture."

Klondike shook his head. "The police won't take me seriously. Never have done. Not with all the many troubles we've encountered down the years. All the criminals who've stuck their noses in. No." He looked up at his old Army comrade. "Besides. You're the best in the business, Mike. I know it. I trust you."

Still, Blakelock looked perturbed. "Kal," he whispered. "I don't think I can do this."

"You can and you will, Mike."

"Why?"

"You know why!"

Blakelock sighed and seemed to deflate into his seat. "Because of our oath…"

"Right."

"Why did I ever agree to that?"

"Why? Because I pulled you out of that minefield in Gastrade. Carried you on my back for miles, over mines and the bodies of our fallen comrades. When we reached camp, you said you'd do anything for me… after I saved your life." Klondike straightened and tried to look official. "Well, today, right here and now… I'm calling it in!"

Blakelock looked at him quizzically. "You wait nearly 20 years. And then you call it in."

Klondike leant across the small table. "I've never felt a threat like this, Mike. Not in all these years. That crazy broad may be coming to kill me."

"Alright." Blakelock took on a business-like tone. "I'll need a recent photograph. Biographical details. Some kind of-"

"Everything you need is in here." Klondike pulled a small manilla envelope from his breast pocket and handed it over.

Blakelock slowly took it, eyeing him queerly. "You really want the works, don't you?"

"Track her down, Mike. Please, for the love of god, just find her. There's a number in there. You can reach me with any updates. Also, a mailbox for telegrams."

Blakelock nodded absently. "And what exactly are you going to be doing Kal, while I'm out trying to find this broad?"

Klondike took a deep breath. He looked around the canteen discreetly. When he spoke, his words came in a bewildered pronouncement.

"I'll be starting out. All over again."

The boardwalks of Atlantic City.

In many ways the backbone of the seaside resort town, the sprawling old-growth pine marina is known for jutting far out into the eastern ocean, and for marking an entry point into a dizzying world of casinos, gaming halls, slot joints and a seemingly endless cavalcade of vaudeville entertainments.

Every grifter out to make a fast buck on the eastern seaboard can be found among the boardwalks, working seamlessly alongside fortune tellers, caricaturists and street entertainers.

At the very far end of the marina could be found an enormous white and gold limestone structure that looked like it had been transported from the world of Arabian Nights.

With glass domes and minarets sprouting out of its corners and a giant, curved archway above the glass entrance doors, the odd-looking building resembled a foreign embassy or even an architectural oddity conceived by an eccentric.

A large purple and green sign above the entry doors screamed down to passers-by the true nature of the enclosure. In garish lettering, it read: RIBBECK WORLD CIRCUS. EST, 1922.

Inside, the domain was like a circus museum. Vintage show posters and flyers adorned the walls and old midway equipment sat in the many corridors that led to offices and conference rooms.

In a giant first floor office at the head of the great construction, the walls were also covered in circus posters and bills, though these ones advertised more recent shows.

A man and a woman sat before a large, ivory desk, looking up earnestly at a figure hovering by a great bay window, which offered a panoramic view of the legendary boardwalks outside. And of the vast Atlantic Ocean beyond.

Eric Ribbeck finally turned to look at them, his face alive with a bright, yet sinister smile. With a magnificent pompadour of snow white hair, tanned but haggard skin and emerald-like green eyes, he certainly did not look his 71 years. He was dressed in his favourite burgundy smoking jacket and held an ornate meerschaum pipe in one hand, as he nearly always did.

"Finally, the pendulum has swung," he said in a grizzled, Texas accent. A proud son of the lone star state, he had settled on Atlantic City in the north-east as the perfect site for his circus headquarters decades ago, despite his southern roots.

"Finally, that damn yahoo Klondike is finished. Out of the picture. Just like I always said. A straight flush was never enough for that sucker… he always wanted more." He chuckled lightly, appraising his confederates.

Veronica Hunslett, his executive assistant, sat to one side. With her blonde hair tied back tightly and dressed in a midnight blue business suit, she looked cold and aloof. The same could be said for Luca Marconi, the old man's bodyguard and de-facto majordomo, who looked like a Brooklyn street fighter with his oily dark hair, scarred face and black leather jacket.

"You were right all along," Veronica purred, still sat emotionless. "He really did bite off more than he could chew with that European tour. Just look at the mess he has ended up in."

"He never should've set sail for England," Ribbeck uttered icily. "That tour was cursed. Cursed, I tells ya. Even if that Italy show was a smash hit, the whole thing was doomed from the start. Whatever the hell happened to that boat of his in New York… that was God's way of telling him he never should've left, you ask me."

"So, what happens now boss?" Marconi scoffed in his New York accent.

Ribbeck still stood before them, clutching his pipe. His green eyes took on a mesmerising glare as he gazed back at the window, and the rolling waves outside.

"I used to dream of the day Kal Klondike would be out of my hair," he whispered in a dream-like tone. "Ever since he left me and started his own outfit back in '52. He has been a constant, and growing, threat to us ever since. Right up to last summer, when his circus reached a level of transcendence. All thanks to that damn Superstars and Stripes show." His face twisted into a scornful ball of hate. Then, he continued: "Well, now it's all over for Klondike and his ragtag gang of misfits. And so, the moment I have been waiting for, yearning for, in every way for two years…now that moment is here."

He crossed back to the ivory desk and stood directly over them.

Veronica glared up at him knowingly. "You're talking, of course, about cherry picking his talent?"

Ribbeck smiled cruelly. "You're god damn right I am."

Marconi chuckled. "So, last year, you offered Klondike half a million for Shapiro and Olsen. And now… what, you can just pick em up for nuthin?"

Ribbeck paced around slowly, puffing on the great pipe. His face was a conspirational mask of deceit. "The circumstances are somewhat precarious, Luca. Our situation is dicey, boy." He eyed his associates shrewdly. "Far as I can tell, all Klondike's talent is now outta contract. So, we can move in and sign em up. But we have to play the long game. I want Klondike's stars under my big top, make no mistake. That has been my dream for two years now. To put on the greatest show on earth. The greatest line-up of all time. Now, that dream is so god damn close I can practically taste it…"

Veronica and Marconi stared at him, slightly unnerved.

"And, so…" Veronica prompted.

Ribbeck snapped out of his reverie. "So, we finally get Shapiro and Olsen on board. But 'we' won't be doing the work. No, we will have us a little help." He snorted, chuckling to himself. "You see, the recruitment process has already begun, people."

With that, he pressed a bony finger into an intercom switch next to his telephone on the desk. "Jean!" He bellowed. "Show our guest up the stairs."

Then, as Veronica and Marconi looked on, mystified, the old man wandered slowly to the office door. Opening it, he looked down the hall, smirked to himself, then glanced back inside.

"Please welcome our special guest, and the latest addition to Ribbeck World Circus…" he held out an arm grandly as a figure appeared in the open doorway. "The leader of the Daredevils, Tip Enqvist!"

The stunt rider crept over the threshold into the confines. He looked almost unrecognisable in a beige suit, his prematurely silver hair neatly trimmed and his ever-present stubble shaved off. Grinning widely, he shook hands heartily with Ribbeck, before ambling over to the others, arms wide as if greeting thrilled fans.

Veronica and Marconi both gasped in alarm, for this was an unexpected development. And an exciting one.

Ribbeck closed the door and followed Enqvist over, offering him a seat to the side of the great desk. The Norwegian rider sat, and the old man stood behind him, placing a hand proudly on his shoulder.

"That's right," he murmured as Marconi grinned up at him. "I snapped up the Daredevils as soon as I heard Klondike went bust. Now…. now we have the hottest motorbike stunt team in America signed up."

Enqvist's grin was as ever-present. "Honoured to be here, Mr Ribbeck. Me and the boys are delighted to sign with America's leading troupe, and can't wait to get started." He turned slightly and glanced up at the man standing over him. "And it's a pleasure to work for you, sir. A legend in our industry. Even back home in Oslo we'd heard of Ribbeck World Circus. Now, to be here, as part of your outfit, it's a dream come to life, man."

Marconi was still staring at the newcomer, almost in awe. "So," he blurted, "does this mean… oh, man! Does this mean that circle of death gig will be part of our show!"

Enqvist smiled like a wisened soothsayer. "The Globe of Death. Or, rather, the all-new Globe of Death. Yes, my man, the new sphere cage is being constructed by your circus's outfitters as we speak."

Ribbeck joined in happily. "The most frightening, most spellbinding act in the country today. Now, it's ours, all ours."

Veronica shifted in her seat, unnerved by the three wild grins encircling her. "You mentioned something about a little help, Eric…"

"The masterstroke in this enterprise," Ribbeck roared, his hand gripping Enqvist's shoulder harder now. "Tip here is the key to luring our golden duo. Last year, our boy was part of Klondike's holy trinity along with Shapiro and Olsen. The top trio. And look what they accomplished. Superstars and Stripes. Arguably the greatest circus spectacle ever. That's some experience… to go through together."

Ribbeck finally relinquished his hold and ambled behind the desk, flopping into the huge antique desk chair. He tapped the pipe against his teeth, an old habit. "So, now you all have a chance to taste such success again, continue the glory… here, at Ribbeck World Circus."

Veronica was startled. "You mean, that's the plan? For Tip here to talk them into joining him?"

Enqvist nodded sagely. "We went through a lot together. I know what to say to hook them in. Sure, we didn't exactly get along but… well, they will see this is going to be the biggest circus in the country. And the richest."

"God damn right about that…" Ribbeck muttered, pipe in mouth. "Besides, those boys are out of work now. Circus work, that is. They need something. Need an income. And my wages will widen their eyes, dammit." Enqvist sat back, a disturbing grimace clouding his hawkish features. "I'll make sure they have no god damn choice but to join us."

Marconi suddenly joined in. "But, boss, what if Shapiro or Olsen have already been snapped up by one of the other promotions?"

Ribbeck's grimace became a dark, menacing scowl. "Then there are other ways to make them sign."

An uncomfortable silence engulfed the boardwalk office.

Enqvist rubbed at his unusually smooth jawline. "They're smart. They'll go where the money is. Now that the Daredevils are here, they'll see the money that can be made."

Veronica was not convinced. She eyed the newcomer. "That is a hefty role for you to play, Tip."

The stunt rider looked her over, his predatory dark eyes displaying lust and aggression. She shuddered.

"Luca, get the drinks," Ribbeck cried, breaking the awkward silence. Then, he looked at Enqvist with a mesmerising glare.

"That kid Olsen," he whispered, "they say, at that Italy show, he did his act on a high wire? For the finale. With Shapiro and Fortune. All of them up there. Is this… is this true? Did it really happen?"

Enqvist looked him straight in the eye. "It happened alright. Damndest thing I ever saw."

Ribbeck shook his head in awe. "There's no end to that kid's talents. Just imagine… all of them up there on a wire, for the finale! My god!"

Enqvist leant forward, smirking. "Maybe you won't have to imagine for much longer, Mr Ribbeck."

The old man roared like a grizzly bear. Marconi returned with a tray of scotches and handed them all out. He remained standing.

Ribbeck held his glass aloft. "Here's to the future! And our new all-star line-up!"

They all cheered at that. Even Veronica.

"I'm drowning! Help me! Help meeeee!"

"Grab my hand, ma'am. I'll pull you aboard. Come on!"

"No, I'm drowning! I…I can't…I…"

Then came the sensation of being plucked from the icy waters like a rag doll, hurled up from the depths by the two burly lifeguards.

She was unceremoniously dumped on the transom, soaked and shivering spasmodically. All she could hear were cries for help, the sound of utter bedlam. She could see her colleagues all in the water – waving frantically, swimming lackadaisically, as the New York coastguard cutter bobbed around them.

Then, she realised even more of her friends were on the boat. All sat around like her, in tight balls, shaking, barely conscious.

She had never been so cold in all her life. The water had been impossibly bitter. Her breath gushed out in great geysers of vapour.

Then, a middle-aged woman knelt beside her, taking her pulse.

"Can you hear me?"

She remained silent, unable to operate her jaw.

"What is your name?"

"Suzi Dando…"

She looked up now, awoken from her reverie by the soft, southern accent. A tall, gangly young man in faded jeans and flower shirt stood over her, smiling widely.

Suzi had been sat on the floor of the old wooden porch in front of the motel, lost in her memories. The flashback had seemed so real.

She looked up and grinned. "Yup. Er, sorry, I was just thinking of… something that happened a while back."

It was as if the young man had read her mind. "It's alright, Suzi. We know what you've been through."

Suzi baulked. "Really?"

"Of course. Hell, you're a celebrity out here, hon." He looked behind him towards a huge Winnebago camper van that resembled an apartment with wheels. "Anyway, we're about set to move on out, so thought I'd give you the heads up."

Suzi nodded as she stood, stretching slightly. "Thank you…Martin, right?"

"Call me Marty. Marty Bertwee, and the Bertwee Five. Boy, are we glad to have a star like you along with us for the season, Suzi."

She managed a smile. "You're very kind."

"We all are. We believe in peace, love and the Christian way. As a travelling singing group, we can spread our message everywhere." He hesitated. "In you, we see a kindred spirit."

She stared at him. He cleared his throat. "Now, you can ride in the car…" he grinned impishly, "or the camper van. Which is it?"

"The camper van," she gushed.

Without further ado, she grabbed a rucksack and valise, which Marty helped her with, and they walked to the Winnebago.

As she climbed inside, she nodded and said a greeting to the two boys and one girl already inside. All teenagers, they were engrossed in a conversation about some kind of gospel music festival.

Suzi placed her belongings neatly in a holdall above a set of cupboards, and paced silently to a small armchair right at the back of the mammoth van.

As she settled down, she pulled a small item from her jacket pocket, a photograph.

Suzi looked longingly and tenderly at the studio shot of Roddy Olsen. Immaculate as ever in his silver waistcoat and purple pants.

That straw blond hair, the sky blue eyes. Will there ever be another like him, she wondered softly.

Of course not. That was just impossible.

Suddenly, without warning, she burst into tears.

"Oh Roddy," she whimpered.

The man known to thousands of youngsters and circus-goers across the country as Corky the Clown was at that moment just simple, plain old John Lone.

Minus his facepaint and wacky yellow and pink suit, the veteran performer looked anything but a professional entertainer as he sat leaning against the bar in O'Reilly's, an uptown watering hole in Nob Hill, San Francisco.

He looked middle-aged, tired and weary as he slumped on the stool, dressed in a brown suit. It was hard to believe this very man regularly performed spectacular acts of juggling, balance and derring-do under the big top.

So, that's that? He kept telling himself, eyeing the tall glass of lager in his hand. He took a long swig. He felt like he wanted to drink away a great inner pain.

Born and raised in Cleveland, Ohio, Lone had accomplished what so many of his generation had yearned to do in their teens – he had run away to join a circus.

He had become a standout performer in no time, regarded by many industry experts as one of the nation's most skilled and dedicated clowns.

He had been with Kal Klondike since the very beginning, along with Shapiro. The three of them had peeled off from Ribbeck World Circus to form a new and exciting promotion in 1952. The hope, the excitement and the success had been overwhelming.

And now… now it was all over.

"Buy you a drink, buddy?"

The soft voice from behind interrupted his thoughts and he looked up, in recognition as well as shock. As he swivelled on the barstool, his eyes widened and his lips burst into a smile.

"Roddy," he gasped. "Where did you come from?"

There stood the Puppet Master, right here in O'Reilly's, in uptown Frisco. But something was different. Corky nailed it immediately. He wasn't dressed at all like Roddy. This version wore an expensive-looking turquoise suit, with shiny Stanco shoes.

"Hello Corky," said the youngster. They shook hands, and Olsen slid on to the barstool nearest to him. The joint was nearly empty, as it usually was at 3pm.

Olsen continued: "I've actually been looking for you, man. I remembered you used to stay in Frisco at the Remington Hotel. So I asked there. They suggested to try a few of the local bars. This was number three."

Corky was still smiling. "I'm glad you came, kid. I was just starting to feel depressed."

Olsen motioned to the beer glass. "Can I get you another?"

"Please."

He ordered a lager and one soda water from a veteran bartender prowling nearby. Then, Olsen turned to face Corky – and really study him. "So, how have you been Corky? What you been up to?"

The legendary clown looked at him dumbly. He sighed. "First season in more than 30 years… the shows are about to roll. And I'm not signed up. To anything!" He drained the contents of the tall glass. "I feel empty. Lost. Without purpose." His eyes went down sadly. "It's not a nice feeling, kid."

Olsen tapped the beer glass. "Looks like you found an old friend."

Corky shook his head. "No, it's not like that, Rod. Just having a few days to myself. I don't drink booze during the season. This is like a holiday."

The drinks arrived and Corky nodded his thanks, taking a gentle sip. "So, yeah, that's it, already. I've been holed up here in Frisco since we all left Cristo." He eyed Olsen speculatively, noting the fine stitch work of his shiny new suit. "So, how about you kid? What, you get a job selling Martinis or something?"

Olsen laughed happily. Then, he leaned over, against the mahogany bar top, and eyed Corky mesmerically. "You're not gunna believe this…"

The veteran clown was instantly hooked. "What?"

Olsen tried to sound official. "I'm going to be running my own circus!"

Corky's eyes widened to the point where it looked unhealthy, as if they might implode. "You what!"

"That's right. Circus manager, no less." He quickly sipped his water. "Have you ever heard of Miles Courtland?"

"Sure. He is a record producer. Discovered a lot of those rock n roll hepcats in leather jackets few years back. What did they call him? The Idolmaker?"

"Right. Well, apparently, it's been his lifelong dream to run a circus. And now, it seems, after selling his record company, he is ready to make a go of it…"

Corky rolled his eyes. "Hardest job in the whole world. Circus promoter. Getting started is the toughest bit." He narrowed his gaze. "Does this bozo know what the hell he is doing?"

"It would appear so," Olsen said conversationally, relaxing in the bar stool. "But, with his money and influence, it's not so much of a challenge. Anything he wants for his circus, he can have. Just like that." He noted Corky's frown and apparent scepticism, and held up a hand. "I've been down into his camp, Corky. On his estate, which looks like something a royal family would preside over. Everything is there, man. And good hands too. Good, experienced people. This… this is serious."

Corky nodded vaguely, and guzzled some beer. "This all sounds insane, kid."

"I know," Olsen muttered. "But everything really is all worked out. We're doing a soft, half-tour, covering California, Washington State and Oregon. Departure is in three weeks."

"Wow," the clown breathed, genuinely taken aback by it all. "That is the damndest thing I've heard in some time. Courtland! Why, I never saw that coming." He turned suddenly to his old colleague. "So, why did he want you… as manager?"

Olsen's beautiful, bright features took on a queer look. "You know what, I just can't figure that out. He says top talent will want to join us if I'm running the show." He laid his hands out.

"But me? I'm just a kid, man. I don't understand it. However, I'm embracing my new duties as best I can. Courtland is handing me out business cards, portfolio sheets, you name it..."

Corky pointed to the bright turquoise suit. "And a fancy new wardrobe?"

"That was my plan." He looked at himself dumbly. "I figured I should look the part."

The clown was rubbing at his salt and pepper hair. "So what, this whole thing just happened out of the blue... just like that, eh?"

Olsen shrugged. "You bet. Courtland sent me a telegram asking me to come and visit him. Said he had the offer of a lifetime. Well, I had nothing else to do. No gigs booked. Now, I'm running a show."

Corky nodded sagely. "Hmm, just like that." Another swig of beer. Then, he said slowly: "And so, Roddy Olsen, the Puppet Master, the big question. What brings you here? To me?"

Olsen grinned like a cherub. "I think you know, superstar."

"Oh my god," the older man wailed. Then, inexplicably, he burst out laughing. It was almost like he was back on the sawdust again.

"So, you want me to join you? That's it, huh? This is a recruitment drive, isn't it?"

Olsen laughed now, actually enjoying himself. "You bet it is, old buddy. If I'm gunna be running my own circus, I want the world's greatest clown on board. After all..." he gave Corky a mock look of innocence. "You're not signed up, you're on a... holiday."

"Dammit all if this isn't crazy," Corky stammered. His head was spinning. "So, what? Courtland wants me?"

"No, Corky, I want you. Actually, I need you. There's a big difference, buddy. I've been given the keys to this guy's kingdom. His own private playset. I need a guy in there with me I can trust. A proven box office attraction, beloved by fans everywhere. I need you, Corky. I need you."

The older man ran a hand over his mouth. "This is all so much to take in. Are you gunna be a, er, player-manager?"

Olsen was all business now. "We have decided I'm going to do the announcing, like in my first season with Kal."

Corky nodded. "That was some season. And a great format."

Then he looked down. A deathly silence suddenly engulfed the figures in the murky bar.

"You want a few days to think about it, Corky?"

Then, the clown looked up, and his eyes looked wide and clear, his face suddenly alive, his adrenaline pumping. "Nope," he blurted excitedly. "You've got yourself a deal, young man. It's been an awful few weeks, but that is the greatest piece of news I've heard in what feels like an eternity. And also the most welcome." Suddenly overcome with emotion, the clown held out a hand. "Thank you, Roddy. I appreciate this. And, my oh my, I simply can't wait to work with you again."

Olsen laughed like a juvenile. "That's the spirit. Welcome aboard."

The two old friends shook hands.

"Alright everybody, sorry to keep you waiting. And now, it's showtime!"

A woman dressed in a silver leotard with black tights over her legs jogged excitedly into the gymnasium.

A large group of teenagers and twenty-somethings, dressed similarly in gym ware and shorts, all looked up hopefully as she entered the hall.

Calston Community Gym Hall, in Bootham Heights, about 100 miles south of Los Angeles, was hosting its busiest practice night in many months. The class, which specialised in trapeze and acrobatics, aimed to produce world class gymnasts and flyers, and had a favourable track record down the years. But today's session was very special.

The teacher in the silver leotard, still smiling emphatically, glanced back to the locker room door. She nodded.

"And now," she panted, "let's have a grand Calston welcome to our special guest coach. I can't tell you how lucky we are to have her. Ladies and gentlemen, let's hear it for… the fabulous Penny Fortune!"

The gaggle of students exploded into applause as a toned woman with long, shiny blonde hair walked casually into the hall, waving in response to the clapping. She wore a sparkling, orange fireball leotard and her bare arms and legs seemed to gleam.

Penny Fortune joined the throng of youngsters, shaking hands, high-fiving and even hugging some in the excited group.

Everyone offered their thanks, and many hurled questions at the celebrity newcomer.

"Miss Fortune, what are you doing now? Now that Klondike's Circus has closed?"

"Penny! What was it like working with Gino Shapiro?"

"Is it true he has retired? Please say it isn't true!"

Penny held up her hands, smiling. "Alright, alright. Listen guys, I will happily answer all your questions later. I promise. There will be plenty of time. I'm with you all day. But first..." she offered a mock smile and ferocious eyes. "I heard there are some pretty good young flyers here. Now, who wants to show me what they can do?"

Several of the animated group nodded enthusiastically, blabbering at the special guest in indistinguishable chatterings.

Penny nodded, clapping her hands. "Alright, that's more like it." She looked up at the class's trapeze rig, some 25 feet above them just below the hall's ceiling. Three rings hung dormant in midair, with a scaffolding unit sat on either side of the rigging.

"Now, let's get a handler upside down on centre ring. And, anyone who fancies it, how about you line up on the left, ready to hit the first ring. Then, we'll start with some basic vaults. Right across to the far side, then back again."

The youngsters all cried with delight, and most raced for the scaffold. A burly young man with mop top hair and a moustache made his way over slowly, playfully pushing his classmates out of the way.

"Hey, you there," Penny cried, grinning, "handler, right?"

The youngster turned to her and saluted. "Right. I can hurl these young suits, no bother."

"I'm counting on it," Penny gushed.

She stood, arms folded, watching the group getting into position for the training drills.

The head coach stood beside her, her face a mask of utter joy and elation.

"I can't thank you enough for this, Penny. Look at the kids! They're getting a real kick outta this. Having a real circus star here to work with them."

Penny smiled demurely as she watched the big handler swing across to the centre ring above them. "It's a sincere pleasure, Anne. I really enjoy it too. I think I'm going to concentrate on coaching for now. There are plenty of schools, just like this one, sprouting up across the West Coast right now."

"I'm sure," Anne replied. She gazed up at the rings. "The circus industry is booming. You…" she let the word linger. "You played a big part in that, Pen."

Penny shook her head slightly. She seemed to bristle. "Yeah. Yeah, I suppose so. It… it gave me so much. Changed my world."

Anne eyed her. "Do you miss him?"

"Who?"

"Him."

Suddenly, Penny felt herself caving in. The confident coach, the powerful demeanour… it all cracked slightly. She closed her eyes. Saw him whirling through the air with effortless grace, high above the watching thousands below. Even at that incredible height, with all those people staring at them, with everything at stake, he would wink at her as he flew across to her ring, ready for her to take his hands and propel him back up to the tent's summit.

"Yes," she finally blurted as she watched the students clamber up the scaffolding. She sighed heavily.

"Every day… in every way."

CHAPTER FIVE

The Sierra Nevada foothills represented a sprawling territory that almost seemed to embody every kind of landform and terrain imaginable.

Rocky outcroppings gave way to dense forest, all lying in the shadow of the impressive Sierra mountain range.

On the other side, prairies and desert land stretched for hundreds of miles.

Nestled between Central Valley, in California, and the Great Basin, in Nevada, it was something of a world of contrasts.

The turquoise Delta jeep pulled to a stop on the dusty lane it had followed for tens of miles. Nothing but rangeland had filled the horizon for more than an hour.

Kal Klondike put the engine into idle and wiped a mound of desert dust off his forehead. Squinting into the distance, he saw the ranch house, about 400 yards off the lane. His eyes then looked straight ahead and he spotted a giant, stone-walled entrance to the ranch itself.

Then, he rubbed at his unusually clean-shaven jawline. There it was. The next stop on his tour of intrigue.

In the three weeks since the disaster of New York, Klondike had received telegrams, phone calls, even visits to Rio Cristo. Offers of employment. Interest. After all, he had been on the cusp of running the world's most celebrated circus before the Floating Top incident. And then it had all come crashing down. Despite the horror of the nautical disaster and its aftermath, his standing in the industry still remained respectable. It had just taken a mighty battering. Through something beyond his control… or belief.

So far, circus promoters from across the country had contacted him with offers. Job titles had screamed at him. Consultant. Deputy manager. Talent scout. Head of bookings.

But no promotion out there had offered him the one role he craved, and believed he still deserved. Circus manager.

The pain he had felt at losing his most-cherished of possessions, Klondike's Circus, was simply impossible to cure.

The way he saw it, the only answer for salvation and even redemption was to start out again. Running a circus. And, dammit all to hell, making it the best.

Everything had changed two days ago. An unexpected phone call late at night, and an offer that finally got his attention.

The Double G Circus. Operated by Colonel Gregory 'Griff' Garrison, owner and proprietor of the Double G Cattle Company, run out of Sidewinder Ranch, Pearson Valley.

Klondike had heard much about the Colonel down the years. Tall stories. Like himself, he was a World War Two veteran, serving predominantly in the UK and the Netherlands. Legend had it Garrison had been part of the elite black ops crew known as the Purple Jackets, or PurpleJacks, who had operated behind enemy lines eliminating spies and interlopers ahead of attacks and top secret missions.

Lots of tall stories.

But Klondike knew little about the Colonel's circus. One thing was for sure, the man's cattle ranch was enormous.

Finally re-engaging the engine, he drove his beloved Delta jeep up to the huge, slightly unsettling entry gates. Giant stone slabs stood on either side of the open gate, with an old-fashioned wild west sign above saying: SIDEWINDER RANCH.

As he drove up the short gravelled pathway that led to the ranch house, Klondike looked all around him, like a kid at a funfair.

Out on the range, cowboys were herding cattle across the prairies. Inside one of several corrals, a wrangler was expertly breaking a fine Kiger Mustang, which had just ceased bucking.

Klondike slowed to a crawl and watched happily. Born in Hell's Kitchen, New York, the notion of being a cowboy had filled his inner being since childhood, despite the geographical absurdity of it. The wild west had been his whole act when he had performed as a knife thrower, adorned in buckskin cowboy attire.

Now, he finally pulled up to the front of the huge ranch house, which looked like a cross between an old military fort and a country cottage. White, stonewashed walls were complimented by Cape Reed thatch tiles on the roof.

Klondike introduced himself as a tall, young cowhand wandered out of the entrance, dressed in stetson, plaid shirt and jeans.

He was led inside the labyrinthine property, which seemed to be full of studies, parlours and small bedrooms.

Finally, they approached a pine door at the very rear of the ranch house. After a knock from his escort, Klondike was shown in.

The room was a surprisingly modern office. Old wild west and Native American artwork adorned the walls, while the ground space was filled with filing cabinets, boxes, and a typing stand.

Colonel Griff Garrison sat behind the behemoth desk at the far end, a huge window behind him bathing his figure in hazy sunlight.

As Klondike entered, he immediately stood and rushed over.

"Kal Klondike. A pleasure, sir."

"Colonel Garrison. Thank you for inviting me down."

They shook hands. Garrison was an inch taller than Klondike. His hair was quartz grey, and was short and neat, like the crisp moustache beneath. He had the same craggy skin as Kal, but his was redder, from years of exposure to the merciless Nevada sun.

The Colonel was dressed in a caramel blazer, with brown leather elbow patches, and sported the obligatory jeans and plaid shirt. Klondike placed him in his mid-60s.

"Come, sit," the host said. "What can I get ya? Beer? Scotch?" He had a gravelly, mid-west voice, that contained a vaguely aristocratic grace. And authoritative. The sound of a man used to giving orders.

"Scotch would be just fine. Thank you."

Garrison quickly made the drinks at a mini bar in the corner and, with a quick glance through the window at the rangeland outside, he settled into an impressive red leather chair behind the massive desk. Klondike fell into the office chair opposite. They drank.

Then, the Colonel spoke. "Madison Square Garden. 1954. The Jupiter Circus talent auction. You remember that, Kal?"

Klondike baulked. Not the opening gambit he had been expecting. "Sure I remember. Why?"

Garrison grinned. "Before right now, that was the only time you and I had been in the same room."

Klondike marvelled at the words. "You were there?"

"I was. Like you, just starting out with my own outfit back then. Trying to get some guys on board… in a quick and easy fashion. Cheap, too."

"How'd you get on?"

The older man cackled. "Bust right out. Didn't recruit anyone. But…" he smiled knowingly, "I learnt a thing or two."

Klondike grinned, warming to his host. "So, we started out about the same time, Colonel?"

"Right." His face seemed to crack slightly. "But where you conquered the industry, made it to the top, got all those TV specials and Las Vegas contracts…" He stopped and added weakly: "My troupe never really caught on."

Then, he looked fierce again. "I've followed your career with interest, Kal. Really, I have. Right back to your throwing days with Ribbeck. I'll never forget that show, Circus of the Stars: Las Vegas, when Gino Shapiro did that death-defying leap to the tall rope. It looked like suicide."

Klondike chose his words carefully. "It was an unbelievable night. In every way."

Garrison smiled, taking a generous sip of his whiskey. He seemed to make a decision. "It would be an honour to have you run my circus, Kal. I'm not going to lie. You, Ribbeck and Zack Wurley are simply the biggest promoters in the country." He frowned. "Listen, I know all about what happened in New York, and I sure am sorry. Thank god no one was killed. But, in my view, nothing changes your standing in our industry. You're still the best in the business."

Klondike nodded his appreciation. "My thanks."

Garrison leaned forward, like an angler feeling a bite. "Surely you've had offers from other troupes? I can't believe I'm the only one?"

Klondike eyed his host squarely. "You're the only one to offer me a role as manager."

The Colonel's face erupted into a victorious smile. "And that's where you belong, right? Calling the shots."

"All I ever wanted, Colonel."

The older man seemed to be trying to calm himself. He spread his arms. "So… how about it, Kal?"

Klondike simply stared back at him. The Colonel was saying all the right things. And it unnerved him.

Garrison sensed the opportunity. "Listen, my cattle empire here at Sidewinder is a multi-million dollar enterprise. I'm pleased to say I'm at liberty to offer you good money, as well as a free hand."

Klondike's eyes widened. "A free hand?"

Garrison waved an arm through the air. "Sure. I mean, I'll be running it with you, but you know… I'll sign the checks, pay the bills, that kind of thing. Hell, I've tried running this outfit for 11 years and ain't never seen a profit."

Klondike nodded. His dark eyes took in the sea of wild west and Native American paraphernalia that covered the wallpaper.

"I must confess, Colonel, I don't know too much about your circus."

Garrison actually laughed. "Like most of the mid-west public then!" He chuckled for a moment, then got serious. "We started out as a wild west circus in 1950. Roping, horse tricks, sharpshooting, knife throwing, a little rodeo, even some singing from country and western stars."

He stood, glass in hand, and hovered by the great window, staring out at the prairie lands. "Over the years, we started to get more traditional. After much advice. Wanted to look like the great Klondike's Circus!" He glanced back. Kal smiled.

"But somehow, all the talent just never seemed to click with the audiences… which dwindled rapidly. Hell, I could never put my finger on it. But, one thing I did understand… part of the problem was I'm a cattle man, not a circus man. I am out of my depth."

Klondike brooded for a moment. "Why did you start a circus in the first place, Colonel?"

Garrison smiled mirthlessly. "Same reason as you probably. It was my dream. Going to the circus shows with my pappy when I was a boy was the happiest time of my life. I always thought there could be nothing better in life than running a circus… bringing all that joy and happiness to so many. It seemed to consume me."

Again, Klondike had to smile. "I sure can resonate with that."

The Colonel brought them back to the present. "Now, I know what you're thinking. You're tempted, right? But you want to see what it's all about. The talent, the equipment. Hell, the damn tent…"

Klondike spread his arms. "You got me!"

Garrison sniggered. He beckoned Kal up.

"Let's go!"

"Seems like we've got a fair bit in common, you and me…"

Garrison almost shouted above the roar of the exhaust from his pick-up truck as he guided the motor down a sandy path that seemed to split his massive ranch land down the middle.

Klondike looked out at the fine Black Angus livestock that roamed freely among the vast open range. Wranglers could be seen on horseback every now and then, like centurions watching over the herd. He was actually enjoying himself.

"You mean as circus promoters?"

"Nope," Garrison looked edgy, serious yet cautious. It was a queer mannerism he maintained. "I'm talking about the army, Kal. Hell, I've seen your record. You're a god damn hero."

Klondike shook his head. "I never quite reached your status, sir. A colonel, no less!"

Garrison was not messing around. "You ever hear about me in the services? Rumours, gossip, the like?"

It was a test. Klondike knew that. He just had to play his hand right. He decided to call.

"They say you were in the PurpleJacks. That's quite an elite squadron."

Garrison grimaced. "The dirty work done behind the scenes. What nobody ever hears about. After a while, got kinda hard to tell the good guys from the bad." The man's sun-kissed face seemed to darken. "I saw you served in Sicily and at the fall of Berlin. Figured you'd heard something."

Klondike stayed silent. No use opening up any old wounds. The issue did not concern him remotely. For now, anyway.

"So look at us both," the Colonel said behind the wheel. He was watching the sandy track intently for potholes and rocks. "Old war veterans. Now in the circus business."

"You couldn't have made it up," Klondike mused.

Finally, the truck came to a clearing at the end of the long lane. It slowed smoothly.

As if suddenly gripped by some form of rapt excitement, Klondike leant forward, then pulled open the door the second the engine died.

Before him stood a circus camp.

It seemed isolated and impossibly removed from civilisation out here on the rangeland.

A small, battered-looking barbed-wire fence encircled the grassy enclosure. The whole thing looked to be under one square mile. Within sat the usual plethora of trailers and cabins found in any circus camp in the world, along with rows and rows of midway stalls and construction equipment. Klondike noticed an entire fleet of fancy-looking Winnebago camper vans all parked to one side. There must have been 20 of them. There seemed to be some kind of rehearsal stage in the very epicentre of the clearing.

Beyond that, on the far side, stood a mini-big top, coloured gold and white. The training tent.

"There it is," Garrison proclaimed proudly. "My baby. The Double G Circus." He eyed Klondike nervously. "Now, I know it might not look like much, Kal. But we're aiming to get bigger and better." He winked. "Under your stewardship, soldier."

Klondike smiled. "No, it looks just fine, Colonel. Just very remote."

"You were a circus train outfit. I know that. We travel in vans. Transporters. A big convoy. As we head into towns, the folks know the circus is coming!"

Klondike nodded. "So that's what that fleet of Winnebagos is all about?"

"Right. Got one ready for you, Kal. 25-footer. Nothing like it on the road."

Klondike smiled ruefully. "That might be just as well. I've got developers and realtors scouring my home right now, about to give me a price."

Garrison placed a hand gently on his shoulder. It actually shocked him. "It's alright, Kal. You come on board with me and my crew, we'll make things right. How, you ask? Well, you'll be involved in something special again. You'll have purpose."

Klondike shook his head. The older man spoke like a college sports coach at times, but seemed to have tapped into his current mood. And depression. It was unnerving.

"So, let's hear the schedule, Colonel."

"Right." Garrison led the way to the small fence, and opened up the simple wire gate. They slowly walked into the camp, as if without care or concern.

Two long lines of circus trailers bordered the gravel path that led into the headquarters. Garrison began talking wistfully, as if selling off one of his prized longhorns.

"We currently operate a 13-city, eight-week tour. We play the major south-west spots mostly. Start in Memphis, then move through Dallas, Houston, El Paso, San Antonio, Tucson, Phoenix, Albuquerque… you get the idea. Our biggest show, every year, is in Balboa Park, San Diego." He finished with a theatrical flourish.

Again, Klondike nodded shrewdly, as he studied the trailers that lay sprawled all around them. "And when do you roll?"

Garrison stopped walking and stood very still. Again, the apprehension showed. "In six days."

"Oh, Jesus…" Klondike groaned. He rubbed his eyes, and wandered around in a vague half-circle, as if confused. "This is getting more and more overwhelming, Colonel. Six days!"

Again, the Colonel placed a comforting hand softly on his guest's shoulder.

"Come on. Come and meet the guys!"

The stars and staff of the Double G Circus were all enjoying some downtime in the crew's canteen/recreation quarters, a red-bricked bungalow that looked like it had stood there for centuries. The massive structure was found right behind the practice stage, so Klondike saw several performers in action as they made their way inside.

Cowboys. All doing horse tricks and hind-leg salutes.

"Those boys are the Riders of the Double G," the Colonel said grandly, waving. The five cowboys waved back, noting the presence of Klondike. "Been here since the start."

They entered the bungalow. A canteen fell on the left, with bench tables stretching beyond them like giant, flat dominoes. To the right, what looked like a large living room seemed to bleed out in the other direction. They entered it.

"Alright, few people I'd like you to meet, Kal," Garrison mumbled.

The pair stood at the head of the great room. Immediately, a giant of Native American descent approached, moving like a loose wardrobe.

"Hondo Cloud," Garrison proclaimed. "I thought you might have a special interest in him, Kal. He's our knife thrower!"

Klondike shook hands. "Pleased to meet you, Hondo."

"A true honour, Kal Klondike," the big man blurted loudly. His hand looked like a bunch of bananas as it crushed Kal's. "You are one of the greatest ever throwers. We are privileged to have you here."Then, as if dismissed, he ambled off again.

Cloud was replaced by a man who looked like he was pushing 80, dressed in a leather jacket and slacks, with porkpie hat.

Garrison again did the honours. "Kal, please meet Don 'Fearless' Peerless. A fire eater extraordinaire. Just don't ask him for a light!"

Klondike politely laughed at the ancient gag. "Peerless, eh? That's a great name for PR. Pleased to meet you."

"How do you do?" the old-timer said in a rasping voice that sounded like its owner was being asphyxiated.

Klondike raised an eyebrow. "How long you been doing this gig, Mr Peerless?"

"Since I was 14," Peerless rasped. Then he grinned, showing a mouthful of brown and black teeth. "So, 10 years!"

They all laughed, and the fire eater left.

Next up came an unusual-looking woman, who strode elegantly over like a princess who had gotten lost. She looked middle-aged, but her skin was soft and smooth and her hazel hair immaculately coiffured. Her dark eyes looked wild and somewhat zany. But it was her dress that garnered most attention.

She wore a Middle Eastern harum-style get-up, coloured indigo, green and brown.

The woman curtsied before them grandly. Garrison was grinning like a pampered cat.

"Please allow me to introduce Miss Arletta LaRue. Our very own… snake charmer."

Klondike froze as he shook the lady's hand. "Snake charmer!" he blurted. "Hell, I ain't never had one of them before."

In an inexplicable moment, Arletta placed her free hand on top of his. "The men, they love it. They see my power over my babies, and are lost in adoration and wonder. My babies obey me. It is, how do you say, spellbinding."

Klondike stared at her. Her voice was warm and smooth, blissful. The accent sounded French. He felt like he was being hypnotised.

Snapping out of it, he gently took his hand back. "Well, that, er, sounds wonderful, Miss LaRue. I look forward to seeing a demonstration."

She bowed gracefully, and floated away again.

As if on cue, another figure appeared before them. But this one looked more like a monster. Seven foot tall, possibly 300lbs, he wore a vest and sweat pants. His muscles were impossibly huge and plentiful, seemingly bursting out of his body. But the face was unforgettable, like a modern-day Genghis Khan, a violent, angry, almost terrifying look. But, for Klondike, recognition ripped through his mind.

"Strongman, right?" Klondike muttered as he got his hand crushed again by the behemoth.

The big man just stared down at him, snarling slightly.

Garrison stepped in. "This is-"

"I know, I know. Soolaimon, the Mongolian giant." Klondike squinted up at the head, well above him. "Did I see you perform for Racey's Circus down in Fresno one time?"

Soolaimon merely stood there, as if in rage.

"The good thing about our strongman here," Garrison muttered, "is that he stays in character all the time. Kind of like a bad guy wrestler."

Klondike nodded approvingly. "Them's the best kind, Colonel. A true professional." He quickly looked up. The giant was smiling.

Then, with a grunt, the musclebound strongman wandered off, the floor echoing with each step.

Garrison continued to lead Klondike around the recreation lounge. He was greeted with warmth and respect by everyone. Some seemed excited to meet him.

He was introduced to all of the Riders of the Double G, as Garrison explained to him that their cowboy tricks and skits filled the entire first half of the show. Then, the floor opened to the "solo stars" Kal had just met near the door. All four of them.

As he was introduced to the circus roustabouts and stewards, he suddenly felt a little lost. Inexplicably, he fell into one of the many easy chairs scattered around the unusual room. It was an armchair, the type popular in the 1800s.

Garrison watched cautiously. "Alright, Kal. We'll wrap it up for now. This must be a lot to take in."

"Damn straight." Klondike removed his hat and fanned at his face.

"What can we get ya? Beer?"

"You read my mind."

One of the stewards, who seemed to be some kind of waiter, hurried off.

Garrison stood over his guest now, one foot up on a coffee table next to the armchair.

"So, what do you think?"

Klondike rubbed at his eyes. Talk about a fast-moving day. He had seen a lot out here. And it had made him think. But he definitely felt something.

"Colonel Garrison," he muttered, suddenly feeling very tired. "The first, and most important, thing I have to do now is see everyone perform. Each act individually. Then the whole damn show. All together. Out in your practice tent."

Garrison grinned again. He looked like a hungry dog straining at a leash. "Yes, yes, sure. You got it. But... but..." he was stammering wildly, and he knew it. He calmed himself down. It was bizarre to watch.

Then, he looked up coldly. That look. There was the look of a Black Ops mercenary again. A ruthless practitioner. He hadn't lost it over the years.

He addressed the seated Klondike with steel in his voice now.

"Mr Klondike. Will you help us? Will you become our manager?"

Klondike gazed up at the Colonel with respect.

The suspense was strangely overpowering in the far corner of the room.

Then, Klondike rubbed at his jaw and simply let the words fall from his lips.

"Yes. Yes I will, god damn it!"

CHAPTER SIX

The Colonel rolled out the welcome mat for his esteemed guest, in every way. Klondike was allowed full use of a small guest bungalow on the ranch grounds. The following morning, he was invited to join the Colonel and his wife Karen for a steak and eggs breakfast in the ranch house's main saloon. Garrison eagerly produced circus posters and flyers for him to pore over as they drank coffee afterwards.

Then, it was time to head down to the camp again. Garrison raced them down the sandy lane in his truck, as if possessed by a new found energy.

At the circus headquarters, the two men wandered excitedly up to the mini-big top, where all performers were now gathering.

Inside, Klondike saw it was set out like most practice arenas he had encountered. There was the usual sawdust-covered circus floor, a low wooden boundary wall around the perimeter, and then just several seats thrown together here and there. They walked through the traditional tent flap, which was positioned next to a fleet of trailers, where each act now waited.

Klondike and Garrison settled into a pair of old oak chairs sat near the flap and looked out at the sawdust arena floor before them.

Kal's eyes automatically darted upwards, to the summit, a domain where so much unforgettable circus action he had witnessed down the years had taken place. He noted there was no trapeze rigging up there. Just the tent ceiling.

"You don't have any flyers," he said quietly to Garrison, still looking upwards.

The Colonel's face seemed to drop. "We did. But they never showed up for camp this summer. Damn yahoos bailed out on us!"

Klondike frowned. "Who did you have?"

"The Bliscoe Brothers. You heard of them?"

"Yeah, I heard of them alright." Klondike's eyes showed understanding. The brothers had a reputation of no showing.

They had been on the California circuit for years. Pulling the same old trick.

Klondike again eyed the tent ceiling. "You still have the trapeze rig?"

"Sure. It's in the storage shed. Along with the touring tent."

Klondike nodded. His eyes fell back down to the sawdust.

"Alright," Garrison said. "We'll run the whole show by ya, Kal. Then you can discuss each act, see it again… whatever, you name it."

"Sounds great. Ready when you are."

Garrison nodded. Standing, he called out to a stetson-wearing steward stood in a wooden booth behind them. "OK, hit it, Bronc!"

A country and western tune suddenly boomed out of the tent's speakers. Then, a smooth old voice proclaimed: "Ladies and gentlemen, boys and girls, welcome to the Double G Circus. We hope you enjoy the show. Please give a warm welcome to our opening act, the fabulous Riders of the Double G… yee-hah!"

Then, the team of 10 cowboys on horseback all burst into the tent. They galloped round in great circles to begin with, before slowing, then beginning random tricks as the mounts continued running in loops. There were headstands on the saddles, switching mounts, riding double and acrobatics that saw the riders hang onto the bottom of the saddles.

Then, five of the cowboys dismounted and led on the sawdust, before the other five took it in turns to vault their horses over them.

Klondike studied the horses. They were all golden palominos, 15 hands high, and in excellent physical condition.

As the riders all remounted and the horses all darted off in different directions, they took it in turns to perform hind leg salutes, all perfectly executed.

In the middle of this showcase, a blond-haired cowboy dressed in silver shirt and stetson rode over to the watching management and suddenly stood on his saddle and performed a somersault, landing before Garrison and Klondike.

"That's Rawley Walsh, the Double G leader. Been with me since he was a teenager," Garrison muttered proudly.

Klondike doffed his hat at the performer, who responded in kind.

Then, the Riders of the Double G all dismounted and broke out into an array of rope tricks with their lassos. The faultless display lasted a good eight minutes, with each cowboy performing a different set of tricks. They were all there, the tall lasso loop, the wide loop, the decreasing circle, and an array of rope hops, where the performers jump in and out of the loop as they spin it around their bodies.

Then, the team were back on their mounts, racing around the arena floor again. This time, a steward wandered into the centre of the sawdust and began hurling plates into the air. The cowboys took it in turns to draw pistols and fire, obliterating each plate with immense accuracy.

Klondike leant over to Garrison. "What's in those guns?"

"Blasters," the Colonel said without alarm. "Caps like firecrackers. They shatter as soon as they hit the plates."

Klondike nodded thoughtfully. Then, he raised an eyebrow as a dramatic drumroll sounded over the tannoy.

Now, the steward was standing in the centre of the stage floor, holding a plate high in each hand. Twenty yards away, Walsh was off his horse… and was now blindfolded.

The veteran cowboy stood on his haunches for several moments. Then, with lightning fast reflexes, he made his draw, pulling out each of his brace of Navy Colt handguns from his holster in a blur and firing.

The two plates shattered instantly. Then, the other Riders began encircling him rapidly, each throwing another plate into the air. Walsh, still blindfolded, fired continuously. Every plate shattered, leaving shards of old white clay covering the sawdust.

The Riders of the Double G all began wailing "yee-hahs" and held their hats aloft to an imaginary crowd.

Then, another drumroll sounded. Walsh, back in his saddle again, rode his horse slowly to the far side of the floor. At the opposite end, another of the team did the same.

The two men stared at each other across the arena.

"Watch this," Garrison whispered, nudging Klondike gently.

Suddenly, after a whip crack sound exploded over the tannoy, the two horses began charging at each other across the sawdust.

Like two jousting knights from medieval times, the pair of riders raced directly at one another.

Klondike leant forward. A nasty collision seemed just moments away as the cowboys got closer and closer. The horses were fearless and direct in their galloping.

Then, in an almost imperceptible, lightning fast move, the two riders leapt from their saddles as the horses brushed past each other. The two men performed a mid-air pirouette, their bodies glancing off each other, and swapped saddles. The whole thing lasted barely one second, and now each cowboy was riding the other one's horse, slowing as they reached the far boundary wall.

Klondike began to clap. Turning to Garrison, he said: "Now, that was impressive."

"Thought you might like it," the older man said, smiling grandly.

Then, the sound of blaring trumpets thundered from the speakers.

The Riders of the Double G trooped off. The horses were breathing heavily, the cowboys all holding their hats aloft.

The stage announcer's voice returned. "And now, ladies and gentlemen, please welcome the human abnormality, the man who eats and breathes fire. Let's hear it for Don 'Fearless' Peerless!"

Peerless wandered casually into the arena, waving at the management. He wore a bright green shirt and what looked like yellow fire department pants.

The old-timer stopped at a long steel desk that a roustabout had just assembled, and began fiddling with a big steel barrel.

Dramatic piano music began blaring down from the tannoy. Then, Peerless drew a long stick, similar to a stream reed, from a pouch on the desk and shoved it into the barrel. He withdrew it, its end now covered in fire.

With a chuckle, he opened his mouth wide, threw his head back and simply dunked the entire stick into his mouth.

Klondike watched in awe. The tip must have been at the bottom of his gut, he thought idly.

Peerless closed his lips, rapidly withdrew the stick, and then leant forward.

Like a mystical dragon from some ancient fairy tale, he blew a mighty ball of raging fire into the air before him, held it for a few seconds, then breathed in again. The small blaze was gone.

"Thank you," Peerless said with a wink.

What then followed was a wild, almost nausea-inducing display of fire eating as Peerless ate the fire sticks, and blew out mini-blazes of all shapes and sizes. Then, he threw into his mouth six fire sticks in one go. Withdrawing them, he fell to his knees and then let the following eruption soar into the air. The enormous cloud of fire that shot into the atmosphere made for a shocking sight. The eerie way it all cascaded back down into the man's mouth was even more unsettling.

Then, a drumroll sounded. For his climax, Peerless lit up two small balls, ping-pong sized. He placed both tiny balls of fire into his mouth, leant back and then spat one two feet into the air, before shooting out the second. He repeated the trick continuously, juggling two inflamed balls with his mouth.

Klondike watched the surreal trick, rubbing at his jaw. It was unsettling to watch, but he could not look away. Despite all of his many years of scouting for talent, he had never seen anything quite like this.

After about 30 seconds, the bizarre juggling act finished. Peerless hastily removed the now unlit balls from his mouth and stood, hands raised, as if cherishing the cheers of an audience.

Klondike and Garrison clapped. Peerless nodded and waved his thanks, then casually breezed out of the tent, as if finishing a day's shift at a workbench.

"Ever had any accidents there?" Klondike whispered.

"Nothing, thank god," Garrison replied. "Don is a smooth operator."

The Texan voice returned on the tannoy. "And now, ladies and gentlemen, prepare to be spellbound by the enchantress of the west. The snake charmer extraordinaire… Arletta LaRue."

There was silence. Two stewards then ambled on to the sawdust, carrying a large black coffin between them.

Klondike frowned as he watched. The duo placed the antique, well polished casket in the centre of the stage floor, where Peerless's desk had been moments earlier.

Then, a queer, almost haunting flute tune rained down from the speakers.

The casket burst open, and there she was. Arletta LaRue. The strange and sensual woman sat up slowly, then stood. She wore a black silk dress that would not have looked out of place at a Broadway cocktail party. Klondike squinted at the unusual display. Then, he realised the coffin was full of snakes. As he focused on the moving masses at her feet, he realised there must have been five or six of the creatures in there, including a python that was now encircling her slender frame.

Arletta began a beguiling dance, moving her body in time to the eerie music, spinning slowly through the air and holding various aerobic poses. The python seemed completely at ease. She gently pulled its head towards hers, and the two stared into each other's eyes. Woman and beast. Then, she held the snake full in her hands above her head, and it became apparent just how large the monster was.

Holding it again around her shoulders, she deposited it back into the coffin, and replaced it around her neck with another. In all, she performed the same dance and hypnotic looks with each of the snakes.

Klondike thought he saw a boa constrictor, mamba, viper and a small grass snake. It was mind-blowing. And frightening.

"What gives with those snakes?" he spat out as he watched. "Are they drugged or something?"

Garrison shook his head. "All under the spell of Madam LaRue."

Klondike grunted. "This will make a lot of folks feel unsettled. Trust me."

He continued to watch with interest, and Arletta began her finale.

Slowly and tenderly, she knelt at the coffin and pulled all of the snakes onto her shoulders. Then she stood, the entire upper half of her frame covered in a grotesque, bizarre-looking ensemble of slippery green and brown flesh. As the snakes all clung to her hideously, she held her arms aloft, and bowed.

Then, holding the mass of creatures earnestly, Arletta simply sat in the coffin again, and then led down, pulling the lid closed over her.

The same two stewards returned to the floor to collect the casket. Hoisting it up, they simply ambled off stage again, transporting the box of horrors and mystery away.

As Klondike watched from his chair on the sidelines, somewhat befuddled, another announcement boomed down.

"Behold, ladies and gentlemen, as the Double G Circus presents to you… the world's strongest man! It's the Mongolian giant…Soolaimon!"

An old-fashioned horror movie theme sounded. Then, with a roar, the circus strongman appeared from the flap. He wore baggy, Arabian Nights-style pants and was shirtless. His chest and shoulders were truly immense. On his head he wore a fur helmet with two horns sticking out of each side, which he soon removed and placed on a medieval-like throne that had been placed at the stage's centre.

Soolaimon began his act by picking up a classic gym barbell loaded with multiple 25kg weights. Hoisting it up above his head like an Olympic powerlifter, he held it in place before turning the huge set of weights around in a circle. In seconds, he was spinning the bar around as if it were a bamboo stick. Keeping the motion going for a full minute, the giant then halted the spinning and, in a shocking turn, held the arrangement vertically by one of the weight blocks, before placing the lot deftly upon the top of his head. Then, he nonchalantly folded his arms, balancing the mighty load.

Next, he gripped the barbell and then hurled it 10 feet into the air. Crouching slightly, he duly caught the immense load in his hands, the effort seemingly causing him no trouble at all.

The Mongolian giant then approached the flap again, walking slowly and methodically, like a robot.

The crew of circus stewards all approached him, as if to shake hands. But Soolaimon lifted the first one up off his feet, seemingly with minimal effort. Placing one hand at the man's throat and the other around his belt, the giant hoisted the steward above his head like the barbell, before then performing push-ups, raising the figure up and down with his enormous arms.

The giant repeated the feat with each of the five stewards, who had extended a hand, before being unceremoniously hauled into the air and used as a human weight bar.

After placing each man back on his feet again, Soolaimon wandered casually to the throne in the centre of the floor, placed his warrior helmet back on and merely lifted the great throne up with one hand before walking off stage with it. He made for the flap and left the tent altogether. And that was that.

Watching by the flap, Klondike frowned. As impressive as the feats of strength were, the strongman act had featured very little showmanship or razzmatazz.

His thoughts were interrupted by the next announcement. "And now folks, get set for the finale of our show. The Double G Circus is proud to present to you… the most wanted man in the west! Deadly with a knife, with hands like crossbows. Let's hear it for the Pride of the Sierras… Hondo Cloud!"

The huge Native American walked in grandly. He was almost unrecognisable from his appearance in the lounge the previous day. Now, Hondo wore his full performance attire, consisting of a caramel buckskin jumpsuit, the arms and legs of which were adorned with tassels. A Comanche-style poncho covered his shoulders. His black hair was combed straight back, flattened to his skull.

Behind him came a woman who looked barely out of her teens, dressed in a similar buckskin outfit.

"Who's the girl?" Klondike asked absently as he watched the entrance.

"Betsy. Been with him since he started out," Garrison whispered.

That same group of stewards had brought out a giant wooden wheel, painted the gold and white colours of the big top.

Within seconds, Cloud had positioned Betsy on the great wheel, tying her wrists and ankles down with leather straps located in the corners of a rectangular formation on the flat surface.

The duo said a few words to each other, then Cloud walked slowly to a small stand 10 yards from the wheel. With a theatrical gesture, he removed a black cloth from the top of the stand, revealing a glittering set of six, long and ferocious-looking Bowie knives sat together in a black leather sheath.

Cloud nodded to one of the stewards, who moved to the large wheel and, with a mighty yank, set it spinning. The wooden disc moved rapidly, spinning Betsy around in wild, blurred circles.

Opposite her, Cloud set the leather sheath in a standing position. He breathed deeply. Then, it happened.

Crouching lightly in a classic thrower's stance, Cloud grabbed at the first knife in the holder, held it behind his right ear, and then hurled it forcefully at the spinning wheel. With a mighty whack, the instrument slammed into the smooth oak inches away from Betsy's right hand.

With rapid velocity, Cloud repeated the move with the rest of the blades. The next three landed barely an inch from her left hand, and either foot. The fifth one embedded itself just above her head. And the sixth slammed into the tiny space between her knees, as she continued going round in complete circles.

Cloud held a hand aloft, as if saluting overwhelming applause.

Then, as the stewards untied Betsy and helped her down, the big man in buckskin opened a drawer on his stand. He removed what looked like a machete. He held the giant blade up, as if for everyone to realise what it truly was.

With Betsy safely away from the wheel, a steward set it in motion, spinning the great disc so it quickly became a blur to all who watched.

Cloud had walked back a good 15 yards from his previous position, putting him more than 20 metres away from the spinning wheel. This time, the Native American moved like a baseball pitcher, keeping the machete behind his frame at arm height, then spinning his body and throwing the great blade with his wrist almost horizontal.

The machete whizzed through the air, planting itself into a small red circle dead centre in the wheel. A bullseye.

Cloud held both arms aloft, as if celebrating a home run or a touchdown. All he got in response was applause from Klondike and Garrison, watching on from the flap.

"Thank you," he called out. Betsy ran over and gave him a hug, then the two idly wandered over to the flap, stopping by the watching management.

Cloud leant on the wooden perimeter wall next to Klondike, and grinned at him whimsically.

"Well, what did you think, Mr Klondike?" His voice was deep and raw.

Klondike looked up at him, then back at Garrison beside him. The show was over. That was it. Now, everybody wanted his opinion.

"You've got a lot of talent, Hondo," Klondike rasped, somewhat bewildered. He turned slightly and noticed all of the talent – the cowboys, the other acts, stewards, everyone – had gathered at the flap entrance.

The old country and western tune playing on the tannoy died abruptly. Suddenly, the practice tent was deathly silent.

Klondike stood up slowly, looking befuddled and awkward. He raised his hands.

"I want to thank you all for this demonstration of your talents," he said loudly, addressing the entire gathering. "It's obvious to me you all have a great deal of potential and skill. Now, we all have to figure out the best way to showcase it. Believe me, that's a skill in itself. But… it's what I do best. What I've been doing my whole life."

"Did you… did you like us, Meester Klondike?" It was Arletta, stood at the front of the group by the flap. She still wore her distinguished black dress, but he could not help but picture her covered in snakes. She was staring at him, eyes wide, almost in fright.

Klondike smiled weakly. "I liked you. That was a unique show… a truly unique showcase. I really enjoyed it."

Those words seemed to appease the group, who all slowly dispersed, creeping through the flap and out towards the trailers. Cloud offered a final handshake to Klondike, saying: "It was a great honour to perform for you, sir. A great honour."

Then, with an arm around Betsy, he too left the practice tent.

Within a minute, Klondike and Garrison were all alone again, sat there on the sidelines.

"Well," the Colonel finally said. "What did you really think? Can you make this work?"

Klondike looked up once again at the tent ceiling high above. Then, he eyed the speakers, the perimeter wall, the sound cabin behind them, and then the flap. His eyes were pensive, alert. He made a curious smelling motion, closing his eyes, as if nourishing the pungent odour of the sawdust.

Finally, he turned to Garrison. "Hell… I'd like to try."

Dusk fell over the Sidewinder Ranch like a deep scarlet dye dissolving into a clear glass of water. The skies quickly turned a dark, glowing red, then faded into the grip of darkness. A Sierra Nevada night skyline, borne of the eternal and merciless sun that graced the prairies day after day.

The crimson skies and darkened hills made for a memorable backdrop across the ranch. Klondike had enjoyed a short walk around the stable grounds after supper and now stood, centurion-like, at one of the galaxy of fences that encircled the fields and corrals.

Leaning against the old oak fenceposts, he looked out across the range as the light fell. A gentle breeze had wafted down from the Sierras, causing him to turn up the collar of his leather jacket and ram his fedora tight around his skull.

He studied the longhorn cattle, as they wandered freely across the ranch land. Singularly and in groups, all seemed content here at Sidewinder. Standing alongside the livestock, Klondike found their grunts and snorts oddly therapeutic as he tried to think in the night air.

It was hard to believe that, barely two months ago, he had overseen a circus spectacular in Rome, a show that would be talked about for years. Seven thousand fans, a roster of American and Italian stars. A finale that had been simply unforgettable. He closed his eyes. He could still hear the screaming fans, the adulation. On the other side of the world.

In a daze, he thought of all the major shows his old troupe had starred in down the years. Circus of the Stars. Superstars and Stripes. The ATV spectaculars. That Las Vegas show at The Golden Dune. His circus had grown bigger each year across the 1950s, eventually reaching the zenith of the industry.

He thought of all his old superstars. Of Gino Shapiro. Roddy Olsen. Corky the Clown. The Daredevils. The Hightops. The talent on his roster had been the envy of every big top in America. Maybe the whole world.

And now… now he was here. Presiding over the Double G Circus. A Mid-West touring outfit. He thought back to the dress rehearsal earlier in the practice tent down at the camp. Then he thought back to Rome. In just a few short weeks, his whole world had turned upside down.

Next, he thought of Jenny Cross. How could it be that his monumental reversal of fortune could all be down to one woman? It seemed absurd. Yet he knew what he saw. That wave goodbye. It would stay with him forever.

Then, curiously, he thought of Lacey Tanner. Dear, sweet Lacey. His muse, mastermind and miracle maker. A woman like no other in this world. They had been apart for two weeks now. To him, it felt like a lifetime already. It seemed inconceivable to not have her presence in his life.

"Kinda relaxing out here at night, ain't it?"

He was awoken from his reverie by the rasping voice from behind. He turned at the fence and watched Colonel Garrison approach, emerging from the rapidly descending darkness like a wraith. He wore a sheepskin jacket, and black stetson.

"Very much," Klondike blurted, nodding at the cattle. "Your cows… they help me think."

Garrison laughed. He held out a hand, and Klondike saw it contained a leather pouch full of cigars.

"La Masouras, from Latin America," the Colonel whispered. "I heard you like em."

Klondike grinned. "More than life itself."

He took one and placed it in his mouth, holding it in place as Garrison offered the flame of a gold Zippo lighter. The Colonel then bit off the end of one for himself, and lit up. The two tall figures in the fading gloom quickly disappeared in a giant purple cloud of thick, hazy smoke at the fence.

"My thanks," Klondike uttered in awe. "That is the greatest."

Garrison nodded, then leant against an upright fencepost and surveyed the cattle dotted around the range as darkness fell.

"I know what you're thinking," he muttered, eyes on the spread. "How did you fall so far? So fast. I saw your face down there in the tent earlier."

Klondike gently inhaled and let the smoke fall from his lips in billows, savouring the taste. "That's not the whole story,

Colonel. I'm happy to be here, really I am. You and your people have offered me a chance. A new start. And I'm eternally grateful."

Garrison looked him over, as if trying to pierce his thoughts. "You weren't overly impressed by my performers, were you?"

"That's not true, sir. I was. But I also feel there is room for improvement. That's why you're hiring me, right?"

The Colonel ignored the question. He tilted his head back. "You think there's any chance you could entice any of your old troupe down here? Y'know… your superstars?"

Klondike baulked, the cigar clamped firmly in his jaw. "It wouldn't be right. They were almost all killed because of me. I put them all out of work, in the blink of an eye. After promising so much. They all – well, almost all – agreed to go their separate ways, just like that. No ill feelings, no demands for cash. They were all signed up… long term. And then it ended." He grimaced and shook his head sadly. "I can't now come calling on them. On any of them. Besides…" he looked at the Colonel uneasily. "The wages in those contracts are A-list pay checks. Some of the biggest in the industry. We… we were making so much green, none of it was a problem."

Again, Garrison nodded calmly. He toked silently on his cigar as the two figures stood still in the near darkness.

"What do you think we need here, Kal? I mean, to make the Double G a real success."

Klondike seemed to wince slightly, then faced his host. "You need stars. Shining stars. In my experience, the true stars in any circus are the flyers, the acrobats. The guys that get people off their seats."

Garrison nodded. "Top flyers are hard to find…"

"Yeah, that's right. But, listen, we got us six days. That's a bit of time to bring somebody in, find some more talent. Maybe unearth a diamond."

"What? You can do that?"

"It's what I do. I've spent years scouting talent."

"But how will you find anyone in less than a week?"

Klondike finally offered him a smile. His dark eyes seemed to twinkle in the moonlight as an enigmatic force appeared to consume him. "I know a guy."

Garrison looked at him in shock. The two men merely stared at each other. The silence of the night suddenly seemed overpowering.

"Thought you boys could use one of these."

They both turned. The Colonel's wife Karen was approaching from the ranch house, carrying a small tray containing two steaming mugs.

"Cooky's black coffee. Texas style. Oughta warm your sides pretty good in this chill." Karen approached and held out the tray. The two men took a cup each.

"Thank you, Karen," said Klondike. He looked at her. She was a small woman with short brown hair and a friendly, relaxed demeanour. "And my thanks for all your hospitality. Putting me up here and all. I sure appreciate it."

"Not at all," she breathed, eyeing her husband. "Why, it's not every day we have a celebrity up here at Sidewinder." She rubbed his arm, and then made her way back towards the ranch house.

"Celebrity…" Klondike moaned quietly. He sipped his coffee. It burnt his tongue. "Hell, I'm bankrupt. I've got developers scouring my winter camp upstate. I'm in debt to about six different organisations. My old backers have dumped me. Nobody in their right mind wants anything to do with me."

Garrison remained impassive. The colonel in him came to the fore. He thought carefully about what to say next. "You know, we haven't talked about your wages yet, Kal. Your budget. The whole package."

Klondike waved a hand through the air, trailing cigar smoke like a sparkler. "I didn't mean it like that." He thought for a moment. "What I guess I'm trying to say, Colonel, is that I'm just grateful to you for giving me this chance. To be a manager again. A leader. A trail boss."

Garrison drank his coffee. "I can see it means the world to you."

"It did," came the bitter reply. "More than anything in life. But then… to have it all taken away like that. It was… well, it was indescribable."

There followed a long, awkward silence. Klondike stood like a statue, staring into nothingness on the edge of the rangeland.

Finally, Garrison placed his mug on the rounded top of a fencepost. He took a deep breath, as if preparing himself for an uncomfortable outcome. Then, he said it.

"Kal... what the hell happened to your outfit?"

Klondike raised an eyebrow at the question he had long expected from his host. He looked to the heavens. His craggy face transformed into a grim snarl.

"We were on top," he began quietly, slowly. "One of the most successful troupes in the country. But when you're at the top of the mountain... the air gets mighty thin. You look down, and you see enemies everywhere, climbing up, trying to get at you. Getting on top is one thing... staying there is the real test. And you never know who is coming at ya. That was part of the problem..."

Another uncomfortable silence. The snorting of the longhorns out in the range punctuated the quiet.

Then, Garrison spoke again. "Who did this to you?"

Klondike glared at him in astonishment. "How... what makes you say that?"

The Colonel was impassive. "Years of intelligence training. Interrogations. You learn signs, signals, mannerisms. You get the idea."

"Yeah..." Klondike whispered in shock. He chose his words carefully. "It's not your problem, sir. I am, er, dealing with it. My way."

Garrison offered a curt nod. "Fine. It's none of my business, Kal, but... I know people. People who may be able to help. You change your mind... you let me know, ok?"

Klondike stared at him, then nodded. "Again, I appreciate it, Colonel. I know a few... people, too. And one of them is kinda handling this for me, in a manner of speaking."

"Good. Then may God go with him."

Darkness settled in full over the mighty ranch. The two men remained at the fence, as if observing some unknown vigil. Both were lost in their own, unspoken thoughts, which were plentiful in number.

The pair of them stood there for some time.

CHAPTER SEVEN

The large mansion house overlooked a beautiful, tropical garden, where palm trees and tall grass were plentiful, while a whitestone patio led to a swimming pool.

Beyond the redwood wall at the back, the monolithic hotels and casinos of the Las Vegas Strip were visible, looming in the distance like planets in an astral plain.

A whole vortex of world class entertainment and gaming, right on the doorstep.

On the first floor balcony, a woman dressed in a beautiful white frock watched over the exotic gardens and pool. A look of sheer satisfaction covered her features.

She had long, straight blonde hair and cool blue eyes, with pale skin and a slender, toned physique, like an athlete.

Leaving the sunlit balcony, she moved through glass doors into a large dining room, that sat grandly in the sunshine gushing through the tall glass doorway.

She seated herself at the head of a beautifully-set dining table, covered in plates of bread rolls, meats, fruits and pastries. There was enough to feed a multi-generational family gathering, yet she was alone at breakfast.

However, none of the rich delicacies and treats on offer caught her attention. Her cold blue eyes locked on to the morning newspaper, which she had already opened to a specific page.

With an ice cool glare, she looked again at the article on page 11, savouring the words of the banner headline…

CIRCUS KING KLONDIKE FACING RUIN…TOURING SHOW IS ALL OVER

She read the first few paragraphs for the third time that morning. The words gave her an eerie, warm feeling, like a bolt of electricity running through her. It was the sweet feeling of victory, she realised.

Now, looking around the opulent surroundings she was immersed in, the feeling was stimulated further. She felt near ecstatic. Her world had transformed, and everything had fallen in her favour. Everything.

"Grace!" she bellowed into an adjoining room. "I'll have my coffee now."

An elderly woman in a black maid's outfit breezed in silently, placing a cup and tiny jug of cream next to her plate. She slid out just as quietly.

The woman doused the cream into the cup and took a long sip. Then, she snatched at a croissant and had a bite. Everything tasted sweet.

"Good morning, darling!"

She turned as an older man entered the upstairs dining area. He wore an immaculate silver suit, and looked almost twice her age.

His receding hair was grey and oily, and he had the look of a former tough guy who was turning to fat through lack of exercise.

Ray Generoso. Her latest meal ticket. A man who had fallen for her instantly over the tables at the Desert Inn.

"Ray, darling, you look wonderful!"

She stood, and the pair shared a passionate kiss.

"You are staying for breakfast, of course?"

"No," Generoso scowled, looking over the great spread with loathing. "I've got to get over to Nero's Palace for a meeting. They need me and the boys to watch over a new delivery of slots."

"Oh, how exciting," she gushed.

He looked at her oddly, then kissed her again. "Enjoy your day, baby. Remember, we've got that function at the Las Vegas Country Club tonight. Wear something real nice, eh?"

"I sure will. I have plenty to try on!"

He chuckled at that, then offered a vague wave and set off down the marble staircase, a grand affair that circled round in a half corkscrew down to the porch.

She watched him stiffly. As soon as the door slammed shut, she returned to the dining table. Greedily, she filled her plate with pastries and fruit items.

Everything tasted good.

An hour later, the woman left the huge mansion house, walking happily into the bright morning sunshine in her dress.

She leapt behind the wheel of a yellow Gran Torino that looked like it had just come off the production line. The motor roared to life, and then it sped away down the home's long, gravel pathway, and onto the main boulevard that led to the city highway.

As the grand vehicle rolled out of the mansion's enclosure, its driver would never know, could never know, that she was being watched.

Mike Blakelock sat behind the wheel of a black Sedan, parked on the curb just behind a row of pine trees that made up the perimeter of the exotic property.

As the Torino breezed out onto the main road, he started up his engine and eased the Sedan along, following the bright yellow motor at 30 yards on the deserted road.

When they reached the main Vegas highway, he was able to drop back to 60 yards. The Torino was easy to follow with its bright, shiny yellow paintwork. He could see it from virtually any distance.

The woman drove into the downtown area of the gambling metropolis, finally parking up in a street filled with stores and restaurants.

Exiting the car, she walked freely along the busy street, drawing admiring glances from men of all walks of life as she breezed past them. Finally, she entered a jewellery store.

Blakelock was practically crawling along the street in his Sedan. He parked directly opposite the door of the store, and was able to watch as the woman in the white dress was shown various necklaces and bracelets.

Several minutes later, she exited the bespoke store, a shiny gold bag under one arm. Reaching her car, she appeared to lock something small in what looked like a mini-safe in the Torino's dashboard.

Then, she was off again, walking briskly down the street, in the direction of the Red Rock mountains that sat beyond the desert city.

Blakelock turned off the ignition and got out. Following the fleeing woman with his eyes, he slammed the car door shut, and pulled on a dark blue jacket.

He crossed the road, saw his quarry moving about 40 yards ahead of him, and began following her.

Men, women, boys and girls, all rushed past him as he moved down the busy street. But he never lost sight of that white dress, and the slender figure within it.

She suddenly turned, and skipped up a short run of stone steps into a large, old-fashioned sandstone building. As Blakelock reached the steps, he looked up. Las Vegas City Art Gallery. With a roll of his eyes, he followed her in.

Inside, the gallery was a labyrinthine complex of white-painted corridors that led from one viewing room to another. Each room contained no more than four paintings.

Blakelock knew little about art, but was certain some of the pieces displayed were classics, and very valuable.

The woman seemed to have a pattern of stopping in each viewing space, dissecting every painting up close, before deftly moving on to the next corridor.

Blakelock stayed well back, able to watch her from a distance as he wandered idly around the complex. As he followed, he ran through his mind once more the strange series of events that had seen Kal Klondike re-enter his life.

He had known Klondike for years, since basic training with the Marines. Back then, he was still called Terry Calder. But nobody had called him that in years, he knew that.

Blakelock had meant every word when he had sworn an oath to help Kal at any time, back in that medical tent in France. The man had saved his life, at great risk to his own. He would help, no matter what. He had just never expected the call to come over an issue like this. A woman. A former lover. But one who had apparently destroyed his beloved circus. A criminal mastermind, it would appear, with contacts and backing.

Jenny Cross.

She now called herself Julia Carson, it seemed. Romantically involved with Ray Generoso, almost 30 years her senior. A former bag man for the mob, who had worked his way up the syndicate chain until he had been offered the role of casino manager at three of the mob's Las Vegas gaming halls. And, as a reward for his long service to the organisation, Generoso had been gifted riches and a share of the profits that he could only have dreamed of.

And now he had Jenny too. A grim picture of what kind of woman he was dealing with was forming in Blakelock's mind.

He began to wonder what he was being dragged into. Klondike had called on him because he trusted his old war buddy. And because he was a professional.

Before he had come to Hollywood to work as a stunt co-ordinator, Blakelock had worked as a private eye in Los Angeles. Utilising many of the skills he had learnt in the Marines and on the battlefield, the New York native had built up a strong reputation… as a first class problem solver.

Now, he watched idly in the shadows of a mighty stone pillar as Jenny Cross viewed an ancient oil painting.

He studied her toned arms, bare under the cocktail dress she wore. Her pale skin, and beautiful blonde hair. Idly, he wondered how many men had fallen victim to her schemes… if it was all true.

Could it really all be true?

Nodding to himself, he made a decision.

"So, what's good here?"

She looked up, somewhat startled, as the man eased himself onto a bar stool next to hers.

Mike Blakelock had changed into a dark blue suit and now looked dapper and sophisticated as he addressed the woman.

Jenny smiled thinly. She was now wearing an Arctic silver fur coat over her dress. "I'm just sticking to my favourite cocktail. Nevada Twilight." She nodded at the tall glass in front of her, which held an unusual-looking green and white mixture.

The newcomer studied the drink. He knew it was her third of the afternoon. He had been watching her from a booth by the doorway for the past half hour.

Gerardo's was a high class cocktail lounge located at the heart of The Strip. With a high society dress code and overpriced wine list, it was a bar where the Las Vegas elite tended to gather. Right now, at 3pm, it was fairly quiet, just a few tables of businessmen discussing casino trade making up the custom.

"Nevada Twilight," Blakelock muttered. "That sounds interesting. And a little wild." He looked her in the eye. "In this instance, I think it could be wildly interesting."

Jenny smiled again. "This is the only joint in Vegas that serves them. They're the greatest."

"Can I get you another?"

She froze for just a second, studying him curiously. Blakelock pretended to look at something in his wallet.

"Sure. Why not?" she finally uttered.

He signalled to a bartender and made the order. Then, looking around, he said: "You know, I've always wanted to come here for a drink. Just never made it. My associates all say it's the best bar in the city."

Blakelock let his gaze linger as he studied the opulent confines. Then, he let it settle purposefully on Jenny beside her. He had caught her looking him over. She let her eyes drop.

He took the plunge. "Say, don't I recognise you from somewhere?"

If she was alarmed or shocked, she did not let it show. It was a question she had faced countless times before, he figured. And she was now putting on an act, his instincts told him.

"You might," she replied sharply. "I used to be a model. Monde, Miss Alesi, various other fashion mags. I'm retired now. Enjoying the, ah, fruits of my past labours." With that, she downed the contents of her cocktail glass.

"Well, that all sounds mighty interesting, Miss…"

Again, she studied him, her ice cool blue eyes showing minor alarm, but also interest. "Carson. Julia Carson."

"Pleased to meet you, Miss Carson. My name is Matthew Black."

They shook hands as the drinks arrived.

Holding his cocktail glass delicately, he held it aloft. "Cheers. Here's to…the fruits of life."

They touched glasses and each took a sip, casually eyeing each other.

"And how about you, Mr Black," she said coolly. "Do you work in the city?"

"Yeah, and about 10 others!" Blakelock blurted with a chuckle. He looked at her. "I'm an oilman in Denver… most of the time. Over the years, we've struck big on some wells across the southern states. So, a year ago I started investing in other interests. An old pal of mine from Princeton talked me into joining him on the board of his casino, The Starlight, north end of The Strip."

He had watched as Jenny's eyes widened slightly as he talked.

"Oh my," she gushed, "that all sounds… wildly interesting, Mr Black. Princeton! Oil! The Starlight! You must be a very busy man."

"Oh, I am. But, over the years, I have come to appreciate life outside of work. The dynamics of spending money, not making it, are what thrill me now." He held out an arm, pointing to the Las Vegas Strip through the tall windows behind them. "I guess I'm in the right place!"

He watched with interest as she took a long pull on her cocktail. She would be drunk before long, if she wasn't already.

Blakelock continued. "It's all very grand. The only problem I have is my enemies. Rival oilmen. All trying to bring me down. Some guys back in Denver even tried to frame me. Have me arrested for market manipulation and illegal drilling. It beggars belief, I tell ya. But I've managed to outsmart them all, every last damn one of them. Now, all is sweet again in my world. Now that each and every nemesis is taken care of. At last."

With those final words, he turned to study her again. She appeared strangely transfixed by his story. Her eyes were glassy.

He probed further. "I'm sorry. I don't suppose you can relate to any of this, Miss Carson." Then, he squinted at her. "Or can you?"

Suddenly, she snapped out of it. She shook her head and grabbed at her glass. "I am sure I don't know."

Blakelock changed tactics. "I'm sure a nice girl like you has never had enemies. Ha! Only admirers."

She turned on the barstool, and gave him a very queer look. To his immense relief, she then giggled lightly, almost purring like a lounge cat. She shook her hair casually, then put the glass to her lips and finished off her fourth cocktail of the past hour.

"It has been a pleasure, Mr Black," she murmured. She stood up, and the magnificent fur coat slipped from her frame slightly.

Blakelock leapt off the stool in a gallant manner. He quickly grabbed at the coat, moved slightly behind her, and placed it over her shoulders again. She adjusted her arms inside.

Turning, Jenny eyed him up and down. "Thanks for the drink. Maybe we'll see each other again…sometime."

"I'd like that," Blakelock whispered.

Then, with a final haughty gaze, Jenny Cross strolled elegantly across the lounge floor, pulling the mighty coat around her again. The tuxedo-clad doorman almost fell over himself opening the great glass door for her. She left, the long blonde hair and giant coat soon lost in the sun-drenched sidewalk outside.

Blakelock watched her go. He waited a full two minutes, then glanced down at the contents of his right hand.

A small, thin pink notebook.

He hadn't tossed a pocket in years. But, evidently, he had not lost his touch. The opportunity with the fur coat had been perfect. He placed the notebook on the bar top. His eyes widened as he read the solitary word on the front cover.

Diary.

He had struck pay dirt.

CHAPTER EIGHT

The Westward Pier Carnival had been running for years in Santa Barbara.

With shows several times a week throughout the spring and summer, the old-fashioned attraction aimed to hook in tourists, travellers and weekenders, while also relying on a host of regular patrons.

The carnival was like a nostalgia trip to times gone by. Laid out across the Santa Barbara waterfront piers were ferris wheels, dodgems, giant slides, and a sprawling midway featuring every game of chance every conceived by a carnie operator.

Fortune tellers, caricature artists, balloon kiosks and cotton candy sellers were everywhere.

A large marquee at the far end of the enclosure offered a live show, often featuring dancers and vaudeville performers.

Kal Klondike wandered idly across the old wooden planks, his gaze going from the cool waters of the Pacific below to the mighty ferris wheels whirling round high above. He was trying to think clearly about the many incidents that had covered his path over the last week, but it was hard to think about anything – the ragtime music blasting out of just about every attraction at the waterfront was somewhat overpowering.

Then, with a grin, he spotted the man he was looking for. Stood next to the wheel of fortune. Just like he said he would be.

Harry Taskman looked like a grizzled gold prospector from another era. With messy grey hair hidden by an old porkpie hat and a ragged white beard beneath, he could have been mistaken for a hobo. And probably quite often was. His brown cloth suit did little to shatter that illusion.

Taskman had always reminded Klondike of Walter Huston's character in The Treasure of the Sierra Madre. Old, rambling, seemingly disorientated, yet wise and astute when it mattered.

In truth, he was a veteran talent scout, whom Klondike had known for years. They had worked together under Ribbeck back in the day, and Taskman had recommended several acts to Klondike down the years.

At that moment, the old-timer was savagely attacking a box of popcorn, as if weeks had passed since he'd last enjoyed a full meal.

"Harry!" Klondike boomed as he approached.

Taskman's wrinkled face screwed up into a smile. "Kal, you old son of a gun. How goes it?" He had a high-pitched Southern accent.

They shook hands warmly, just as the big spinning wheel hit the jackpot, causing a teenage couple to shriek with delight.

"All the better for seeing you, old buddy," Klondike rasped, putting an arm around him and leading him away from the crowd at the wheel. "Like old times, meeting up at a California carnival."

"Sure is," Taskman said, finishing the popcorn and tossing the box into a huge garbage bin by the pier rail. "I was shocked when you called me asking for help, Kal. I didn't think I'd ever see you again, things being the way they are."

Klondike nodded ruefully. "Things don't always turn out as you'd think."

Taskman nodded and took on a sombre look. "I sure am sorry about what happened to that ship of yours. And everything else. Sounds like your troupe was on top of the world after that tour of Europe. But now, I guess…" he let the sentence hang.

The pair walked idly along the great pier, past a semi-circle of spectators watching a man juggling plastic pins while balancing on a unicycle.

"It's alright," Klondike uttered. "I told you on the telephone about my latest venture. Hell, I'm starting out again, Harry. From scratch."

Taskman began fiddling incessantly, rubbing his fingers together. "You didn't give me much time. For anything!"

"Hell, I know Harry. I just need talent. I've got the guts of a show at the moment. We need some star power."

The old-timer studied him shrewdly. "Just what kind of a show is that Garrison running down there in the Sierras?"

Klondike shook his head. "At the moment… one that isn't making any green. It's up to me to help change that."

They continued walking, joining a steady stream of patrons wandering from the pier attractions to the tent at the far side. It was a circular marquee, the kind used at old horse shows, and was painted pure white.

The duo moved inside and saw a mini-arena of seats drawn out in a large circle. In the middle was a three-foot tall, wooden wall that encircled a small stage of about 30 yards in diameter. The floor within was covered in sand.

"Alright, Harry. What have you got for me?"

Taskman grinned. "Rollerskates."

"Roller what?"

"Come on, Kal. All the kids are doing it now. They don't walk or run, they skate."

Klondike rolled his eyes. "You made me come all the way out here to watch rollerskating?"

Taskman smiled knowingly. "Just you watch."

Klondike was about to protest further when an announcement suddenly boomed out over a PA system. They both sat down.

"Ladies and gentlemen, here for a 12th consecutive night at the Westward Pier spectacular, please give a warm round of applause for the new sensation of the ages… California's own speeding superstars… The Rollergirls!"

Several screams of delight rained down from the seats around them. Then, Klondike looked down at the stage as a steward opened up a door hidden within that small wooden wall.

Then, from out of nowhere, six women dressed in bright purple leotards zoomed onto the stage floor, as if propelled by rockets.

They burst onto the sand in single file, and proceeded to roam around the space in lightning fast circles.

Klondike's eyes fell to the floor and studied the skates. All he could make out was some kind of red boots with small wheels beneath. Then, he watched the routine with interest.

The Rollergirls were racing around the perimeter with super fast velocity. Then, after several laps, the team began performing tricks, throwing in somersaults, handstands and flying pirouettes, all the while returning their skates to the ground and continuing to zoom around the stage floor.

Then, as a cheer broke out, the six flyers all leant forward and picked up even more speed, before somehow mounting their skates to the mini-wall that enclosed them. Each one skated along the vertical base for several seconds, mounting and then returning to the ground, and seemingly defying gravity, as their bodies took on an almost horizontal slant.

The action never slowed. Next, the flying women in purple skated close together, forming a huddle of sorts. Then, three of the flyers crouched as they skated, allowing the other trio to place their skates on to their shoulders. Incredulously, what followed was a mesmerising sight as three of the team skated around the stage, each carrying another lady, standing, on their shoulders. The transition was seamless, and the stunt was made to look easy, with the shoulder mounted skaters all stood still, perfectly balanced.

The shoulder standing came to an end as each of the high-placed flyers leapt off their escorts, and continued to fly across the sand in a blur.

Then, the Rollergirls came to a sudden standstill. As the spectators all watched in earnest, one of the team, seemingly its leader, led them into the very centre of the clearing. A steward had placed a small circular stand before them, which looked like a half-dome and measured about two metres wide.

The lead skater climbed into the small interior, and was joined by one of her team-mates. The duo joined hands and began spinning round repeatedly within the half-dome.

As silence gripped the marquee, the pair began bolting around in circles at supersonic speeds, becoming a blur of purple.

Then, the second skater inexplicably leapt into the air, placing her legs around the other's waist. The first woman gripped her ankles with her hands and, suddenly, she was spinning her flailing partner round and round at a breathtaking pace.

It was almost frightening to watch, looking for all the world as if the woman being propelled around in lightning fast circles would smash her head or arms, or maybe be flung wildly to the floor beyond.

But the spinning looked almost balletic, despite the velocity.

After about two minutes of maddening whirling, the lead skater finally began to slow her pace, and pulled her companion closer to her frame. The carried skater grabbed at the leader's shoulders, and then deftly pulled up her legs and flipped herself off, before landing on her skates and continuing to glide smoothly around the half-dome. The whole act was breathtaking, and as fluid and professional-looking as a Las Vegas cabaret routine.

The spectators, seated and standing in ragged formations across the tent, applauded heartily. The Rollergirls all began skating slowly in another big circle within their enclosure, waving and blowing kisses to the watching fans.

Thirty yards back, near the entrance, Taskman nudged Klondike as they watched the skating sensations.

"So, what'dya think, Kal?"

Klondike had not stopped smiling since the shoulder carrying. He winked at his old friend.

"I think we've got a live one here, pal."

Pamela Hotch was still breathing heavily, her face and neck drenched in sweat as she listened to Klondike's proposal. Her bright purple leotard was soaking wet with perspiration, and her skin looked red and somehow inflamed.

She was standing in the foyer of the Rollergirls' massive, industrial-sized trailer, chatting with Klondike, as the rest of her team lay sprawled on armchairs and couches in the lounge area just behind. They all looked breathless and hazy, as if they had all just run a marathon.

"Alright, alright," Pamela was saying. She was older than the others, maybe 30, and had a hardened, streetwise look that matched her Brooklyn accent. With long, straight hazelnut hair and pugnacious features, she came across as feisty and alert.

"So what's this circus of yours called again?"

"The Double G Circus. Out of Sidewinder Ranch, in the Sierras."

"Sounds like an episode of Bonanza," Pamela said with loathing. "And you want us to come over there, to your 'Sierras', and live with your people and tour with them too?"

Klondike remained cool. "That's how a circus works, Miss Hotch. We all travel together to the shows. It's a two-month engagement. You get your own trailers, plus three squares a day, at the ranch and on the road. You get $200 each per show, and no charges, for anything." He saw her mentally mulling it all over.

He threw in an incentive. "It will make for great publicity for the Rollergirls. You'll be playing to audiences all over the Mid-West. Just imagine…"

Pamela looked back at the other five skaters. They were all too exhausted to respond in any manner. She wiped at her brow with a white towel, which she then threw around her neck. "We never pictured ourselves riding with a circus, Mr Klondike. I ain't never heard of rollerskaters performing in a circus show."

Klondike leant against a cabinet in the narrow foyer, standing just inside the trailer door. "Miss Hotch, I've been in this business since I was 16. Talent spotting for more than 10 years. And I am telling you, you girls have what it takes to be stars. Superstars! Circus crowds will love your act, trust me. What I saw out there in that marquee was very special. Unique, unusual and… sensational."

Pamela stared at him, unmoved. It was as if she just didn't trust the visitor. She leant back slightly, resting her spine against a breakfast bar. "I've heard plenty about you, Mr Klondike. You had the number one circus in the country. Ain't that right? You were the manager of some of the biggest names in the industry. And now look at you! You're here, trying to sign me and my girls up, at a pier show!"

Klondike tried to remain calm. "I've scouted out some of the biggest names in circus history. And now I'm here… because I believe in you. I'm offering you…. you Rollergirls, the opportunity of a lifetime. To be superstars. To have fans screaming your names across the country." He stopped, trying to give Pamela his most sincere look. "Now, Miss Hotch, what do you say?"

Pamela finally cracked a little, looking downwards, concerned and a little worried. She rubbed at her elbow. Another look at the others, and again they all ignored her. It was obvious the team was used to Pamela doing all of the negotiating, essentially making her their manager.

Finally, she spoke, this time in a softer, less hardened tone. "I'm sorry, Mr Klondike. We thank you for your interest, and for coming to watch us in person. But… well, you see… this just isn't us. Roaming around the Mid-West, with some kind of cowboy show. I just don't think it's going to work. It's too much… too much for us. It ain't gunna work out. I know it."

Klondike felt his shoulders sag. The bitter sense of defeat tugged at his every emotion. But he knew the feeling well enough. He smiled and waved a hand through the air.

"That's alright, Miss Hotch. I understand. I really do. I'd like to thank you for your time." He raised his voice, so all of the team could hear. "You Rollergirls are a talented crew. My congratulations." Then, to Pamela, he added: "If you change your mind, you know where to reach me."

He extended his hand. Pamela took it, surprising him with the strength of her grip. "Thank you. See you around."

He smiled again. "I hope so."

Then, he was gone, out the trailer door and into the night again. The Westward Pier backlot was a giant field covered in trucks, vans, trailers and vehicles of just about every description.

As Klondike walked gently away from the Rollergirls' enormous trailer, Taskman appeared out of the shadows and fell into step beside him.

"I can tell they said no. That's too bad."

"It sure as hell is," Klondike mused, looking sadly out to sea. The Pacific looked dark and foreboding now at this late hour. "They've really got something with that act."

Taskman watched him shrewdly, his nose twitching slightly in the breeze. "So, what are you gunna do now, Kal?"

He sighed. "You got anything else for me, Harry?"

The old-timer shrugged. "Nuthin that you'd go for, my friend. There's all manner of acts in carnivals like this up and down the west coast. But you want elite performers…"

"I want stars, dammit. Superstars." Klondike tried to calm himself. His frustration was mounting. "We need flyers, Harry. Something to build this show around. A headliner. A franchise builder. Someone real special."

Taskman nodded silently as they walked slowly towards the Westward Pier parking lot. "You've just left it too late, Kal. Anybody worth having is signed up to a big top by now. The season is under way for most circuses. You know that. You're scrambling around for talent now. Ain't no other way to put it."

"Yeah, I know," Klondike drawled. He looked up to the night sky. "Someone real special," he repeated, as if entranced.

Taskman frowned. "You've known a few of them."

"Yeah, I sure have," he whispered ruefully. "The best of the best."

The camera crew finalised their positions on the set. An elderly director watched everything studiously, pacing around like a predator ready to strike at any moment.

They were gathered outside the Meredith Building in Sunset Hill, off Hollywood, for the first of their many off-set location shoots. This scene involved the lead character of the movie jumping off the first floor balcony of the immense building, and landing in the backseat of a convertible… about to be driven away by the woman he loves.

As the movie officials all took a last look at the Cadillac convertible in the street, the director glanced up at the balcony above him. It was a long drop, he thought for the hundredth time that morning.

He turned, agitated, as he surveyed the growing swarm of excited spectators standing by a small plastic fence used to seal off the street for the production. Members of the public loved to hang out around movie sets. Anywhere in the world.

Inside the foyer of the Meredith, a group of actors and actresses smoked and drank coffee, exchanging small talk and gossip.

Just beyond them, by the stairwell, Gino Shapiro watched the group with mild interest. He wore a dark brown suit, with a black rollneck beneath. His eyes caught sight of the movie's leading man, Richard Lewis, who was dressed identically. Lewis caught his gaze and smiled, offering a slight wave. He then returned to talking to his leading lady, a beautiful Hollywood starlet dressed in a red blouse.

Shapiro nodded at the pair and couldn't help but smile. His jet black hair had been styled into a quiff to make him look more like Lewis. The life of a stunt double, he thought idly. Looks are everything out here in Hollywood.

Outside, the director made an announcement through his loudspeaker. "Alright, everybody out here for a final run-through. Then, it will be action stations people."

The groups of actors and actresses headed out the glass revolving doors, led by Lewis, all still chatting and laughing among themselves.

Shapiro followed behind, along with the second unit director, who was to supervise his leap from the balcony.

Suddenly, as Shapiro followed the ensemble outside and down the granite steps towards the camera crew and Cadillac, a mighty cheer erupted from the watching group of fans stood beyond the set's perimeter fence. Women screamed. Applause broke out.

Richard Lewis turned towards the spectators, grinning widely and holding a hand aloft.

Then, someone from the public group screamed: "Look… it's Gino Shapiro!"

More cheers and gasps emanated from the onlookers. Frenzied comments floated across the street to the film-makers.

"I can't believe it's really him!"

"He's turned his back on the circus to do stunt work… can you believe that?"

"The hell with Richard Lewis. That's what a real star looks like!"

The excitement seemed to simmer through the group watching across the street. Then, in one giant act of unparalleled unison, everyone – camera crew, director, sound man, actors and actresses – all turned as one and stared at Shapiro.

Gino stood there on the bottom step, smiling sheepishly and waving a hand softly through the air. "They know me, you know, from the circus," he said weakly.

The elderly director was incredulous, standing at the front of the film crew. "These people… they're all here to see YOU!"

Shapiro looked across the film set, and nodded. "Circus fans. They, er, follow their heroes."

One of the supporting actors snarled, crying: "Then why don't you go and serve them some cotton candy, pal!"

Shapiro remained cool. He was about to respond, when a female voice shrieked: "Gino, I love you!"

The watching group all laughed.

By the camera, the director seemed to snap. "Alright people, let's get on with this…"

But the entire film crew were looking from Gino to the spectators and back again.

Then, Richard Lewis broke away from the production team and ambled slowly over to Shapiro at the steps.

The two men, dressed identically, stared at each other for several moments. Then, Lewis said: "What are you doing here, Gino? You belong on a bigger stage than this… a stage all of your own." He gestured to the watching public across the street. "I think those guys have just confirmed that."

Shapiro forced a smile, looking across the set at the excited onlookers. Then, he looked down sadly, hands in pockets.

"Si, is true. But, alas, my stage is gone. Finished." He looked up and eyed Lewis directly. "There is only one true stage for me. And it was taken away from me."

Lewis nodded vaguely. "I understand… I think. But, listen man, there are other stages. Surely?"

Shapiro looked back at the excited members of the public who had screamed his name. His mind slipped back through time.

"Not for me, amigo."

Hullabazoo Toys Inc.

Located in Barbary Street, San Francisco, the famous old store was an emporium of nostalgia, beloved by children, parents, enthusiasts and purveyors of hand-crafted collectibles.

Roddy Olsen could not help but feel a deep sense of sentimental emotion as he entered the shop. He had first visited some 10 years previously. Back when he was a teenage kid with big dreams.

Now, he walked confidently to a door at the back of the ground floor, passing shelves cluttered with teddy bears, woollen figures, plastic soldiers and cowboys, and intricately carved wooden animals.

Knocking once on the door, he breezed through and found himself in a large workroom, full of shop benches covered in tools and lines of sheet plastic and odd-shaped pieces of fabric.

A middle-aged woman wearing a long, knee-length brown work coat was hunched over a small sewing machine, pulling a piece of fabric taut. She looked up at the sound of the door closing. Recognising Olsen, her face burst into a beautiful smile.

"Roddy…" she breathed. She stood up. "How wonderful to see you. So glad you could come, in person."

"Carolyn. Are you kidding? I wouldn't miss this for anything." He approached the woman and they hugged briefly.

Carolyn Adams had worked at Hullabazoo for decades, since the site had opened. Olsen had met her years earlier, as a teenager. He had come to this store a long time ago, asking if anyone could make him a puppet.

Now, he was back. And it felt like an almost spiritual odyssey.

Carolyn could not stop smiling, her trademark octagonal glasses perched on the end of her nose. "Look at you", she gushed. "You still look so young. So fresh. Like when you first came to me. You've hardly changed at all."

Olsen rolled his eyes. "Yeah. Everybody still calls me 'kid'."

"I'm not surprised." She studied him for a moment, wiping her wrinkled hands on an old cloth. "So, I hear you are working for Miles Courtland now. I read about it in the Chronicle. What, er, what's he like?"

"Real nice." Olsen glanced around the work room, looking awkward and unsteady.

Carolyn smiled wisely. "I'm sorry. You want to see my work. I'm stalling it all. Come!" She gestured to the back of the large workshop, where a long desk held a range of parcels, boxes and packages.

"No, I'm sorry," Olsen whispered. "I don't mean to appear rude. It's just that… well…"

"I understand, Roddy. Come, here we are."

She stood in front of the long table, pulling a neat, two-foot tall velvet bag towards her. She placed a hand gently inside. "Ready?" she said.

"Oh my goodness, yes."

With a grand flourish, she pulled the loose bag down, revealing its contents.

It was impossible. There, on that old table, sat Rusty Fox. Not the Rusty Fox sitting at the bottom of the Atlantic, alongside so many props and accessories from Klondike's Circus. No, this was a new creation… identical in seemingly every way to the original.

"Oh my god!" Olsen gasped, staring almost hypnotically at the puppet. He delicately touched the figure's cheek. "It's him. Carolyn… you've done it! You've brought him back."

The older woman was grinning uncontrollably, her heart warmed. "Well, I did create him, all those years ago." She ran a hand over Rusty's trademark quiff hairdo. "It wasn't as complicated as you'd think. What with all those pictures you gave me. They covered every conceivable angle."

"Thank you," Olsen said in a trancelike voice. Then, as if under a spell, he picked the fox puppet up and placed his hand into the holder. The act came to life again. It was magical.

Rusty looked at the ventriloquist and shook his head. "Not you again!" came the unmistakable New York accent.

Carolyn clapped her hands with delight. Then, with an almost hyperactive cackle, she moved back a few steps and produced another of the velvet bags. This time, she stepped back and allowed Olsen to do the honours.

Roddy placed Rusty Fox back on the table and approached the new bag, as if afraid to touch it. Then, with a deep breath, he grasped at the soft material and slowly, deftly, pulled it down.

He laughed uncontrollably, almost spasmodically, as the unforgettable face of Napoleon, his old army puppet, glared up at him. Removing the bag completely, Olsen studied the GI figure, feeling its white imitation hair, long nose and green military fatigues. The army cap he wore was as recognisable as his black boots.

Olsen steadied himself, clutching at a support beam near the low ceiling.

"I don't know how to thank you, Carolyn. You've… you've somehow brought Rusty and Napoleon back to life. It's… it's so completely fantastic. You are a genius."

Carolyn had been watching the unveilings proudly. "And Tony Tan is on his way, should be finished by the weekend," she said, referring to Olsen's other trademark character.

Grinning like a hyena, Olsen had placed Napoleon on his arm and was staring down at him with utter glee.

"Napoleon, you're back," he said.

The old soldier stared up at his controller. "Yes, but unfortunately so is that damn fox. The slimy little maggot!"

The snarling voice echoed through the workshop.

Carolyn shook her head. "It looks like a lot of fans out there are going to be very happy."

Olsen seemed to quiver. He placed Napoleon back on the long table, next to Rusty.

"This is just extraordinary," he uttered. "I feel like I'm in a dream."

"I guess now," Carolyn began, "you're all set. All set to be a star again."

Olsen gazed at the puppets, then looked across at Carolyn. "Yeah," he said quietly. "Yeah, that's right. Only this time… this time it will be different."

CHAPTER NINE

The Double G Circus practice tent was a hive of activity as performers worked on routines and roustabouts raced around, eagerly fixing apparatus and moving props.

Just outside in the main corral, the cowboys were orchestrating a training session of their own, going through their saddle tricks in the dry morning heat.

Within the tent, each of the performers were practising their routines, each finding an individual corner or space on the sawdust.

And in the middle of it all, going from act to act, Kal Klondike roamed around like a football coach on the sidelines, calling out instructions and observations as he patrolled the floor like a drill sergeant.

He had just approached the mighty Soolaimon, who was practising his barbell swinging act, thrusting the mighty weight bar around his head with little effort.

Klondike looked up at the giant, hands on hips. "Listen, buddy, we need to work on a very important factor of entertainment here… called showmanship."

To his shock, Soolaimon slowly lowered the barbell, before dropping it to the sawdust with a mighty thwack. The strongman glared down at Klondike, then softened.

"Never been my strong point." His voice was deep and rasping, but he had an accented American tone.

Klondike practically exploded. "My god! So you can talk! It's a miracle."

The giant actually smiled. "I stay in character most of the time. But, well, you're the boss now, so, well…"

"Yeah, I get it." He looked up at the so-called Mongolian giant. "Listen, I got a few ideas for ya, buddy. It will help. Trust me. It will enhance your character."

Soolaimon stared at him awkwardly for a long moment, folding his immense arms. Then he grunted. "Alright. I can do that."

Klondike breathed a sigh of relief. "Thank you. I'll come over to your trailer tonight."

He patted the strongman on his meaty elbow, then wandered slowly over to where Hondo Cloud was hurling knives like clockwork onto another of his spinning wheels. Betsy watched at his side.

Klondike studied his throwing, then glanced at the wheel. It was essentially painted to be a giant dartboard, with a bullseye in the middle and multiple sections running across its diameter.

"Nice throwing, Hondo," Klondike breathed. The Native American had thrown five knives in his latest spell, one had hit the bull, and four were imbedded around the small, foot-long red circle.

Cloud unleashed his sixth knife. It slammed into the oak, a foot above the bullseye target.

Klondike immediately ripped that last blade out of the wheel and approached the thrower.

"Try this," he said softly. He placed himself beside Cloud, put the leather knife handle in his palm, then delicately pulled the big man's arm back behind his head. However, he kept manoeuvring it further back than Cloud had done. His bent elbow now rose, so it was almost in line with his nose.

"Now," Klondike said in Cloud's ear as he titled the throwing arm back. He indicated for the thrower to crouch, and gave a little push on the wrist, which raised the upturned elbow a little higher. "Balance so that the point of your elbow is level with that bullseye."

Cloud nodded in understanding. "OK, it's level now."

"Right. That is your crosshair. Your sight guide. Now, when you release your forearm forwards, aim it to that elbow point. Where it had been a second earlier. Then release."

He moved back a step. Then, Cloud propelled his throwing arm forwards, releasing the knife. The Bowie blade hit the oak wheel, an inch above the bull.

Cloud turned to Klondike beside him, nodding slightly. "I see how this works. A good system, Mr Klondike." He looked back to the wheel, then at Kal again. "Was that, er, your formula in your old throwing days?"

Klondike nodded, walking over to the wheel and withdrawing the blades. "One of them. I had many systems. Tricks of the trade, pal. There are quite a few."

He carried the knives in a bundle, and deposited them on to the small wooden stand next to Cloud. Then, he patted the Native American on the arm. "You're a great thrower, Hondo. You can be one of the all-time greats. I promise you. Now, why don't you practise some with my technique. Then, see how the results compare with your method. You'll find it helps to have different ideas."

Hondo and Betsy both offered their thanks.

Klondike turned and wandered idly toward the small boundary wall that encircled the arena floor. Turning to the flap, he saw a tall cowboy in silver shirt and stetson making a beeline for him. Rawley Walsh. The leader of the Double G Riders.

"Good morning Kal," the gruff cowboy barked. They shook hands. "I've been meaning to ask," he continued, "me and the boys have been keen to hear your view on our act. It's been kinda hard to, you know, have a private chat these past few days."

"Yeah, I hear that," Klondike said, watching Hondo make his stance for a fresh throw.

Walsh continued. "Well, we know you had the Range Riders at your old circus. And then you had Duster Williams on that European tour. The king! Now, I don't want to compare myself with him, but... well, we've all looked up to those guys and would like to know how we compare."

Klondike nodded, folding his arms and leaning against the waist-high wooden fencing. "You're all stars, Rawley. Really, you are. I watched your act the other day. There aren't many people in this country who can do what you did. I promise you. I'm delighted to have you and your boys onboard."

Walsh fiddled with his hat and smiled awkwardly. "Well, it's different having someone like you here, Kal."

Klondike squinted at him. "How's that?"

"Well, you know, you ran the greatest big top in the country. Everyone here knows your name. Hell, we're all still in shock the Colonel managed to recruit you. Here! To our show."

Klondike nodded slowly, ruefully. "Yeah. Well, I'm still a little in shock myself at what's gone down these past few weeks."

He straightened. "But I'm delighted to be here." He patted Walsh on the shoulder. "And I want you and your boys to know, you're a great cowboy team." He leaned in closer, so their faces were inches apart. "But I can make you one of the best in the land. Trust me! Just keep on training and practising. We'll try and come up with some new routines for you, too. Just keep it up, Rawley."

Walsh's eyes had widened at the lofty praise. He hovered off balance for a moment. "You got it!" he finally exclaimed, and then wandered back outside, heading for the horse corral.

Klondike watched him go happily, then turned back to the arena floor, and the action before him.

Hondo Cloud. Arletta LaRue. Don 'Fearless' Peerless. Soolaimon the Mongolian strongman. And the Double G Riders. That was all he had. The whole show.

In his mind, he tried to picture what his new circus poster would look like. No one had even designed one yet, or even thought of it for that matter. A storeroom behind the tent held various old banners proclaiming the stars of the show, but they had been used repeatedly for years. There was nothing new or extraordinary.

Feeling a pinch of anxiety, Klondike stood watching his new acts practising. Then, once again, his eyes subconsciously rose upwards, towards the tent's summit. Where the trapeze rigging should have been. A circus without flyers, he thought to himself. Like a baseball team without any sluggers. It just seemed foreign and inane to him, in every conceivable way. How could a circus show work without any flyers? He kept his eyes fixed on the ceiling, and almost saw imaginary figures flying and vaulting through the air.

Then, inexplicably, his reverie was interrupted in the most explosive way imaginable.

"Can you feel the magic tonight?"

The familiar voice from behind made him jump, and he practically fell over himself in shock.

He was grinning before he had even turned around. He faced the flap.

There he was. The bearlike figure of Heavy Brown. Full of brawn and power, but with the cherubic face of a New Hampshire choirboy. He was smiling enthusiastically as he waded into the tent, through the flap.

"Heavy! What in god's name are you doing here?"

The big ringmaster was chuckling. "You thought you could get rid of me that easily?"

The two lifelong friends embraced by the wooden perimeter wall that encircled the stage floor. They hugged, holding each other as if reunited after years of anguish.

Klondike held him by the shoulders. "God damn, it's good to see you again, old buddy."

Heavy could not stop smiling. "Well, you kinda ran out on me back in Cristo. I didn't know what to do. Eventually, I got word you had come over to the Double G."

Klondike nodded as if in a dream. "Yeah. I'm sorry. I needed a fresh start after all that happened. I… I just needed to get away."

"I know, Kal. I know."

"But, hey, how the hell did you find me? And how in heavens name did you get all the way down here, to the camp? This ranch is like a private nation of its own."

His question was answered as he caught sight of Garrison and his wife Karen strolling arm in arm up to the flap outside. Both had knowing grins on their faces. The Colonel nodded.

"So you've met my new boss," Klondike muttered.

"I've had the grand tour," Heavy exclaimed. "It's like a whole playground for cowboys out here. I love it."

"It's a long way from Rio Cristo. And Vegas. And, hell, just about everything else we've become accustomed to over the years."

Heavy looked up and around at the white and gold circus tent. "And yet, it feels like home. It's a circus, ain't it?"

Klondike smiled as Garrison and Karen joined them on the sawdust.

"Look who showed up!" the Colonel barked. "The ringmaster who needs no introduction."

"The best bawler on the west coast," Klondike said.

Karen was looking around the practice tent in awe. "We've never had a ringmaster here before. An actual real, live announcer!"

Klondike stared at her, then glanced suspiciously at his old friend. "What exactly does that mean? I thought this was just a casual visit."

Heavy just kept on grinning. "Come off it, Kal. If you're gunna be running a circus, you think I'm gunna miss out on the action? After all these years?" He eyed the performers before them. "Besides, it looks like you need me. As ever!"

Klondike huffed slightly. Then, he had to smile. "Hell, I guess we do at that." He nodded towards Garrison. "We'll have to go over terms and wages with the Colonel here and-"

"Yes, yes, yes, don't worry about all that," Garrison stammered, waving a hand. "Mr Brown here is just happy to be signing up. Ain't that right…Heavy?"

"Sure as hell is," the big man replied, rubbing his hands together.

"Alright," Klondike drawled. He slapped Heavy on the back. "Let's go get a cup of coffee. I have a few things to fill you in on."

"I can't tell you how sorry I was to hear about Daryl. Man, that was terrible news. And god awful timing."

"Yeah," Klondike grimaced. "The worst of everything. I went to the funeral in Frisco, in a way representing all of us from the circus. No sooner had the casket been lowered into the earth, his partners tell me all financial support for Klondike's Circus is being axed. Just like that."

Heavy shook his head slowly. "Jesus. It's been like a month from hell."

The two old friends were sat at a corner table in the camp canteen, within one half of the giant redbrick bungalow that served as the circus headquarters. The place was deserted, bar an elderly steward wiping down tables.

Both had a steaming mug of coffee, and Klondike had just lit up a cigar. "I can't even begin to tell you how hard this has all been. From the ship, to New York, that speech in Cristo, Daryl's death… the emptiness of it all has been overwhelming." He sighed. "I had offers from other big tops, but none as manager. Until the Colonel called me up and invited me down here."

"So, you agreed to run his circus, right off the bat?"

Klondike nodded, taking a slurp of coffee. He planted the cigar in the corner of his mouth.

"I'm hoping this venture will be my salvation, Heav. Hell, Rio Cristo is about to be sold off, any day now. The realtors and surveyors have been swarming round the place for days. They're all very excited about such a unique sale. Argh, it just makes me sick. I think of all the time, effort and money we threw into that camp. And now… now it ain't even gunna be a camp no more. Just some vacation paradise for a country club sucker, getting rich off the stock market or some such nonsense."

Heavy tried to sound optimistic. "It should sell for a hell of a lot of green. More than what you paid for it anyway."

"Yeah. And that will pay off the lawyers and the harbour authorities in New York. And whoever the hell else comes crawling out of the woodwork, looking for a fast buck."

They sat there in silence for several moments. Heavy studied his old friend. When they had met as 12-year-old boys running with a street gang in Hell's Kitchen, they had been dirt poor and without hope or purpose. From that low point, the duo had enlisted with the Marines, served across Europe, joined America's number one circus, and then peeled off to form their own troupe. It had been one wild ride. Now, they were joined again, reunited in this new and largely uncertain venture. Far from home, in every way.

Heavy glanced out of the canteen window, at the seemingly endless packs of wranglers out on the range, watching over the cattle. He thought of all their old friends from Klondike's Circus.

"It seems incredible," he mused softly, "how we've all now gone our separate ways."

Klondike toked on his cigar, watching the deep purple/grey smoke waft above them. "Have you heard from any of the guys?"

"I've heard… things," Heavy replied. "Lacey is now working at a top LA public relations agency."

"Where she belongs, I guess. She's the best in the business."

Heavy huffed. "In terms of the talent, I heard Gino is working in the movies for now. Corky, I dunno. Suzi joined some kind of travelling folk band. And The Daredevils-"

"Signed with Ribbeck." Klondike looked at him oddly. "I heard about that one. It made the front page of Star International."

Heavy's eyes widened. "Did you hear about Roddy?"

"No. What happened?"

"Well, the word is he's joined a new circus troupe, owned and bankrolled by Miles Courtland."

"Courtland! What the…"

"Yeah, I know. But they say young Roddy is gunna be circus manager!"

Klondike visibly shook. "Jesus!" He thought it over. "Well, that will be a hell of a thrill ride, I'll give him that."

Then, he looked downwards, suddenly upset. How he missed them all. "My superstars," he whispered sadly. "What talent we had, Heav. All under our big top."

Heavy tried to sound upbeat. "Well… we've got talent here, haven't we? New stars. New acts."

Klondike could not help shaking his head angrily. "We're a touring wild west circus. We've got no flyers. No clowns. No publicity."

"What in hell have you got?"

Klondike just sat there, still shaking his head. Heavy studied him, then nodded, as if in understanding.

After a few moments, Klondike said: "Are you still sure you wanna join me here, Heav?"

There wasn't even a second of hesitation. "Sure as sure, pal. I'm in, Kal. You know that."

"And…what do you think of the Double G Circus?"

"I think we can make it work, man. We can do this!"

Klondike eyed him. "What do you really think?"

Heavy ran a meaty hand through his thinning hair. He looked deadly serious. "Why don't we let THEM, the paying public, decide, eh?"

Klondike nodded at that. Then, he fished a pack of gold-trimmed playing cards out of his inside breast pocket. "Well, seeing as, I guess, this is the start of the season… we might as well carry on with our old tradition."

Heavy grinned owlishly. "My draw?"

"You bet."

Klondike placed the pack, face down, on the canteen table. Heavy took a deep breath and cut the pack, revealing his card to Kal.

"Six of diamonds," Klondike muttered.

Heavy turned the cut pack and studied his card. "Now, what can that signify…"

The banter was interrupted by a teenage roustabout, who burst into the bungalow porch and spotted the duo in the canteen.

"Mr Klondike," he cried, walking briskly over to their table. He wore a denim dungarees, stained with dust and dirt. "There's some people up at the ranch house… say they're here to see you."

Klondike looked up, holding his cigar before him. "Is that right? Someone wants to join the circus, no doubt?"

"Looks that way, sir," the youngster rasped, slightly out of breath. "Only these girls are the damndest bunch. They arrived in the biggest trailer I ever saw. Six ladies. All dressed in purple tracksuits. Call themselves… the Rollergirls."

Klondike jumped to attention. "Where are they, kid?"

The teenager looked startled. "Why, up at the house, sir. Parked by the main corral."

"Thanks son." He looked across at Heavy and grinned. "Looks like our luck may be turning… already!"

With that, he set off at a brisk walk, towards the doors, the youngster struggling to keep pace.

Heavy stood, then glanced down at his card again. He frowned, puzzled. "Six diamonds…" he whispered mesmerically.

Then, he made to follow the others.

"So, what made you change your mind, Miss Hotch?"

Pamela Hotch looked almost unrecognisable from Westward Pier. Now, she wore her hair long, under a fashionable beret, and had a loose vest-top under her open tracksuit jacket. She looked like an all-star cheerleader at a post-match social gathering, Klondike thought.

"Several things," Pamela replied coolly. "The pier boss just offered us a contract through till September. But he only wants to pay us the same fee he's giving us now, as freelancers. It ain't right. Also, his behaviour has been unacceptable… he gives me the creeps."

The Rollergirls were all milling around the front veranda of the magnificent Sidewinder ranch house, watching the cattle and curiously eyeing the cowboys as they rode past on their stallions.

The giant Rollergirl trailer was parked in the huge, dust-soaked driveway, its mass blocking out part of the view of the rangeland.

Pamela was standing inside the open veranda, alongside Klondike and Heavy. She still seemed uncertain, wary and on her guard.

"And then, there was something you said to us the other night. About branching out… performing across the country." She looked around at the endless prairies that surrounded them for what appeared infinity. "Well, me and the girls talked about it the next morning. The more we talked, the more we came round to the idea. It sounds… well, it is…"

"Exciting!" Heavy blurted from the corner.

Pamela glared at him, then back at Klondike. "Well, yeah, I guess. Appealing, certainly."

Klondike nodded wisely, smiling like a proud tutor. "The lure of the circus has ensnared us all at some point down the years, Miss Hotch. We've all felt the pull, the attraction. The magic."

"No finer way to live," Heavy put in, as he settled into a rocking chair on the wooden decking.

Pamela still looked irked somewhat. She smiled wanly. "Well, yeah, so we kinda talked ourselves into it, you might say. At the end of the day, it was down to joining your circus or staying on at the pier." She rolled her eyes and watched her team of skaters, five women in purple tracksuits, all wandering around freely in the dusty plains. "When we really thought it over, this seemed like the better bet."

Klondike eyed her, cigar still clamped in the side of his mouth, like an extension of his jawline. "This pier boss… he give you any trouble?"

She shook her head. "It's not like that. He's just a sleazebag. He looks at someone and calculates a way to make green outta them."

There was an awkward silence as they stood by the door to the house, the range dust swirling spectacularly before them.

"So," Klondike finally announced. "You're ready to join the Double G Circus?"

Pamela nodded. "We are. And we're all set to go, Mr Klondike." She pointed at the trailer, with its trucker-style driver's cab at the front end. "Everything we need, everything we own, is in there."

Heavy was appraising the mighty motor from his rocking chair next to her. "Did you drive that thing all the way down here, miss?"

"I sure did." Then, she smiled deliciously at him. "I'm very talented, you know."

The two men laughed.

Heavy studied her. "Aren't you a little young for all this, Miss?"

She pouted. "I'm older than people think."

"You kidding? I've got socks older than you."

This time, they all laughed.

Klondike placed a hand on Pamela's shoulder. "Come. Let me show you all around." He nodded to Heavy. "Hell, our roster is growing every hour!"

As Pamela made her way to round up the other skaters, Klondike called to her. "One more thing, Miss Hotch."

She turned, and smiled again.

He smiled back. "Welcome to the circus."

CHAPTER 10

"I can see steaks. Sun-blushed potato fries. Two full glasses of Bordeaux claret. A table at Santino's. Idle conversation. And, of course, you and me. Now, what do you say, Lacey?"

She gazed, unimpressed, at the speaker. Her bewildering violet eyes studied him, but with abject disapproval.

Steve Franklin. Head of studio accounts at Montpellier and Cavani. Tall, with reddish brown hair, and a fresh suit for each day of the week. Important, powerful and successful... yet with the attitude of a playground bully, and the reasoning of a juvenile.

Lacey sat back in her leather chair at her huge corner desk in the open plan office. She grimaced internally as he watched her, as if surveying a museum exhibit.

"I am flattered, Steve," she began coolly. "It is very nice of you to ask. But, the truth of the matter is…" she tried to think of a diplomatic way of putting it, then abandoned the ploy. "I'm just not interested. Sorry."

He frowned, as if offended at not getting his own way. "You know how hard it is to get a table at Santino's?"

She nibbled at her pen tip and simply whispered: "No."

Franklin stood up from his position sitting on the edge of her desk. "Alright, alright. Why don't you think it over, huh? I'll come back over and we'll talk, huh? Give it some thought, over the next few days. OK?"

This time, she looked up at him, almost in pity. "No."

Now, he looked mad. He grunted something, then turned and stormed off. Lacey idly watched him disappear. She noted the run of heads peeking out from desk booths, all watching Franklin race off, before turning to look at Lacey again. She could only imagine the onslaught of rich gossip about to be unleashed.

She shook her head, and tried to focus on the press releases piled up before her. The office block was quiet again, and she began to read.

Then, she was interrupted again. But this time by a friendly and familiar voice.

"Well, well, this is a long way from the circus train."

Lacey looked up instantly, and practically cheered aloud.

There before her stood a small, balding man with horn-rimmed spectacles and reddish skin, dressed in a brown suit and carrying a briefcase.

"Richie!" she squeaked. She leapt up and raced over to the little man before her, embracing him tenderly.

Richie Plum hugged her back. "Wonderful to see you Lacey. How are you?"

"Fine, fine. Back in LA, promoting movies, as you can see!" She held both of his hands in hers, and gently guided him into a seat at the desk, opposite hers.

Plum had joined Klondike's Circus alongside her three years earlier, as part of a banking deal. Like her, he had grown to love the industry and had become a key component of the operation in his role as finance manager.

After the Floating Top disaster in New York, Plum had stayed on in the Big Apple to handle a few legal issues with the harbour authorities, and also to oversee the various salvage projects, which yielded little.

In truth, Lacey realised she had forgotten all about him what with everything that had happened these past few weeks.

She patted his hand. "What have you been up to, Richie? I'm so sorry, I haven't been in touch at all. After Kal announced he was breaking up the circus, I had to find a job. And, well, everything moved so fast. And now, here I am." She motioned for him to speak.

"Looks like you came up trumps, as always," Plum said, glancing around the modern office in awe. He cleared his throat. "New York was a nightmare. I had to get out. As the sole representative of Klondike, it felt like everybody wanted a piece of me. I got back to Rio Cristo and, oh my, what has happened to the place? It was all so depressing to see the real estate people scouring over it all. I could see... could see it was all over." He sighed. "Anyway, I read in Star International that you had come here and I, well... I thought..."

Lacey laughed and clapped her hands with delight. "You thought you would see if you could join me, eh kittycat? Like old times, back in Frisco?"

At that, they both dropped their heads simultaneously.

"I was sorry to hear about Daryl," Plum whispered. He shifted nervously in his seat. "He was a wonderful man. And a fine leader of men."

Lacey took a deep breath. "Kal went to the funeral, I believe. I had just moved back down here, to LA. Then… then I heard about it."

The two figures sat in silence for several moments, each lost in their own private thoughts.

"It all seems inconceivable, doesn't it?" Plum whispered. "How everything has changed, so fast. All the people we looked up to. Now out of our lives. Kal. Gino." He looked at her. "Roddy."

"Roddy…" she said in a throaty tone. Her face dropped. "I never even said goodbye."

Another uncomfortable silence followed.

Then, Plum leant forward, looking awkward, as he often did. "Listen, Lacey…" he murmured, his face looking redder with each passing moment. "Do you think Montpellier and Cavani might take me on? As an accountant. Or clerk. Or something!" He gulped heavily. "You seem to be doing well here. Maybe, er, you could put in a good word? And we can work together again…"

Lacey wiped at her eyes, then smiled beautifully at Plum. Boy, had he missed that smile.

"Nothing would bring me more joy, Richie."

She stood, pressing down the creases in her eye-catching crimson pantsuit. He watched her, as if hypnotised.

"Come," she breathed. She hauled the little man up, placed her arm through his, and practically marched him off towards the executive offices at the end of the corridor.

"Montpellier and Cavani would be lucky to have you. Now, let's put in that good word."

On the other side of Los Angeles, the bellhops and porters at the exclusive Beverly Hills Hilton stared unashamedly at the famous face walking casually down the entrance aisle, heading to the Oracle Bar at the far end of the complex.

Gino Shapiro looked, as ever, like a million dollars, in a silver suit and lilac tie, his beautiful white teeth shining against his dark almond skin.

He entered the sprawling barroom enclosure with a nod at the maitre'd and made his way through a labyrinth of elegantly decorated tables, until he reached the far side.

Then, with a half smile, he approached a small table at the end of the line. A sole occupant was looking up at him.

"So, we meet again, dollmaker," Shapiro greeted, grinning now.

Roddy Olsen stood, surprising the newcomer by also donning a suit, though his was a sober navy blue.

"Gino, good to see you."

The two shook hands warmly, Shapiro gently slapping the other's arm. They looked at each other. Gino's sheer black eyes locked on to Roddy's seagram baby blues.

For several years, the pair had been arch-rivals as the two unequalled, undoubted stars of Klondike's Circus. Both had fought for top billing on the show. The beloved veteran flyer and the young upstart ventriloquist, performing an act many were unwise to.

Their rivalry had become legendary within the circus world.

But then, during that incident-filled European tour earlier that year, everything had changed. The pair had finally come to blows, all over a woman sent by a rival circus promoter to ensure Klondike's troupe imploded.

After the fight, and an apology from the interloper, the beautiful and dazzling Carla Selenzy, the pair had found an unlikely respect for each other. And that newfound harmony became even more pronounced during the tour's sensational final show in Rome, where Shapiro and Olsen had actually performed together, in a breathtaking high wire routine.

But no sooner had the two superstars finally come to respect each other and get along, than the whole operation was delivered a mortal blow in New York.

"Always a pleasure to see you, Olsen," Shapiro was saying, still smiling widely. "It feels, ah, like a big event, meeting up now, after all that has happened."

Olsen had to grin. "There was a time I thought we would never, y'know, meet up for a drink."

"I know, Olsen. I know."

They both sat down at the large mahogany table, that was covered in a gold and green linen cloth. A waiter magically appeared. Shapiro ordered a martini, Olsen a soda.

"You're looking good, dollmaker," Shapiro purred, eyeing him like a hungry alligator. "Working for a millionaire suits you, eh?"

Olsen laughed. "I'd say the same about you, Gino. Look at you! You're more a movie star, not a movie stunt double."

"That's what all the people say. And everyone wants me back under a big top. Me? I'm not so sure. I, ah, enjoy the time away, no? In a new project. For now, at least."

The two both looked at each other for a moment.

Olsen leant back. "Just doesn't feel right, does it?"

Shapiro frowned. "What? Us meeting like this?"

"No. Us meeting here in Beverly Hills when the circus season is under way. We should be out there… on the circus trail."

Shapiro scratched his chin. "When does your season with Courtland actually get going?"

"It's a small tour. The first one ever for this troupe. We still got a few weeks till we go."

The waiter brought the drinks on a silver tray. The two men held their glasses aloft, as a sign of respect, then sipped.

"This is nice, huh?" Olsen blurted.

"What do you mean by that, kid?"

"Us getting along like this. Talking, drinking, catching up. How everybody always wanted it to be between us."

Shapiro thought it over. Slowly, he lit a cigarette, letting the smoke unfurl over their table like shrouds of mist across a coastal bay.

"I only wish that's the way it was." His eyes took on a dark, faraway look. "Now, after all that's happened, it somehow just seems irrelevant."

Both men looked downwards, thinking their own private thoughts. It was all very sombre at the table, until a booming voice snapped them both out of their trance.

"Well, just look at this! Gino Shapiro and Roddy Olsen. The two greatest stars in world circus. Together! Right here at the Hilton."

They both looked up at the grand proclamation, and at the figure now standing before them.

Tip Enqvist looked almost unrecognisable from his days with their old troupe. Clean-shaven, with his premature white hair gelled and neat, looking immaculate in a pin-striped dark suit, the grizzled stunt rider appeared more like a city executive than a biker.

Shapiro and Olsen both stood and shook his hand, offering brief pleasantries. Neither had seen him since the day of Klondike's farewell speech at Rio Cristo.

"And now," Enqvist rasped as he joined them at the table, "make that the three greatest stars in world circus!" He laughed over-enthusiastically, running a hand through his oily hair.

Enqvist settled, seated next to Olsen. "Look at us, together again, eh? The three aces from Klondike's Circus. Reunited at last."

Shapiro stared at him. "How could we refuse your invitation for drinks? And in the grandest spot in LA?"

Olsen nodded. "I, for one, am intrigued about why you wanted to meet us both, Tip."

The waiter reappeared then. "A bottle of Dom Perignon," Enqvist roared without even looking up. "Three glasses. Ice bucket."

Shapiro raised an eyebrow. "Ribbeck is paying you too much, it would seem."

Enqvist scoffed. "Correction. Ribbeck is paying. For everything." He lit a cigarette, keeping it in the corner of his mouth. "So, you heard, eh?"

"Of course. Everybody heard. It's big news, amigo. A big spring signing in our world, the circus world."

Olsen tried to sound pleasant. "It's a fantastic move for you, Tip."

Enqvist suddenly smelt an opportunity and decided to run with it. "Not just for me," he murmured, his grey eyes wide. "For the three of us." He paused in an attempt to create suspense. The other two both looked at him, in shock. He grinned, his voice falling to a conspirational whisper. "I have brokered a deal, my friends. Wait till you hear the specifics." He grinned like a hyena, holding the cigarette before him as he leant in, over the table.

"I have put in place a deal like nothing this industry has ever seen before, boys. For us three to become the highest paid performers in circus history. The contracts are all drawn up. It will be like before, with Klondike. Only this time, we three will be gods among men. Nothing will be denied us. Power, glory, fame. Posters, signed photographs everywhere. TV appearances, offers for endorsements. Wealth... and women!" He laughed aloud as he finished his pitch. The eyes were wild and manic now.

Olsen looked across at Shapiro, bewildered. The trapeze ace was studying Enqvist, as if amused.

"And you are here to promise us all this... power, eh Enqvist?"

"And more," the stunt rider said in a flash. "Think about it. A mansion in the Hamptons, vacation home in Malibu." He sneered as he spoke. Then, he looked directly at Shapiro. "All you have to do is come with me, Gino. Come and join us... join us at the biggest, most expensive circus in the world. The greatest!"

Shapiro remained impassive. "So, you are asking us to sign for Eric Ribbeck?"

"But of course!" Enqvist rasped. "Who else but the great Eric Ribbeck could make such a golden life, eh? Who else could promote the three aces? Enqvist, Shapiro, Olsen. We belong together, boys. Let's make it happen. Let's repeat our successes from last year. And, damn it all to hell, let's get rich!"

He broke off as the waiter returned, placing a crystal ice bucket on a stand beside their table before pouring champagne into three tall flutes.

Enqvist dismissed him before snatching up his glass and holding it aloft. "And now, my friends, we can recreate the old days, with Ribbeck World Circus. And, this time, the crowds will be larger, and the glory will be greater. Just wait till you see what he will pay us!"

He took a long swig of champagne. Shapiro and Olsen watched him, somewhat taken aback.

"I don't know if you've heard," Olsen said quietly, "but I've already signed up for another troupe. Courtland and Co, out of Sacramento. We're moving out in two weeks for our tour and-"

"The hell with Courtland!" Enqvist snapped. He looked Olsen over with savage eyes. "What, you want to be the front man in some rich boy's vanity project?" He laughed. "No. No, my friend. Not Roddy Olsen! You belong on the grandest stage of all, our dear golden boy. In the greatest show of all. And I... I can make it happen, my boy."

Olsen frowned. "I've given Mr Courtland my word. We've shaken on it. I'm not turning back on that. Sorry, Tip."

"Are you crazy, man!" Enqvist suddenly roared, shocking the other two. "You are prepared to walk away from a half million dollar contract? From wealth beyond your wildest dreams? Just cuz you gave your word? To some rich country club sucker? No! Come on, Roddy! Think!"

Olsen felt himself backing away from his former colleague. The man's eagerness was almost terrifying. Something felt very wrong.

"I'm sorry, Tip," he said quietly. "But I'm now working for Courtland."

Enqvist looked like he was about to explode, but somehow kept it together. "Think of all that Ribbeck's money can buy you, kid. You'll be a megastar. You'll have everything."

Olsen simply looked away. "I had all that already... with Klondike."

"Klondike almost got you killed, god damn it!"

"He also took me from obscurity to stardom."

Enqvist grunted, downing the rest of his champagne. The bitter taste of defeat filled his conscience. He turned to Shapiro. With an effort, he tried to look charismatic again.

"I know this picture I have painted appeals to you, Gino. With your love of wealth, fame, women, riches... at least I can count on you to join our enterprise."

Shapiro stared at him blankly. "You seem to be forgetting one important factor, amigo." He leant forward. "I worked for Ribbeck once before. I thought he stank then, and I still think that now."

Enqvist swatted a hand through the air. "Argh, that was a long time ago, my friend. A different era. Now, it's not the same. Back then, Eric was building his brand, man. Now, he is an international businessman. A leader of the highest calibre. Only the best of the best appear in his shows." He paused, thinking frantically. "You belong with us, Gino. At the top. The very top."

Shapiro took a deep breath. Everybody waited. Then, he seemed to snarl across the table.

"Just where do you get off talking to me like this?" he barked. "Calling me your friend, acting like we's old pals or something. You used to insult me back when we toured together. You were jealous of me, jealous of my fans." He gave Enqvist an unnerving look. "And now... now, look at you! Coming to me. Doing old Eric's bidding. Pleading! In desperation."

He rose, standing before the table. He hadn't touched the champagne. "I have seen what el patron Eric's money does to people. I have seen the corruption, the filth... his entire circus is covered in it. And now, Enqvist, I see it has had the same effect on you...campesino!"

Enqvist finally snapped. "You're making a big mistake, flyer."

"No, you are, biker. By being an errand boy for that snake. I spit on you and your orders."

With that, Shapiro turned on his heel and stormed off, quickly disappearing between the rows of ornate tables. Gone.

Enqvist watched him ruefully, slipping down his chair slowly.

He turned to Olsen. "This can still work, kid. Together, we can make him see what's right. Come on, let me take you out to Atlantic City. It will blow your mind."

Olsen shook his head, trying as always to remain respectful and polite. He simply said: "I'm sorry, Tip."

Then, he too was gone, standing up and slowly wandering away.

All alone now, Enqvist sat sprawled on his fancy leather-backed seat. With a grunt, he grabbed at the champagne bottle and took a long pull.

He felt himself sink a little further down his chair.

"God damn it! Those stupid, dust-eating yahoos!"

Ribbeck's voice crackled down the telephone line, sounding like an out of control buzzsaw.

Enqvist, standing in a Hilton phone booth next to the Oracle Room, held the phone an inch from his ear. His tie was loose now, his white shirt dishevelled.

"I played out the pitch, just like we said. Both of them were adamant though. They ain't gunna sign."

"Did you mention the half million?" Ribbeck squawked.

"You bet I did. They didn't seem to care, man. I just don't get it. What the hell is wrong with these guys?"

On the other end of the line, 3,000 miles away at his waterfront office in Atlantic City, Ribbeck screwed up his face in disgust. "Some performers live by a different code. A code of conduct. My conduct is what these peons have a problem with. God damn them!"

In his phone booth, Enqvist looked up as a group of well-dressed VIPs waltzed into the glorious hotel lobby. He recognised several of them from the movies. Truly, he was a long way from home.

"OK," he blurted down the phone, "so what do we do now, Eric?"

"You… you get the hell back here and join the circus train with the rest of your boys. As for that hothead Gino and young Olsen… well, let's just say there are other ways…"

Enqvist frowned. "Other ways? What other ways?"

"None of your god damn concern, boy! Just get back here and ready to ride that yellow sickle of yours."

Enqvist winced inwardly but remained cool. "Right. I'll be on the overnight."

In Atlantic City, Ribbeck merely hung up. He looked up from his desk, lost in thought.

Slowly, as if in some kind of trance, Ribbeck rose from his antique captain's chair and paced across the luscious carpeting to his old pinewood drinks cabinet.

Sloshing brandy into a large goblet, he took a long, lingering sip and made his way over to one of the many retro pictures that adorned the office walls.

Mounted between the vintage circus posters from yesteryear was a large, framed photograph, taken from an air balloon, many years earlier.

It showed the famous Ribbeck big top. Purple and green. Its fabric rising high, seemingly into the sky. Surrounding the great tent on all sides was an impossibly large crowd of people; a sea of humanity, enveloping the massive big top. Thousands of them. Fans. The public. All desperate to get inside, to get in and view the most spectacular show of them all. The event of a lifetime.

As Ribbeck studied the arresting sight, he smiled to himself. He took another sip of brandy.

"To know greatness is to know godliness," he whispered to himself. He thought it over. The greatest circus of all time. No matter what, he told himself, that honour belonged to him.

And nothing, or nobody, would deny him his destiny.

CHAPTER 11

Rollout day duly arrived for the men and women of the Double G Circus.

For Kal Klondike and Heavy Brown, it was all a far cry from what they had always been used to.

For years, the duo had overseen the colossal operation that involved loading up their circus train, filling carriage after carriage with equipment, stalls, tent construction materials, vehicles of all shapes and sizes, food and drink, animals and an army of roustabouts.

At the Sidewinder Ranch, rollout day was much less ceremonial and nowhere near as hectic.

The fleet of camper vans Klondike had spotted on arrival at the circus camp were loaded up with the minimum of fuss. The ranch cowhands joined the roustabouts in the work details, and a swarm of helpers seemed to descend on the circus headquarters, all knowing their specific jobs.

By mid-morning, the supply trucks were ready to go. It seemed incredulous to think that an entire circus midway, as well as the tent itself and a plethora of seats and equipment, were all tucked inside a dozen or so lorries.

There were several elongated flatbed trucks, transporting groundhole punchers and forklifts, and a range of enormous Mack trucks, their cabs almost six feet off the ground.

Klondike had watched in awe as crates of metal folding chairs were all lined up and shoved into the interior of a Mack by one of the forklifts. His own circus tent had used grandstands with bleacher-style seats, all connected together in the big top by scaffolding.

In this new venture, a plethora of these simple chairs would be set out in rows, encircling the arena floor. It all seemed so straight forward.

The talent all made their personal RVs as comfortable as could be, before settling down for the long drive to Memphis for the opening show of the season.

Inevitably, the prairie dust swirled uncontrollably across the ranch lands as the trucks all rumbled to life, before departing, like a convoy of desert liners. The circus caravan, as such operations were known, soon left the boundaries of the Sidewinder Ranch and headed out towards the Sierras, and the canyons and plains beyond.

The camper vans all slowly followed in their own time. As each one drove through the old wire fence that separated the circus operation from the ranch, the old holding camp felt a little more deserted.

Outside the bungalow, Klondike and Heavy watched the last of the accommodation vans make its way out onto the gravel trail that led up to the ranch house, and the main highway. They could see the Rollergirls' huge trailer leading the convoy of RVs out towards the open road.

Klondike pointed to a pristine white motorhome the size of a touring coach, parked next to the cowboys' practice corral.

"Well, old buddy, that's our home for the next two months."

Heavy wandered across to the giant vehicle. "Smartest looking RV I ever saw. We could probably fit half the troupe in there!"

Klondike joined him, moving ahead and opening up the door. They went inside, nodding in approval as they took in the huge main salon, which contained a dining table, two couches and storage cupboards. Two berths at the rear contained beds.

"There's a table for poker, a radio for baseball, beer in the fridge… all you could ever want," Klondike said wistfully.

Heavy grinned. "Next stop, Memphis!"

The duo moved back to the doorway as they heard footsteps in the gravel outside.

Griff and Karen Garrison were wandering over, looking proud and content.

"You're the last to leave, boys," the Colonel barked.

"And what about you?" Klondike asked.

"I told you, I'll see you in Memphis on Saturday. We've got a Belgian bull arriving this afternoon and I have to oversee the arrival. It's one big son of a bitch, so we need to be wary."

Klondike nodded absently. "Well, me and Heavy are just about set. This is it. The start of a whole new adventure." His face broke into a grin. "The Double G's greatest season yet!"

Garrison smiled too. "I sure as hell hope so, Kal." He moved forward to the trailer, extending his hand. "I want to thank you, Kal. For coming here, for giving us your expertise. Hell, for believing in us. You too, Heavy. It means a lot to us here."

"My pleasure," Heavy called.

Klondike took the Colonel's hand. "There's a long way to go. Anything can happen."

"Yeah," the Colonel drawled. "And from what I've heard about you two, anything and everything has happened during your years on the road."

Klondike smiled. "You're well informed, Colonel."

Then, in an unexpected gesture, Karen walked over, moved into the doorway and hugged both Klondike and Heavy. She seemed emotional.

"Thank you both for joining us," she gushed. "No matter what happens, we will never forget it. Now, just make our circus the best spectacle you can."

"Yes ma'am," Klondike said, doffing his hat.

"We won't let you down, ma'am," Heavy offered.

They all shook hands again, then Klondike and Heavy headed back inside the trailer, slamming the big door closed behind them.

As Garrison and his wife stood watching, arm in arm in the now deserted circus camp, the big motorhome roared to life.

With Heavy at the wheel, the sleek camper rolled along to the gateway and began climbing the gravelly path back towards the ranch house. And the adventure that lay beyond.

As Garrison watched the behemoth chug away, the dust clouds swirling across his land, he closed his eyes.

"May God go with you, gentlemen."

March 21: New York Waterfront. Malloy Pier. Departure…

Mike Blakelock tapped his ballpoint pen against the open page, the tip touching the diary entry.

"March 21," he whispered to himself. "That fits. She was there."

He was sitting at the small roundtable in his motel room, studying the stolen diary under the dim light of a small desk lamp.

Jenny Cross's diary had turned out to be so much more than he had imagined. Rather than random names and places that would mean little to anyone aside from its owner, the little pink book read like an official service ledger. Dates, times, names and meeting points were all chronicled in a precise, almost scholarly manner. The code was the same for each entry. Date. Place. Event.

The only inconsistency was the occasional appearance of names written beneath various entries. One name, in particular, appeared in many of the New York appointments.

Zane.

Idly, he wondered who, or what, Zane was. Or represented. Deep down, he knew it was something bad.

Blakelock took a sip of his coffee, poured into a paper cup from a pot across from his room in the lobby. Then, he lit a cigarette and gazed idly out of his motel window. There, over the motel pool, were the bright neon lights of the Las Vegas Strip. No matter where you went in the desert city of sin, you were never far from those bright lights.

His dark eyes returned to the diary on the roundtable before him.

New York. She had been there many times over the past year. And, it seemed, she had been there for both Klondike's departure from the Big Apple… and his return.

Was that a smoking gun? Not exactly. But it put her in the right place at the right time. Although none of that really mattered. He believed everything Klondike had told him. His old army buddy was the most honest and trustworthy fellow in his life. Always had been. Ever since that minefield in Gastrade. All those years ago.

With a huff, Blakelock rifled through the pages of the small pink diary.

None of it made sense. She was a former patient at a mental institution. Tried and convicted of conspiracy to commit murder.

Yet here was a schedule befitting a society heiress. It was astonishing. Cocktail parties. VIP nights. Casino openings. Even a movie premiere.

He returned to today's date and read the entry.

June 6. Wilmington Mansion. Summer ball.

With a sigh, he stood up, downing the rest of his cold coffee. Time to move.

Wilmington Mansion was located south of the Strip in Paradise Valley, eight miles from downtown Vegas.

A sprawling, 12-bedroom manor house, it was the summer residence of one Thomas Wilmington, deputy head of the Nevada Gaming Board and, as such, one of the most influential men in the city.

His wife Gloria often entertained the great and the good of the city's high society in quarterly balls, centred around the seasons. Tonight's summer ball was as grand an occasion as any for the Wilmingtons, with a host of casino owners and board members all flocking to the mansion for cocktails and canapes.

Many of the guests had gathered in the library, on the ground floor facing the mansion's magnificent imperial staircase, which was a whopping 10 feet wide and covered in gaudy purple carpeting.

At the library entranceway, Ray Generoso stood talking shop with a gaggle of casino executives, all resplendent in textbook tuxedos.

As always, the streetwise Generoso felt ill at ease and uncomfortable in a suit, discussing finance and business transactions, sipping champagne. But, alas, this was his life now, and he was not complaining.

His dull grey eyes studied the grand mansion lobby as he half-listened to the conversation around him. He searched the doorways and reception rooms all around him like a security dog, seeking his quarry. Then, his eyes followed the grand staircase upwards until they reached the vast landing above, where many guests had gathered to stand by the marble railings and watch the party in full swing far below.

Then, he spotted Jenny. And immediately frowned. Looking dazzlingly beautiful and elegant in a turquoise cocktail dress, she was just finishing a flute of champagne, placing it on a passing waiter's tray, and grabbing at another, all in one movement.

She took a long sip on the fresh glass, before catching Generoso's stare from down on the floor. She waved at him cheerfully from the landing. He forced a smile and waved back.

Jenny studied Ray with her cold blue eyes. It never ceased to amuse her how uncomfortable he appeared at functions such as this. Surrounded by old money, intellectuals and entrepreneurs. She smiled with contempt at how pathetic it all was. Then, she idly wondered how long it would be until she moved on. The thought was truly tantalising. Enthralling.

"Don't I know you from somewhere, ma'am?"

The voice from behind shook Jenny from her reverie. She brushed at her hair, and turned slowly.

There stood a youngish executive, immaculate in a black tux, with his hair combed in the popular quiff style of the day.

She smiled coyly. "I've been told I have one of those faces…"

The man grinned. "Sure. I thought you were out of the movies or something. Or maybe a show! There's plenty of them out here."

She eyed him, intrigued by the notion of toying with the younger man. "You're very sweet. Are you a casino boss or something?"

"Or something…" the man echoed. "I work as pit boss down at Martinelli's joint on Fremont Street. You know, the Silver Streak?"

"Oh, how exciting," she murmured, already losing interest.

Then, the brawny figure of Generoso came heaving up the staircase, looming behind the newcomer.

The man sensed his arrival, and turned excitedly. "Hey Ray!"

"Hey, beat it kid," Generoso muttered, looking ill-tempered.

The younger man vanished into the crowd of guests instantly.

Genoroso rounded on Jenny by the ornate railings, high above the grand lobby.

"Follow me," he whispered angrily into her ear, before storming off past the gathering and into a study opposite the landing.

Jenny looked around nervously, downed the rest of her champagne, then followed dutifully, skipping across the marble tiles on her sleek high heels.

She followed Generoso to an open balcony, beyond a large desk and bookcase. Moving past a silk curtain, she entered the veranda, instantly feeling refreshed by the cool night air outside.

Below them was an immense garden the size of a football field, surrounded by forestland that somehow appeared sculptured.

There, on the edge of the balcony, Generoso hovered menacingly, looking irate and uneasy.

"Is anything wrong, darling?" Jenny said smoothly, wandering over to him. "You look like you've-"

"The hell with me," he snarled. "What are you playing at, doll? I've been watching you. Constantly. You've just slugged your seventh glass of bubbles. You're uneasy on your feet. Swaying, for Christ sakes."

Jenny gawked at him, looking pale in the moonlight outside. She put a hand on her chest. "I thought the idea was to enjoy ourselves…"

"Have you got any idea how many important people are here tonight? Have you? Huh? Half the moneymen in the city are in this cash pit." He ran a hand through his thinning hair. "All of them… looking at me. Judging me. Wondering what the hell a schmuck like me is doing here. Knowing that I don't belong! That I'm nothing but a mob boss. Placed here by capos in New York." He cursed to himself as he paced the balcony. Then, he glared at her. "And… as if that's not enough, I got you, my gal, drinking like a god damn catfish, out on her feet!"

Jenny glared at him, more than a little afraid now. "Ray, darling, I can assure you-"

"I don't want to hear it, baby," Generoso whispered. He seemed to cool slightly, touching her bare arm. He was nervous, she could see that. "Just lay off the booze until we leave. Another hour should do it. Just so we's been seen here, with the others." He ushered her inside again, back into the study.

He was gentler now. "You can manage that." It was a statement, not a question.

Jenny shuddered. She looked through the study door, at the well-dressed guests thronging all around on the landing. She closed her eyes. Then, she briefly thought of all she had been through over the past year.

"I can manage anything."

Just over 80 yards away, hidden in the trees that bordered Wilmington Mansion's immaculate gardens, Mike Blakelock lowered his binoculars.

He was standing directly in front of an oak tree and immediately behind another, blended in like a shadow in his black coveralls and leather gloves.

He had been observing the mansion for an hour, catching brief glimpses of Jenny and Ray Generoso as he shifted his glasses from window to window, eyeing the many well-dressed dignitaries as they quaffed champagne and merrily exchanged small talk.

He had never, ever expected to see the couple in full view. But his pulse had quickened the moment he saw Generoso burst onto the balcony high above the garden. When Jenny had appeared moments later, he had zoomed his high-tech glasses in on the scene, feeling like the pair were practically on top of him.

He watched. Jenny was facing the garden. Generoso had his back to him. With a firm effort, he tried to read the woman's lips, but soon realised he was woefully out of practice. It had been years since he had taken on a case like this.

The couple on the balcony appeared to be having some kind of confrontation. But then, just as quickly, the situation seemed to cool again. They slowly moved inside the house again, slipping past that fancy silk curtain.

Blakelock applied the maximum zoom on his military grade binoculars. He frowned as the figures disappeared completely beyond the curtain. The balcony appearance had been all too brief.

He lowered the glasses. Then, with a shock, he froze all over.

A security guard, dressed in some kind of antiquated grey uniform with a patrolman's cap, had appeared at the far edge of the woodland, and was slowly moving towards his position.

Blakelock did not panic. The guard was eyeing the mansion, but appeared to be ready to pounce at any sign of a disturbance.

With the smooth, slow and silent movements of a predatory cat, Blakelock crept backwards, his feet padding gently across the twig-infested ground. He merely melted away into the woodland, like a receding shadow. The guard was possibly 30 yards away, but was still watching the back of the house.

Confident he hadn't aroused any unwanted attention, Blakelock finally turned around and paced briskly though the trees. He came to the six-foot high stone wall he had cleared earlier.

Keen for a quick getaway, he ran the last few paces to the wall and vaulted up on to its summit, swinging his legs over before launching himself down onto the roadside beyond. He landed with an almost silent thump.

And almost collided with another guard.

The man in the same grey uniform stared at the intruder in shock.

"Hey!" he blurted in astonishment. That was as far as he got.

With lightning fast reflexes, Blakelock smashed his fist into the guard's solar plexus with blistering force. The man wheezed in pain as he doubled over.

Blakelock hopped to the flailing figure's side, then placed his hand flat and high in a well-practised move. Then, in a blur, he brought the flattened hand down onto the back of the guard's neck in a textbook judo chop.

The guard crumpled to the floor like a rag doll.

In a flash, Blakelock was gone. Head down, he sprinted across the deserted gravel road. His black Sedan sat on the corner, by the junction for the main highway.

Reaching the motor, he threw the door open and fired the ignition in seconds. There was no telling how many guards were patrolling the perimeter. Or if anyone had seen him knock one of them out.

Seeing no sign of life down the lonely old road, he pulled the Sedan off the kerb and slowly rolled away, towards the highway.

Just another late night driver heading towards Sin City.

As he pulled onto the main road, he studied his rearview mirror for several moments. No one was following. The night was dead. He breathed a sigh of relief.

It could have gone a lot worse.

CHAPTER 12

The Beale Recreation Fields in downtown Memphis had always been a happy hunting ground for Klondike in his many years of running a circus troupe.

Capacity crowds, commercial exposure, knockout reviews and legions of fans had been the norm for Klondike's Circus during its visits to Tennessee during the glory years.

Now, Klondike wandered idly across the Beale grounds as the Double G Circus encampment dominated the parkland.

The seemingly endless sea of camper vans and trailers stretched out almost to forever at the far side of the field, while teams of roustabouts erected the midway stalls and booths in the park's centre. Beyond that, the groundhole puncher had just completed its work and a large team of shirtless men had just begun raising the big top. The pristine white and gold tent slowly inched higher and higher into the sky, soon dominating the park and covering much of the horizon. Like a great sea monster emerging from the depths, the behemoth rose and rose, standing like a monolithic skyscraper of hardened polyester, above its kingdom of cotton candy booths and shooting galleries in the midway.

Klondike watched the team of roustabouts erecting the great tent. Already, a small flatbed truck was heading to the big top, carrying the great stacks of foldable chairs.

As he watched the sea of activity all around, it struck him something was very different to the encampment process from the old days. He realised the interest from the general public was almost non-existent.

In his Klondike's Circus days, folks would swarm across the camp, hoping to catch a glimpse of some of the stars while being entertained by the clown team, who would hand out posters and balloons for hours.

Now, as he watched the men and women of the Double G Circus go about their work, he saw the whole operational machine was all business. No fans. No dignitaries. Just the work details.

As Klondike wandered slowly around the freshly erected big top, glancing up in awe at its majesty, he was joined by Heavy, who also could not stop staring at the great tent before them.

"Well, it's not our old red and blue, but I kinda like this white and gold," the ringmaster muttered.

"Sure is a fine tent," Klondike said.

He watched as a roustabout pulled up the tent flap, which was enormous, and secured it open. The small flatbed slowly rumbled inside.

The two old friends looked on as the army of roustabouts, all dressed in cowboy attire, roamed around the tent, like ants on a quarry.

"It's all so very different," Klondike whispered.

Heavy turned from the tent and watched the midway assembly operation. The Riders of the Double G were all on their horses, slowly riding across the Beale grounds among the stalls and trailers.

"A new beginning," Heavy drawled. "For us both." He thought for a moment. "I guess we're fortunate that we're still doing what we love. What we were made for. Running a circus."

"Damn straight," Klondike said. He watched the cowboys as they rode, all laughing and smiling. "And, I'll tell ya what, old buddy. I can't wait to see this new team of mine in action. In front of the paying public."

Heavy nodded. "Tell me again about the order, Kal."

Klondike turned back to the tent. "Well, the Riders of the Double G here open the show. Then, Rawley Walsh does his solo spot. Then Don 'Fearless' Peerless with his fire-eating. After that, Arletta LaRue the snake charmer. Then we have Soolaimon the Mongolian strongman. The Rollergirls then do their act. And then Hondo Cloud. For the finale, if you can call it that, I've got Walsh and Cloud to perform together. Taking it in turns to knock down glass bottles on a fake bar top."

Heavy looked at him knowingly. "A shooter and a knife thrower. Your areas of expertise."

Klondike pulled off his hat and ran a hand through his jet black hair. "Walsh and Cloud are the star sluggers in our batting order, Heavy. I've watched all these guys practise every day for a week. I'm not sure how to describe a lot of what I've seen...

but I sure as hell like those two. And so will the public. So, they go on last."

Heavy watched the cowboys as they rode back towards the newly-erected stable block by the trailers. "And, like you said, no clowns, no flyers, no stunt riders."

Klondike pointed to the colony of trailers at the far end of the field. "Garrison has got everything back there for a full, three-ring circus, pal. Trapeze rig. Wires. Nets. The works." He laughed mirthlessly. "It's almost as if we're waiting for a flyer to fall into our tent."

The duo both looked up in unison as Arletta LaRue appeared from within the commotion of the midway set-up. Dressed in a black leotard, she was trotting gracefully across the grass like a ballerina, performing pirouettes and twirls like a seasoned dancer. She appeared to be singing to herself.

Heavy glanced at Klondike, eyebrows raised. "What the hell is her story?"

Klondike grunted. "You want mysterious femme fatale, like outta the movies… you got it with that one. I can't figure her out at all. Don't really want to. They say she is French, but from Turkey. Raised by gypsies and travelling carnivals. Hell, even Garrison doesn't know her background." Klondike seemed to wince as he watched Arletta perform another balletic jump as she pranced across the field, disappearing behind a supplies truck. "But her act is unique and different, and I ain't never seen nothing like it. There's just one issue… she carries those damn snakes into the big top in a coffin. What in hell are the fans gunna say about that?"

Heavy shook his head. "I guess it's all part of the mystique. What makes her special, different… an attraction."

Klondike had to chuckle. "That's the spirit, old buddy. Hell, who knows, we could really be onto something here."

"Well," Heavy replied, "come Saturday night, I guess we'll know for sure."

And that was the truth.

"Ladies and gentlemen…"

Heavy strode out onto the sawdust in his customary scarlet jacket and black top hat, booming his introduction into the microphone.

As he walked into the centre of the big top and looked up, he quivered slightly at what he saw.

The mighty tent was well under half full. And that was probably a generous estimate. The rows of seats, placed on steps of wooden planks in a giant circle that formed a perimeter to the stage floor, looked forlorn and empty. Small gaggles of spectators sat congested in little groups, leaving yawning chasms of available chairs everywhere. The brown oak of the empty chairs dominated the seating fairway, the patrons resembling small pleasure craft in a vast ocean.

All in all, there could not have been more than 250 spectators attending the opening show. As Heavy strode out into the arena, the atmosphere was silent.

Undeterred, the ringmaster made his all-new introduction: "Welcome to the fastest-growing circus spectacular in America today. The grandest, the wildest, the most incredible blend of action and excitement on offer anywhere in the world. Where cowboys roam… and roller girls whirl. The wild west brought to life, in a show of magic beyond your imagination!"

He held his hand aloft at the grand speech. However, he was again met by silence. It actually felt like an empty arena, like a dress rehearsal in front of nobody.

"And now," Heavy roared, "please welcome our opening act. The wild riding, sharp shooting, kings among cowboys! Give it up for the Riders of the Double G, featuring the master blaster, Rawley Walsh!"

A vague applause smattered across from the seats. Heavy gulped heavily, before walking off as majestically as he had entered.

The Riders of the Double G all erupted from the flap on their magnificent golden palominos, and straight into their customary laps of the arena floor. The horse tricks began, as the cowboys performed saddle headstands, swapped mounts and leapt from their stirrups, as the beasts ran in mighty circles over and over again.

Heavy finally reached the flap enclosure, the long-time home base of Klondike during any and all performances. A perfect partition had been left between the rows of seats, enabling the acts to get in and out, and Klondike stood pensively by the tent fabric, the open flap leading to a small, tunnelled polyester enclosure and the trailers outside.

Heavy joined Klondike on the sidelines. The nearest spectator to them was about 20 seats away. The waves of empty chairs were completely unnerving… and a foreign aberration to the two veteran circus men.

"Jesus Christ…" Heavy muttered, eyes locked on the rows of seats. "Memphis used to be one of our biggest gigs. A true circus town. What… what the hell gives tonight?"

Klondike shook his head. "That was a different troupe. A different big top. Those people came to see some of the biggest superstars of our time." He nodded towards the sawdust, where the cowboys were beginning their roping routine. "This… this is another world entirely. Try as we might, we have to make the best of it."

The cowboys executed their plate shooting act with their usual stunning accuracy, as the noise of blasting caps and smashing china reverberated eerily throughout the tent.

The Riders of the Double G's act was met with applause, although it was hard to hear in the vastness of the great tent.

Rawley Walsh's solo shooting and blindfold act also attracted a mild ovation, but nothing more.

As he performed his lightning fast draw and shot two plates from the hands of a steward, all while wearing the blindfold, all that could be heard throughout the big top was hearty clapping, like a school group inside an assembly hall.

Klondike wandered out slightly towards the sawdust, trying to glimpse who was actually in the audience. He saw mostly youths, teenagers and school kids, folk who probably preferred seeing their cowboys on TV or in movie theatres. Walsh had performed the real thing right here in front of them, with his lighting fast draw and shooting. It was like a western brought to life. But none of the spectators really seemed to care.

After that came the high-speed, mid-air saddle swap routine, which had so impressed Klondike back at the camp on his first day.

The bold and daring act drew a louder ovation, but that was about as good as it was going to get for the cowboys.

In the end, Walsh and the Riders all rode back to the flap after their act, in virtual silence.

Heavy strode back out onto the sawdust. "And now, ladies and gentlemen, please welcome the human abnormality, the man who eats and breathes fire. Let's hear it for Don 'Fearless' Peerless!"

The veteran Peerless somehow appeared a further 10 years older than he had last week, Klondike thought idly. Walking out onto the sawdust at a painfully slow pace, he also looked drunk.

As dramatic piano tunes blared over the tannoy, the old-timer made it to his table in the centre and began covering his sticks with fire and dunking them into his mouth.

Klondike winced as he sensed, rather than saw, an unfavourable reaction from the audience. The fire-eating simply unnerved many of those watching.

Peerless's finale, juggling two inflamed ping pong balls in his mouth, was met with shrieks of alarm and panic. It was as if those watching feared an inferno might break out in the tent at any moment.

Klondike's worst fear had been realised – the old man's act was simply too disturbing and alarming for many.

Peerless left the sawdust to another vague smattering of applause.

Heavy took a deep breath as he faced the fans for his next introduction.

"And now, ladies and gentlemen, prepare to be left spellbound by the enchantress of the west. The snake charmer extraordinaire… Arletta LaRue."

Two stewards ambled to the centre of the arena, carrying the large black coffin between them.

When the haunting flute tune floated down from the speakers, the casket burst open, and Arletta LaRue emerged like a wraith from the realms of the occult.

A gasp emanated from those watching. Klondike shook his head. He could only wonder how many spectators would be scared, offended or plain dumbstruck. He asked himself why he had allowed Arletta to perform this scene of macabre. But, again, he realised it was impossible to look away once she began her beguiling, almost hypnotic dance, while deftly lifting her squadron of snakes one at a time.

The climax of her act, as she hoisted up all five snakes onto her shoulders, was met with screams and a fast, wild round of applause. A mix of appreciation and alarm.

Everyone in attendance then watched, dumbfounded, as Arletta clutched her array of snakes, and simply sat in the coffin again, and then led down, pulling the lid closed over her.

As the stewards collected the black casket and hefted it back to the flap, a slow, bemused ovation reverberated around the dome.

Heavy returned to the floor, holding one hand aloft as he spoke.

"Behold, ladies and gentlemen, as the Double G Circus presents to you… the world's strongest man! It's the Mongolian Giant…Soolaimon!"

As the old-fashioned horror movie theme sounded, the circus giant came striding out menacingly, trying his best to resemble an otherworldly monster, snarling and flexing his enormous muscles in his Genghis Khan attire.

Soolaimon raged and over-acted as he went through his spinning barbell routine. Again, a bitter silence gripped the sparsely populated big top.

Then, a pair of circus stewards raced over to him, allowing themselves to be lifted high above his head, as he performed push-ups with their frame before dropping them back to the ground like dolls.

Soolaimon then lifted up his ceremonial throne with one hand and nonchalantly carried it back to the flap.

But the lack of applause all around the big top was unbearable, a deafening silence. As Soolaimon trudged past, still carrying the mighty throne with one hand, Klondike tapped him on the back. But the big man angrily shrugged him off. Klondike watched him as he disappeared through the tunnel and out into the trailer enclosure. Then, he looked back to the seats.

It was hard to contemplate such a sparse, uninterested audience after years of screaming, over-excited crowds, who had flocked to see his shows for much of the past 10 years. Again, he felt a deep wave of nostalgic pain as he looked over all those damn empty chairs. Again, he saw Jenny Cross waving goodbye.

"And now, ladies and gentlemen, please give a warm Memphis welcome for the new sensation of the ages... America's stunning speeding superstars... The Rollergirls!"

Klondike snapped out of his reverie as the rollerskating team exploded out of the flap to the sounds of fervent rock n roll music on the tannoy.

The group looked like stars, resplendent in their purple leotards, their skates a sparkling silver.

As the Rollergirls whizzed round the arena floor, and the rockabilly tunes roared across the big top, the watching spectators seemed to come to life somewhat, clapping to the beat and cheering the dazzling skating tricks.

When the skaters zoomed up onto the small wooden wall separating the audience from the sawdust, everyone seemed to applaud heartily. Their balancing acts and somersaults impressed everyone.

Then, when Pamela Hotch and her training partner, Sharon, performed their daring, high-speed spinning routine in the small metal half-dome, there were finally cheers and fans on their feet applauding. The spinning duo were little more than a blur as they completed their ultra-fast turns, Pamela clutching Sharon's ankles with a seeming ironclad grip as she expertly, incredibly manoeuvred herself around and around.

Watching on, Klondike said a silent prayer of thanks that the team had agreed to join his new troupe.

When the high-speed spin act finished, the Rollergirls performed two laps of honour, skating slowly and waving to an audience that had finally been enthused.

As they headed for the flap, Klondike shook each woman's hand. Pamela raced towards him, then expertly skidded to a halt one yard away, laughing as he impulsively shielded himself. He glared at her with mock anger.

"An excellent performance, Pamela," he said, somewhat embarrassed.

She grinned like a juvenile. "The girls all love it. In a huge tent like this. It's just wonderful." She looked around at the empty seats. "Tough crowd though, boss man. We were, ah, expecting a little more."

Klondike scowled. "Yeah, well, we're gunna work to put that right during the tour."

With her long brown hair stuck to her scalp and her entire frame drenched in sweat, Pamela smiled, then tapped Klondike on the arm and skated slowly into the tunnel, in the wake of her team-mates.

Heavy grinned at the exchange, before marching back out onto the sawdust.

"And now folks, get set for the finale of our show. The Double G Circus is proud to present to you... the most wanted man in the west! Deadly with a knife, with hands like crossbows. Let's hear it for the Pride of the Sierras... Hondo Cloud!"

The huge Native American walked in like a local dignitary, looking like an actor on a movie set in his caramel buckskin jumpsuit and tassels, with the Comanche-style poncho covering his shoulders. Betsy, as ever, followed just behind him, as a team of roustabouts assembled the giant gold and white-painted wooden wheel.

As Betsy was tied down on the great round platform, Cloud positioned himself at a tall stool 10 yards away.

A deathly silence filled the big top.

Cloud then revealed his set of six shining Bowie knives sat together in the black leather sheath on the stool.

Cloud nodded to one of the stewards, who moved to the large wheel and, with a mighty yank, set it spinning. The wooden disc moved rapidly, spinning Betsy around in wild, blurred circles.

Crouching lightly in his classic thrower's stance, Cloud dispatched his set of knives with stunning velocity, and remarkable accuracy.

The killer blades formed a circle around Betsy's frame as she span around, head over heels, over and over.

His throwing was met with another polite ovation, which sounded like it had emanated from a small touring group such was its lack of warmth.

As Betsy was untied and guided away from the wheel by a steward, Cloud produced his machete and the roustabouts set the wheel spinning again.

With a triumphant Comanche wail, Cloud hurled the giant blade straight into the heart of the bullseye.

This time, there were a few cheers and hearty applause. But the fact there were so few fans in attendance almost made such expressions of delight appear ridiculous.

At the flap, Klondike watched Cloud wave to the crowd in the centre. He looked forlorn and alone.

Klondike half-turned as Rawley Walsh appeared through the tent tunnel and stood beside him. It was time for Klondike's new grand finale.

"Do us all proud, Rawley," the circus manager muttered.

Walsh nodded. "Let's see how many of these folk have ever seen a gunslinger drawing against a knifeman."

Heavy paced out onto the floor again. "And now, ladies and gentlemen, boys and girls. Behold, as The Double G Circus proudly presents our grand finale. The world's greatest knife thrower, Hondo Cloud, draws blades with the fastest gun in the west, Rawley Walsh. Who is the most dynamic? The most deadly? You decide! And now, please welcome back the Sierra Nevada gun wizard, Rawley Walsh!"

A wave of clapping broke out as Walsh walked slowly, purposefully onto the sawdust.

While Heavy had made his announcement, the roustabout crew had quickly set up a makeshift, western saloon-style bar top, actually made from plywood. The bar was placed in the centre of the floor, with 12 empty whisky bottles lined up.

Cloud stood on one side of the bar, 10 yards from the structure, his sheath of knives on the high stool next to him. Walsh stood on the other side, his right hand poised by his holstered Colt.

They stood perfectly still. Then, Heavy began the countdown.

"OK, folks, this is it. Get ready. Five. Four. Three. Two. One. Fire!"

Walsh again executed his lightning fast draw, hoisting his Colt from the holster, before systematically firing at the bottles on the bar top. Each blasting cap smashed the glass of the six bottles on the left of the plywood base.

Cloud plucked out his knives and threw them one at a time at impossibly high speed, like a Gatling gunner firing out ammo.

The six bottles on the other side of the bar smashed one after another as the blades impacted.

Although Walsh had comfortably dispatched his bottles faster than Cloud, both men raised their hands in celebration after the glass had all smashed, splattering over the plywood and sawdust below.

Applause followed, again no wild cheers and exclamations, but hearty applause from impressed patrons. The cheering lasted seconds, though, and then back came the awful, glaring silence.

With a shrug, Heavy came back onto the floor.

"Have you ever seen anything like it, folks? Rawley Walsh. Hondo Cloud. Our wild west stars, faster than electric lightning!"

His grand announcement garnered little reaction from anyone watching. With a glance at Klondike at the flap, the beleaguered ringmaster continued, with his closing address.

"We hope you have enjoyed the wonder, the glamour and the sheer excitement of The Double G Circus folks. Now, let's hear it for the stars of the show, the dynamos of the Double G! Here they come!"

With that, the Riders of the Double G came riding out into the arena at a show ring trot, followed by the Rollergirls, skating leisurely. Walsh leapt up and mounted his horse as it was led to him by a steward.

Arletta, Peerless and Soolaimon merely wandered out onto the sawdust, joining Cloud and Betsy in the centre, and waving to the vague applause that now permeated the grim atmosphere all around.

Klondike grimaced as he watched the gathering in the middle. It looked, and felt, awkward – enforced and uninspiring.

The cowboys and the Rollergirls completed a lap of honour, all waving and smiling at the patrons, many of whom were now leaving the big top.

Then, the performers all arrived back at the flap en masse, seemingly keen to exit and return to the salvation of their trailers.

Klondike remained at the flap and watched the troupe, his troupe, all flee the performance arena. Just like that, everyone was in the tunnel and back in the field outside.

Klondike glanced around, bemused, at the rows of chairs. By now, the whole tent was practically empty. Within 60 seconds of the show ending, the whole place was like a crypt.

Heavy had brought up the rear of the grand finale procession, but was now walking in a daze as he neared the flap. He wore a look of pure disbelief.

"Kal…" he breathed, "what the hell was that?"

Klondike shook his head, lost and dismayed. He looked up at his old friend.

"That," he stammered, "was our opening show."

CHAPTER 13

The debriefing began the following morning after breakfast.

Performers and crew all piled into the great tent, where the chow line was set up along with tables and chairs for everyone.

The circus encampment was silent as everyone lined up inside the big top, talent mixing with roustabouts as Cookie, the tour caterer, handed out plates of ham and eggs.

Klondike was in his trailer, heating up a pot of coffee at the kitchenette.

There was a sharp rap at the door, then Garrison entered. He was dressed in his favourite caramel blazer with jeans.

"Morning Kal."

"Colonel. You're just in time for coffee."

Garrison studied him. "You look like you could use something stronger."

Klondike poured two mugs and handed his visitor one. The two men stared at each other for several moments.

"Last night," Klondike spat out. "That crowd. Or lack of one. Is that... normal here? You normally play to 200 people?"

Garrison looked him in the eye. "It happens."

"Not to me it doesn't. Or any show I lend my name to."

"Is there a problem, Kal?"

"Damn straight. We just played a circus show to a crowd of 200 odd teenagers who couldn't care less. Hardly anyone turned out for us... and those who did weren't exactly enthused. We had 1,500 chairs in that big top. Now, I wasn't expecting a capacity last night but, damn it all to hell, I thought we'd have something. Hell, even when I started out in Coney Island I played to bigger crowds."

Klondike took a deep breath, trying to cool. He sipped his coffee. Garrison watched him curiously.

"And then there's the talent," Klondike continued. "None of them had listened to a word I said. Soolaimon still has no idea what showmanship is. Hondo ignored my throwing tips. Peerless looked drunk, like he didn't belong. And Arletta... well, I just don't know what to make of her gig." He snarled to himself, hands on the kitchenette worktop. "Hell, the only act that impressed anyone was the Rollergirls."

Garrison leant against the breakfast bar. "Your act. Your recruits."

Klondike nodded. "Right." Then, he stared at the Colonel incredulously. "Are you telling me what happened out there last night... that.... that was normal for you guys? Hell, that big top was dead. Dead, man!"

Garrison frowned. "Well, I thought having your name attached to the circus might shed a few tickets. Attract more fans."

Klondike shook his head. "We needed more publicity. More press. I haven't seen a single one of our posters anywhere in Memphis since we landed. It's like... like no one knew we were here."

"Just what are you saying?"

"I'm saying this whole circus is a mess, god damn it!"

"You want out, Kal?"

Garrison's fierce directness shocked him. Klondike stood and faced the Colonel. It was a confrontation. Heated and intense. Klondike studied the older man. He looked ready to go to war.

"Hell no," Klondike finally said, cooling off. He sipped his coffee. Garrison did the same. Kal wandered across the lounging area and stood by the saloon window, gazing at the white and gold big top as several roustabouts spilled out, ready for the mammoth disassembly job.

"Listen, I signed up to this and I gave you my word. That means I'm gunna try my damndest to turn it all around. For you, for me and for them… the people."

"Glad to hear it," Garrison said, softening.

"It's just that... well, I never experienced anything like last night before. It was a big shock."

Garrison wandered across the confined space and joined him at the window. "I did tell you we had been struggling for a long time, Kal. I said this was a big job."

Klondike watched absently at the window as Peerless, still dressed in his fireproof shirt, blundered out of the tent flap, as if lost.

"Yeah..." he growled. "I guess you did at that."

He thought for a moment. "What the hell were the gate receipts for last night?" He shuddered. "I don't even wanna know."

He looked back out at the circus camp all around them. The disassembly operation was underway. "You know, we're never gunna be a success if we don't make money. My job is to generate a profit for you and your people, Colonel. We need to get this tent full. We need a take, a proper take, on the door and on the midway."

Garrison nodded thoughtfully. "There's still money available to you, Kal. To recruit more acts. To get talent in."

Klondike held his arms out. "Who? Everyone is signed up, under way on a tour with another big top. It's just too late, dammit."

Silence followed. The two men were lost in their own independent thoughts.

The grim atmosphere was broken as Heavy burst into the trailer, holding a newspaper aloft.

"Morning boys," he called. "I got us a Memphis Recorder. The newsstand didn't have any other locals."

Klondike took the offered copy and nodded his thanks.

Garrison patted the newcomer on the back. "Great job last night, Heavy. I can't tell you how welcome it was to have a ringmaster out there."

As Heavy helped himself to some coffee, Klondike sat at the dining table and irritably swept through the pages of the Recorder. Then, he stopped… and his face dropped. He began to read aloud.

"The Double G Circus rolled into Memphis last night... and the circus fans ran the other way.

Barely 250 spectators turned out for the touring company's opening night at Beale Recreation Fields, possibly a record low turnout for a circus show in Tennessee.

Of course, several thousand had been expected to witness the resurrection of Kal Klondike, the big top's new manager. The enigmatic Klondike had just returned from a much-heralded tour of Europe with his own troupe... before his circus ship blew up in New York Harbour... and a wealth of lawsuits and allegations blew up in Klondike's face.

The former knife thrower has taken on a management role with this little-known western touring show now. But he'll probably wish he'd never bothered. This opening show of the tour lacked one crucial detail... pizazz!

Indeed, there was little sparkle or razzle dazzle about any of the Double G's acts. Certainly nothing that would have been associated with Klondike's Circus.

This show felt like a wild west exhibition... from 30 years ago. All played out before a plethora of empty seats. The circus was in town... but nobody in Memphis seemed to care."

Klondike scrunched the paper up and deposited it onto the trailer's carpeted floor.

Heavy poured his coffee, looking down at him.

"Pizazz..." he muttered.

Klondike eyed him, then turned to Garrison, who was hovering over the table.

"Listen, Colonel, this is gunna be a battle. To win the press over. To get the fans in." He glared at the discarded newspaper below him. "And having my name attached to your circus seems to be diminishing it, not enhancing it."

Garrison pulled his leather cigar pouch from a breast pocket and offered Kal one. "I have faith in you, Kal. We all do."

Klondike took the offered cigar. "And I appreciate it."

Garrison nodded. "If you need me, I'll be in my executive trailer."

With that, the Colonel ducked out of the narrow confines.

Heavy joined Klondike at the table, casually pulling the obligatory deck of cards from his jacket pocket.

Klondike leant back, thinking about the review.

How he missed Lacey Tanner. It was like a part of himself now ceased to exist, without her there. He had long ago lost count of the amount of scrapes she had disengaged him from.

Lacey could single-handedly turn most dire situations around. He knew that.

But right now, he especially felt her loss.

The public relations ace was in a class of her own when it came to press releases, posters, flyers. Generating excitement and energy around an upcoming show. Drawing up a press conference at a day's notice. Creating interest and excitement in the brand.

There was truly no one else like her.

Watching Heavy as he shuffled his cards, Klondike sadly wedged the giant cigar into the corner of his mouth.

Idly, he wondered just what she was doing at that exact moment.

"Montpellier and Cavani."

Lacey practically shouted the greeting into her telephone receiver. Then, with a cattish grin, she began cheerfully fielding questions from a reporter about an upcoming movie release, from a studio promoted by her PR agency.

As she effortlessly gave directives down the phone, a young assistant, a girl of no more than 18, crept over and held up two posters for her to study, pictures of a recently signed studio starlet.

Without pausing in her monologue on the phone, Lacey pointed at the poster on her left, then winked at the girl.

She finished the call and began frantically scribbling notes on a yellow office pad.

Sensing another visitor she looked up, then smiled beautifully at Richie Plum, who was approaching, a newspaper held before him.

As expected, Montpellier and Cavani had gleefully offered Plum a job in their finance department, purely at Lacey's recommendation. Just like that.

Now, though, the little man looked troubled.

"Richie... what's wrong?"

Plum laid the copy of Star International on her desk before her, opened at an inside page.

"We were wondering what old Kal was up to," he mused. "Take a look at this."

Frowning, she looked down at the page. The banner headline screamed:

CIRCUS KING KLONDIKE HITS ROCK BOTTOM
She began to read, fearfully...

He had been heralded as the greatest circus man in America just a few short months ago.

But, last night, the great Kal Klondike watched over his latest big top offering, a painful mish-mash of cowboy stunts and old-fashioned carnival acts, all played out before a shockingly low turnout of barely 250 spectators.

The Double G Circus opened its season in Memphis, Tennessee, and things can only get better.

From a bunch of cowboys riding bareback in endless circles, to a so-called Mongolian strong man who simply twirled around gym weights, this was an uninspiring procession of acts seemingly thrown together at random.

The finale, if you can call it that, saw a gunslinger and a knife thrower take turns to smash glass bottles on a bar top. And this passes for big top entertainment today!

It is hard to fathom how a circus boss who had recently conducted a grand tour of Europe no less could end up presiding over such a lacklustre event. How a great entertainment general who had brought us trapeze king Gino Shapiro, ventriloquist Roddy Olsen and stunt team The Daredevils, now manages a roster featuring a snake charmer and a fire eater.

Klondike's Circus, the great Klondike's Circus, is of course dead. That shipping disaster in New York saw to that. But Klondike himself has seemingly found it impossible to cleanse the grime of that fiasco off his skin, the only troupe now willing to take him on this ramshackle western carnival.

And so he has gone from putting on shows in front of thousands, not to mention live TV specials, Las Vegas spectaculars and international events, to this sad, backwater parade of pitiful paucity.

How the mighty have fallen...

Lacey looked away, her bottom lip quivering.
"Oh Kal," she whimpered.
Plum stood over her, head bowed. "Looks like he abandoned Rio Cristo altogether. For this... this Double G Circus."

"I'd heard a rumour," Lacey breathed. "Heard he may join a smaller big top. Kind of start out again."

Plum shook his head. "It ain't right. A man like Kal... messing around with some carnival troupe. Getting humiliated." He rubbed at his balding head, the skin reddening. "Hard to comprehend just how it all came to this."

Lacey looked out of the office window, at the swarming LA streets down below.

"They all pulled out."

Plum frowned. "What's that?"

Her face had paled as she stared transfixed at some indistinguishable spot on the golden horizon outside.

"They all pulled out. The sponsors. The backers. The dignitaries. Addison Incorporated, after Daryl died. Claude Hershey, at the Golden Dune in Vegas. Steve Irving and the team at ATV. After the ship disaster in New York, nobody wants to know Klondike's Circus. Nobody wants to touch it. Everybody quietly stepped back. Pulled out. Now... now Kal is all alone."

Plum chewed it over. "Well, it sounds like he may have found some new friends. And surely Heavy will have gone to Memphis with him?"

Lacey was lost in thought, her beautiful violet eyes wide and fraught. She slowly turned to face him.

"I shouldn't have left Rio Cristo like that."

"You said he closed the circus. That it was all over. That everything finished."

Silently, she lit a cigarette, reaching for her own personal seashell ashtray sat in the corner of her mighty desk.

"Finished... not everything is finished." Then, the beguiling eyes bored into Plum with electrifying sharpness.

"Me and Kal will never be finished."

More than a thousand miles away, the colossal Sherman Brothers circus train was holed up in Canyon Creek, Denver.

An incredible 46 carriages full of animals, grandstands and portable cabins, and a whopping 28 staterooms of the highest quality.

The great locomotive sat adjacent to the creek itself, where the entire circus encampment was now up and running, a shanty town of stalls and midway attractions that led, bewilderingly, towards the Sherman big top, a beautiful red and purple, double peaked tent, that could have leapt straight from the pages of a fairy tale.

There were many circus camps just like it across the United States. This one was different, though – it looked rich, opulent, as if it contained attractions only fitting for the privileged elite.

As roustabouts and various guests and local dignitaries paced leisurely across the camp, Jonathan 'Doc' Irwin strode purposefully alongside the train at the creek's edge. Dressed in his stars and stripes tracksuit, the legendary performer left no one in any doubt he was a celebrity.

The veteran flyer shook hands with various passers-by and well wishers, and waved at fans who had infiltrated the troupe's sanctum. He even stopped for several photographs with youngsters in a touring group.

Finally, he reached the very end of the mighty train. The executive cab. Heaving himself up onto the vestibule platform, he knocked sharply on the carriage door, before simply entering.

Within was a sumptuous, carriage-long stateroom, immaculately decorated with mahogany panels and shiny, well-varnished tables and chairs.

At the far end, Gerry Sherman sat behind a huge oak desk, covered in newspapers and manilla files. He didn't look up.

Irwin approached, marvelling as always at the incredible display of framed photographs that sat on every conceivable worktop. There were images of Gerry, his father, brothers, cousins, uncles, and various ancestors, all pictured at varied times throughout history with a famous circus star in the classic handshake 'signing' pose. A firm grip and a big smile.

Irwin reached the desk. "You wanted to see me?"

Sherman finally looked up from his paperwork. A great bull of a man, with receding hair and a huge neck, he cut an imposing, fiery figure in his dark brown suit, a dark cheroot perched in the side of his mouth. He managed a smile. "How you been, Doc?"

The small, bald man in the flashy attire grinned. "Just fine, Gerry. Feel like I could go on forever."

Sherman chuckled. "You look like it as well." He studied Irwin, in admiration. Or was it smug satisfaction, that he, Gerry Sherman, had enticed the great Doc Irwin to perform in his big top?

"You're doing great, Doc. I just want you to know that." He paused again. "The All American. You know, we got kids coming to shows now in your stars and stripes tracksuits. Snapping up your posters. All wanting to see the legend in person. It's really, truly wonderful… the aura you have brought here."

Irwin stood still, hands behind his back. "Glad to have helped, Gerry. And to have inspired the kids to pursue exercise and fitness, instead of… well, who knows."

The two men stared at each other for several moments.

Irwin raised an inquiring eyebrow. "Why do I get the feeling this isn't a nice, social call?"

Sherman frowned, and his whole cheery make-up seemed to evaporate. "Doc," he murmured, holding the cheroot before him. "You know as well as anyone, running a circus is a fretful business. Full of pitfalls, unforeseen issues. Expense. Trepidation. Hell, I've been involved with our firm since I was 11. Owner and manager since I was 24. I have seen it all in my time. And more."

He took a deep breath. Irwin stood perfectly still.

"Unfortunately, as things stand, the books just don't balance out any more. Our outgoings dwarf our incomings. And the difference is quite significant. Our costs are just rising and rising. It's the price of success… of being popular. We're bringing in more green than we ever have… and yet, well, it is just never enough.

"We are shelling out merchandise, confectionary, all sorts of junk in the midway. But, every week, some god foresaken piece of machine needs replacing, at great expense. Another unforeseen fee for a park or a field. Another talent scout or road manager needs paying. It just never ends, Doc."

Irwin looked down at him glumly. "I sure am sorry to hear about that, Gerry. But I, er, well, I don't see how that directly affects me."

Sherman stared at him for a long moment. He exhaled a frantic breath.

"We're making a few changes, Doc. And one of them affects you."

Irwin remained impassive. "How's that?"

Then, Sherman looked away, ruffling his paperwork. "We are cancelling your All American Association. The passes are being withdrawn. Permanently. As of right now."

Irwin looked ready to explode. "What? You've got to be kidding me, Gerry!"

"I'm afraid not. Those passes are costing us money, entry fees. We just can't allow it anymore. I'm sorry. We need maximum take on the gates now. It's imperative."

Irwin looked crestfallen. "Those passes go to children from orphanages and care centres. I've been handing them out for more than 20 years now. The All American Association is a staple of my career, dammit. It's a tradition that's been with me since I started out. Since I became famous. I can't… I can't just cancel it."

Sherman held up a hand. "I understand it's important to you, Doc. But, the fact of the matter is, you're giving out 100 free passes for every show. That's five dollars missing from our take for each pass. It's costing us too much."

A deathly silence filled the executive carriage.

Irwin ran a hand over his smooth, bald scalp. His green eyes were sad and vacant. "Profits," he mumbled sadly. "That's all you people care about. Making dough. Staying in the black."

"I'm running a business, for Christ sakes. Not a god damn children's charity."

Now, Irwin was mad. "Those children have nothing, dammit. Nothing! No family. No money. No hope. They're there waiting for us in every town. The one highlight of their year. The All American Association. Getting their passes. And you…" he glared down at Sherman. "You and your partners want to take that away from them." He stood there, shaking his head in disgust.

Sherman remained impassive. All business. "I'm sorry, Doc."

Irwin turned slowly, as if in a dream. He began walking towards the door. He turned at the far end of the carriage.

"Sorry isn't good enough, Sherman. It never will be."
Then, he left.

153

CHAPTER 14

"And now, ladies and gentlemen, prepare yourselves for a never-before-seen wild stunt, as Rawley Walsh and the Riders of the Double G present… the Saddle Swap!"

Heavy roared the promo into the mic, before holding his arm aloft and retreating back to the tent flap.

On the sawdust, Walsh, resplendent in his all-white country and western outfit, sat atop his palomino at one end of the big top, while his partner, Durwood, followed suit on the other side.

Klondike had been determined to make more of this stunt, and firmly believed it was a show-stopper. He had arranged for more build-up, including Heavy's new introduction, and more bravado, featuring the two cowboys slowly face each other like medieval jousters, to build up suspense.

It was the Double G Circus's Dallas show, and some tweaks had been made to the performances. However, despite Garrison's aides slapping circus posters and flyers all over the city, the attendance was still alarmingly poor. The tent was barely half full, possibly a thousand fans. An improvement on Memphis, if nothing else.

Now, as a whipcrack sounded over the tannoy, Walsh and Durwood raced at each other on their mounts in the tent's centre.

The audience seemed genuinely tense, fascinated, as the horses sprinted towards each other in a seeming show of death defiance all around.

Klondike watched earnestly, feeling the crowd's tension.

As the mounts came together in a terrifying-looking spectacle, Walsh and Durwood leapt simultaneously. They body-checked, spun around and, while Walsh just missed his saddle but managed to cling on to the leather horn, Durwood flew calamitously through the air, sprawling on to the sawdust in an undignified heap.

A mighty hush of stunned disbelief rippled through the seats. Klondike closed his eyes, putting a hand over his face.

All was silent. Then, to the immense relief of just about everyone present, the fallen cowboy rose to his feet, dusting himself down with his stetson. He looked around dumbly, then headed after the now roaming riderless horse.

"He's ok, folks," Heavy cried grandly into the mic. "He's just fine. They make them tough in the Sierra Nevadas. And none tougher than the Riders of the Double G!"

There was no applause, not even a relieved clap. Durwood launched himself back into his saddle and then the entire cowboy troupe performed a lap of honour, the palominos trotting slowly around the arena floor. Muted applause greeted them, and it didn't improve when Walsh performed a hind-leg salute on his mount.

Klondike finally removed his hand from his face. He glanced around at some of the patrons sat around him. Many stared in shock at the cowboy team, unimpressed at seeing a fall. Another mistake.

Klondike glanced back at Garrison, who had joined him at the flap for this show. The old colonel was stood in the tent doorway, leaning inside. This enabled him to keep an eye on the trailers in the field beyond. Garrison's steely grey eyes seemed to burn as he glanced at Klondike. The two men stared at each other.

At the edge of the sawdust, Heavy looked at Klondike, awaiting a signal to continue. Klondike merely nodded.

"And now, ladies and gentlemen, please welcome the human abnormality, the man who eats and breathes fire. Let's hear it for the red hot Don 'Fearless' Peerless!"

Another weak round of applause followed. And it got milder as Peerless wandered in, as if in a daze, to the centre of the floor. He briefly held up an arm to acknowledge the crowd. But that was about as good as it got.

Klondike studied the old-timer in the green fire-proof pants. He looked like he had been hypnotised.

Then, Peerless began lighting his fire sticks at his little table before placing them with ease into his mouth.

The spectators around the flap merely stared at the old man, many in shock, some in disinterest. Others in distaste.

Peerless's finale, when he juggled the flaming dough balls with his mouth, was met with a few laughs, but nothing more.

Klondike stepped backwards and muttered to Garrison: "This isn''t working. Look at him! No one cares. He has got to show some showmanship. Some charisma. He looks like a machinist… a damn factory worker! I've told him to liven it up."

Garrison shrugged. "People come because they think he might get burnt… or worse!"

Klondike watched as Peerless slowly wandered off stage again, pumping a fist in the air as he departed in an almost death-like silence.

Again, Klondike rubbed a hand over his face. The endless apathy from these spectators was driving him mad. He felt like he could not go on. The whole experience was draining. Maddening, almost.

Heavy's next introduction penetrated his inner thoughts. "And now, ladies and gentlemen, prepare to be left spellbound by the enchantress of the west. The snake charmer extraordinaire… Arletta LaRue."

The four stewards entered the big top carrying the great black coffin.

Klondike stared in dismay at the pale faces filling the seats around him. He could practically taste the discomfort.

The whole show, the whole tour, was beginning to feel like a cataclysm. A nadir for his career… and the industry in general.

Changes had to be made. But he only had these few acts to work with.

Uttering a quiet expletive, he watched Arletta begin her eerie snake dance.

"God help me," he whispered to himself.

"Why, it's that handsome Gino Shapiro. Here, in the typing pool!"

He smiled to himself as he overheard the secretaries chatting excitedly while he waltzed past.

A vast patrol of women, some surely teenagers, all sat alert at their desks, staring up at him in awe as he strode along, heading to the executive offices.

Shapiro had been summoned to a meeting with Bob Gelznick, executive producer of the movie he was working on. Here he was, in the big house. The Avalon Pictures studio block in Hollywood. Now, he weaved his way around the endless desks and booths in the studio bullpen before finally reaching the final office at the far end. Dressed in a shiny sky blue suit and pink shirt, all who saw him quite rightly baulked at the sheer magnificence of this superstar guest.

"Come on in, Gino," Gelznick wheezed as he met his visitor at the door. He ushered Shapiro into his enormous, penthouse-like office.

The trapeze ace whistled as he entered, looking out the vast floor to ceiling bay windows at the Hollywood hills beyond. The vegetation looked luscious and sprawling, as if they were stationed on a tropical island in the South Pacific.

Gelznick motioned him to a cream leather couch by the windows. An elderly man in a grey suit, the movie executive looked like he had been involved in Hollywood since the days of silent pictures, his voice as hoarse as an ogre's.

"What can I get ya, Gino," the older man said as he approached a bar in the office's corner.

"Coffee would be fine, thanks."

Shapiro sat on the ultra-comfortable couch, arms spread on the backs. "Santamaria… this office is like a palace!"

Gelznick cackled. "That's how we judge success out here, son. The bigger the office, the greater grosses you've got." He poured himself a scotch, despite the early hour. "And we've been grossing out of the ball park these last few years." He eyed his guest shrewdly. "Richard Lewis has been a big part of that."

The executive producer walked slowly to the couch, placing a china cup and saucer before Shapiro on a lounging table. He held his whiskey as he sat in an armchair to his guest's side.

Gino sipped his coffee, nodding in satisfaction. "Richard… he is a good kid. A true movie star, no?"

The old man smiled wanly. "What would you say if I told you that, last week, you received more fan mail than Richard Lewis?"

Shapiro tried to chuckle. "Fan mail, I always get. It's because of my circus career. Nothing to do with movies, señor."

"I beg to differ." Gelznick sat upright, hugging his glass slightly. "You know, Gino, all sorts of figures are suddenly interested in our once-ailing studio since we brought you on board. Now, I know you're only a stuntman at the moment. But… it would seem the possibilities are endless. I mean, for a man like

157

you. With your looks, your body, your charisma. People are taking note, Gino. And that is gunna help us, no end."

Shapiro shifted slightly in the great couch. "What kind of people, Mr Gelznick?"

The old man's eyes widened insanely. "Money people. Investors. Angels, we used to call them. Guys who want to throw a million bucks into our studio, to see their kind of pictures get made. It's a tantalising prospect. We welcome all investment, of course." He threw Shapiro a queer, cock-eyed look. "We have just brought in a new angel today, in fact. And, hell, let me tell you, son, he has a great deal of interest in you. Even wanted to meet with you, right now. Today! At Avalon."

Shapiro stared at him. "What! A moneyman wants to meet me, you say?"

Gelznick smiled smugly. "That's right. I think you will recognise him, son. In fact, he is waiting for us in our garden outside."

"What is this?" Shapiro blurted, taken completely off guard.

The old man merely stood, motioned for Gino to do the same, and then padded slowly across the great office to a white door at the end of the sprawling bay window. "Come!"

Unsettled, Shapiro followed, leaving his coffee behind.

Gelznick opened the door, and motioned with glee to a beautiful, utopian outdoor gazebo, that seemed to sit placidly among the tropical plants and low-hanging tree branches. Shapiro slid outside, and suddenly noticed a figure within the gazebo leaning on a railing and staring out at the Hollywood hills, with his back to them.

Gino felt an unusual sensation as he crept out towards the figure, who wore a flowery hula shirt and white pants. Recognition blurred in his conscience, overwhelming him.

Gelznick, still in the doorway, called out an introduction.

"Here he is, Eric, the great Gino Shapiro!"

Gino froze all over at the gazebo entrance, his eyes wide in fright.

The man in the flowery shirt slowly turned, and revealed himself. Thick, white hair. Golden, leather-like skin. Thin, sparrow-like arms and neck. Green eyes that glinted like antique jade.

"You!" Shapiro cried.

Eric Ribbeck smiled broadly, looking upon Shapiro like an art collector gazing upon a prized Picasso. Admiration. Awe. Excitement.

"The debonair king of the air. My, it's been a long time."

Shapiro sneered, reeling slightly. He took a step into the gazebo in the tropical garden, staring at Ribbeck as if struggling to believe it was really him. "Not long enough." He marvelled at the older man, how he retained such a powerful poise, after all these years. "What in Sam Hill are you doing here?"

Ribbeck kept smiling. He reached for a cocktail sat on the edge of the railing by his hand. "You didn't tell him?" he called to Gelznick.

The producer grinned and took a step back inside his office. "Oh, I told him. Now, I'll leave you two to catch up. Enjoy the gardens. What's mine is yours, my friends." Then, he was gone.

Shapiro could not stop staring at Ribbeck. It was a surreal, shocking moment. "I can't believe you're here…" he whispered.

"I can't believe it's you. After all these years. I haven't seen you since… since…"

"Atlanta. 1952. The last show of the season. Before you ran out on me." Ribbeck took a long, purposeful sip of his exotic-looking drink. Then, he slammed the tall glass down. "Yeah, I remember Gino. I remember all too well. You god damn rattlesnake, you! Leaving me for that yahoo Klondike. And Corky too! I never forgot that night."

Shapiro frowned. "You're lucky I didn't report you to the cops, old man. The amount of dirt I saw in your outfit."

Ribbeck held up a hand irritably. "Never mind all that, dammit." He took a step forward in the morning sunshine, which glinted majestically off the white stone of the gazebo. "I am not here to talk about the past. Only the future. Or, more to the point, your future, Gino."

Shapiro shook his head. "I have nothing to say to you, old man."

"You don't even want to hear my proposal for you?" Ribbeck turned to a small iron roundtable and retrieved from an ashtray his beloved ivory meerschaum pipe. He held it to his mouth and tapped the stem gently against his teeth, a long-time habit.

Shapiro looked at him blankly. "You've invested in Avalon Pictures…"

Ribbeck sneered. "I'm buying them out, dammit." He let the words sink in. "Avalon and Gelznick have been struggling for years. Despite all this –" he waved a hand around the gardens and studio block – "these suckers are constantly in the red. But I wanted to add a movie studio to my empire and, well, the spurs all seemed to fit the boots and so here we are."

"What the hell do you want with a movie studio?"

Ribbeck puffed lightly on the pipe. "We are going to make films about my circus. Documentaries, shorts, feature presentations for movie theatres… what goes on before the main attraction. It is the next step in my entertainment empire." He diverted his gaze and looked down at Shapiro. It was a well-practised look, one of pure power and superiority. "Which brings me to you, Gino."

Shapiro simply stood there, gaping at him. He felt his chest puffing out subconsciously. "What the hell is this?"

"In essence, I now run Avalon Pictures," Ribbeck said conversationally. "That means you work for me, son. Now, this whole project of making circus films out here, filming our shows… you are going to be a big part of that. In many ways, it is going to be all about you. Because…" the old man seemed to savour the words, enjoying the tantalising moments as he uttered them. His eyes were ablaze, his voice over-animated. "Because, Gino Shapiro, you are now, once again, working for Ribbeck World Circus! This deal today has sealed it."

Shapiro was truly dumbstruck. He clenched his fists. "You must be outta your god damn mind, campesino! You think I would work for you? Ever again? After all you did back then?"

"The contracts are signed!" Ribbeck hissed quickly. "You work for Avalon Pictures. I… I am Avalon Pictures, god damn it!"

"You're delusional, old man!"

"No, Gino, I am a visionary. A revolutionary. And, damn it all to hell, I am going to make you rich beyond your wildest dreams. The biggest star in world circus. Don't you see? This is going to change your life. You're back with the biggest circus on the planet."

"Save it, old man. I already heard it all from your lap dog, Enqvist. He may have been seduced by your money and your nonsense, but not me!"

Ribbeck snarled, jabbing the air with his pipe. "Don't be a fool, Gino. Think about it. Your movie career will be over. Every big top in America has departed for their season. Where will you go?"

Shapiro grunted. "Come off it, old man. I am Gino Shapiro. There isn't an outfit out there that wouldn't want me."

"You belong to me, god damn it!"

"I don't belong to anybody! The hell with you and your money!"

Ribbeck roared like an ox. He flung his prized pipe back onto the table, where it nearly shattered.

"Listen, you damn appaloosa… if you're not gunna perform under my big top, then your movie career is over, dammit! Your contract with Avalon is over! You're fired!"

Shapiro, chest heaving, took a step closer, his dark eyes wild with fierce loathing. Alarmed, Ribbeck backed into the railing.

"Now, you listen, amigo," Gino snarled, "the day I work for you again… will be the day I die."

He made to turn and walk away. Ribbeck groaned and called after him, a last, desperate attempt to win him over.

"Why the hell don't you just join us, god damn it? Think of all the riches, the glory. It will all be yours. Everything you've ever dreamed of. I can make that happen, Gino. For the love of god. You belong with me! With the greatest show on earth! Why can't you see that!"

Shapiro stopped and turned around. "Oh, I can see it, old man." He thought for a moment, looking over the luscious gardens all around. "You forget one thing, amigo. My love is for the circus itself. Not the money, the fame, the adulation, the commercialism. The champagne and caviar. No! For the industry. What is more important than anything is that the industry succeeds. You understand me, campesino?"

Ribbeck looked at him in disgust. "Not a god damn word, you oily son of a bitch!"

Shapiro nodded, in subtle understanding. "Of course. And that… that is the difference between us."

With that, he shook his head and marched to the door, heading back inside the office.

All alone in the grand gazebo, Ribbeck stared at the closed door in disbelief. Then, he turned and gazed over the Hollywood hills.

"Unemployed," he murmured acidly. "The damn yahoo would rather be unemployed than work for me."

He grabbed at his drink. This time, he downed the lot.

Outside in the baking hot Hollywood streets, Shapiro stormed down the sidewalk. He reached a silver sedan parked on the corner and got in.

Andros Murphy was at the wheel, waiting and listening to a ball game on a portable radio. He looked up in alarm as Shapiro got inside.

"What happened, Gino?"

Shapiro swore, running a hand through his shiny black hair. He looked at his old friend. "I'm sorry, amigo. I think I just got us fired."

Murph was incredulous. "What? From the picture?"

"From Avalon Pictures. The whole studio."

Murph shook his head. "What the hell happened in there, man?"

Shapiro stared at the traffic, the sunshine taxi cabs that seemed to dominate the streets. "There's a new moneyman at Avalon. And we don't exactly get along."

"What are you talking about?"

Shapiro eyed him seriously. "Eric Ribbeck."

"Ribbeck!"

"Right. He is the studio's new investor. It appears they have rolled out the red carpet for him, the campesinos." His eyes seemed to drop. "It was all a ploy to get me to sign for his circus. The whole damn thing. That man... he will never quit."

Murph looked at him. "So you told him to go to hell, right?"

"But of course."

Murph nodded. They both sat there in silence for several moments.

Finally, Shapiro spoke in a low tone. "I'm sorry, Murph. I've screwed this all up for you. The movie work. As long as you're associated with me, I fear your days here are numbered too."

But Murph was impassive. "It's alright," he said slowly. "Like you, I promised I would never work for that son of a bitch Ribbeck again. No matter what."

Shapiro tried to smile. "It would appear, my friend, that we need to rustle up a new gig. Come, I owe you one now."

"You got any suggestions?"

"Sure. We find us some circus work, amigo. Doing what we do best."

"I thought you said you could never work for another big top, after Klondike?"

Shapiro smiled wanly. "I didn't count on being blackballed out of the movie industry like that." He grabbed at his old friend's shoulder. "Come on, Murph. We can put our old act back together."

Murph sat there bewildered. "We haven't performed together in eight years, for Christ's sake."

Shapiro nodded slowly, his mind racing. He patted Murph's immense shoulders, his bulging chest muscles.

"Time for some practice."

CHAPTER 15

COWBOY CIRCUS SHAKES UP HOUSTON… BUT NO ONE CARES!

By Cobi Spanning, Texas Review Journal

The Double G Circus brought its wild west antics to the Cattle Club in Houston last night – but big top fans stayed away.
Barely 500 spectators made it into the troupe's mighty white and gold tent for the show, meaning a vast swathe of empty chairs dominated the seating area.

The only thing more embarrassing than this pitiful spectacle was the actual talent on show, which was low key and low fare but, alas, high in admission price.

The main attraction of this Sierra Nevada-based travelling show is the recent addition of the great Kal Klondike to its ranks.

Of course, the legendary circus manager was left unemployed and, seemingly, undesired after his all-conquering promotion Klondike's Circus was involved in a disastrous and controversial ship sinking in New York harbour while retuning from a European tour earlier this year.

Now, the fallen idol of Klondike is acting as manager for this ragtag group of cowboys, gunslingers and carnival clouts.

And the good people of Houston were most certainly not impressed by their routines, barely breaking into cheers or applause throughout this 90-minute horror show.

Whether it was a group of cowboys riding endlessly around the tent in a circle, a snake charmer who looked like she had been drugged, a geriatric fire-eater who was drunk, or a musclebound strongman merely lifting up weights, there was little to excite, entertain or enlighten. And the fans responded in kind.

In fact, many had left long before the circus's climax, which saw a gunslinging cowboy and a knife thrower smash up glass bottles on a fake bartop.

Somehow, this unholy manner of hillbilly claptrap is still classified as entertainment… in some quarters, at least.

The Double G Circus tour continued west. But as the mass convoy of camper vans and trailers roamed from city to city, each stop felt like a lost cause.

El Paso, San Antonio, Rawlson… some of the biggest circus towns in the territory. Klondike had played them all with his old troupe down the years. To much acclaim.

But now, as manager of the Double G, everything felt like a colossal struggle. From trying to generate publicity and media interest in each city, to ensuring the roustabouts had set up the tent and midway correctly. Even rousing the talent and explaining how they could improve… it all felt like an uphill struggle.

Then, he was back in his trailer with Heavy as they drove for hours on end to the next stop. How he missed his glorious old circus train, the Barrowman Express. The whole locomotive had probably been sold for scrap in California, he had mused to himself during one long road voyage.

As the circus convoy headed to its next playing field in Albuquerque, New Mexico, Klondike realised he was on a hiding to nothing. Simply put, he had arrived on the scene too late. That was the dilemma. Joining up with Garrison just days before the tour began. It was an impossible scenario. There had been no off-season. No tune-up. No chance to plan anything – the order, the training programme, even the work details for the crew. No, there had been no time for any of that.

Instead, he was flying along, clutching at straws. Trying, desperately, to conjure up a way of turning the Double G Circus around… of making a profit. Of finding his salvation, perhaps, with a new success story.

He knew the answers would not be found in Albuquerque. But there were still six more dates after that.

Time. For anything to happen. Maybe even a miracle.

As if some divine heavenly force had answered his prayers, the Albuquerque show crowd was touching on 2,000. Still some way off the 2,500 tent capacity, but a significant improvement on what the Double G had experienced so far on this tour.

And, finally, the audience seemed enlivened by the wild west action of Rawley Walsh and Hondo Cloud.

The Saddle Swap routine drew mighty cheers and applause, as did Walsh's blindfolded shooting. Then, Cloud's knife throwing act drew rapturous ovations from all within the big top. The Native American acknowledged the cheers by briefly juggling three of his blades, another of Klondike's suggestions, which went down a treat with the fans.

At the show's finale, the sight of Cloud and Walsh performing together seemed to enrapture the watching patrons, who applauded the action heartily, producing the loudest cheers of the night.

Finally, after seven frustrating, exhausting shows, Klondike's initial, game-changing plan had come to fruition – the fans being excited at seeing the show's big two stars performing together, in a grand finale.

The Albuquerque crowd had seemed to enjoy the wild west elements of the show, right from the off. Klondike and Heavy had noted this from the audience reactions – the excitement and glee on the younger fans' faces as the cowboys rode out. And even seeing a real-life Commanche in Cloud was a real treat for many.

Now, in a big top filled with raw energy and excitement – at last – Klondike folded his arms as he watched alongside Heavy at the flap, as Walsh and Cloud faced off, eyeing each other 20 yards apart, with the plaster wood bar covered in green glass bottles between them.

The lively crowd grew silent. The two figures stood still, as if in a showdown in the old west, ready for the draw. Then, a female voice sounded over the tannoy. "Five. Four. Three. Two. One. Draw!"

Walsh whipped out his Colt 45, as Cloud hurled his Bowie knives in machine-gun fashion, one after another, from the leather pouch now mounted on his right shoulder.

The explosion of glass in the arena's centre was cataclysmic. Shards flew everywhere in a 10-yard circle of destruction. It looked like the bottles had been blown up by an unseen detonation. In another of Klondike's new ideas, Cloud then ended the sequence by hurling a final knife straight towards

Walsh, across the sawdust. The cowboy aimed his revolver and fired a shot, smashing the blade clear with a perfectly aimed cap. The routine worked perfectly… on its first outing.

As the knife deflected harmlessly through the air, away from Walsh, the two performers pointed at one another in an 'I'll get you next time' gesture. Then, the crowd were on their feet, as applause rained out across the circus floor from the seating circle. Children called out in wonder, and there were audible cries of delight.

Klondike closed his eyes and cherished the cheers. It felt like years had passed since he had last heard an ovation. A real one. He smiled, bemused and warmed all at once.

Then, Heavy waded gloriously out on to the sawdust again, waving at the fans.

"Have you ever seen anything like it, folks? The fastest gun in the west, Rawley Walsh. The Comanche knifeman, Hondo Cloud. Our wild west stars, faster than electric lightning!"

He held a hand high. "We hope you have enjoyed the wonder, the glamour and the sheer excitement of The Double G Circus, folks. Now, let's hear it for the stars of the show, the dynamos of the Double G! Here they come, Albuquerque! Your circus superstars!"

An all-new sound erupted from the PA system, a dramatic song from an old Italian opera, which in itself was astonishing.

Then, the Riders of the Double G came riding out into the arena, this time at a strong gallop.

They were followed by the Rollergirls, who skated out into the arena at a furious pace, whizzing past the horses, dangerously close to the fans in the front rows.

Soolaimon marched into the big top – carrying Arletta and Peerless on his mighty shoulders. The two smaller figures waved enthusiastically at the cheers.

While all this was happening in the centre, Walsh and Cloud were walking around the perimeter of the sawdust, high-fiving the patrons on the front row and uttering their catchphrases to the children.

Then, both jogged out onto the sawdust as all the performers gathered in the centre of the big top. Just as the opera music reached a pulsating climax, electrifying the tent, the performers all held their arms aloft in unison, a choreographed move designed to make the team look like a unit. A troupe.

It worked, and the audience all cheered as one.

At the flap beyond, Klondike smiled again. His small tweaks had transformed the show's grand parade from a mirthless procession akin to a village funeral into a fan-friendly, dramatic final act, a salute to the spectators and a last hurrah.

Sure, it lacked the grandeur and spectacle of the Klondike's Circus grand parade, where the performers had sat in Cadillac convertibles that had performed a lap of honour in the tent while Suzi Dando had sung her beautiful song.

But this, this fitting conclusion to the show – his show – was something. And the crowd seemed to like it.

Klondike clapped his hands merrily at the flap as the troupe all exited the big top, every single one of them waving to the fans as they left. The applause followed them out.

The cowboys on their horses and the Rollergirls were the last to leave the arena, all acknowledging the cheers.

As the Rollergirls slowed to a stop by the flap, walking awkwardly in their skates, several teenaged boys sat nearby rushed towards the partition in the seats, seemingly ecstatic. They called out wildly.

"You Rollergirls are great! We love you!"

"Where are you playing next, girls? I'm gunna get my whole crew to come along!"

The skaters all smiled happily at the praise.

Pamela Hotch, who was bringing up the rear, nodded knowingly as she caught Klondike's eye at the flap. Then, in a whirl, she span around on the spot at lightning speed, before jumping into the air, and landing in the splits. The gang of teenagers all cheered again.

She looked at them seductively.

"There's so much more where that came from, boys. All you have to do is get yourselves to Tucson, next Saturday night." She smiled devilishly from the ground. "We'll all be waiting…"

The boys all cried out aloud, before chatting excitedly among themselves.

Pamela somehow leapt to her feet, and lumbered out on her skates.

Klondike watched her at the flap, and followed as she moved through the exit and out into the tent tunnel that led onto the playing field. Once outside, they both stopped, breathing in the cool night air and looking out at the moonlight. The black blanket above was full of stars. A shanty town of trailers and vans seemed to stretch for an eternity ahead of them. They could hear the commotion of the spectators all leaving the big top on the other side of the great tent.

"That was quite a stunt you pulled for those boys," Klondike muttered, his eyes on the night sky.

Pamela's eyes gleamed. "All part of the show. The tricks of the trade. You know how that works, Kal."

Klondike grunted. "The more of that kind of thing you girls can whip up, the better. We need as much advance publicity as possible."

She turned to him and grinned. "You can count on it… boss man." She looked back and eyed the enormous circus tent behind them. "Now, that felt like a smash hit show. At last! Fans cheering. Children laughing. Seats with actual people sat in them, not empty again. Why, that ovation my team got at the end was loud, excited." She chuckled. "It looks like this tour has finally got some zest! Some interest."

Klondike nodded, studying her. "Your team are a big part of that, Pam. Hell, the people love you guys. I'm just so glad I talked you all into joining us. We need you! The Rollergirls give us something extra. Something magical."

Pamela huffed. "I was beginning to wonder if we'd made a mistake hooking up with you, Kal."

Slowly, almost imperceptibly at first, she began to roll away from him on her skates, moving as slightly as a leaf in a light breeze. The woman in purple inched away into the night, heading towards the mass of trailers.

With expert control of her skates and balance, she whirled around, rolling backwards, and called out to him.

"Now, I'm not so sure anymore. You may have something here, Kal Klondike. Goodnight!"

Klondike watched her disappear into the circus encampment. With a slight chuckle, he turned and looked back once again at the mighty circus tent behind him. The light from the moon and stars was astonishing, such was its intensity. And the big top was so immense, it blotted out half the sky from where he stood. It was an effect he had always found awe-inspiring.

"Just like old times," he whispered to himself.

The Montague was one of the most opulent eateries in all of California. Nestled in Santa Monica Bay, on a cliffside overlooking the mighty Pacific, the ancient Whitestone building was decorated in modern, early 1960s chic furniture. Its heavily varnished mahogany tables seemed to shine, while cream marble tiles covered the floors.

The exclusive restaurant catered for the privileged and the elite, and its prices reflected that.

Completely at home in such grand surroundings, Eric Ribbeck sat at a central, booth table, nourishing a goblet of Bordeaux wine as he studied a newspaper. It was before lunchtime, and the restaurant was hardly busy at this early hour.

Ribbeck savoured the peace. Dressed in a burgundy blazer with a white cravat at his throat, he looked every inch a blueblood aristocrat, a far cry from his roots as the son of a Texas cattle baron.

The old man smiled smugly as he re-read the newspaper report, a review of his circus's show from last night, more than 1,000 miles away in Minneapolis.

The headline screamed:

DAREDEVILS STAR AS RIBBECK CIRCUS CONFIRMS SUPERIORITY!

With a mild chuckle, he began to read the review...

Motorcycle stunt team The Daredevils were the stars of the show last night as Ribbeck World Circus roared into Minneapolis – and blew us all away!

Rider Tip Enqvist and his team of stunt bikers left the audience at the Belle Longton Showground stunned into disbelief with their astonishing Globe of Death act.

The Daredevils were circus boss Eric Ribbeck's star off-season signings as he strengthened what is surely the world's greatest line-up of big top talent.

They have joined Ribbeck's stalwarts – trapeze ace Dirk Tempest, wild bird trainer Clint Martinez and beloved clown Calypso – to form what this correspondent (a long-time circus-goer) believes is the greatest roster ever assembled. A team of comic book superheroes, if you will.

And what a joy to behold it was to see them all in action. And all under the magnificent green and purple big top synonymous across the USA with first class entertainment.

And seeing Ribbeck's latest additions The Daredevils in action was truly a delightful treat for this circus fan. The Globe of Death routine simply has to be seen to be believed, such is its impossible enormity. Death defiance as never seen before… in this world at least.

I can only recommend everyone and anyone, who ever enjoyed a thrill, to check Ribbeck's tour schedule and find out when he's coming to your territory. You won't regret it – if you are lucky enough to get a ticket!

Ribbeck could only smile with sheer contentment as he savoured the words of the report. He had read it three times since arriving at The Montague.

Better still, there were 10 more newspapers sat in his limousine out back, all carrying equally effusive reviews for Minneapolis. It was his six show of the season, but already the critical acclaim was through the roof, while commercially his troupe was booming. Six shows, six sell-outs, with hundreds being turned away at the box office.

He laughed with absolute pleasure. Now, there could be no doubt. Ribbeck World Circus was America's number one. The figures and the reviews spoke for themselves.

Ribbeck's glistening green eyes took in the article's accompanying picture, which showed Tip Enqvist sat on his motorbike at the top of the Globe of Death ramp, holding his helmet aloft as the spectators stood and screamed.

Silently, he congratulated himself on acquiring the Norwegian stunt team. It had not exactly been hard. Once Enqvist had heard about the money he was offering them, the deal was virtually done.

Licking his lips as he devoured another sip of the Bordeaux, Ribbeck felt his pulse quicken at the prospect of rejoining his circus in Minnesota that weekend. Of the six shows so far, he had attended only one due to his various business dealings around the country. And that brought him back to his meeting today, at The Montague.

Absently, he looked back at the newspaper report, then down at the leather-bound menu beside it on his table. But his mind was elsewhere.

He was doing well, he thought. But yet still he craved more. More!

The voice from behind made him jump.

"Mr Ribbeck."

The old man shook himself from his reverie, his green eyes darting upwards in alarm.

A short man with wavy, curly brown hair and a reddish, freckly face was hovering over the table, dressed impressively in a brown pin-stripped suit, complete with a pink cravat.

Miles Courtland. He needed no introduction. Ribbeck recognised him instantly.

"Mr Courtland," he said in his croaky drawl. He rose slowly and the two men shook hands. The old man gestured to a seat.

Courtland, looking as excited and agitated as ever, slipped into the vinyl bench seat opposite. "This is indeed an honour," he chirped.

"It is I who am honoured," Ribbeck mused, though he hardly sounded genuine. "Having a great musical impresario like Miles Courtland entering our industry. My industry! I am delighted by the news, and wish you every success. Come…" he poured a generous helping of the crimson-coloured wine into a spare goblet and thrust it in front of his guest. "A toast. To success in your latest venture."

Courtland accepted the glass and took a long sip. He raised an inquiring eyebrow.

"Thank you. Though I must confess, Mr Ribbeck, to some surprise at your invite. Lunch, here at The Montague. After all, we are now going to be competitors."

Ribbeck snapped out of his warm and pleasant demeanour. "Hardly," he uttered. Then he smiled again. "But, as a trusted and long-standing custodian of the circus industry, I felt it my duty and a fitting measure to offer you my best wishes… and those of my contemporaries and allies." The old man smiled devilishly. "Allies," he said again. "There is a lot to be gained from being my ally."

Courtland gaped at him for a moment. Then, he nodded in understanding. "So, that's it, huh?"

Ribbeck was impassive. "What's that, sonny?"

Courtland lost much of his warmth and charm. "You want a union. Between my circus and your… your empire."

Ribbeck glared at him. Sharp as a tack and with a mind that processed business first, and relations last. He was impressed.

"I like the look of your outfit," the Texan drawled. "You've put it together real fast. All that talent. Assembled in a matter of weeks. My compliments, son. You are quite the taskmaster. As we say in Texas, a prime ranchero."

Courtland stared at him. "Is there something you want to propose… Eric?"

Ribbeck grinned wisely, his steely eyes adding a savage undertone. "Like I said, I like what you've done… Miles. What you're doing. Now, your new troupe is set to depart this Thursday, right? And your whole schedule is all mapped out, real professional and totally faultless."

Courtland had lost all pretence of nicety. "Can you please get to the point?"

Ribbeck leant forward eagerly. "How would you like to become a Ribbeck World Circus developmental promotion?"

"A what?"

"It is basically an affiliated group working and performing under the Ribbeck promotional banner. I have several throughout the southern states. So, we'll swap talent, promote each others' shows, help each other out, you get the idea."

A deathly silence filled the booth. Courtland merely stared at his host, his face showing little emotion. Ribbeck well knew the younger man had experienced a wealth of business deals down the years, negotiated multi-million dollar contracts with stars from across the world. He was no fresh-faced choirboy, even if he did resemble one. More a hardened showbusiness veteran, comfortable handling the country's most elite media moguls.

As the two men stared at each other silently, like chess masters in a championship match, a young waitress gently approached the table.

"Are you gentlemen ready to order?"

More silence. Then, it was Courtland who answered. "No… we are not."

The female in the white shirt backed off as smoothly as she had approached. The two men's eyes never left each other.

Finally, after what seemed an eternity, Courtland spoke quietly. "This is about Roddy, isn't it?"

Ribbeck squinted at him. Again, he was impressed by the record producer. "What makes you say that, son?"

"Ah, come on, man. I've followed the circus industry for years. Spoken to a lot of top people. It's no secret you covet Roddy. They say you see the kid as the missing piece in your mighty jigsaw… the act that will truly make your troupe the greatest of all time. I might've guessed this whole meeting would boil down to the kid."

Ribbeck frowned but remained cool. "You're wrong, Miles. I already have the greatest show on earth. Without question. Getting Olsen onboard isn't going to suddenly achieve that. But the fact remains… the kid is an otherworldly talent. A god damn ace! He belongs with the best… the very best. And what's more…" he leant forward again, his leathery face a mask of power and superiority. "I want him. Chances are, when I want something, son, it's gunna end up in my hands. Like so many straight flushes…"

Courtland rolled his eyes. He looked about at the fabulous decor all around. The antique porcelain figures resting on stands, the marbled tiles, and the oil paintings covering the walls.

"I appreciate your interest in Courtland and Co," he finally said, wearily. "But I must decline your offer, Eric. I've planned and organised this enterprise from the very start. It's my baby. And, well, I intend to keep it that way. Right through to the finish line. We'll go our own way and see where the road takes us. That's part of the fun after all, right?"

Ribbeck's face was a weathered mask of contempt. "So, you're going solo, eh? Just like that? You start a damn circus out of nothing. Set up a holding camp, what, in your back yard so I hear? And then you just roll... you and your people..."

Courtland frowned. "That's the general idea."

Now, Ribbeck was enjoying himself. It felt like he knew what Courtland's answers would be, and already had his next statement ready. It was an unnerving sensation for the younger man. "Of course," Ribbeck drawled, "you'll have all the necessary paperwork? Membership of the National Circus Alliance? Without that, you can't legally put on a show anywhere."

Courtland finally cracked slightly. "I have my circus licence. All the ground permits. They were obtained months ago. What the hell is this alliance?"

Ribbeck sat back, grinning with satisfaction. "The NCA runs the industry in this country, boy. You obviously failed to look them up when you started out. That tends to be the problem when you act gung-ho and try to rustle up a touring show, like saddle tramps setting up a rodeo. Hell, you rushed all this, boy, and I-"

"I asked you a question, dammit!"

Ribbeck glared at him. "The NCA is a membership organisation, consisting of a committee of long-standing big top owners and stock holders. Between us, we govern the industry, maintain order and...grant permission for new circuses to tour within our jurisdiction."

Courtland rolled his eyes yet again. "I notice you said 'we'."

"Damn right. I don't just sit on the board, son. I run the place. You newcomers to the trade just don't get it... here, in the United States of America, I am the circus industry, dammit! It runs and exists through me now. The others will vote however I vote... no one goes against me. Not when we're voting on a greenhorn like you." He folded his arms smugly. "So you see, Courtland, I have all the influence. All the ace cards." He narrowed his eyes. "All except one... one ace of the sawdust."

The younger man shifted in his seat. "How do I know any of this is for real?"

"You can look it all up, investigate. But I really don't see the point. You know I'm telling the truth, you know who I am, and that's the end of it."

"So, it seems I have a choice. Join you and become a, what was it, 'territorial promotion' for your business. Or I try and win some favour with these NCA cronies of yours?"

"You can try and win some of them over, Courtland, but there just isn't time. Your first ever show is set for Saturday night. You're screwed, god damn it!"

Courtland finally seemed to deflate. For the first time since he had dreamed up his circus adventure, he felt somewhat out of his depth.

"We've sold tickets," he whispered fiercely, "spent a fortune on advanced publicity. Arranged land permits, licences. And you want to ramrod all that just cos some boardroom of traditionalists has to rubber-stamp everything?"

"You've got a lot to learn, son," Ribbeck spat out. "Like showing respect to this industry and those who control it. I told you before, you should've got your house in order when you started out. Anyone worth a damn in the circus world would have told you not to go against the NCA. Now... it's too late."

Suddenly, Courtland shot up, standing at the table and leering down at his host. "My circus isn't over! It's just been delayed."

Ribbeck held up his hands. "Good luck telling that to the people of... wherever the hell your first show was going to take place."

Courtland stared at him in disgust for several moments. Then, with an almighty huff, he left the table and stormed out of the joint. Gone.

The Texan watch him go, disappointed and satisfied in equal measure. It was an unusual sensation.

As he sat there brooding, the young waitress returned. "Would you care to order now, sir?"

Ribbeck eyed her, and nodded. He glanced down at the long-forgotten menu before him. Then he looked up at the space his visitor had just vacated.

"God damn yahoo," he muttered to himself.

"Good evening, ladies and gentlemen. My name is Tony Tan, and I've come here tonight all the way from... the bar!"

The diminutive puppet with the tanned features, thick black hair and giant eyebrows, dressed in a black tuxedo, came to life.

Tony Tan was placed on Roddy Olsen's arm, as the young ventriloquist horsed around outside his trailer in the sprawling Courtland estate.

Olsen stared at the puppet by his side. "Are you going to sing for us tonight, Tony?"

The figure hiccuped. "I sure am, Rod. What is the song for tonight, man?"

"Bye Bye Blues."

"Saddest song I ever heard…"

"What? Bye Bye Blues?"

"Oh, I'm sorry, mack. I thought you said, Bye Bye Booze!"

Several young roustabouts who had been standing watching all burst out laughing at the exchange. Corky was stood with him, and chuckled at the sketch.

The holding camp within the grounds of the mighty estate was filled with trailers and trucks, as workers dashed around endlessly, like ants around a woodpile.

Olsen fiddled slightly with the puppet, adjusting the grip. The youngsters all slowly filed away, wishing him good luck.

With a happy sigh, Corky joined him by the doorway of his trailer, eyeing little Tony Tan mischievously.

"So, your girl back in Frisco finished work on this little fella?"

Olsen grinned at him as he slipped the puppet off his arm and deposited it, all so gently, into his beloved leather suitcase.

"Right. It arrived with a courier this morning." The youngster seemed elated. "Now, the band is all back together. Rusty, Napoleon and Tony, all alive and… and… well, with me again."

Corky nodded, staring at the suitcase. "And not at the bottom of the Atlantic…"

Olsen closed his eyes. "It's all so hard to comprehend." He looked at his great friend. "I know the originals are all gone. Sunk off New York like everything else. But, well, these copies from Hullabazoo are the nearest thing I'm ever gunna get to them. They're all identical, finished to perfection. And it feels like… like I have my guys back in my life again." He glanced at Corky impishly. "I guess this must all sound crazy, huh?"

Corky shook his head fiercely. "No, not at all, man. Hell, I've never known a ventriloquist who didn't think of his puppets as family. You take care of them, Rod. And, well, they will take care of you, in a way."

Olsen nodded mesmerically. He hauled up the great suitcase and deposited it inside the doorway to his trailer.

Then, he looked about at the endless manor grounds all around them. Everything, and everyone, seemed to be in the shadow of the gothic Courtland mansion, that lingered on the horizon like a mighty dreadnought in the ocean. Within its shadow, vehicles of all manner were parked in a jumbled mess, while the roustabouts and stewards carried equipment across the grass, all lost in their duties and errands.

Olsen glanced sideways at Corky. "Still glad you joined me, buddy?"

Corky grinned. In a polo shirt and jeans, and minus his facepaint or any real indication of his true profession, the legendary clown looked like one of the roustabouts right then. An everyman.

"Sure I'm glad," he wheezed. "I'd still be sat on that barstool if you hadn't tracked me down." He squinted into the sun as he studied the various midway stalls as they were loaded onto flatbed trucks, all around them.

"Besides, there's just something about a circus rollout. The excitement. The anticipation. The open road ahead. Magic time, as we used to call it…"

The clown looked happily into the afternoon haze, and Olsen followed his gaze.

Then, both seemed to stand to attention as a figure burst out from among the trailers, pacing rapidly towards them. In an expensive brown, pin-striped suit, he looked somewhat out of place among the circus workforce.

"Mr Courtland," Corky exclaimed as the figure approached, standing before them by the trailer. "Is everything alright?"

Courtland looked ill at ease. Sweating profusely in the dry heat, and with his hair looking an unkept mess, the music mogul's breaths came in short, sharp gasps.

He put his hands on his hips, staring at the duo. "It's off!" he bellowed.

Olsen and Corky stared at him. "What?" they said in unison. "It's off! It's all off!"

"What's off?" Corky asked.

"The circus, dammit! We've been called off. The whole thing has to be postponed. For now, at least. We've got a problem!"

Olsen was incredulous. "Mr Courtland! What are you talking about?"

The tycoon was mad, his manner completely out of character. "I just told you, man. We got a problem! A big problem! And it's managed to smash our circus."

Corky moved closer to Courtland. "You're calling it off? After all this? All the planning, the investment, the outlay…"

Courtland quivered, and held a hand over his eyes. Was he crying? "I'm sorry, boys. It's all outta my hands."

Olsen was lost. "Mr Courtland… what happened? Can you tell us?"

Suddenly, Courtland looked up, staring straight at him with vacant, maddening eyes. "You're part of it, Roddy!"

Olsen baulked. "What?"

"That's right. And, for the first time since all this got under way, I've started thinking I'm in over my head!"

Corky remained calm. "What is this problem, sir?"

"The problem," Courtland snapped, still glaring at Olsen, "is a man. One Eric Ribbeck!"

Olsen and Corky froze. The name hit them like ice-cold fingertips across the spine.

"Ribbeck…" Corky murmured, in shock.

"Looks like he's aiming to put us out of business – for good!" Courtland cried in an animated manner.

Olsen shook his head. He motioned to the door of his trailer behind them, and looked at Courtland sincerely. "Why don't you tell us what happened, Mr Courtland?"

The record producer stared at him, and nodded slowly. "It's simple really, kid. Old man Ribbeck wants you in his troupe. He'll do anything to get you. Even close us down!" He nodded grimly, his face fraught. "Now, well, now I guess you are free to join him, man. We haven't got a show as it stands."

Olsen stared at him, frozen to the spot. "You mean… you mean all of this is because of me?"

"It's all about you, kid! Everything! It always has been." Courtland rubbed at his eyes, pulled at his wavy hair. "Even me getting started as a circus boss… it was only because I could boast having the great Roddy Olsen on board. With Corky the Clown backing him up. You guys were the dealmakers… I pinned everything on you!"

Olsen glanced at Corky, then back at the boss. Suddenly, it all seemed very quiet in the holding camp.

"Like I said," Courtland whispered, "now you can join Ribbeck. And cement your legacy as a global superstar."

Olsen squinted across at him. Then, he looked up at the heavens, his mind a whirlwind of alternating notions.

He had never met Eric Ribbeck face to face. Yet, the circus legend had been an ever-present, a constant antagonist, during his years at Klondike's Circus. Throughout his rise to stardom. Ribbeck was always there, scheming in the background, as Klondike's greatest rival.

Now, Olsen looked downwards. "Ribbeck…" he murmured grimly. His eyes seemed to glow, a strange and eerie sensation. The other two watched as he stood, transfixed. Both felt unnerved as he continued, in a strange, distant tone.

"It's always been Ribbeck."

CHAPTER 16

Klondike pulled his beloved Delta jeep into a small parking lot by the edge of the River Grande and leapt out.

Flagstaff, Arizona. They had made it to Arizona. Slowly, surely, they were inching closer to California with each show.

California. In his mind, the home of the circus. A land rich in carnival goers and big top fanatics. Somehow, in his head at least, everything would be alright once they reached that West Coast. Any circus show worth a damn attracted a crowd out there.

Arizona was similar, in his long experience on the road. He liked the people out here. Genuine, honest and humble.

Now, Klondike paced anxiously across the asphalt of the seemingly abandoned parking lot, joining a rugged gravel path that ran alongside the soft grey water of the Grande.

Not a soul in sight. Perfect, he thought.

He kept to the slender path as it ran parallel to the river for about 100 yards. Nothing but forestland stood all around, oaks and redwoods springing up in every direction, with the river running though it all like a divider.

Then, squinting into the afternoon sun, he saw what he was looking for.

A bench and, more importantly, a figure sitting upon it.

Klondike upped his walking pace until he reached the seat. He looked around, everywhere. Then, satisfied, he sat down next to the man, who didn't look up or show any emotion at all.

"For Christ's sake, Mike, you can't get much more remote than this."

Blakelock glanced at him, shrugging. "You can't be too careful, Kal. I'm still not entirely sure who I'm dealing with."

Klondike raised an eyebrow as he settled into the bench. "Oh? That doesn't sound promising."

Blakelock nodded slightly. He looked confused, tired and alone. "I'm getting too old for this crap."

Klondike nodded. "Like I said before, I appreciate anything you can do for me."

"The way things are right now, I got more questions than answers."

"Alright, Mike. What have you got for me?"

With a sigh, Blakelock retrieved a large manilla envelope from a satchel he had placed on the bench next to him. Delicately, he began removing items.

"Your girl Jenny is a player. I'd say she's been playing people all her life. In one way or another. Right now, she is playing a whale."

He handed Klondike a large black and white photograph. It showed a stocky, well-built middle-aged man with a bulldog expression and thinning hair.

Klondike frowned. "Who's this? Al Capone?"

"You're not far off, Kal. The name is Ray Generoso. Former bag man for the mob. Now a casino floor manager for the Rhinestone, and several others downtown. Influence. Power. And… the current lover of our Jenny Cross."

Klondike felt his face drop. "Jesus. Is this for real?"

"Uh huh. They've been an item for some time, it would appear." He handed across another image, which showed Generoso in a cafe seated opposite a blonde haired woman in a white dress. Klondike's eyes seemed to sting as he recognised his former lover. A woman he had once promised everything. He shook his head.

Blakelock continued casually. "I believe she was seeing him on top of another. A mark. Up in New York. She would've been playing them both along at the time… at the time of the ship disaster. You ask me, she pulled the plug on her New York relationship after the ship went down, and relocated to Vegas full-time. The entries in her diary would suggest as much."

If he was surprised Blakelock had accessed Jenny's diary, Klondike did not show it. He knew Mike was a thorough professional.

"So, she's hooked up with this casino whale. What exactly is she doing, Mike?"

"The ultimate society girl, as far as I can tell." He thought for a moment. "When I spoke to her, it was obvious she was deluded. Anyone could tell she was lying. She uses a false name. Julia Carson. She spoke as if she was a VIP. But everything has come together through Generoso. He is connected with the Vegas elite. I imagine he sees Jenny as a trophy… an award for his years of hardship serving the syndicate.”

He handed Klondike a trace-copy of what looked like a page of diary entries. “Study these dates,” he said. “I think you’ll find her movements all tie in with your departure from, and return to, New York. She was there, Kal!”

Klondike grimaced sourly as he looked over the copy. “I knew that already, god damn it! I saw her. She waved goodbye to me as my ship blew apart. I can’t get that image outta my mind.”

Blakelock looked him over. “Well, these printouts help prove it.”

Then, Klondike looked up from the paper and out at the river. His nostrils flared and his eyes went cold. “She took everything!” he snarled. “Took everything from me! Damn her to hell.”

All was silent for several moments. The slight rush of the water, the swaying of branches in the light breeze the only sounds.

Then, Blakelock spoke softly. “She’s a mess, Kal. Psychologically. She’s living a life that isn’t real. Hopping from one meal ticket to another, for Christ’s sake. And then… then there is her drinking. It’s way out of control, Kal. And it’s causing problems between her and her lover boy.”

Klondike nodded. “That’s some nice work, Mike.” He turned back to the photo of Generoso. “Now… I need you to come up with a plan.”

Blakelock stared at him. “A plan? For what?”

Now, Klondike turned to him and looked deadly serious. He said the word with chilling finality. “Payback.”

“Oh…” Blakelock gasped. He thought for a moment. “Well, I had given that some thought.” Then, he leaned in closer, in a conspirational manner, despite their remote setting. “Why don’t we let Generoso handle that? Hell, he could nail her for us.”

Klondike frowned. “What do you mean?”

“Hell, I’ve got enough dirt here…” he patted his satchel, “enough notes, photos, to make him turn on her. He thinks she’s Julia Carson. Former model. But, he has no idea about this…”

He pulled another item from the satchel. This time, it was an old newspaper clipping. Klondike felt his blood run cold as he read the headline.

CIRCUS STAR HANDED SENTENCE IN MENTAL HOSPITAL OVER SHAPIRO TRAPEZE INCIDENT!

"That's from the Las Vegas Herald," Blakelock continued. "Somehow, old Ray hasn't figured out who he is living with yet. It won't take much for him to uncover the truth."

Klondike's dark eyes were on the photograph accompanying the newspaper article in Mike's hands. There was Jenny, in her orange fireball leotard, stood arm in arm with Gino inside a circus tent. His tent. He closed his eyes.

"How in the hell," he whispered savagely, "can someone just recreate themselves like that? Start a new life? Over and over again? She served time in that hospital. Somehow got out early. And now… now this! Living the life of a Vegas socialite. How is it even possible?"

"A dangerous and deluded woman," Blakelock said casually, as if conducting a college lecture. "She has the power to make men, some men, do whatever she wants. She is a pathological liar. And, worst of all… she enjoys it."

Klondike stared at the river straight ahead. "Jesus…"

Blakelock watched him for a moment. He decided that was enough for now. "Listen, I'll keep tracking her. If you want me to. But, you ask me, your best bet for nailing her is to leave it to the big guy, Generoso. This guy is trouble, man, real trouble."

With a sigh, Klondike stood. Blakelock joined him.

"OK, Mike. If you say that's the way to rumble, I say you're right." He studied his old friend, and tried to smile. "I can't thank you enough, Mike. For all this."

Blakelock nodded solemnly. "It's my debt to you, Kal. I wouldn't be standing here now if it weren't for you, man."

They shook hands warmly. "Let me know what happens," Klondike said quietly. "With this Mafia sucker. With everything."

"You bet, Kal."

Then, Klondike turned and simply walked back down the path, following the straight trail back to the parking lot.

Blakelock watched him go. Then, he slowly began placing the clippings and pages back into his satchel. He shook his head.

"That crazy broad."

The Double G Circus encampment was setting up at the Yewtree Recreational Grounds in Flagstaff, ahead of Saturday night's show.

Klondike pulled into the parkland just as the dying rays of afternoon sun fell across the horizon.

Yewtree was an immense grassy field surrounded by old cattle corrals that had become part of the area's wild west tourist attractions. The whole place felt rustic and preserved.

After parking his jeep by a line of flatbed trucks, Klondike wandered casually around the circus camp, checking in with performers and staff.

After patrolling the grounds for several minutes, he headed for the newly erected big top, sat proudly at the head of the encampment and dominating the site.

As he crept inside, Klondike paced past the seats spread out in rows around the tent perimeter. Then, subconsciously, he glanced upwards. Up there. To the summit. The trapeze zone. The newspaper headline ran though his over-animated mind once more. That's where it had all happened. Up there!

"Kal! I thought I might find you in here."

He turned suddenly. Griff Garrison was approaching, a cheerful expression dominating his rugged, leathery features.

"Ah, Colonel. How are you? Sorry, I've been running a few errands today."

"Not at all." Garrison joined him on the sawdust, at the head of the seats. "I've just been talking to Sally, our finance manager. She said the take for Albuquerque is out of sight! Midway was almost double any of our other stops. The box office take was easily our best so far. The tent was almost three-quarters full. And, well, as far as anyone can tell, the reaction from the fans was positive." He squinted at Klondike, seemingly satisfied. "Things are looking up, Kal. Well done."

Klondike nodded slightly. "It's a start, Colonel. Nothing more. Our first six shows were nothing less than a disaster.

Barely 200 spectators. Falls, mistakes, mishaps from the talent. All adding up to a very poor take."

Garrison bristled slightly. "You expected more?"

Klondike took a pace back, folding his arms with a knowing look. "Colonel… we're not making any money. I'm not giving you a profit. That's the reason you brought me in. Right now, we're running at a loss. Now, until we start getting capacity crowds, excited circus fans, into this tent, and some major publicity floating through these territories… this is going to be one long, uphill struggle."

Garrison looked at him. Then, his grey eyes shifted around the tent, taking in the great walls of fabric enveloping them. An empty big top was always an eerie place to be.

"It's not all about profits, Kal. The circus is my passion, my lifeblood. Just being involved, delivering for the fans… hell, that's something worth living for."

Klondike smiled. "I forget you're a millionaire cattle baron."

The Colonel laughed. "Raising cattle is my bread and butter, son. But this, the big top, this is my passion." He bent down and ran a hand tenderly through the sawdust at their feet. When he spoke, his voice came out in a dreamlike whisper. "Many has been the time… I've imagined, merely imagined, my circus being a smash hit. On TV. All over the papers. The talk of every territory. All over America." Then, he looked up sharply. "You've lived that dream, Kal. You've been to the top of that mountain. Conquered it all."

Klondike just watched him, nodding. Almost sadly.

"When I invited you to be our manager," Garrison continued, in that mesmeric tone, "I imagined your aura, your successes, would rub off on the Double G. That, somehow, we would make it to the top. Because we had you… to guide us there."

Klondike smiled wanly. "If there is one thing I've learned in the circus world, it's that you never know what action is coming in the next town, the next stop. That's kind of why we all love it." He chuckled. "Things can change. Fast."

"Kal!"

They both turned at the feminine voice emanating from the flap.

It was Karen, Garrison's wife. She was dressed in a country and western shirt with jeans, and looked about ready to saddle up.

"Kal, there is a call for you. The guy said you're not going to want to miss it!"

She joined them by the seats, smiling astutely.

"Thanks," Klondike blurted. "But where the hell is the telephone exchange? I haven't seen one since I joined."

The couple laughed. "No, silly," Karen giggled. "The call came in our trailer. Out back. You can't miss it."

"Yeah, I know the one," he mumbled. He stared at Garrison. "You have a telephone in your trailer? What the hell!"

The Colonel shrugged. "We travel in style, what can I tell ya!"

With a chuckle, Klondike headed for the flap and went out into the field.

"This is Kal Klondike."

A soft, gentle voice answered him. "Good evening, sideburns."

Klondike froze all over. He had to be hearing things. Only one man, in all these years, had ever referred to him by that nickname. It was one he had never taken to. But none of that mattered right now.

He took a deep breath, feeling his pulse quicken. "Is it really you?"

"But of course." There was a pause. "Reno, 1949. The final of the Rochivelle poker tournament. You and me. And you beat me with... of all the lousy hands, a busted flush."

"Jesus Christ! It is you!"

Klondike was standing in the living room of the enormous executive trailer, feeling like he was enjoying the confines of a luxurious penthouse suite. Everything looked immaculate, from the shiny white oak-panelled kitchenette to the spotless washroom at the back. He felt like his head was spinning, so he sat on the leather couch next to the phone stand.

"Jonathan Irwin," he said grandly into the receiver. "The All American. The pleasure is all mine." He tried to think clearly.

"Now, what on earth can I do for you? And how the hell did you find me?"

A soft chuckle came down the line. "You're not even gunna ask how I am? After all these years…"

"I'm in shock it's you, Doc! It's been, what, 10 years?"

"Almost 11. Way back. When we were both flying high with Ribbeck World Circus. Me, literally. You, metaphorically."

Klondike smiled widely, lost in time momentarily. "It sure is nice to hear your voice again."

"Likewise, sideburns." The voice was gentle and dreamlike, akin to a children's storyteller. "I heard you had joined the Double G as manager. And, well, after a little digging around, one of my associates in LA found a number for the so-called Sidewinder Ranch. And the boy there gave me this number."

Klondike pictured in his mind the small, diminutive Doc Irwin. His bald, gnome-like head and agile body. Performing breathtaking acts of derring do on the high wire, in his resplendent stars and stripes singlet. "I've heard lots about you down the years too, Doc. Tales. Mostly tall tales. I read you were with the Sherman Brothers now."

"Up until yesterday. I just quit. As I have my entire career, I've remained freelance, so there was no contract. I'm walking out on Sherman."

Klondike leant forward eagerly. "What happened?"

"Long story. Let's just call it a huge difference of opinion."

Klondike allowed a stony silence to prevail. Then, he spoke tentatively. "Did you hunt me down just to reminisce about the good old days?"

Irwin suddenly sounded more business-like, losing the good-natured patter. "I have found myself in the enviable position of being able to pick and choose my projects, Kal. My work. Freelance. It opens up so many doors. That's why I insist on working that way."

Klondike felt his heartbeat surge. Irwin continued on the other end of the line. "I see a troupe I like, I get in touch. Some big shot promoter wants to bring me in for a top show, we work something out. You get the idea." He took a deep breath. "I've read about what you're doing down there, Kal. With this Double G Circus. Building a brand. Trying to reinvent yourself after what happened to your old outfit. It's admirable. And… well, it's exciting."

Klondike was on the edge of his seat. He felt like he knew what was coming, but was almost too scared to say it. Even to think it.

"The fact of the matter is," Irwin continued, "your venture sounds like the most interesting story in the American circus world right now. I am intrigued. But, also, I have seen the reviews. Heard about your empty seats. The lack of interest. The accidents and mishaps."

Another deathly silence followed. It was all too much for Klondike.

"Doc, I am…"

"I'd like to help you out, Kal."

There it was. Irwin finally said it. Words Klondike could only have dreamed of. Coming down the telephone line like a spell from the heavens.

"You can't be serious!" he blurted.

"I'd like to help you out," Irwin repeated. "If you'll all have me, that is!" He chuckled now. "I've had offers, sure. Looked at a few circuses that recruited heavily in the off season. But… well, there is something about the challenge that the Double G offers. The feel of it all. It appeals to me now, at my age."

"I can't believe what I'm hearing, Doc."

"And there's something else." Irwin paused again for effect. "There's you, Kal. You! Yes, it's been over 10 years, but I remember you all too well. A fair, decent man. And, what's more, a circus man, through and through. A man willing to put the success of the industry, of the art form, above everything else, even himself."

Klondike was almost laughing now, not in mirth but in shock. "You got me," he blurted.

Irwin sounded genial again now. "So, how about it, Kal? I'm offering my services to you. To the Double G. Are you interested?"

"Am I interested?" Klondike repeated in a dreamlike manner. "In recruiting Doc Irwin into my big top? Hell! The All American. One of the most famous and beloved circus performers of the past 30 years. A legend of the industry and a transcendent figure in entertainment." He cackled down the line. "Yes! Yes, I am most certainly interested in having you join us."

Irwin laughed too. "That's wonderful. I am in Salt Lake City right now. I can join you guys in Arizona by tomorrow night."

"It just gets better and better."

"One thing," Irwin said, serious again. "We can work out my pay when I get down there. But the whole thing is off unless you agree to my one and only condition."

"I know, I know," Klondike said, surprising them both. "Your All American Association passes. I haven't forgotten, Doc. And I heartily endorse them. Don't worry, no one is going to mess that up. One of the finest traditions in our industry, you ask me."

"Glad you see it that way, Kal. This sounds like a deal."

Klondike's heart was pounding like a jackhammer. The whole conversation, with a voice from the past, had been a surreal exchange. An unfathomable development.

"One more thing," he whispered, grinning wisely. "Can you still do that bicycle routine? On the high wire?"

Irwin chuckled down the line. "Every night, Kal. It's still the perennial crowd pleaser. Now, then, forever. Even after all these years."

"God damn!" Klondike exclaimed. Then, he paid solemn tribute. "Thank you, Doc. I can't believe you have called like this, after all this time. But thank you… for thinking of me."

"I often think of you, sideburns. You were always one of the good ones."

Both men were silent on opposite ends of the telephone line. Lost in their own solitary thoughts.

Then, Irwin simply said: "I'll see you tomorrow, sideburns."

He hung up. That was it. A potentially season-saving deal, all over and done with in just minutes.

Klondike still sat on the leather couch with the receiver in his hand, marvelling at it all. He finally replaced it on the telephone stand.

Then, feeling somewhat giddy, he looked up at a picture hanging on the trailer wall. It showed Garrison and Karen in full rawhide gear on their ranch back in the Sierras. He looked at the Colonel's cheerful expression. As if in a dream, he spoke to the image.

"What till you hear about this, Colonel."

CHAPTER 17

Shapiro swung expertly on his ring, heaving his arms back and forth to build up momentum, pushing his straight legs high, and then away again. The swinging made his ringseat fly like a wild pendulum in seconds.

As it flew backwards, towards the wall of the tent, he hung by his arms loosely. As it came back towards the centre, his body tensed, like a stalking panther.

Then, as it reached the full arc of its swing inwards, he released his grip and flew upside down into the air, flying straight up a good 10 yards. With minimum effort, he allowed his body to turn in midair, and he descended feet first, seeing the safety net far below.

Arms wide like a skydiver, he saw the figure of Andros Murphy swinging up towards him, upside down on his ring with his legs holding his weight on the seat. Murph had his hands out as he swung upwards in perfect, textbook fashion.

Shapiro grabbed at the hands, then let Murph carry him past the centre of the tent, as they swung together.

He then released himself as the ring flew towards the summit. This time, with all the momentum, he darted vertically, tucked his knees into his chest, and performed a quick-fire double turtle roll, before emerging straightened up, arms wide again.

Murph came back on his repeat swing, clasped the hands again, and this time hurled him back towards the first ring.

Shapiro vaulted through the air, securing his grip on the ring and hauling himself up into a sitting position.

The whole exhibition had lasted seconds.

Now, as Murph performed a midair sit-up and cradled himself in his ring again, the two flyers sat there, 30 yards in the air, gently rocking back and forth.

They were in a smaller, old-fashioned big top, the tent a dazzling design of pink and brown stripes. Below sat the safety net, the sawdust stage floor and a handful of onlookers.

Shapiro, panting slightly, grinned across at Murph, as the two sat on their rings at the tent's summit – Gino in his fireball orange singlet, Murph in a red and white bodysuit.

"What I tell ya, amigo. We still have our chemistry up here. Some things, you just never lose."

Murph seemed ecstatic. "You're right. I can't believe it. It's like all those years have never been and gone. It's crazy."

Shapiro put a hand high on the rope, twisting to look around at the vast empty seats below. "No. We are professionals, Murph. Dedicated. Switched on. That is why we still have the magic, no?"

Murph nodded. Then, he looked down. Way down. "See ya at the bottom, pal!"

With that, he seemed to perform a forward roll off his ring and plummeted down through the air like a stone. His huge body turned about halfway to the ground, and he landed on the net feet first, with a mighty cheer.

Shapiro stood on his ring and, with a cry of "Santamaria", somersaulted off into midair. He too landed on his soles, dragging the net surface five yards down before he was thrown back into the air again. On landing, he crawled to the edge of the black netting, gripped the cord at the side and rolled off headfirst, his arms swinging him down to a standing position on the sawdust.

As he slapped Murph on the back, several watching roustabouts clapped heartily. Then, all fell silent as a woman approached from the tent's flap.

She wore jeans, a denim shirt and black leather boots. In her 60s, with silver hair tied back in a mighty bun and with reddish skin and blue eyes, she looked a formidable presence.

Martha Stanwyck. Emigrating from Poland in the 1920s, she had worked as a stablehand for ranches across the western states before becoming first a horse performer, then a manager, and then one of the hardest-working circus promoters in America. A no nonsense boss woman, she had built up a reputation as a shrewd and astute circus promoter. One who had come up the hard way, from the very bottom.

"Not bad, boys," she muttered in her nasal, accented voice. "Looks like you are still at the top of your game."

"Thank you, Madam Stanwyck," Shapiro said, bowing slightly. "Really, it is like riding a bicycle. You never really lose the connection."

"Yeah," Murph blurted. "We got our rhythm up there, alright."

"Fine." Stanwyck said the word with chilling finality. She looked back at the trapeze rigging high above. Then at Shapiro again. "Ok. Like I said earlier, we have a spot spare here due to Dan Jupiter's hand injury. He'll be out maybe three weeks, the doctor says." She looked at them both again coolly. "The spot is yours if you want it. I'll pay what we agreed earlier." Then, she frowned, as she often did. "Jesus… you'll be the highest paid performers on our roster. And for what? Standing in for Dan Jupiter and his girl…"

Shapiro looked befuddled, but quickly came around. "You need flyers, Madam Stanwyck. Well, we are the best in the business."

"You're not wrong there, Gino. I saw that devil drop you did on TV back in '58. That crazy stunt in Vegas that almost got you killed. And that flag trick on Superstars and Stripes. Who could forget that?" She took a step forward and eyed him sternly. It was an unnerving look. "There aren't many flyers in the world who can match that. And I should know! We've gone through enough here."

Shapiro bowed again. "We thank you for your appreciation, madam. And we won't let you down."

She continued staring at him. Then, she nodded in a kind of gesture of respect. "Alright then. Help yourselves to a trailer each out back. The vacant ones are at the far edge of the lot. Chow time is at 7pm in the marquee." She went to move off, then paused slightly. She spoke over her shoulder. "You'd ever told me Stanwyck's Circus would have Gino Shapiro under its big top… hell, I've said you were crazy. Funny how things turn out."

They watched her stride away. "Hilarious," Murph muttered.

The duo shook hands with the roustabouts that had watched their rehearsal. Everyone slowly wandered away, back to their duties.

Shapiro and Murph walked around the perimeter of the big top, taking great interest in their new surroundings.

There were standard aluminium grandstands erected in mammoth blocks, joined by bolts, encircling the arena floor. Everything looked fresh and modern, even the smooth sawdust at their feet.

They stopped and looked up as a group of roustabouts unfurled a giant sheet banner across the top of a block of seats.

It read: STANWYCK'S CIRCUS PROUDLY PRESENTS…THE KING OF THE AIR, GINO SHAPIRO!

Murph eyed his companion. "They didn't waste much time…"

Shapiro admired the banner and its luscious paint work. "Pretty fancy printing job."

One of the roustabouts looked down at them from the stands. A big bull of a man, he wore a stetson, buckskin shirt and jeans, and had a huge moustache over his lip and a square jaw. "All of this," he bellowed down at them, "just for you, superstar."

Shapiro looked up at him awkwardly. "Thank you, friend. We are delighted to be here."

The man grunted as he helped position the giant banner above the stands. His fellow workers ignored him. "Never saw me any royalty before…" he murmured loudly.

Shapiro and Murph looked at each other, then shook their heads. They moved away, heading towards the flap, having completed their circle of the arena.

Another pair of roustabouts were slowly rolling in a knife thrower's spinning wheel as they neared the exit. Idly, the duo watched.

"Er, excuse me, Mr Shapiro, sir."

Gino practically jumped at the soft voice from behind. He turned swiftly and found himself staring at a young man of no more than 20 years old. He had thick reddish/blond hair, a face full of freckles and a tiny, agile physique. He was dressed in lumberjack shirt and jeans, like the other helping hands all around.

Shapiro smiled. "What can I do for ya, kid?"

The youngster walked towards them across the sawdust. "The name's Rogers. Tommy Rogers. I'm with the work crew here. But, well, my dream is to be a flyer. Just like you boys!"

Shapiro and Murph exchanged a knowing look, smiling wisely.

"I'm a county finalist gymnast," the newcomer continued. "I would've made the state finals, but I could't afford the bus fare to Oakland. Instead, I started practising trapeze at a local performing arts school. Then, I got a job here at Stanwyck as I thought I might get a break. But Dan Jupiter ain't interested in training me. No matter how hard I try and impress him."

Shapiro nodded intently. "I'm sorry to hear that, kid."

Rogers looked up excitedly. "I was wondering, sir… if maybe you could teach me a thing or two, perhaps. Y'know, while you're here? I sure would appreciate it. I reckon I've got everything it takes to succeed. I, well, I just need that guidance… that polishing…"

Shapiro studied him. "How old are you, Tommy?"

"19, sir."

"And where you from?"

"Dalton, Pennysylvania."

"Pennsylvanian, eh?" Shapiro nodded calmly, eyeing the youngster. "You look like a poster boy for Harper's Apple Pies, you know that?"

Rogers stared at him. "Huh?"

"You look like Howdy Doody," Murph put in. "The American boy next door. It's, er, a good look."

"Exactly," Shapiro added. "The look of a star."

Rogers licked his lips, eyes wide. "You reckon? So… so, you'll help me, sir? Train me some?"

Shapiro moved beside the youngster and slapped him on the back. "Kid, I haven't had time lately to practise myself, let alone train any newcomers. I've been bouncing from job to job, trying to stay in shape. Me and Murph here need to get some hours in on the rings and fast, now we've got this gig lined up."

Rogers looked crestfallen, but smiled gamely. "I understand, Mr Shapiro. And I thank you for taking the time to talk to me. You guys need anything, anything at all, you come to me, ok?"

Shapiro nodded. "Thank you, Tommy. We appreciate it."

The youngster jogged off out of the flap.

Murph watched him go. "We're making friends faster than a star quarterback at a new high school, man."

Shapiro laughed. "Yeah. Offers coming in from all angles, it would seem."

They ducked out of the flap and into the meadow beyond.

Later that night, Shapiro opened the door to his newly appointed trailer and stepped out into the clear night air.

Bakersfield, Southern California. The sunsets were immaculate, the sky full of stars, and the air wholesome and clean.

He had seen hundreds of circus camps in his life, and nothing separated this one from any of the others. Trailers parked in endless circles, all pointing to the all-encompassing big top.

Murph had heard about Dan Jupiter's injury and had immediately put in a call to Martha Stanwyck. She had hungrily accepted their services, even sending a driver to pick them up in Los Angeles and escort them to the camp. It had been a whirlwind, he thought. But, then again, it always was with him.

Shapiro ducked into the chow marquee, and ambled over to a small bar in the corner. Dressed in his trademark orange tracksuit, he drew the attention of all the various performers sat around drinking at the tables.

He nodded at a burly bartender stood drying a glass. "You got a sarsaparilla back there, pal?"

The man grinned. "The recognised drink of the cowboy! Why, sure we have."

He handed Shapiro a glass bottle of pink liquid. "Much obliged," said the flyer, taking the bottle and walking out of the marquee again.

Outside, he opened the bottle and downed half the contents in one. The camp was quiet at this late hour, the incessant chirping of the crickets thus seemed deafening.

As he slipped between two trailers on his way back to his temporary home, he suddenly felt a presence behind him. He turned rapidly.

There, barely five yards behind him, was a large, well-built man, dressed in denims, his face dominated by a massive moustache and square jaw. Shapiro instantly recognised him as the roustabout who had tried to rile him earlier in the tent.

The two men stared at each other in the night, feeling somewhat enclosed between two large trailers.

"Can I help you with something, friend?" Shapiro said.

The man looked angry, eyes wild. "I'd say you've done enough, superstar."

Shapiro rolled his eyes. "And just what is that supposed to mean?"

The roustabout didn't seem to hear. "I heard how much Miss Stanwyck is paying you to be here. And I want you to know something, superstar… I'm disgusted! Why, there's some of us work crew labourers ain't gunna see that kind of money all season. Or next season. Or in a lifetime!"

Shapiro held his arms wide. "You want it? Learn to be a flyer!"

The man dismissed his point. "I been watching you, Shapiro. You breeze in here, like a damn VIP. Everyone bowing down to you. It makes me sick, dammit!"

Finally, Shapiro snapped. "You have a problem, big man? Why don't you do something about it, eh?"

"Why, you rotten son of a bitch!" The roustabout surged towards him, putting his hands up. When he was a few steps from Shapiro, he threw a ferocious looking right hook towards his quarry's jaw. Fortunately, Shapiro saw it coming and blocked the blow with both hands. However, the sheer brute force of the punch made him step backwards, where his foot went straight into a small tin full of laundry pegs. He stumbled, and fell to his knees.

Instinctively, trying to regain some balance, he threw a wild uppercut. His attacker had leapt forward, and the blow hit him clean on the nose. He roared like an ox.

Shapiro pulled the tin off his foot and made to stand. Then, the now enraged roustabout was on him. He pounced upon Shapiro and threw a meaty forearm around his neck. Then, he squeezed with all his might.

Shapiro could not believe the strength. He was trapped in the headlock, and found he could barely move. He grabbed at the massive arm, but could not break the hold. Then, he tried to move, pushing his feet into the grass. Nothing happened.

"I got you now, superstar," the big man wheezed as he maintained his grip on Shapiro.

Gino gasped wildly, then began to feel himself passing out. He nudged an elbow into his attacker's midriff. Still, nothing happened.

Suddenly, a new voice erupted in the clearing.

"Hey! You!"

The roustabout turned as he kept the pressure on the headlock. He saw a youngster sprinting towards him, before slamming a metal trashcan lid into his skull. The big man immediately released his grip and threw his hands to his head, calling out in agony.

The new figure raised the lid above his head and smashed it down onto the larger man's back. He cried out again.

The youngster pushed him to the ground. "Get out of here! Right now! And don't ever come back."

The roustabout picked himself up clumsily and made to run for it, stumbling dumbly through the darkness as he kept his hands around his bruised head.

Shapiro was sprawled on the grass, rubbing at his throat. He had never known such a ferocious grip. Finally, he looked up to glimpse his saviour. His eyes widened.

There before him stood young Tommy Rogers, holding a hand down to him. Shapiro accepted it, and was surprised by the teen's strength as he hauled him to his feet.

"Tommy…" he wheezed, massaging his neck.

"You alright, Mr Shapiro?"

"Yeah, thanks to you, kid. Another minute, my lights would've been out. Santamaria!"

Rogers looked out into the night, trying to spot the attacker. He was gone, vanished into the darkness. "That guy was a bad apple. We all knew it. Sure doesn't belong in no circus."

Shapiro stood straight, and put an arm around Rogers' slender shoulders.

"Thanks kid. I mean it. That was a very brave thing to do."

"Anytime, sir. Just glad I was out walking and heard the disturbance."

He patted Shapiro on the back. "You need a hand with anything, Mr Shapiro?"

"No, no. Thank you. I am good. Just need another sarsaparilla. That ape knocked the last one outta my hands, god damn it."

"Alright then. I'll say goodnight, sir."

Rogers made to wander off.

"Come by the tent at nine tomorrow…" Shapiro called out to him.

Rogers turned. "What for?"

Shapiro baulked. "What for? Why, your first training session of course!"

Rogers grinned like a baby. "I thought you didn't have the time."

Shapiro smiled at the youngster, whose enthusiasm was strangely contagious. He had a certain spark, a warm and carthy charm.

"I'll make the time, kid."

CHAPTER 18

Doc Irwin's arrival at the Double G Circus was almost an event in itself.

A beautiful, gleaming Ford trailer painted in glorious stars and stripes patterns – like a giant American flag on wheels – floated majestically into the camp in Flagstaff, his horn blaring out the first line of the US anthem.

Everybody associated with the Double G – performers, management, roustabouts, cowboys, even idle fans who were passing by – all gathered at the front of the big top in awe.

As the big motor parked in the centre of the midway, the side door opened – and there he was.

Doc Irwin emerged from the elegant confines, delighting the watching crowd by wearing his stars and stripes tracksuit. As if directed by a conductor, the entire gathering began applauding as one outside the tent. Irwin waved happily as he disembarked his trailer and paced across the gravel towards the assembled group.

Many watching could not believe how small he was, barely five feet tall, and also how old he looked. With his bald head and rubbery skin, Doc hardly had the look of a beloved hero.

But the All American was a superstar in every way, and his feats on the high wire were the stuff of legend. His tracksuit alone looked like a garment fit for an Olympic idol.

As Irwin approached the crowd, everyone seemed to surge for him at once. He shook hands with everyone, signing autographs and even posing for several pictures.

Finally, he spotted Klondike by the flap. His old colleague had not changed one bit, right down to the brown leather jacket and fedora.

"Kal!" he exclaimed as they shook hands warmly. "Great to see ya! This is all so nice. Thank you for coming out to meet me. Everyone!"

"Welcome to the Double G, Doc!" Klondike boomed, grinning broadly. "Hell, once everyone heard you were coming, no one was going to miss it. And we saw that fancy motor of yours from a mile away!"

He turned, to an excited-looking older man behind him dressed in a business suit. "Doc, I'd like you to meet Colonel Griff Garrison. Owner and founder of the Double G Circus. Colonel, meet the All American, Jonathan Irwin."

Garrison practically exploded as they shook hands. "Mr Irwin! What a pleasure to meet you. I can't thank you enough for joining us down here. It is a wonderful, magical moment for all of us here at the Double G."

Irwin could not stop smiling. "Colonel. It is a sincere pleasure to be here. I thank you all for having me."

"I am at your service," Garrison proclaimed, before ushering Karen in front of him. "My wife, Karen."

"Mrs Garrison, a pleasure."

"Oh my lord," Karen squealed. "Thank you so much for joining us, Mr Irwin. I still can't believe it. I saw your act once in Salinas. You were out of this world!"

Irwin bowed. Klondike put an arm around him and motioned for Heavy to approach. "You remember Heavy Brown, ringmaster extraordinaire?"

"Of course," Irwin said, gazing at the big man with fondness. "I almost didn't recognise you without that scarlet jacket and top hat."

"Welcome, Doc," Heavy said warmly. "So good to see you again. After all these years."

Next up was the sensuous and unmistakable figure of Arletta LaRue, who bowed before the newcomer before offering him a decorative wreath of white carnations, placing it grandly around his neck.

"Our All American, we welcome you," she purred. "I am Arletta, the snake enchantress. What an honour it is, my sir, to have you here with us."

Irwin glanced awkwardly at Klondike, before nodding happily. "Thank you, Miss Arletta. I, er, can't wait to see your act."

Several more introductions were made, before the gathering slowly dispersed. Klondike, Garrison and Heavy showed Irwin around the camp, pausing at the shooting gallery in the midway, where the Colonel poured them all a soda from the refreshment kiosk.

"So, what do you think?" Klondike asked as they stood around.

Irwin grinned, squinting into the sunlight. "It's beautiful," he mused.

Garrison sipped his drink. "We've got a show on Saturday night, of course. We thought you might like to sit that one out and have a full week's training before making your debut next week, in Phoenix?"

Irwin looked at him humorously. "You're not paying me to train, Colonel."

Garrison was incredulous. "You mean you'll perform here? In two days' time?"

"You've got your wire set up?"

"Sure," Klondike answered, "we got it out, dusted it down and had it assembled this morning. But… well, we didn't think you'd feel up to performing right away. Hell, you've only just got here."

"Think nothing of it," Irwin mumbled, swatting a hand through the air. "So, how about I take my trailer into town, rustle up some interest, meet a few people and try and sell y'all some tickets?"

Garrison's face was a picture of utter delight. "Mr Irwin, that would be incredible. Thank you."

"No problem." Irwin finished his drink and turned. "Just let me freshen up a bit and I'll start the publicity drive." He headed for his trailer.

The others watched him go. Klondike spoke quietly in Garrison's ear. "You know those new posters we've ordered from the printers?"

"Sure."

"We need them now. Right now! We need to get Doc's picture on every street corner in town. In every shop window. And not just here. In Williams, Gumley, Harrisonville and Yuma. Everyone needs to know he's performing here on Saturday night."

"Right, right," Garrison said, quivering slightly. He ran a hand through his silver hair. "Gawd, I can't believe this is all happening."

Heavy grinned boyishly as he watched Irwin climb the steps into his trailer. "Doc Irwin. Boy, oh boy. How many more fans do you think he'll put on the gate?"

Klondike squinted as he studied the big top before them. "I want it that we need a bigger tent." He slapped his hand against Garrison's shoulder.

"This is it, Colonel. This is where it all takes off."

Saturday night arrived in what felt like a heartbeat. Suddenly, it was showtime, and the staff and performers of the Double G Circus found themselves playing host to a night the likes of which they had never known.

The big top was, finally, playing host to a capacity crowd, with not a single ticket left in the box office to hand over.

Garrison and Klondike's mass, rapidly-conceived publicity drive had paid dividends. The new circus posters, featuring a full size body picture of Doc Irwin in his stars and stripes singlet covering the whole page, had indeed been put up across the territory. Word had spread, and a kind of euphoria had quickly gripped Flagstaff.

The big top was full of eager, excited fans, many of them youngsters, most with their families.

Standing at the flap, Klondike finally felt a warm, content feeling of delight as he watched the spectators all tucking into their cotton candy and hot dogs. The tent was buzzing, at last, and it was the most welcome feeling imaginable.

As the Riders of the Double G opened the show, Klondike was joined at the flap by Garrison. Then, a few minutes into the opening performance, Irwin himself ducked through the entranceway to watch the acts. Decked out in his show singlet under the stars and stripes tracksuit top, he stood just behind Klondike, largely out of sight.

"Come to check out your new team-mates?" Klondike muttered over his shoulder.

Irwin nodded as he watched the cowboys perform their saddle tricks. He spoke quietly. "Let's see what you've got, sideburns."

Unfortunately for Klondike and his new star signing, the first three-quarters of the Double G Circus's Flagstaff spectacular were full of misfortune.

During the Riders of the Double G wild west sequence, one of the cowboys fell off his mount and was trampled by a following horse. He managed to rise to his feet and reclaimed his mount, but the shocked gasp of the capacity crowd was an unwelcome development.

Worse was to follow during the Rollergirls' routine. For the first time in several years, one of the skaters slipped during their high-speed laps of the arena floor. Although she was fine and able to continue, there were more agitated and worried fans on their feet, shocked at seeing a potential disaster.

"That doesn't happen," was how Pamela put it as they skated out of the arena afterwards.

But perhaps the most deadly blow followed in Hondo Cloud's knife throwing act. On this occasion, one of his blades missed the top of Betsy's skull by mere millimetres, causing the young woman to scream in terror at the very near miss. The bloodcurdling sound had reverberated around the tent.

At the flap, Klondike had pulled the performance right then and there. There was no way the duo could continue after such an occurrence.

The big top had fallen silent as Hondo and Betsy trudged off the sawdust. Several stewards helped a shaken Betsy through the flap. Cloud looked at Klondike and shook his head sadly as he exited the arena.

It had been the worst build-up imaginable to what was supposed to be the biggest climax the Double G Circus had ever known.

As the spectators all gaped in shock at the knife thrower's wheel as the roustabouts hastily removed it from the sawdust, Klondike shook the emotions from his head. He looked across at Heavy, on the edge of the sawdust, and nodded.

This was it. The big moment. But it had not transpired as he had imagined.

Heavy strode out confidently to the centre of the floor. The audience were now deathly silent.

"And now, ladies and gentlemen," the big man in the top hat roared, "we come to our feature attraction. The Double G Circus is proud to present to you a legend of American entertainment. One of the greatest living performers in the circus world today. He has joined the roster this week, and is making his Double G debut right here this evening, in front of you all. So… please give a warm Flagstaff welcome to the wonder of the high wire, the All American… Doc Irwin!"

The crowd's silence was swiftly erased by a hearty ovation as screaming and clapping fans showed their adoration for the All American.

Doc Irwin came jogging out on to the sawdust, resplendent as ever in his stars and stripes singlet, and with an American flag tied around his neck. He high-fived several patrons in the front row, before donating the flag to a little girl being held aloft by her father.

Then, he jogged across to the gleaming, exotic-looking high wire platform that had just been wheeled in by the roustabouts.

Two scaffolding platforms, 25-feet high, stood 30 yards apart. They were covered in stars and stripes placards and bunting, looking like carnival floats from a July 4th parade. The platforms were bridged by the high wire, a two-inch thick plastic cord that ran hard and firm through the air.

Everything was set, as a patriotic marching band score began playing on the sound system.

As he rose majestically up a side ladder to the top of the nearest platform, Irwin gave a final wave to the cheering fans. Then, he began, stepping out onto his favourite perch. The high wire, his second home for almost 40 years, and a spot where he was an unequalled master.

He began his routine by merely walking straight across the wire. Once he reached the far platform, he then made a return journey… this time walking backwards, at the exact same speed he had completed the first leg.

Walking in reverse all the way back to his starting point, he stopped halfway and executed a perfect splits jump, his legs practically horizontal beneath him before duly arriving back on the wire.

Reaching the platform, he then set off again, this time seemingly jogging along the ultra-thin wire, before launching himself into a set of cartwheels, spinning himself in beautifully choreographed loops as he rolled effortlessly along the plastic cord, around and around, arriving at the far platform with a flourish.

The fans were on their feet, cheering this spectacular show of human agility and death defiance.

At the flap, Klondike and Garrison watched in muted wonder at the tiny man in the US flag-inspired outfit. His small frame had become a blur, a red, white and blue whirlwind as he span across the wire.

Klondike smiled with relief, not pleasure. The mishaps from tonight's show seemed to have been forgotten by the spectators, who were spellbound by the high wire act. He also felt a deep sense of nostalgia, having not seen Irwin perform his routines in a decade. It was all as polished and precise as he remembered it all those years ago.

Next, Irwin removed a four-metre walker's pole from a chest within the platform. Then, he opened a duffel bag and pulled out a pile of perhaps 20 white dinner plates. Standing perfectly still at the edge of the wire, the pole lying against his frame, he deftly placed the load of plates onto the top of his head. Grabbing the pole and placing it horizontally across at his midriff, he then began a slow walk across the cord, the plates remaining rigid upon his clean, bald head.

Another hearty applause greeted him when he arrived at the far end.

Relinquishing the pole and plates, he next grabbed for a skipping rope, sat at the edge of the platform roof. As the entire auditorium held its collective breath at the sight of the little man preparing to start skipping across a high wire, Irwin threw the little rope over his head, leapt on to the cord... and he was off.

In just seconds, he had hopped across the wire, propelling himself over the skipping rope continuously as he surged across.

This act drew wild cheers from the audience, amazed the performer hadn't fallen, or even slipped.

As he waved at the fans encircling his high wire get-up, Irwin ducked into the scaffolding platform below his perch. When he emerged again, he was carrying an old-fashioned bicycle.

It was time. Time for Doc Irwin's most celebrated act. One he had performed on television, for two presidents, and royal dignitaries all over the world.

At the flap, Klondike shuddered slightly. He turned to Garrison beside him, who had been joined by Karen and even several of the other performers, all desperate to see the All American.

"Just watch this..." Klondike said. Garrison nodded, all smiles.

Then, on the high wire, Irwin mounted his bicycle and rode across slowly, beeping his horn when he got to the far edge. True to form, he then rode the bike backwards across the wire, drawing more incredulous cries from the crowd.

Then, when he reached his platform, he dismounted. What followed was an impossible sight.

Irwin rested the bicycle on the edge of the wire, half still on the plastic sheeting of his scaffold tower. He led on top of the bike, so that his chest was firm on the saddle. Then, lining up his arms, he placed his hands into the pedals and pushed down hard. With a sudden jerking motion, he expertly lifted his legs into the air and pushed his chest off the saddle.

Inexplicably, he was performing a handstand atop the bicycle, his hands on the pedals and his small body lying vertically straight, pointing upwards. The bizarre sight became an abnormality when Irwin then began peddling with his arms, driving the bike across the high wire with his hands, while maintaining the handstand.

Many in the audience looked like they might faint. Mouths gaped, eyes stared wildly. No one had ever seen anything quite like this.

Klondike quickly diverted his eyes away from the unbelievable sight high above and scanned the spectators all around him by the flap. What he saw delighted him, a sea of astonished, incredulous faces, all gazing upwards in awe.

Irwin slowly propelled the bicycle across the high wire, his agile body remaining perfectly straight and still like a pillar as he guided himself across.

And then, once he reached the far side, an anguished yet playful howl reverberated from the audience as he began riding back across – going backwards again.

For the duration of the bizarre-looking 30-yard voyage, Irwin's frame remained as stiff as a rock as he held his handstand perfectly, his arms rolling around like harvesters as he drove himself along.

When he finally reached the platform, Irwin expertly allowed his chest to fall to the saddle before flipping himself up into a standing position again.

The ovation was thunderous, like nothing the Double G had ever known, as Irwin waved to the fans in a great 360-degree arc, bowing grandly and holding his arms aloft.

Then, Heavy's voice was booming across the PA system again. "Have you ever seen anything like it in your entire lives, folks? The wonder of the wire, Doc Irwin. Let's hear it for the Double G Circus's latest signing! The All American! Our death-defying, dynamic Doc!"

As Irwin began climbing down one of the ladders within the scaffold unit, the applause was constant, many in the crowd still utterly mesmerised by what they had witnessed moments before.

Heavy continued on the microphone. "And now, ladies and gentleman of Flagstaff, please show your appreciation for all of the many stars of the Double G Circus, whose pleasure it has been to entertain you this evening."

The many mishaps the show had endured earlier were now seemingly forgotten, as everyone remained on their feet to applaud the Double G roster.

The cowboys came out on their galloping mounts, the Rollergirls sped into the arena for a few more laps of the stage floor, and the mighty Soolaimon strode out, carrying Don Peerless and Arletta LaRue on his hulking shoulders, the latter two waving happily at the cheers from all around.

After the Rollergirls and the cowboys had performed several laps of honour, drawing loud applause from all sides of the big top, all of the talent assembled in the tent's centre. As the opera music blaring out from the tannoy reached its climax, Soolaimon picked up the tiny Irwin, who stood on the giant's shoulders.

The music stopped, all of the talent held their arms aloft and Irwin, standing cleanly on top of Soolaimon, put both thumbs in the air, before expertly somersaulting from his lofty perch and down to the sawdust.

That was it. The show was over.

The capacity crowd remained standing, applauding heartily.

The talent all headed for the flap. Klondike was delighted to see Irwin, Walsh and Cloud all high-fiving circus patrons in the front rows, and gleefully signing autographs. Irwin seemed content to speak to everybody, and posed for pictures with several children. He was still out there after every one of his new team-mates had headed for their trailers.

Klondike had stayed at the flap, patting all of the performers on the back as they departed. Then, he merely watched Irwin greet the fans near the exit enclosure.

The big top was nearly empty now, but still Irwin greeted anyone who wanted to meet him, shaking hands happily, never appearing tired or fed-up.

As Klondike watched on the periphery, Garrison approached behind him, from outside in the flap tunnel.

"He's the real deal, that one," the Colonel muttered.

"A man of the people," Klondike agreed. "And one who never lost sight of what the circus is truly all about. The fans. The paying public."

Garrison shook his head in awe. "I still can't believe this. Suddenly, out of nowhere, we have a legend… one of the biggest names in the industry, right here under our big top." He placed a hand deftly upon Klondike's shoulder. "And I'm all too aware that I have you to thank for it, Kal. You made this all possible. He came here for you."

Klondike nodded absently as he watched Irwin chatting to an elderly woman, before high-fiving a passing steward. Sweat cascaded down his neck and bare shoulders.

The tent was almost empty now, the thousands of fans all out in the meadow beyond.

"Hell," the circus boss said dryly, "it looks like Doc got us out of jail tonight. That whole show was a disaster... right up until he came on."

Garrison frowned. "You really think that?"

Klondike smirked slightly, still watching Irwin as he finally made his way towards the flap, his lean, taut body draped in sweat.

"I think... I think we've just found our saviour."

CHAPTER 19

EVEN THE DOC CAN'T SAVE CIRCUS OF SHAMBLES!
By Tom Price, Arizona Herald

He stands as one of the most heralded performs ever to set foot under an American big top.

But this morning, Jonathan 'Doc' Irwin must be wondering what on earth he has let himself in for after debuting last night for the little-known Double G Circus, out of Sierra Nevada.

Indeed, the opening three-quarters of this big top offering at the Yewtree Rec, Flagstaff, was an ungodly mess, highlighted by mistakes and poor professionalism.

One of the circus's team of cowboys fell off his mount during a saddle trick – and was then almost trampled to death by his team-mates.

The Rollergirls – exactly what they sound like, a team of women in short leotards whirling round the circus floor – were a breathtaking sight... until one of them went flying and almost broke her neck.

Worst of all, the good people of Flagstaff were almost witness to a horrendous accident when knife thrower Hondo Cloud (his real name, apparently) nearly embedded one of his instruments of death into his assistant's skull. The poor girl screamed and had to be led away by backstage staff.

Entertainment, you say! I ask you.

Into this fulcrum of amateurish nonsense then strode the great Doc Irwin. How the mighty have fallen. To see the All American, a star of stage and screen for several decades, lower himself to this level of indecency, working for a wild west carnival in essence, was just too depressing for words.

To his immense credit, Irwin's act was as faultless as ever, finally offering the paying patrons something to cheer. His standing ovation ensured the Double G Circus's show ended on a high note. But the truth of it is, this was far from a success. And everybody present last night knows it.

All Doc Irwin achieved was saving this mish-mash of a touring company from having its tent ripped down by disgusted circus goers, demanding their money back.

Well, doctors can perform miracles. And, last night, this Doc saved his boss from a mortal wound… but he failed to find a cure for the show's one major ailment – failure.

Mike Blakelock looked up from the newspaper, scanned the tennis court again, then glanced back at the review. With a bemused frown, he tossed the copy of the Arizona Herald onto the dashboard of his Sedan.

Then, he focused on the court again.

There was Jenny Cross. Purple sweater. White tennis skirt. Hopping across the court like a teenager, blonde hair flowing beautifully in the gentle breeze.

He was sat in the parking lot of the Red Rock Health Club, just south of Vegas. Behind the wheel of another rented Sedan, he settled back in his car seat and looked around idly. The exclusive club provided health and leisure activities for the rich and their cronies, the dignitaries of Sin City, of which there were many.

The main health centre, a huge Whitestone complex, sat to his right. A row of 12 tennis courts bled out before him, stretching across the club's endless grounds, surrounded by palm trees and cactus plants.

Rubbing at his face, Blakelock tried to concentrate on Jenny's match. Not that it was much of a match. She was playing one of the club's professionals, a one-time ATP touring rookie, who now looked and played like he was past it.

The tennis match seemed to come to a conclusion as Jenny swatted at a serve, missed, and then ran playfully towards the net, laughing and gushing. The pro met her at the net, and the two shared a long embrace.

Blakelock watched with interest, reaching for his binoculars and studying the tennis pro. Thick brown hair, large moustache, strong muscular build. California beach tan. This could get interesting, he thought idly.

As he watched from his car in the parking lot, Jenny and the tennis pro wandered leisurely away from the courts and into the clubhouse.

Blakelock watched. Then, with a huff, he picked up the newspaper again.

"La Caliguria, the pearls of Magellan."

The store assistant held aloft the exquisite, sparkling pearl necklace in hands covered with spotless white gloves.

Jenny eyed La Caliguria intently, her blue eyes shining almost as brightly as the immaculate turquoise pearls as she gazed at them.

"I'll take it."

She was in EH Houghton's, the bespoke Las Vegas jewellery store, south of the strip in Paradise Avenue.

The shop was like an exclusive museum, with various artefacts displayed in glass cases along the velvet-lined walls, and customers wandering about the aisles, taking interest in various pieces.

La Caliguria was a necklace that simply screamed of wealth, opulence and, in her eyes, acceptance. Jenny eyed it hungrily as she hovered in the store, wearing her Arctic silver fur coat and a white trouser suit beneath.

"One moment," the assistant uttered. She placed the necklace on a velvet-covered holder and then disappeared through a curtain into a back room. Moments later, she was replaced by an older woman, who looked stern and alert, a giant pair of spectacles dominating her wrinkled face.

Jenny frowned as she approached.

"Meredith Hawkes, co-partner. How may I be of service, ma'am?"

Jenny stared at her in shock. "I am buying this necklace, La Caliguria."

The woman looked at her for a moment, and then studied the beautiful necklace sat between them.

"A beautiful addition, and a wise choice, ma'am." She cleared her throat. "Might I ask, ma'am... will you be purchasing this piece with cash, cheque, or perhaps another method of payment?"

Jenny stared at her in anger. She pulled up the collar of her immense fur coat. "Do you make it a habit of insulting your customers, Miss Hawkes?"

"I mean no offence," Miss Hawkes said rapidly. "However, this pristine piece is priced at more than 10 thousand dollars, so we need to know if, ah, certain arrangements are required for payment."

Jenny kept staring at her. The woman remained impassive, as if she had this type of conversation every day.

"I intend to pay using credit."

"From what line?"

Again, Jenny frowned. "Mettasina Gaming. The Generoso account."

Miss Hawkes gave an almost imperceptible shake of her head. "Oh, I'm very sorry, ma'am. We do not recognise that account here."

"What?" Jenny hissed. "What are you talking about?"

"We have no association with the Mettasinas. Or any of the… er, casino owners, for that matter."

Jenny took a step forward, scowling. "I want that necklace!"

"And you can have it, ma'am. We just need an accepted payment method. Cheque, perhaps?"

Jenny sneered, suddenly looking cruel and ugly. "Do you know who I am?"

"No. But I know who Mr Generoso is."

"Aha! Then you will know not to disappoint him. Not to turn him down. Or anything in his name." She smiled contentedly. "Now… shall we continue with this purchase?"

Miss Hawkes surprised her by smiling. "I am afraid not." She looked from side to side. "Now, good day to you."

Jenny glared at her, with pure hatred in her eyes. A furious concoction. Slowly, she removed one of her silk gloves. Then, holding it before her steadily, she suddenly slapped it across the woman's face. Miss Hawkes shifted involuntarily and closed her eyes as the soft material kissed her cheek.

Both women seemed to stand there in shock for several moments. But Miss Hawkes's reaction was not that which Jenny had hoped for. Still, she remained cool, staring back at Jenny with a bemused expression.

Finally, Jenny turned. "I'll be back. With my people."

Then, she was gone. The glamorous woman in the giant fur coat.

As she breezed out of the store, she stumbled slightly in her high heels and almost fell.

That made Miss Hawkes smile.

"Give me another."

Jenny pushed the tall cocktail glass to one side and prepared to welcome a replacement.

She was seated at the bar of the downtown cocktail lounge. Now, she was far from the exclusive health resorts and jewellery stores of southern Nevada, instead rooted in the heart of downtown Vegas, a seedy cesspool of vice and squalor. A world of gamblers, hookers, strippers, alcoholics and grifters.

She attracted many curious glances as she slumped at the bar of the darkened saloon, the blonde in the exotic fur coat and beautiful white shoes. But she now looked somewhat dishevelled, defeated, as if living the life of an elite society heiress was somehow too much. As if she had cracked, and was now back at her true home. She certainly did not fit in here.

The bartender produced another expresso martini. She hungrily grabbed at it, raising the big glass to her lips with both hands and downing half the brownish contents with one gulp. Then, she held the glass before her in a sign of near-worship, as if it contained a precious elixir for eternal life. Then, she finished the drink and signalled the barman for another. Yet another.

Blakelock watched from a corner table in the darkened joint, possibly 20 yards from her. He was nursing a tall glass of beer, which he had barely touched. A baseball cap was pulled low over his face, though he was convinced Jenny Cross would never recognise him. Or even remember that they had met.

Watching her was an extraordinary experience. On entering the bar, she had resembled a countessa from Europe. Now, she looked almost like a vagrant. Her drinking was mind boggling.

Blakelock struggled to take his eyes off her. Casually, he lit a cigarette and sipped at his beer.

"Damndest broad I ever saw."

He looked up at the gruff voice. An elderly man in a cheap suit had been walking past his table, before noticing his spellbound gaze… and seeing the woman at the bar.

"Yeah," Blakelock blurted. "She looks a mess. Must've got lost down Paradise Avenue."

"You got that right," the old-timer mumbled. "I see her in here often. Knocking back them cocktails. Without worry. Then stumbling outta here. To god only knows where. Dressed to the nines!" He shook his head. "Damndest thing…"

Blakelock nodded. He watched Jenny light a cigarette, accepting a lit match from the over-eager bartender.

"Yeah," Blakelock muttered, even though the old-timer had moved on.

"She's the damndest alright."

It was a glorious sight for all present to behold.

The immaculate green and gold big top, filled to its magnificent 8,000 capacity attendance. Excited fans cheering in the grandstands all around, forming a great stadium of sound and electricity as they applauded the acts and screamed with delight.

Giant green banners and posters proclaiming RIBBECK WORLD CIRCUS seemed to be hanging everywhere. The audience seated around the performance arena contained pockets of junior fans dressed in yellow and black jumpsuits, the recognised fan clothing of The Daredevils.

At that moment, those spectators were in absolute ecstasy. The Daredevils were mounting the ramp, heading into the Globe of Death. It was happening, right now, the ultimate act of death defiance. And the crowd were going crazy for it.

The globe itself, which resembled a great round cage, was sat in a support frame in the tent's very centre, as the motorbikes had whirled round it at high velocity.

As the bikers all slowly headed into the massive, caged metal sphere for the mind-blowing act, the last rider to head up the ramp to the cage door was of course Tip Enqvist.

Reaching the top of the ramp and the threshold for the sphere, in which his team-mates were performing ultra-fast loops in all directions, Enqvist made his usual gesture. Removing his yellow helmet as he sat prone on his motorbike, he raised a fist and began pumping the air emphatically, whipping the fans into a wild frenzy as the noise of the exhaust dominated the big top.

As he held his arm aloft, Enqvist squinted into the main grandstand, his eyes taking in the VIP enclosure directly alongside the mighty tent's flap area. He saw a line of men in smart business suits watching on, and quickly made out Eric Ribbeck, sat among them in a burgundy suit with white cravat.

Waving at the crowd, Enqvist gave a special, one-off salute to Ribbeck, far away in the stands.

In his seat, Ribbeck grinned with satisfaction. He gave Enqvist a wave happily.

Then, in an instant, Enqvist was inside the Globe of Death. The door slammed shut. And the rider zoomed around in great circles, somehow avoiding all of his team-mates as he flew around in all directions.

In the audience, one of Ribbeck's associates, seated next to him in the stand, whispered into his ear, above the roar of the bikes.

"You've got a winner there, Eric. Well done getting these guys on board. Just look at these fans."

Ribbeck smiled smugly. "Welcome to the greatest show on earth."

An hour later, Ribbeck sat sprawled at the giant antique desk inside his plush executive carriage within his circus train.

They were playing in Des Moines, Iowa, and the circus was riding high after another sell-out performance. Their 12th in a row. Gate receipts and midway take were off the scale. But, more important than any of that, Ribbeck World Circus was growing in popularity at a rapid rate.

At that moment, Ribbeck was happily filling his pipe with apple scented tobacco behind the great desk.

Veronica Hunslett, his executive assistant, watched him curiously across the desk. It was like an art form, working that beloved pipe.

"So… you agree with my idea? About the new merchandise? We need more… the Daredevils adorning more items. You heard that reaction, Eric? The one when they first came out and then… then that ovation when they finished the Globe of Death! It blew my mind."

"Yes, yes," Ribbeck muttered as he concentrated on the pipe. Finally satisfied, he struck a match and held it at the bowl, inhaling through the stem as great wafts of caramel grey smoke filled the carriage. "Right as usual, Miss Hunslett. See to it."

She nodded. "What did the investors make of it tonight?"

Ribbeck cackled. "Hell, they loved it. They saw the fans screaming Tempest's name. Screaming Martinez's name. Then they saw those Daredevils. God damn! Those boys were practically drooling. I could see the dollar signs in their eyes!"

They both looked up abruptly at a sharp rap on the stateroom door. Then, it opened and Luca Marconi walked in slowly. He looked shocked, as if he'd seen a ghost.

"Someone to see you, boss…"

Ribbeck's eyes were on some paperwork spread out on the desk before him.

"What? At this hour? Here?" He looked up, then frowned. "Luca? You alright? You look sick, boy."

"Mr Ribbeck…" Marconi said dumbly. He had a vacant look on his rugged, scarred face. "You're not gunna believe this. It's… it's Roddy Olsen!"

Ribbeck stared at him with wild, hypnotic eyes. The pipe slipped out of his mouth and he caught it before it smashed into the desk.

"Wh…what?"

Then, in what felt like slow motion, the door behind Marconi opened further.

And then, there he was. Dressed in his faithful green anorak and jeans, Roddy Olsen strode in purposefully.

His baby blue eyes were on Ribbeck, the old man behind the desk. In that moment, nobody else existed in the distinguished train carriage. He walked up to the mighty desk and hovered over the veteran circus man. This was it, their first ever face to face encounter. It felt like an event to both men.

Ribbeck stared at him, in awe and wonder. His cold green eyes twinkled like antique jade. But for the first time in years, he was lost for words.

"Roddy…" he breathed, gazing at the youngster in a dreamlike fashion.

"Finally, we meet," Olsen said.

"You… you came to me! You are here. On my train."

Olsen took a deep breath, his eyes still locked on Ribbeck. "I had to come. All the way here. To face you. And tell you something."

As the confrontation took shape, Veronica and Marconi said nothing, simply staring at the youngster who had boldly marched into the executive carriage. It was a move none of them were used to.

Ribbeck was still misty eyed, as if having an out of body experience. "God damn, boy," he whispered, "how I have dreamed of this moment. Seeing you. Meeting you. Damn, you are like a golden fleece, son, a beautiful idol…"

Olsen frowned. "I don't get what-"

"I've been watching you, Roddy," the old man continued in an airy tone, slow and awestruck. "I've been watching you. All these years. Your shows with Klondike. The TV work. Vegas. I've read the reviews. Marvelled at your magic. And now… now you're here. You have come, Rod, to where you belong. With the best. The best of the best."

Olsen shook his head, tired of it all. "I came here to tell you what I think about you and your outfit." He took another deep breath and steadied himself, as if preparing an assault. "I think you stink, Ribbeck! You and your dirty tricks! Your cronies and your deals. You've been riding roughshod all over this industry for years. Walking all over people, wrecking their lives. Screwing guys over, and leaving misery in your wake." He paused, his blue eyes now full of fire as he glared down at the man behind the desk. "Well, I'm here to tell you it all ends now, Ribbeck. You've screwed over Courtland, wrecked his dreams. And all to get me on board with your outfit. Under your big top. Well, it ain't gunna happen, old man!"

Ribbeck stared at him in astonishment. It had been many years since anyone at all had talked to him in such a fashion, even tried to. Within seconds, Marconi approached Olsen and grabbed his arm.

"Alright, that's enough, babyface. You don't know who you're talking to."

Olsen shrugged him off forcefully. Then, Marconi grabbed at him again.

"It's alright, Luca." Ribbeck held up a hand, a shaking hand. He tried to focus on Olsen.

"You don't understand, Roddy. You belong here, boy. This is the greatest show on earth. We are about to become the biggest circus in the history of the business. Don't you understand, dammit! The greatest of all time." He stared intently at the youngster now, lines and creases suddenly covering his caramel, leather-like skin. "Yes, I want you! Everybody knows that. I want the best circus there has ever been. That is my obsession. And you, Roddy Olsen, you will be the MVP. The star of that show. The face of the franchise." He thought desperately for a moment. "With a free hand in your material and workload. The largest salary in circus history. Dammit all to hell, boy, all this and more can be yours… if you'd just sign a contract with me. With the best!"

Despite the rousing speech and offers, Olsen remained impassive, as Marconi backed off.

He leaned over the desk slightly. "You're riding high now, Ribbeck. But you're not going to be the best. And I'm gunna see to it that your days at the top are over." He snarled angrily, glaring down at the old man. "I'm not signing with you. Ever! Instead, I'm going to use my fame, my following, my fans… to help bring you down!"

Ribbeck was again astonished. An extraordinary, pained look fell over him, as if a mortal wound had been administered. He looked up in desperation. "But why, dammit?"

Olsen screwed up his nose. "Because of all the pain, the suffering you've caused, Ribbeck. Your schemes and threats, to put people like Miles Courtland out of business. Hell, you're not a circus man, you're a damn outlaw. You and all your people." He smiled, his eyes suddenly lightening up slightly. "But me, and my people… we are real circus folk. And we're going to pull the chain on you, pal."

That made Ribbeck growl like a riled lion.

With that, Marconi grabbed at Olsen's shoulder and violently spun him around. "Alright, you little punk, that's enough…"

As Olsen turned, he threw a lightning fast right cross straight into the unsuspecting Marconi's jaw. The New York tough guy was completely unprepared and flew over backwards, crashing into an antique coffee table and lantern.

Ribbeck and Veronica stared in shock at the events. Both remained seated.

Olsen backed away slowly, shaking his right hand in pain. He reached the door.

Ribbeck glared at him now, his look of awe and wonder replaced by one of fire and venom. "You've made a very big mistake today, Olsen. I offered you the world, a life most mortals can only dream of. And instead you spit in my face."

Olsen stood in the doorway, a strange look of triumph marring his youthful, innocent features. "You said you've been watching me my whole career, Ribbeck. Well, you can go right back to watching. That's all you'll ever do. Because I'd rather work as a backstreet busker than ever turn out for you."

Then, he was gone. The oak door slammed shut as he left the executive carriage.

As Marconi wearily rose from the floor, clutching his jaw, Veronica sat like a statue, dreading her boss's response.

Ribbeck slowly rubbed his beloved ivory pipe. Then, with a mighty snarl, he hurled it wildly at the far wall, the antique piece shattering into a mess of shards.

The deathly silence that followed was bitter. Perfectly matching the old man's mood.

CHAPTER 20

"Did you really perform for the President?"

Doc Irwin grinned, nodding happily. "Right. Actually, two presidents. Truman back in '52. Then good old Eisenhower the following year. Ike was in the audience for a TV charity gig I was invited to."

Irwin was holding court with a small group of circus performers in the canteen tent. The Double G had arrived in Phoenix the night before, and the circus encampment had slowly been erected that morning. Many talent and staff had quickly made for the canteen once it was up and running, urgently seeking refreshment to help combat the dry, Arizona heat.

Irwin now sat at the head of a table in the small marquee, surrounded by Pamela Hotch, Arletta LaRue, Hondo Cloud, Betsy and several of the cowboys.

The others sat staring at him in awe and wonder as he happily regaled them with tales of his long career at the top. He sat in his customary Stars and Stripes tracksuit, a white towel around his neck, while he sipped a tall glass of milk.

Arletta was asking most of the questions at the table. "And how about royalty?"

"Why, yes, ma'am," Irwin said, still smiling. "King Gottfried of Switzerland, during a European tour some years back. And then there was King Baudouin of Belgium, who came to watch a show I was in at Madison Square Garden."

The others leaned towards him, spellbound. Beyond them, scores of roustabouts were entering and leaving the canteen tent, gulping down glasses of yellow lemonade and patting their faces with wet flannels. Another of the Riders of the Double G joined the table, having helped himself to some lunch at the long buffet tables.

"I heard about your All American Association, Irwin," the cowboy mumbled as he sat himself down at the far end. "Helluva thing, helping the kids out like that."

Irwin nodded down the table at him. "I thank you. Means more to me than any of this... the money, the fame, the prestige.

No, it's all about making the fans happy, you ask me. Giving them a show. Nothing else matters." He looked down solemnly. "For some, coming to the show wasn't always possible. That's why I came up with the idea of the passes."

The assembled group all nodded slowly.

"How do you do that bicycle act, man?" Cloud suddenly blurted, eyes wide. "None of us have ever seen anything like that."

Again, Irwin grinned happily, arms folded as he sat back. "Practice, Hondo. It all comes down to practice. You keep doing it, the same routine, over and over, until you don't have to think. It all becomes a part of you. You're no longer performing the act... it has become you... it's in you, as if it had always been there. Like you and your knives."

Cloud nodded slowly. He put an arm around the youthful Betsy beside him. "Yeah. I guess so."

Pamela stared at the wire walker intently. "Why do they call you Doc, Doc?"

Again, a wisened grin. "Hell, that began way back. When I started out." He leant forward, a determined look on his gnome-like features, like a coach giving a team talk. "I always kept myself in the best possible physical condition, folks. Sought advice from medics, physiotherapists, healers, fitness gurus, you name it. After a while, I became an expert on the human body. Muscles, bones, anatomy. Began to understand injuries, and why certain muscles wouldn't work when you wanted them to. I analysed rest periods, relaxation modes, warm-ups, therapies. After a while, the troupe I was riding with... well, all the guys started calling me Doc. Said I was an expert on physical conditioning. Ha! And, you know, it just kinda stuck, as these things do."

The group all seemed delighted with the explanation. The wide-eyed Arletta leant forward. "You have kept yourself in fantastic shape, Mr Irwin."

He smiled, slightly awkwardly. "Thank you, ma'am."

Suddenly, everybody seemed to sit up and look to the marquee entrance as Kal Klondike wandered in, with Heavy at his side.

The circus boss smiled wryly as he noticed the assembled group at the table, with Doc at its head.

"Well, well," he drawled. "Looks like story time with Doc Irwin."

Irwin laughed. "Something like that." He gestured to the others. "Just getting to know my new team-mates. Quite the crew you've assembled here."

"Damn straight." Klondike stood next to the table with Heavy.

"Alright, we're gunna run a few training drills this evening. Say 7pm sharp. This Arizona desert heat is something else, and we need to be sure we're acclimatised by Saturday night. It's, well, it's dryer and warmer than we're used to."

Heavy nodded, rubbing at his forehead with a towel. "Just nobody stay out in that sun for too long."

Klondike gazed down mesmerically at Irwin. "You ready to smash it out of the ball park again, Doc?"

Irwin grinned. "You bet, sideburns. All the way." Then, he looked around at his comrades' alarmed expressions. "Er, I mean… yes sir, Mr Klondike."

Klondike laughed. Then, with a nod, he wandered casually across to the drinks station and poured two beakers of water, handing one to Heavy.

"I can only imagine what fresh escapades await us here," Heavy muttered as he downed half his glass beaker in one go. "It's been an incident-filled tour. And, hell, I didn't even think there was gunna be a tour."

"Same escapades, just under a different banner," Klondike murmured.

As he drank the ice cold liquid, his dark eyes settled on the far side of the canteen tent.

One man sat all alone. Don Peerless. He was hunched over a coffee cup, of all things in this heat.

Klondike frowned as he watched the old-timer brazenly remove a large hip flask from his breast pocket, and pour a generous measure of booze into the coffee. Then, with a satisfied sigh, Peerless sat back and enjoyed a long sip.

Klondike finished his beaker of water. He squinted across at Heavy beside him, and shook his head.

"Argh, we're getting closer to home now, here in Phoenix. But, you know what, it still feels like we're in a different world."

Heavy stared at him. "But we're making the best of it."

With a nod of acceptance, Klondike tapped his old friend on the back and nodded towards the doorway. "Come on."

With immaculate elegance and grace, like a hand glider rolling with the winds, the small, lithe figure in white shorts and vest whirled through the air, propelling itself from one ring, high into nothingness, before deftly grasping the next one, and repeating the motion.

Back and forth the whirling figure flew, swinging expertly between the three trapeze rings like an angelic entity.

After several moments, the flyer came to rest upon the ring on the far left side of the trapeze rig, hauling himself up into a sitting down position, panting wildly.

The resplendent, old-fashioned big top was completely empty, its grandstands deserted and the sawdust floor bereft of activity. The tent's shiny pink and brown fabric looked brand new in the morning light.

Directly below the trapeze rig on the stage floor, Gino Shapiro stood gazing upwards. Dressed in his orange tracksuit, with a white towel around his shoulders, he held a coffee in a plastic thermos cup before him, but had yet to take a single sip. Instead, he had stared upwards, astonished at the young marvel flying high above.

He turned to Murph, stood beside him in a red shirt and white shorts. The big man looked impressed.

"Santamaria," Shapiro breathed, "it looks like we've got a natural here, Murph."

"You said it, pal."

Up above them, Tommy Rogers sat swinging gently on his ring. He finally smiled, still slightly out of breath. Finally composing himself, he rose slowly to a standing position on the tiny, swinging plastic platform that supported him. Then, with another effortless vault, he propelled his tiny frame through the air, like a dart, his arms reaching out and clutching the tall rope several yards from the ring.

Clinging to the rope like a jungle sloth, he began hauling himself down, slithering faster and faster as the ground grew nearer.

When he hit the sawdust, he laughed joyfully and jogged over to Shapiro and Murph. "Well, what did you think, guys?"

Shapiro stared at him, his gaze one of shock and respect, all blended together. "Tommy," he murmured. "Your skills are exceptional. Where did you acquire them?"

Rogers could not stop smiling. "It's like I told you, Gino. I'm self-taught. I learnt all this from watching other guys. These past few years. Hell, seeing as how no one would give me a shot, a chance to train with them… seemed my best bet was to practise alone. Train alone. Copying what I saw every night from my rigging position." He nodded to himself, glancing up at the rings again. "I sure have seen a lot of flyers in action down the years."

Murph was incredulous. "You learnt all this just from watching? Hell kid, that is crazy."

Shapiro was appraising the youngster. "Where did you practice, kid?"

Rogers smiled impishly, pointing to the summit. "Up there. Once the show had finished. And everyone had gone home. Why, no one was going to clear away the rigging until the next day. I just took advantage."

Murph stared at him. "Now, that really is crazy, man. You taught yourself trapeze… on the fly. By night."

Rogers shrugged. "Seems to me I had no choice. If I wanted to be a flyer. A real flyer."

"Bravo, Tommy, bravo," Shapiro said, finally sipping his steaming coffee. "An incredible story. Almost worthy of a movie, eh Murph?" He chuckled. "No, that is very impressive, kid. I salute your spirit and determination… and your guts. Taking matters into your own hands like that. You have il coraggio."

"Thanks, Gino," said the youngster. "That sure means a lot, especially coming from you."

An awkward silence filled the dormant big top. There was something about an empty circus tent that always created an irksome atmosphere.

Rogers took a deep breath. "So, what do you guys think? You reckon, maybe one day, I could join your act? Huh? Maybe as a warm-up guy? Or a jobber? Or maybe as an apprentice…"

Shapiro and Murph exchanged a quick look. Gino smiled warmly, and approached Rogers, placing an arm around his shoulders.

"Maybe one day real soon, Tommy," he whispered. "And sooner than you think. You have shown me today you are already on the path to stardom, I feel."

Rogers practically exploded, rubbing his hands across his face and shaking. He seemed to hop up and down, like a puppy. "Oh, Gino, Mr Murphy, that is fantastic. I can't thank you enough. For everything. And anything you can do for me. Just this here today, right now, it means the world to me. Finally being able to show an expert what I can do."

Shapiro tapped him on the back. "We'll have another session. Tomorrow. Same time. Maybe you can show us something new from your, ah, repertoire of skills."

Rogers laughed joyfully. "You bet!"

He thanked them both again, shook hands, and jogged sprightly across the sawdust to the flap. His pale skin seemed to blend in with his white shorts and vest.

Shapiro and Murph watched him leave curiously.

"Well, I never saw that coming," Murph announced.

"This season seems to be producing more surprises than the last 20 put together," Shapiro said dryly. Then, he smiled. "But that was a surprise most welcome."

Their musings were interrupted as a group of roustabouts in plaid shirts and jeans marched across the sawdust towards them, carrying a large pommel horse between themselves.

As Shapiro and Murph watched idly, one of the group addressed them, with a sly grin.

"Don't mind us, your majesty. Just the servants, assembling the kingdom. We'll be out of your way in no time, highness."

One of the others joined in. "Yeah, superstar. Y'all be sure not to break a toenail or pull an eyelash there. That'll cost Miss Stanwyck another hundred bucks!"

The gang all laughed heartily. They hauled the massive gym horse across the floor, struggling to maintain its weight.

Murph watched them pass by. "You ever get the feeling we're not wanted, pal?"

"Yeah, by everyone, except the boss lady." Shapiro glanced down at his plastic cup. "Come on. I need some more coffee."

They headed towards the tent flap.

Lacey Tanner threw a gentle wave as she saw Richie Plum breeze into the cafe, glancing around nervously, attempting to locate her.

She was sat at a corner table of The Coffee Pot, a popular diner joint a few blocks away from the executive offices of Montpellier and Cavani, just off Sunset Boulevard in downtown LA.

The joint was full of suits, discussing the movie industry and various showbusiness avenues, all while downing cups of coffee and devouring endless plates of ham, eggs and pie.

Plum spotted her through the thronging masses of the breakfast rush hour. He weaved his way over and plonked himself down in the vinyl bench seat opposite her in the booth. They exchanged pleasantries.

"Sorry I'm late," he muttered. "Still finding my way around this city. It's like a hornets' nest. People everywhere."

Lacey smiled. She looked somewhat conservative in a grey trench coat and black beret. "You'll get used to it, baby. Los Angeles is a city of magic. Of stars and dreams." She held her coffee cup before her, perched by her lips. "Of opportunity."

Plum looked at her, bemused. A waitress appeared and he ordered coffee, plus a refill for Lacey.

"Well, it's going to take some getting used to, I can tell you that. My new apartment is down in Tropicana Heights. But I can't sleep. Too much noise. Just… people. Everywhere!"

Lacey smiled demurely, somehow putting him at ease. "It really meant a lot to me, Richie. That you came out here. To join me." She laughed. "Tracking me down like that."

Now, Plum smiled. "How could I not, Lacey?"

She nodded happily. "OK. Now, tell me, please… what did you find?"

Plum immediately hauled up his beloved briefcase, and removed various files and newspaper clippings. Lacey could not help but smile as she watched him go to work.

"All sorts," he mumbled. "And most of it not good."

They paused as the waitress returned with two steaming mugs of coffee. Again, Lacey held hers before her, poised.

Plum continued, studying the papers he had assembled on the diner table. "To begin with, Kal's new enterprise, this Double G Circus, seems to be lurching across the south west states, attracting negative reviews and not a lot of commercial appeal. However…" he looked up with a wry smile. "I don't know how old Kal did it, or if he was even involved, but the Double G unveiled their new star signing at their last show in Tucson on Saturday. One Doc Irwin…"

Lacey's beautiful violet eyes widened, and she gasped. "Irwin? Oh my lord, what a coup. He is a legend of circus folklore."

"Yes. Yet an ageing one, of course."

Lacey nodded slowly, lost in thought. She watched the diner patrons, business people all arguing and shouting, ensconced in their own private little realms within the cafe. "What about the others?"

Plum knew who to mention next. "Roddy," he breathed.

Lacey immediately shot a glance at him, one of concern, alarm.

"What-"

"Well, his career seemed to be on the up and up after signing with that new circus outfit, Courtland and Co. After all, Miles Courtland is one of the wealthiest figures in the entertainment industry. But… well, it would seem that Courtland and Co's season was finished before it even started."

"I don't follow."

Plum looked at her meekly. "Eric Ribbeck. Apparently, according to the trade journals, old man Ribbeck closed the troupe down. Just like that. All because Miles didn't have the correct licences, paperwork. The rumour is .. well, they say that…"

Lacey closed her eyes. "He did it all to force Roddy to join his troupe."

Plum looked downwards. "That's right."

"And Corky was out there with him, wasn't he?"

"So they say."

"But Roddy turned Ribbeck down."

"I have no way of knowing."

"He did. Roddy would never work for him. Not ever."

Plum raised an eyebrow. "Well, Enqvist joined up with the old man."

Lacey waved a hand through the air and screwed her nose up. "Tip is a mercenary. An animal. He'll go wherever the money is. Especially money like that. Roddy is a different beast entirely."

They both sat in silence for a moment. Lacey lit a cigarette as she thought of Olsen. Of their history. What a rollercoaster ride it had been. So many ups and downs, personal and professional. It now seemed impossible, fantastically impossible, that they were so very apart, living such separate lives. Inhabiting different spheres of existence.

She shook her head, forcibly exorcising the many memories from her conscience. "And what of Gino?"

Plum tried to smile. "Our dear Gino has been a busy hombre. He was a stunt co-ordinator on a movie, Big Top Showdown. Another circus epic from Hollywood. Interestingly, that picture is financed by Avalon Productions." He looked up from his notes. "Who recently welcomed a new investor. Guess who?"

Lacey rolled her eyes. "Eric Ribbeck."

"Bingo. After that, it appears old Gino left the studio."

Lacey nodded, her eyes wide. "Just like with Roddy. He tried to ramrod Gino into his troupe. Jesus! The man is a shameless rogue. Trying to make everyone dance to his tune. Just as always. No matter what the cost."

Plum looked at her weakly. "It would appear so." He glanced back at the many sheets of paper before him, fiddling with a newspaper clipping. "And now, just last week, Gino has resurfaced at a circus. Stanwyck's Circus, in fact. Out of Fort Worth. But currently pitched up just down the road. In Bakersfield."

"Bakersfield?" she panted. "So close…"

Plum showed her the clipping. "He signed some kind of contract with this Stanwyck woman. It made the newspapers."

She tried to smile. "That one is big news. Wherever he goes."

Plum nodded. "He sure is." He put the clipping in a pile with the other pieces of paper, and pushed it all gently to one side. He looked at Lacey, who seemed lost in thought, cigarette in hand. An awkward silence engulfed the table.

Plum gulped heavily. "So, er, where exactly does that leave us, Lacey? I mean, what are we even doing here, going through all this?"

She leant back in the booth bench seat, and took a long drag on her cigarette, exhaling a mighty cloud of smoke that briefly formed a ceiling above them at the table.

Her expression looked saddened, lost. But the eyes had some of their old sparkle. Something was happening. Plum just knew it.

"It would seem," she finally exclaimed, in a melodramatic tone, "that our old parish has become lost and broken."

Plum leant forward and eyed her knowingly. "Without its guiding light. Its guardian angel."

She giggled. "Oh, Richie! Please!"

He looked at her seriously now. "Don't you miss it, Lacey? Surely you miss it?"

Lacey looked downwards, then forcibly stubbed her cigarette out in the glass ashtray. She took a deep breath. When she spoke, it was in a quivering whisper.

"Endlessly, Richie. Endlessly."

CHAPTER 21

"Ladies and gentlemen…"

The Double G Circus big top was filled with enchanted families, curious teenagers and legions of males in their pale Arizona stetsons for the Phoenix extravaganza.

The show was not quite a sellout, goggles of empty seats could be seen here and there among the throngs of spectators. But they were close to capacity.

As predicted, it was a warm, dry and somewhat suffocating atmosphere that night in the tent. Scores of hands waving folding fans under their jawlines created an almost rhythmic motion across the lines of seats as everyone tried to stay cool.

Heavy Brown stood in the centre of the floor, microphone pressed to his lips.

"Welcome to the fastest-growing circus spectacular in America today. The grandest, the wildest, the most incredible blend of action and excitement on offer anywhere in the world. Where cowboys roam… and roller girls whirl. The wild west brought to life, in a show of magic beyond your imagination!"

He held his hand aloft in a grand gesture, but there was little reaction from the audience, almost as if the spectators were too hot to say or do anything.

"And now," Heavy roared, "please welcome our opening act. The wild riding, sharp shooting, kings among cowboys! Give it up for the Riders of the Double G, featuring the master blaster, Rawley Walsh!"

A conservative applause broke out across the rows of metal folding seats as the Riders burst through the tent flap on their pristine palominos, galloping wildly into the big top before performing their customary laps of the stage ring. The fantastic repertoire of saddle tricks followed as the cowboys "yee-hawed" and zoomed around in great circles.

Heavy had retreated to the flap enclosure, where Klondike stood, leaning ramrod straight against a tent post, arms folded.

"I sure hope those horses have been watered," Heavy muttered as he took his place alongside the circus boss.

Klondike squinted at the cowhands from the Sidewinder Ranch as they performed their routine. "One thing I've learnt from my time with the Double G," he mused. "Those boys know their business. No doubt. They know horses better than any cowboys I ever met. They're a credit to ranching, and horsemanship."

As the Riders went around the stage floor again, performing an intriguing, fast-paced blur of headstands and leaps, Heavy wandered back on to the sawdust.

"And now," he roared into the mic, "legendary cowboy Rawley Walsh and his partner, Joe Deckland, will perform the outlandish, the impossible master display of horseback wizardry… the Saddle Swap."

The cowboy tricks came to an end and the horses all moved to the outer edges of the stage floor. Then, as was customary, Walsh and Deckland manoeuvred their mounts to opposite ends of the sawdust. Both backed up until their horses were practically in the front rows, on either side of the big top.

The two men on horseback faced each other. Then, as Walsh gave a subtle nod, the display began.

Both palominos charged forward after an invitational tingle from their riders' spurs. The Saddle Swap was under way, the spectators holding their collective breaths as both horses charged towards each other in that frightening, jousting action.

But something was wrong. Klondike noticed it from the flap, 50 yards away. Walsh's horse, which was charging in his direction, looked like it was having a seizure as it bolted forwards with all its might. Its eyes were wide, wild even, and it was drooling from the mouth.

Klondike stepped forward to the edge of the sawdust and was about to point out the abnormality to Heavy, when disaster struck.

The beautiful golden palomino suddenly lurched downwards as it ran, its front legs dropping alarmingly as the beast sunk to its knees. A miniature dust bowl seemed to erupt from the ground as it fell. The horse came to a screeching halt, head tucked into its chest, as its hind legs flew upwards. The sickening motion hurled Walsh from his saddle violently, the rider catapulted a good 12 feet into the air, before landing with an almighty thud on the sawdust. The cowboy yelped in pain as he sprawled in the dust cloud.

The whole incident had lasted just seconds. As Walsh landed on the ground, the audience in the big top seemed to gasp in horror as one, as hands shot to mouths and eyes widened in shock.

Klondike didn't even think. He raced out on to the sawdust in a wild sprint, Heavy a yard behind him.

Several of the Double G riders had beaten them to the stricken Walsh, who lay flat on his back, grimacing like sin. The cowboys all knelt around their fallen comrade, forming a protective shield of humanity.

Klondike and Heavy finally arrived, and looked down at Walsh.

Klondike leaned over him, placing a hand on one of the Riders.

"Rawley? Rawley? Are you alright?"

Walsh squinted up at him, his face a contorted mask of agony. "I can't move my leg," he gasped in horror. He turned his head slightly, looking downwards. "I landed on my damn ankle. Now, I can't feel anything…"

Klondike didn't hesitate. He signalled to one of the roustabouts who was hovering nearby, on standby. "Call an ambulance. Now!"

The youngster disappeared, racing towards the flap.

Klondike turned to two of the cowboys alongside him. "Let's get him up, boys."

Two Riders helped haul Walsh up, gently and in one steady motion. Each took an arm around their shoulders, before two others delicately lifted up each of Walsh's legs at the thigh. Then, they slowly waded out of the tent.

Klondike walked a pace behind them, nodding to Heavy, who quickly brought the mic to his lips.

"He's alright, folks. He's ok! They make their cowboys tough in the High Sierras. He'll be back in the saddle in no time." He paused for a moment. "Ladies and gentlemen, on behalf of all of us here at the Double G, we apologise for what you all just witnessed. This is a live show, folks, and, as such, sometimes accidents do happen."

He watched as several of the other cowboys helped Walsh's horse pace back towards the flap. The palomino had slowly risen to its feet again after the shocking fall. It appeared to be fine now. Not even shaken.

Heavy continued, watching the horse wander away with the riders. "Now, let's hear it for the Riders of the Double G! And a big hand please for our star cowboy, the fastest gun in the west, Rawley Walsh!"

A polite, subdued and somewhat bemused round of applause followed. Stunned faces dominated the watching crowd. Alone now on the sawdust, Heavy could practically taste the surprise all around. And it was a sour taste.

As the cowboys disappeared down the flap, Heavy spoke again.

"And now, ladies and gentlemen, please welcome the human abnormality, the man who eats and breathes fire. Let's hear it for Don 'Fearless' Peerless!"

"Alright, Raw, the ambulance is on its way. Just sit tight."

Klondike tapped the cowboy on the shoulder as he rested on a deckchair in the middle of the now deserted midway.

Several of the cowboys were still present, having grabbed Walsh some water and a milk crate to rest his leg on. They now milled around nervously.

Klondike stood over Walsh, concern clouding his rugged features.

"That was a nasty bump you just took, cowboy."

Walsh gritted his teeth and glanced up at him.

"Broken ankle. I promise ya. Done it several times before. I recognise the pain."

Klondike squinted down at him, wiping his brow. "I'd say you're lucky if that's all you got. That horse tossed you into the air like a damn rag doll."

He looked up at the sound of a siren on the horizon. "What I tell ya. Here's that ambulance. They'll take good care of ya, Rawley."

Walsh looked up at him sadly. "I'm sorry, Kal. That damn ride. She ain't never down nothing like that before. I don't understand what happened."

One of the other Riders spoke up. "It's the heat. Causes sunstroke. Giddiness. Just like with us humans."

Klondike nodded. "He's right. That horse just flipped, just like that."

He frowned suddenly as he caught sight of Heavy, waving furiously at him across the midway from the edge of the flap tunnel. That was wrong. Very wrong.

Klondike patted Walsh on the shoulder and addressed his team-mates. "See he gets to the local hospital alright, fellas."

Then, he set off at a sprint towards the big top again, racing over to where Heavy stood in the short, five-yard long felt tunnel that led inside.

"Kal!" Heavy exclaimed. "Check this out. You won't believe it!"

Klondike rushed through the small enclosure and stood on the edge of the seating area. A sea of embarrassed, shocked faces emanated from every corner of the audience. Klondike looked up at the stage floor. Then, he frowned and cursed.

Peerless was lighting up fire sticks… but was struggling to stand up straight. The veteran was weaving around his small desk on unsteady legs, wobbling and almost falling. He had two lit fire sticks in his hands. He dropped one back on to his desk, then made to shove the other into his mouth… but missed. Instead, the lit stick rested on his right shoulder, upon the fireproof fabric of his yellow jacket, the flames licking his cheek.

A woman screamed, and several spectators stood in alarm.

Klondike raged as he watched in utter disbelief. "The son of a bitch is drunk!" he whispered savagely.

Then, without another thought, he once again raced on to the sawdust. In a daring display, he grabbed ahold of the loose fire stick by its base, resting upon Peerless's shoulder. The tiny blaze licked his fingers as he pulled it clear. He rapidly hurled the stick onto the metal table, then ducked and grabbed a safety blanket from a drawer under the surface. Then, he smothered the sticks entirely, extinguishing the flames.

Peerless stumbled around behind him. "Hey, man, wha… what the hell are you doing?"

Klondike turned, ignoring him. He could smell the whiskey, even over the gasoline. Throwing himself forwards like a bucking bronco, Klondike threw his head and shoulders downwards towards Peerless's midriff and then effortlessly hoisted him up on to his mighty shoulders. Yet more gasps emanated from the crowd.

Without another thought, Klondike paced rapidly towards the flap, an irate Peerless lying on his shoulders.

As the strange-looking abomination comprising Klondike and Peerless charged out of the flap, Heavy quickly paced out on to the sawdust. A team of roustabouts had already come out to take away the table and fire equipment.

Heavy closed his eyes and took a deep breath. Then, he raised the microphone to his lips. "Ladies and gentlemen, once again, we are sorry you had to witness that. I don't know what gives with our guys tonight. Too much sun?"

He laughed gingerly into the microphone. Then, inexplicably, he caught sight of a face, one face, in the throng of hundreds all staring right at him. It was a little girl. Looking straight at him. She was crying.

Silently, Heavy cursed to himself. It was all wrong.

Klondike kicked down the front door of a wooden supplies cabin and hurled Peerless off his back, dumping him unceremoniously in a heap on the oak planks below.

The old timer snarled in pain as he writhed, rolling around several times in a pitiful display. He glanced up angrily at Klondike and made to stand, grabbing at a stack of folding chairs, only to slip back to the floor again.

"You're drunk, Peerless!"

Klondike roared down at him in utter disgust. He hovered over the fallen man, like a prizefighter after scoring a knockdown.

Peerless continued writhing around on his hands and knees, before finally making it to his feet, in slow motion. He swayed as he rose.

"What the hell do you think you're playing at, dammit?" Klondike spat out, looking ready to unleash a torrent of blows at the older man. "You turn up for a performance drunk? Drunk as a skunk! You must be outta your mind."

Peerless leant against an old metal tank in the cabin's far corner. He managed to speak. "I been performing like this my whole life, god damn it." His voice was a gravelly wheeze, like gas escaping from a split pipe. "Ain't no one ever had a problem before!"

"I don't give a damn, Peerless. You're a drunk. A bum. A god damn liability. And I ain't got no place in my big top for a juice head."

Peerless steadied himself, eyes wide in fright. "What are you saying, Klondike?"

Klondike's eyes narrowed. "I'm saying you're through here, Peerless. You just committed the ultimate sin – you let the fans down!"

Suddenly, a new voice interrupted the confrontation.

"What the hell is going on here tonight?"

Klondike turned in alarm. There stood Colonel Griff Garrison, in his finest cream suit and stetson. The Colonel looked bewildered as he hovered in the doorway of the cabin.

"I'm hosting the Phoenix City Council delegation tonight, on what was supposed to be one of their biggest nights of the year. Instead, what they've seen is an embarrassing disaster. And we're only two acts into our show, damn it all to hell!"

Klondike held up a hand. "What happened to Walsh was an accident. The horse was sick. This…" he pointed to the quivering figure before them. "This is something else. Old Don is drunk. Look at him! He went out there drunk! And that…" he gazed at Peerless with savage, murderous eyes, "that is an unforgivable move, sucker."

Garrison eyed Klondike curiously, then gazed at Peerless. He appeared conflicted. Peerless looked at him in desperation.

"Alright, alright," the Colonel muttered, somewhat befuddled. He pointed angrily at the fire eater. "I've told you about your drinking, Don. Repeatedly! Don't you ever learn?"

Peerless held out his hands. "Hell, Colonel, how many people you ever see doing what I do? Huh? Ain't no one can eat fire like that. You half to be half cut to manage it… immune to the fire, the burning.”

Garrison glared at him. He pointed again. “This is your last warning, Don.”

“Woh! No, no, no,” Klondike snapped, cutting in. “We’re beyond that now.” He looked Peerless over in disdain. “I said you’re finished, Peerless. And I meant it. You’re through here. Now, beat it! Get your belongings together, get in a cab… I don’t care! Just beat it!”

Peerless crumpled to the floor in despair, moaning slightly.

Garrison took a step towards Klondike, and whispered quietly. “Don’s been with me for 10 years.”

Klondike moved his head away and looked the Colonel in the eye. A stone cold stare. “He went out drunk. That’s the point of no return. I can’t work with a man who would do a thing like that. Not ever.” He took a deep breath, his head reeling. “I’m sorry, Colonel. He has to go. Now. Right now. Or else…”

Garrison frowned. “Or else what?”

Klondike exhaled loudly. “Or else I go.”

The Colonel stared at him for a moment. Then, he nodded curtly. “Alright.” He looked down at Peerless again. “You’ve disgraced us, Don. Now, you have to pay the price.” He hesitated slightly. “I’m sorry. You’ve got 20 minutes. The boys’ll help you get it together.”

Then, the man in the crisp suit was gone, storming off back to the tent.

Klondike watched him go, trudging angrily across the gravel. Then, he looked one final time at Peerless, slumped on the cabin floor.

And then, worst of all, his dark eyes crept across to a commotion by one of the big top exits, some 20 yards away.

Scores of spectators were leaving. Barely 30 minutes into the show. Many seemed to be rushing, as if desperate to put some distance between themselves and the great tent.

As he watched the patrons hastily exiting, he turned slightly, and caught sight of a Double G Circus poster on the cabin wall next to him. He seemed to address the colourful flyer as he spoke, his voice coming in a deep, bitter whisper.

"Just when I thought I was on the up, they go and drag me back down again."

240

CHAPTER 22

NIGHT OF SHAME AT THE CIRCUS

By Pat Latimer, Phoenix Herald

The Phoenix big top spectaculars have been warming hearts and minds for decades.

Last night, the latest circus show in town chilled my heart and froze my head.

The Double G Circus was playing at the Phoenix Recreation Grounds. But little did any of the scores of paying fans realise... that a disaster was about to ensue.

Firstly, the show's star cowboy Rawley Walsh fell off his horse, almost killing himself as he landed at an awkward angle in the chipper.

Never mind. The gunslinger was hauled off the floor like yesterday's garbage, led away by his pals out back. The show must go on, you see.

Children in the audience were crying, actually crying. Yet still the next act was slung out before us all.

And what an 'act' this was.

It is hard to imagine the potential damage and mayhem a drunken fire-eater could cause. This one, the ironically named Don Peerless, wandered out on stage while barely able to stand, no doubt with little idea what town he was in, or that he was even conscious.

Then, the drunk actually began lighting fire sticks and trying to place them down his neck – but missing – to add to the madness before our very eyes.

Fortunately, and hilariously, a big guy in a hat raced onto the stage and carried this drunk away, like a piece of trash, before he could inflict any damage on the tent... and its bewildered inhabitants... save of course for the inherent despair this ungodly mess inflicted upon our souls.

The show then returned to some semblance of normality. We were 'treated' to a bunch of girls in purple lycra whirling around

Lacey Tanner gently placed the newspaper on her desk. She had stiffened as she read the review. Now, she felt a wave of emotion capsize through her very being, crashing down on her like a tidal wave.

Silently, she felt tears forming in the very corners of her eyes.

She looked across her cluttered desks. What a mess. Newspapers, magazines, journals and studio portraits were everywhere. A giant roll-a-dial sat like a pillar of wisdom within the vortex of news materials. And then, just beyond the hideous mess, sat the concerned, yet cherubic face of Richie Plum.

He was staring at her. Sadly, with a touch of regret.

"I wish I hadn't brought that copy of the Phoenix Herald up," he muttered.

Lacey shook her head. She sipped her coffee and fished out a cigarette, letting it hang limply in her mouth.

Plum leaned across the desk. "You seem perplexed Lacey. Almost lost. You know, I remember that look from back in-"

"This has to stop!"

It was a dramatic statement. She lit her cigarette, the giant violet eyes suddenly alert and now focused upon him.

The wild hubbub of the Montpellier Cavani office seemed to suddenly be extinguished, as if the two of them existed only in a bubble, outside the confines of the bustling PR enclosure. Bodies raced by, wild calls and exclamations zapped across the office floor, but they no longer seemed to feel or hear them.

Plum rubbed at his face. "Er… what?"

"I said, this has to stop." She eyed him coyly now, calming slightly, her face a mask of intrigue once more.

"I know," Plum said quietly. "But, what? What has to stop?"

"This!" She held the copy of the Herald high above her head, before slamming it angrily onto the desk. Several office staff peered over at her, alarmed at the uncharacteristic tone. She ignored them all.

Lacey stood and looked down at Plum before her, holding the cigarette as she crossed her arms. "These hideous reviews. The scalding condemnation. From everywhere!" She visibly shuddered. "The fact Kal is presiding over this cowboy circus, this mess, when he deserves so much better." She exhaled wildly. "It isn't right… and it cannot go on."

Plum nodded vaguely. "You and I are, as usual, in complete agreement. But…"

She held up a hand. "But nothing, Richie. Kal is our confederate. In many ways, strange and beguiling ways, he is our saviour. Yes, that's right. Our saviour. Look back at our lives before we joined up with Kal's circus back in 58, upstate in Santa Cruz. Do you remember, Richie? Do you really remember? Working in bank buildings, office blocks…" she looked around idly. "In places like this?"

Plum was lost in her gusto. He merely nodded some more.

"And then," Lacey continued theatrically, "the thrill of the open road. Or rails, as it were. Travelling the country, playing to some of the biggest crowds in big top history. That lifestyle… what it did to us."

"I can still remember boarding that old train the first time, in Santa Cruz." Plum sat back, smiling. "Oh my, the fears I had. Those staterooms. So small, yet graceful."

Lacey peered at him whimsically. "You see. Kal and his circus changed us in ways we don't even fully recognise." Her giant eyes darted back to the newspaper, as if it represented a diseased, contagious alien life form. "Now… now, we have to help him."

It was a grand declaration, noble and dramatic. Her theatrical manner had Plum on the edge of his seat now.

"What do you suggest, Lacey?"

She looked fierce and determined. "That show was in Phoenix last night. So they'll be heading out tomorrow morning."

Plum nodded dumbly. "Er, yeah."

"And the next show is in San Diego, a week Saturday?"

"So what?"

She grinned devilishly. "We have a matter of days, Richie!"

He gaped at her. "For what? What are we doing? And where are we going?"

Lacey was alive and full of electricity now. She paced around the big desk. One hand span the roll-a-dial dramatically.

"To heaven. If I have anything to do with it. And, what's more…" she stood behind him, placed her hands playfully on his shoulders, and whispered gushingly in his ear.

"We're not going alone."

Colonel Griff Garrison ran a hand through his thinning grey hair and paced across to the window of his executive trailer.

With a mighty huff, he glanced out at the circus encampment, which was slowly being disassembled all around him.

Roustabouts and cowboys were everywhere, taking down stalls and lifting wooden cabins on to the back of flatbed trucks. Beyond that, the rigging team was preparing to take down the mighty big top, which was now covered in support ropes and netting.

Garrison watched for several moments, always amazed at how rapidly the world his team had created could be so easily dismantled and erased. By tomorrow, the recreation grounds would be deserted again, the sea of trailers and stalls a distant memory.

"Alright," he finally said, angrily. "I thought we were on a roll. They told me the Double G is on the rise. Ticket sales soaring. An actual fan base. People going crazy to see us. And then…" he looked downwards, lightly brushing his moustache. "And then last night. That opening! Those reviews! Suddenly, after a night of misfortune, everyone hates us! What the hell!"

Now, he turned to face the living room of his grand and immaculately furnished trailer. There was fire in his grey eyes, and a touch of disbelief.

Kal Klondike was also standing, stirring a cup of coffee by the breakfast bar. He faced the Colonel with an equally downbeat expression.

Doc Irwin was seated in an armchair by the main coffee table, strikingly dressed in his stars and stripes tracksuit, the obligatory white towel around his neck.

"What happened to Walsh was misfortune alright," Klondike said quietly, raising his coffee cup. "But Peerless… that no-good son of a bitch disgraced us and embarrassed us." He cursed. "I been in this business 20 years, and I'm telling you… incidents like that can stay with a troupe. Can be very hard to get over. Make fans, the media forget all about you. That drunken bum may have tarred our big top… for good!"

Garrison eyed him anxiously. "In your opinion, Kal, what is the best way to get over something like this? Eliminate it from everyone's memory?"

Klondike laughed mirthlessly. "Hell, you whip out something from the other end of the spectrum. A show that dazzles, enchants. Blows the fans' minds. Then, nothing else matters. Just the show. The next show. The stars. And the glory."

Garrison stared at him. He nodded. "Well, we got work to do. Without Rawley on board, the bottle shooting act with Hondo is out." His eyes suddenly cooled. "What's the hospital report on Rawley? Have you heard, Kal?"

Klondike nodded, sipping his coffee. "They've reset his ankle. He has to stay on there for a few days. May be discharged next week. But, well, it goes without saying his season is over."

"Reading some of those reviews this morning," Garrison said dryly, "you would think *our* season was over too."

Klondike was impassive. "We've got 10 days till San Diego. That's a long time to prepare."

Suddenly, Garrison turned his sharp gaze to Irwin, who had been sitting calmly, sipping a tall glass of milk.

"Alright, Doc. Let's have it. What do you think?"

Irwin smiled thinly and held up his hands. "Hey, Colonel. I'm just here to help you guys sell some tickets. I'm not initiated in show management."

"Ah, come off it, Doc!" Garrison snapped. The hero worship and adulation he had bestowed upon Irwin on his arrival had seemingly evaporated in the past few days. Now, he addressed him like he was any other hand in the outfit. "You've been involved in circuses for longer than any of us. You've got a feel for which way the winds are blowing."

The two standing men looked down at the diminutive Doc. "Alright," he said quietly. "What happened with that damn fire eater was a disaster. And you're right, Kal. It's hard to get over something like that. People remember such incidents. But…" he tried to look, and sound, optimistic. "The show must go on, fellas." He rubbed at his shiny bald head. "All I can suggest is some new tweaks to my act. I'll have a think and try some new stunts… or, rather, old stunts that I haven't wheeled out in a while. Something fresh for the next crowd."

Garrison looked down at him. "Tweaks. Stunts." He shook his head.

Klondike took on a defensive stature. He felt obliged to. "Listen, Colonel, if it wasn't for Doc here, we would be in an even bigger mess. Doc and his legend have kept us in the black. For now!"

The Colonel nodded. "You're right. I just… well, after what happened last night… hell, I was out there in the seats, with the dignitaries. The suits. They were…" he swallowed hard. "They were appalled."

Klondike downed the rest of his coffee and placed a hand on Irwin's shoulder. "Leave it with us, sir. We'll come up with something."

He sounded infinitely more confident than he felt. With Irwin at his side, they left the huge executive trailer, and paced down the tiny step ladder out into the dry Arizona morning heat.

"I'm gunna practise some on my mini-wire," Irwin said calmly, "and try a few things."

"Keep it mind-blowing, Doc."

Irwin slowed and studied the circus boss. "It's alright, Kal."

Klondike stopped, and stared at him, frowning. "What's that?"

The veteran stood still, folding his arms. "You're following a path that's right. Chasing a dream, but it's something you believe in. You believe in the Double G. You're standing up for it." He squinted into the morning sun, taking in the rapidly disappearing big top encampment all around. "You're standing up for what you believe in. Nothing finer in this world, you ask me."

Klondike thought for a moment. "Do you believe in the Double G, Doc?"

The smaller man smiled. "Wouldn't be here if I didn't, sideburns."

There was a momentary silence as the two figures, both long-standing custodians of the circus world, looked each other over.

Then, Klondike nodded and slapped Irwin on the shoulder. "Thanks Doc. Catch you later."

As Irwin peeled off towards his unmistakable stars and stripes-decorated camper van, Klondike walked slowly, disconsolate, towards the big top, which was slowly falling in on itself, like a great air balloon being deflated beside a hangar. It was mesmerising, almost melancholy, to watch the great sheets of fabric fall away, creating a field of white and gold on the dusty grass all around.

His ears perked up as he heard the sound of tiny wheels crunching in the soft gravel of the pathway behind him. He half-turned, and tried to smile.

Pamela Hotch was rolling to a stop alongside him. She wore shorts and a purple t-shirt with The Rollergirls logo emblazoned across the front.

"Our beloved tent has been dealt a mortal blow," she said with a cheeky grin. Then she turned to face him. "Like our show, perhaps?"

Klondike grunted. "Never. These things happen. We move on."

Pamela nodded vaguely. "If you say so, boss man."

"I do." He turned again and studied her. "You know, we'll be looking to you Rollergirls to really smash it outta the park in San Diego. We need… well, we need superstars, Pam. You guys have got that star power. That uniqueness. Hell, we need our stars to shine next week. Brighter than ever before."

"Why, Kal, it sounds like you're now dependant on us," she said playfully. Then, she got serious. "Listen, you've given my girls a spotlight. A major spotlight. You can rely on us. I promise. We won't let you down."

He nodded. "God damn glad to hear it, Pam." His dark eyes turned back to the fallen tent, the scores of roustabouts picking it up, in great clumps of polyester fabric. "You Rollergirls offer the fans something they won't get in most circuses, in most towns. Something different and original. I thought that the first time I saw you all in that pier show. The speed, the danger."

He turned to her, with a sudden look of concern. "Just, for the love of god, no falls or mishaps. I beg you. We can't take any more. That fall Linda had a few weeks back was a nasty bump." His eyes narrowed. "How is she doing, by the way?"

Pamela waved a hand through the air wistfully. "Fine. All fine. All part of the game, boss man."

He nodded. "Listen, when we hit San Diego, how about the five of you go skating through town, around the harbour and the tourist areas, handing out flyers and spreading the word?"

She smiled demurely and folded her arms. "All dressed up in our purple stage suits and make-up?"

He smiled back. "Damn straight."

Pamela giggled. "Sure. May well whip up some interest in the circus."

"May well get some gangs of teens following you… all the way to the big top."

With a sigh, he looked around idly at the work crews, all packing away the great tent and the midway stalls. It was like watching a small township getting demolished. All traces of commercialism evaporating with each work detail.

Then, his dark eyes fell back upon Pamela Hotch, staring up at him, as if in anticipation.

He wiped his brow. "Say, this heat is unbearable. You wanna slip on over to the canteen and get a-"

"I'd love to."

She propelled her legs into motion and began gliding along the path on her dust-covered skates.

He struggled to keep up.

CHAPTER 23

The remnants of the much-hyped, but never launched, Courtland and Co Circus lay scattered across the seemingly endless grounds of its owner's sprawling estate.

Broken-down tents, empty trucks, scores of shipping containers and an eclectic collection of fairground stalls sat in a jumbled mess across the once-elegant gardens of the gothic mansion.

The assembled pieces now resembled disorderly debris from some mighty explosion, lying around at random across the estate of Miles Courtland, who had not been seen in days.

Roddy Olsen and Corky watched over the disjointed collection, depressed and aghast by what they saw. They had been walking around the manor grounds, in sheer dismay, taking in all of the many attractions and midway stalls Courtland had accumulated over the past few months, which would now never see the dust of the circus trail, and instead lay abandoned and, seemingly, left to rot. It was an overwhelming, sobering sight. The world of a child's nightmare, a world no one ever wanted to experience.

The two friends came to a stop at a carousel, of all things. The great, multi-coloured plastic unicorns speared on the mighty steel holders looked jaded, bereft of magic and magnificence.

Olsen leant against the edge of the carousel platform, stuffing his hands into the pockets of his favourite green anorak.

"My god, what a sight," he breathed, dejectedly. "All the components of magic time. Just without the magic."

Corky nodded grimly, his eyes darting around the barren stalls, as if expecting an ambush at any moment. "Like a damn funeral wake. Say, where the hell is everybody, anyway?"

"I guess everyone headed out when they heard there was no season. The roustabouts need to sign up to another outfit, while they can. If they can!"

"And what of us two?" Corky murmured sadly. "We've stuck around…to oversee the demise." Suddenly, he ran a hand through his thinning hair in disgust. "What the hell is this? A whole circus operation, a whole schedule, blackballed at the last minute. All those fans out there, left disappointed. Makes me sick."

Olsen shook his head. "I feel for Courtland. This was his dream. His mission in life."

Corky frowned. "Where the hell is he, anyway?"

Olsen pointed up at the giant, imposing mansion house, that seemed to cast an ominous shadow over everything.

"The house staff say he has hardly left his room, these past few days. Sick, apparently."

"Jesus!"

Olsen patted his old friend on the shoulder. "I guess it's time we move on, Corky."

The clown was incredulous. "To what, for Christ's sake?"

"What is it you used to call it? Hound dogging from town to town, looking for action?"

Corky laughed, but his face was pained. "Living like a ham and egger? You're a superstar, Roddy, god damn it! Any circus in the land would be glad to have us. But..." his eyes took on a mischievous look. "I say we contact some of the networks, Rod. And the casinos in Vegas. We've still got a lot of favour out there, man, a lot of interest. We need a big score, and that's where we'll find it. Something big. TV and stage work. Despite everything that's happened this year, the big shot executives will still want us on their shows."

Olsen nodded thoughtfully. "OK. Let's do it. Maybe, between us, we can devise a new kind of show. But let's concentrate on bookings first." He shook his head, feeling overwhelmed. "If only we had some representation. An agent. Someone to handle the deals..."

Corky slapped him playfully on the back. "The first step is getting the hell out of here, Rod." He looked around distastefully. "Hell, we stay around here much longer, our bodies are gunna start decaying, like all these stalls."

"Alright," Olsen said sadly. "I'll get my stuff from my trailer and we can head down to LA." He glanced at his watch. "We can make the midday train and be there for dinner."

Suddenly, he looked up, as if sensing some form of otherworldly existence. Squinting into the deep morning sun, he studied the far end of the gardens.

Two silhouettes were visible against the brightness, like ghostly apparitions in the hazy sunlight. They appeared as shadows in the sunny backdrop, but they were real… and they were heading towards the carousel.

Olsen frowned. He pointed over to the duo, and Corky followed his gaze, also frowning.

As the shadows approached, it soon became possible to distinguish a woman in a dress and a small man, in shirt and tie. They were heading right for them.

Olsen continued to watch them. "That's funny," he muttered, "who on earth can that be? Wandering through the estate, and at this early…"

Suddenly, he froze all over. His body went stiff as a rake, his blue eyes bulging. Corky sensed his alarm, and grabbed his arm.

Olsen shook his head. "No! It… it can't be!"

Then, he shifted away from the carousel platform, deftly stepping forward like a dog sensing a treat. Then, he was off, racing towards the newcomers like a long lost relation. Behind him, Corky grinned widely and started to jog after him.

Olsen ran faster through the grass, until he was just yards from the two visitors.

"Lacey!" He cried in sheer delight. "Lacey! You're here! Oh my god!"

Lacey Tanner, dressed in a beautiful, flowery summer dress, ran also, and the two embraced in the garden like lovers reuniting after a wartime separation.

They hugged warmly, wildly. She held his face in her hands, smiling uncontrollably. "Roddy! It's you!"

"I don't believe it," Olsen was blabbering. "You found me!"

"Always, Roddy, always." Still holding his face, she kissed his forehead. "How I have missed you."

Olsen finally turned and gave Richie Plum a slightly less joyous embrace. "Hey Richie! How ya doing?"

"Just fine, Rod," the little man cried happily. "Great to see ya!"

Corky joined the happy reunion, hugging Lacey and lifting her clean off her feet. "Boy, oh boy, am I glad to see you again, Lacey!"

He shook hands with Plum. "And Richie! It's been ages! What happened to you, man?"

Plum rolled his eyes. "I was tied down in New York after the ship disaster. It was… complicated."

Corky nodded solemnly. "We can only thank you, Richie."

Throughout the whole exchange, Lacey and Roddy were smiling at each other, as if in some kind of trance.

She gazed into his baby blue eyes. He in turn was captivated as always by her huge, all-consuming violets.

"You're here," Olsen said dumbly, in awe. "Out here, after all this."

"We never said goodbye," Lacey whispered, eyes dancing.

"Don't tell me that's what this is? A long goodbye…"

"No," she said gently. "It's the opposite. It's a new beginning. Or a plan for one. A great big welcome back."

Olsen could not stop smiling. He turned to Corky, who looked utterly bemused by it all.

"You've heard about what happened to us out here?" said the clown.

"I know everything!" Lacey cried theatrically. She was suddenly all business again. She pulled on a pair of black designer sunglasses, that looked like they were on loan from Grace Kelly. "More than you boys think. And there is much to discuss, kittens. These past few months we have all… become separated. So very disjointed. So very disappointed."

The four of them stood in the huge, meadow-like gardens, all eyeing each other keenly, as if sensing salvation from one another, from within. It made for a strange, surreal atmosphere.

Corky spoke up. "Word is you got work at some fancy LA publicity studio…"

Lacey nodded. "Work, yes, Corky. But not a purpose. Just an emptiness. A nothingness."

They all looked at her blankly. Like a starlet at a studio audition, the mesmerising Lacey positioned herself between the three men. She smiled as they all gaped at her.

Corky finally broke the silence. "It's real great to see you again, Lacey. But, er, what are you doing here exactly?"

She actually laughed. "On a mission, you might say."

Still the blank expressions encircled her.

Lacey continued. "There's been a lot of big news in the circus world so far this season. I heard about what Ribbeck did to this troupe. And I've heard a whole lot more, boys. A whole lot of bad. About a man we all owe plenty."

Olsen stepped forward. "Kal."

She turned to him. "Right, kitty cat." She lowered the sunglasses down her nose and looked at him. "Have you heard?"

Olsen looked at Corky, and both shrugged. "We ain't heard nuthin' Lacey," Corky stammered. "What the hell happened?"

Lacey spoke quietly. "Kal is in trouble…"

Olsen and Corky stiffened. The clown spoke again. "You want to tell us the whole story, Lacey?"

She half-smiled. "Oh yes, Corky. And so much more."

Olsen studied her. "Like what?"

She turned again, and smiled beautifully at him. An extravagant, overwhelming look, of beauty and elegance and goodness. Pure warmth. How, oh how, he had missed such looks. He could only smile back.

"Well," she said softly, looking at each of them.

"I'm calling it the rescue plan."

The great and the good of Bakersfield society were gathered under one roof at the city's most celebrated landmark, the historic Sheridan Hotel at the heart of downtown.

The setting was the mayor's annual fund-raising ball, known as the California Capital. Held every summer at the Sheridan, the grand gala evening consisted of cocktails and a three-course dinner, followed by a charity auction. Local celebrities, dignitaries, sports stars and TV personalities were all on hand to show their face and do their bit, and all were expected to bid generously for the donated items in the auction later on.

The money raised would all be transferred to the mayor's chosen charities, and the whole shindig was essentially a celebration of Bakersfield and its citizens. At least, the wealthiest ones.

Gino Shapiro looked like a Las Vegas cabaret singer as he wandered casually across the packed Sheridan ballroom, looking resplendent in his classic tuxedo, his jet black hair combed straight back against his scalp.

Even though the circus was set to leave town the next morning, Martha Stanwyck and the stars of her troupe had been invited to the gala evening, considered illustrious visitors by the mayoral staff. When the mayor had heard that the great Gino Shapiro was currently touring with Stanwyck, he had eagerly sent out a further invite to the trapeze star that morning, delivered to the circus camp by courier.

Now, Gino patrolled the floor, receiving a string of pleasantries from passing dignitaries, many of whom recognised him instantly.

With a wry smile, Shapiro slithered up the grand stairwell and walked along the landing above, where men in shiny tuxedos chatted excitedly to women in extravagant cocktail dresses.

He spotted a lone female leaning against the pine bannister, looking down at the thronging masses in the ballroom, many of them dancing to swing tunes softly played by a brass band situated in a gazebo stand in the far corner.

The woman wore a dazzling red dress, and had straight black hair and pale skin. She appeared awkward, nervous perhaps, as if feeling she did not belong at such a lofty public occasion.

Shapiro crept up beside her, and joined her at the bannister, staring down at the extravagant frocks on display below on the dance floor.

"My, my," Shapiro muttered airily, looking straight down at the many assembled guests, "quite the crowd. I feel like I'm at an Oscars party."

The woman nodded, then turned to face the newcomer. Her face seemed to explode into an excited grin. "Oh my god! It's you!" she squealed.

Shapiro laughed lightly. "It is? And who is that?"

The woman gripped the bannister rail, staring at him in awe. "You're one of the circus people! The trapeze artist."

He bowed gallantly and held out a hand. "Gino Shapiro. Pleased to make your acquaintance, Miss…"

"Ackers. Kim Ackers."

"What do you know? I thought you were Audrey Hepburn…"

She laughed over enthusiastically. "Well, she's probably in here somewhere! There are a lot of stars here tonight."

Shapiro took her hand and kissed it quickly. "And surely you are one of them, Miss Ackers. An actress, perhaps?"

She laughed gushingly, one hand on her chest. "Oh my goodness, no! How could you think such a thing, silly. I work in the mayor's office. Administration. I had to help organise all this."

He chuckled. "My sympathies…"

She laughed also. "Well, it isn't all that bad." She took a deep breath. "It meant I got to meet people like you, Mr Shapiro."

He smiled enchantingly. "Well, I have to say that-"

"Well, well, well, if it isn't the debonair king of the air!"

They both turned in shock at the new voice that erupted beside them.

A middle-aged woman dressed in a beige business suit was standing there, staring at Shapiro. She held a notebook and pen, at the ready.

Shapiro gazed at her. "Excuse me, madam, but this is a private conversation."

The woman seemed oblivious. "You don't remember me, do you Gino?"

"Nope."

"Janet Mulverhill. California Today."

He shook slightly. "Ah, yes. Now, I remember. That reporter from San Jose, right? Always following the big circus companies, looking for a scoop."

"You nailed it." Janet eyed him coyly, bringing the notebook up in front of her and making a note. Gino watched her nervously. "Now," said the reporter, "what's all this I hear about your loan spell at Stanwyck's Circus coming to an end?"

"What?" Shapiro was genuinely stunned. "What's that you say?"

"Oh…" Janet said conversationally, "I heard from a booker that Dan Jupiter has recovered from his wrist injury now, and is ready to resume his duties."

"That is false, madam," Shapiro snapped. "Jupiter is nowhere near ready. And, besides, Miss Stanwyck loves my act and-"

"That's not what I heard!"

"What!" Shapiro shook his head, incredulous. "What is this talk? Who you been talking to, senorita?"

Janet had an impassive look. "What happened to your date?"

"Huh?" Shapiro had forgotten Kim Ackers completely. He turned. She had gone. Vanished. Just like that. He looked around desperately for that red dress, but quickly gave up.

He turned angrily to the journalist. "Anyone ever tell you you've got lousy timing, Miss Mulverhill?"

"Yes, and with great frequency."

He stared at her. She remained unmoved. "And yet still, you don't change your ways, eh? Still snooping around, notebook in hand, pouncing on whoever catches your eye."

She raised an annoyed eyebrow. "You're big news, Gino. Face it." She moved a step closer, suddenly looking fierce with determination. "I know you're about to move on, Gino. You'll have no choice once Jupiter is back. People will want to know what big top you'll be performing for. Where they can see you. You've got a fan base, big shot, and the public are interested." She watched him coyly. He stared at her in dismay.

"Alright, alright," she said quickly. "How about a different tact? A new angle." She cleared her throat. "What's all this about that kid you are training? Rogers, is it? You and Murphy are training him up, right? They say he could be the next big thing. How about I do a feature about the kid?"

Shapiro felt like his head was about to explode. "In the name of Sam Hill! How do you know all this stuff? It is impossible!"

Janet smiled smugly. "It is my job to know."

Shapiro signalled to a passing waiter, who held a silver tray of champagne flutes. Reluctantly, he grabbed two glasses and held one for Janet. She accepted.

"Santamaria," he murmured. "You are a real piece of work, Miss Mulverhill. Can you predict the future too?"

They both took a sip of champagne. She savoured the taste, then looked curiously over Gino's shoulder. She smiled oddly.

"Well, I can predict who your next female admirer will be. Maybe your next date, no?"

He grunted, taking a further, longer sip. "Why don't you enlighten me?"

Janet smiled. "She is coming straight for you now. She is truly beautiful. With long, flaming red hair. Cinnamon skin. Enormous eyes. And, boy, can she wear a ballroom gown! She is looking straight at you."

Shapiro looked at her quizzically. Then, he turned. And his eyes almost popped out of his skull.

There she was. But like he had never seen her before.

She was adorned in a beautiful white frock, with straps over her shoulders, and a plunging neckline. Its beautiful material flowed to her high-heeled silver shoes, with a slit at the thigh. Her skin was the colour of a peach, and seemed to shine under the bright lights. A green, seashell-style leather handbag clung to one shoulder.

"Lacey!" Shapiro cried, his voice a curious, uneven whine. "Santamaria, look at you! My goodness, you look like an empress from a Venetian ball. Like an angel from the heavens."

Lacey walked over elegantly, batting her eyelids at the attention. "Gino Shapiro! I thank you. And this from a king, no less."

Shapiro was trying to remain calm. But it was difficult. "What… what on earth are you doing here?"

She raised her beautiful violet eyes and let them settle on his chestnut browns. "Why… looking for you, of course!"

"Ha! I told you!" the forgotten Janet Mulverhill blurted.

Lacey did not avert her gaze in the slightest. Shapiro addressed the reporter. "Do you mind, Miss Mulverhill? We are old friends. You understand?"

Janet was already getting prepared to move on. "Oh, I understand alright." She winked at him. "Just remember what we talked about, huh?"

She disappeared into a crowd of well-dressed dignitaries. Shapiro returned his gaze to Lacey, who had not stopped eyeing him the whole time. It was unsettling, overpowering, and she knew it. She smiled at him playfully, so very comfortable in this role.

"Madam publicist," Shapiro finally stammered. He signalled again for the waiter, who rushed over with his tray. He grabbed a flute for Lacey, and she held it before her. Still, the gaze remained.

Shapiro swallowed hard. "You… you were looking for me?"

"Why of course, baby," she whispered, head held back. "And you aren't hard to spot, are you now?"

He shook his head. "But here? Now? How did you even know I was here… tonight?"

She smiled deliciously. "I knew you were here, in Bakersfield. With the Stanwyck show. I saw this mayor's ball was on tonight, and figured it was worth a shot. Then, I saw your name on the guest list downstairs. It seemed this would be the best way to get you!"

She slowly fished a pack of cigarettes from her handbag, and placed one delicately between her lips, the eyes never leaving him.

Shapiro felt like a gunslinger from the old west as his hand shot to his hip pocket to retrieve his lighter in under one second. He held the light for her. She blew a long cloud of thick smoke into the air above them.

Shapiro felt spellbound as he watched, but shook himself out of it. "And how did you get an invite to this ball?"

She held the cigarette before her, as she often did. "Connections, baby. It's what I do."

Shapiro could not help but smile. "You know, you are one of a kind, Lacey. There is no doubt about that."

He held his champagne flute out before him, and they touched glasses. "Cheers," she purred. "Here's to the future."

Shapiro tried to get serious. "Why were you looking for me?" He cocked his head. "Are you looking for a date for the Met Gala?"

Finally, she cracked a little, shaking slightly with laughter. "Well, you certainly look the part."

"And so do you, Lacey." He straightened up. "But, seriously, why have you come?"

Lacey's uber-confident demeanor seemed to soften. She finally stopped eyeing him, and surveyed the vast swathes of VIPs gathered below on the dance floor. Then, she shot a look at him again. A sharp look.

"I heard about what Ribbeck did to you. At Avalon Pictures. That was scandalous."

Shapiro frowned. "It happens, sometimes. Especially with that treacherous dog." He leant on the bannister, looking her over. "I heard you had gone back into PR again. In Hollywood. This is good, no?"

She stood in line with him, leaning on the rail. Guests passing by stared in admiration at the striking couple.

Lacey took a deep breath. It was time.

"We need you, Gino."

"We? Who's we?"

She turned to face him. "Klondike's Circus."

Shapiro stared at her. He shook his head. "You and I both attended a meeting at Rio Cristo, barely four months ago. I seem to remember hearing the words, 'Klondike's Circus is over.' I saw Kal like I never saw him before, ever. He said it was finished. Everything. You were there, Lacey."

Suddenly, she felt emotional. She grabbed at his tux jacket. "It doesn't have to be over. Just because he said. He finished the circus because of his guilt over the ship sinking. Surely, you can see that, Gino?"

"Well, yes, but…"

She held up a hand. Her entire persona seemed to have diluted. Suddenly, she looked like she might cry. It was an extraordinary transformation. Shapiro sensed it, and held her arm.

Lacey shuddered slightly. "Kal is in trouble, Gino."

That did it. Shapiro stared at her with stone cold vision. "What? What trouble? Tell me, Lacey. You must tell me now."

She nodded vigorously. "If I tell you, will you come with me? Now? Right now?"

There was no hesitation. "Of course. Let's go. You lead the way."

And, just like that, the striking couple, who resembled a leading man and glamorous co-star from the latest Hollywood blockbuster, strode towards the grand stairwell together, arm in arm.

It was a dramatic exit, befitting of their dazzling appearance.

"And now, the stratosphere is reserved for us… and only us."

Eric Ribbeck spoke the grandiose words like an ancient soothsayer prophecising the dawn of a new era. With a twisted grin and wide, staring eyes, he had the look of a man possessed, lost in some deep, full-blown vision.

Seated at the antique ship captain's desk in his executive train carriage, he was proudly surveying a sea of papers, many covered in figures and notations. The words were said to Veronica Hunslett, as many of his wisened musings often were. Veronica sat opposite him at the desk, conservative as ever in a plain grey suit.

Ribbeck, dressed in his favourite burgundy smoking jacket, was grinning across the mighty desk at her. And it was somewhat unnerving.

The circus train was stationary, just outside of Seattle, Washington. They had arrived the previous evening, with the encampment operation now underway outside.

But none of that mattered to the ruler of this vast empire right now. Ribbeck had spent the whole morning going through figures and financial reports. Now, he smiled like a predatory reptile.

"The stratosphere… yes, that heavenly place I have long referenced. Well, Miss Hunslett, now we are all but there." He chortled lightly to himself, fiddling as ever with his ornate Windsor pipe. "The take over the past five shows has been enormous. The reviews breathtaking. And the fan club membership is going up by more than one thousand people every single week."

He leant back in his huge, throne-like leather chair. "And so, we are there, doll. Finally, on the cusp! On the cusp of becoming the world's greatest circus show of all time. We salute Barnum and Bailey and the Ringling Brothers, and their fine efforts for the past century. But, my god, now we are replacing them. Finally assuming their title of the greatest show on earth."

Veronica smiled thinly as he took a deep puff on his pipe. "Congratulations, Eric. You have led this team to the very summit of the circus industry. Now, you stand at the top, the very top. Of that, there can be no doubt now."

Ribbeck purred at the praise like a contented tabby cat. "The fabled stratosphere. The great, white buffalo in the herding range." He leant forward, and his caramel, leathery face took on a hardened look, as he stabbed the air with his pipe. "I said we'd get to the top. And that no one could ever stop us. Nobody, dammit!"

Veronica shuddered internally, but gave an airy laugh. "Of course."

There was a sharp rap at the carriage door. Seconds later, a steward dressed in an immaculate white jacket walked in quietly, gliding over the beautiful Oriental rugs and polished mahogany floorboards to the great desk. He held a small cardboard box.

"Sir," he announced. "The prototype for the Ribbeck World Circus lunchboxes has arrived."

The steward placed the box swiftly before Ribbeck, before smoothly pacing out of the carriage again.

Ribbeck glanced at Veronica and cackled again. Then, like a beggar offered a plate of gold, he grabbed excitedly at the box and ripped it open.

Gasping in awe, he removed a shiny, plastic green lunchbox, examining it as if it were a priceless archeological treasure.

Equally entranced, Veronica stood and paced over to stand behind him. She was mightily impressed. The box contained a dazzling illustration on its cover, featuring the Ribbeck World Circus logo, top centre, and the famed green and purple big top throughout the background.

Interspersed across the cover were comic book-like drawings of Dirk Tempest, Clint Martinez, Calypso the Clown, the Ribbeckettes dance troupe and, jutting out from beneath the circus logo, the Daredevils in their yellow jumpsuits.

"Oh my god, Eric!" she stammered. "This is incredible! What a fantastic design."

"They've taken the bronco to the bull pit with this one," Ribbeck drawled. "What a sensation!" The old man was unusually animated. His green eyes glistened like antique jade.

He looked up at her knowingly. "Another rung on the ladder to greatness, doll. The kids will snap these boxes up."

He placed the extravagant lunchbox back on the desk. "Just think," he mused, "every town we play in… we'll have a superstore on hand, full of merchandise. All for the fans to snap up. Not a gift shop, or a merchandise stall. But a superstore! That's what we'll call it. And these…" he lovingly tapped the lunchbox before him, "these are just the start. Before long, the green coming off the merchandise roll will form a massive part of our profits."

Veronica nodded shrewdly as she returned to her seat. "It is the future, Eric. Mass merchandising will be everywhere one day soon."

"And we've taken the first bold step," Ribbeck snarled.

At that moment, Luca Marconi entered the carriage, merely tapping on the door as he walked in. He hauled a large pile of newspapers under one arm as he paced across the stateroom, before offloading the bundle with a thump on to the antique desk.

"They's the papers you ordered, boss."

"Thank you, Luca."

The bodyguard caught sight of the lunchbox. "Hey, that's real neat. Would you look at that? I gotta hand some of them out at the Bullseye Club in Brooklyn, man."

Ribbeck ignored him. He spoke in a brisk, business-like manner. "What's the word on the circuit, Luca? You hear anything?"

Marconi hovered over the desk awkwardly as the other two eyed him. "Nuh-huh. Nuthin, boss. I been in touch with all our pigeons last night and this morning. There ain't no moves. No shaking. Nothing's happening out there on the trails, boss."

Ribbeck nodded sagely, tapping the stem of his pipe against his teeth, as he usually did.

"Where's Zack Wurley's troupe playing this week?"

"Crankton, Arkansas."

Ribbeck sniggered with contempt. Then, he held his pipe before him. "And Klondike?"

"Klondike!" Veronica cried in alarm. "What do you…" she tailed off as the old man held a hand up to silence her.

Marconi grinned slyly. "That sucker is on his way to San Diego."

"San Diego…" Ribbeck whispered, as if in awe. "That will mean Balboa Park. Beautiful location. A golden harvest for most troupes."

Marconi sneered. "Yeah… most troupes, boss. But not that lame redneck outfit Klondike's rolling with."

Ribbeck eyed him seriously. "No news from Klondike's crew?"

"Not since that disaster in Phoenix. They stunk the place out, even with the great Doc Irwin on board."

Ribbeck continued rattling the pipe stem against his teeth. "They'd stunk out every rec from Memphis to Arizona. Yet Irwin still joined them. Wanted to join them."

Across the desk, Veronica frowned. "What are you saying, Eric?"

"I'm saying what I've been saying for 10 years now. That god damn yahoo Klondike is never through. Just when you think he's finished, he comes up outta the horse manure smelling of roses."

Marconi folded his arms. "He still worries you, eh boss?"

"You're god damn right he does. We've been through too many duels, me and that one."

Veronica leant forward, her pale face a mask of reason. "Eric, you just said it yourself. We are on the stratosphere. Klondike? He's working in a drunk depository, his name forever tarnished by that disaster in New York."

A stony silence filled the majestic executive carriage. Ribbeck's cold green eyes fell back to the lunchbox. What a glorious age we live in, he thought idly, where such novelties were now common place. He shook his head.

"The stratosphere," he whispered, seemingly in wonder. "We are there now. I… I can practically taste it."

CHAPTER 24

The Delano Rossiter Health Spa was a hideaway for the privileged elite of Nevada society.

Beautiful and spacious suites were occupied by politicians and casino chiefs, and more often than not their wives, lovers and mistresses.

The complex boasted five swimming pools, and whirlpool spa tubs, saunas, steam rooms and a magnificent tropical garden.

Nestled deep within the Red Rock mountains, the site resembled a futuristic kingdom with its glass buildings and space age domed roofs.

Deep within the immaculate, marbled hallways and corridors, a network of small rooms served as massage parlours.

Jenny Cross was led face-down on one of the fine, leather padded massage tables, her head placed to her side, and her arms deftly draped on a soft silk pillow. A fluffy towel covered her naked body from the waist down.

She was lost in the comfort and sensual feeling of the massage, her mind subdued as she felt herself seemingly drift into beautiful tranquility.

Towering above her stood a huge, musclebound young man decked out in tight shorts and polo shirt, his hands gently caressing her back and shoulders, like a master healer feeling out some unknown ailment.

"Can you go a little higher, Anthony," Jenny whispered, eyes tightly closed on the bench.

Anthony grinned sheepishly. He moved his hands. "Your skin is so soft and clear, Miss Carson. What is your secret?"

She stirred slightly below him. "Fine living."

The massage continued deftly, the strong, smooth hands moving towards her shoulders and trapezius muscles.

Fine living, she thought idly as she led there. Maybe now it was. But that hadn't always been the case. Years of struggle. Being taken advantage of by promoters, flyers, hustlers, and just about any other schmuck looking to make a fast buck on the West Coast.

Then, prestige. Respect. The lover of one of America's greatest circus managers. And a position as his star flyer under the big top.

That feeling of exhilaration and power had been shot down when he left her. Then came the truly overpowering emotion of her conscience, that had consumed her like nothing before or since. The single most powerful emotion she had ever known.

Vengeance. Redemption. That thirst for hitting back.

All throughout the horrors of her stay at Wrangways Mental Hospital. With every instance of abuse – both mental and physical – the thirst had stayed within her. Controlling her.

Then, after she had tricked Dr Thornton into releasing her from that hellhole, everything in her life had been all about planning her revenge. That hit. And then, finally, that glorious moment had arrived.

Her mind a whirl, she slowly visualised in her head that warm spring morning back in April, when the Floating Top ship had blown up and sunk in New York harbour. She had watched, unemotional, with a face of pure stone, as the liner had disappeared rapidly beneath the waves.

Devouring it with lust from the fake harbour patrol launch she had commandeered, the feeling she had experienced as the vessel went under the waves was indescribable. Untouchable. It had felt like everything she had worked for, all she had dreamed of, was finally accomplished.

She had struck a mortal blow, not just on her perennial nemesis, but on his empire. His entire world. His beloved circus. It had all been vanquished… by her hand. And it tasted delicious.

Since that fateful day, she had enjoyed the carefree life of a socialite. The girlfriend of a casino big shot. A trophy to him, but in her eyes a reward for all her years of suffering. It was the sort of lifestyle she now relished, despite her distaste for Ray Generoso.

She shook internally as she led there. Being placed on his arm was a small price to pay for living like royalty out here.

And, besides, Ray Generoso wasn't forever. Already, she was planning her next chapter. And possibly running away again…this time abroad. Maybe to Europe.

"Don't I know you from somewhere, Miss Carson?"

Anthony's high-pitched voice brought her, reluctantly, back to the present, and the Delano Rossiter Health Spa.

The question was thrown at her on an almost weekly basis. She enjoyed playing with her answers, just for the hell of it.

"Television. I used to play bit parts in shows. Cop programmes, mostly." She grinned to herself. "Then, I took early retirement and came out here to Nevada to enjoy the action. And the glamour."

Anthony chuckled. "Well, there's plenty of that out here, Miss Carson."

She kept her eyes closed beneath him. "And so much more."

Then, with a contented sigh, she let her mind drift once again. With a slight tingle, she pictured her next Martini. It would be waiting for her at the bar when the clubhouse opened at five o' clock. Not long now.

"And so much more."

She looked so young, impossibly innocent, in the picture. Like a Hollywood starlet posing for her first studio shot. A beautiful, pale face and rich, straight blonde hair, her taut and lean figure covered in a red and blue leotard.

Mike Blakelock studied the youthful figure in the snap. She was like a child, full of longing and hope. His mind wandered. It was hard to believe the girl in this photograph had become an unhinged maniac. An alcoholic. One who lived a fantasy. And a soul full of hatred and scorn.

He was sitting at the desk in his small motel room in downtown Vegas. A significant mound of reports and newspaper clippings sat before him, clustered around a glass of bourbon and a plastic ashtray filled with cigarette butts.

He was in the process of placing the papers into an industrial file, inserting each piece neatly into a cellophane holder, as if preparing a business proposal. He was being sure to file the papers in chronological order. The reason? To fully illustrate the alarming fall and rise of Jenny Cross.

He looked again at the portrait of Jenny as a young flyer. His dark eyes drifted down to the small headline beneath the picture.

YOUNG TRAPEZE GOLDEN GIRL JOINS KLONDIKE OUTFIT.

In many ways, that had been the start of it all, he mused.

Blakelock placed the clipping in the file, near the front.

He shook his head, and reached for his smokes. Lighting up, he took a sip of bourbon, and looked over the many stories and articles he had amassed over the past few weeks, all through his research and backtracking.

He worked under a faded desk lamp, which sat at the edge of the table, its feeble glow barely illuminating the clippings, and somehow giving them a dark, macabre feel.

His eyes took in another headline, the next in line.

TRAPEZE QUEEN CROSS IN RINGS HORROR! PARTNER ALMOST KILLS SHAPIRO…THEN HERSELF!

The accompanying picture showed a shaken Jenny, in a brief, shiny leotard, being led away from a giant crash mat by a team of police and security guards inside a big top. Shocked faces filled the background.

He shook his head yet again, then glanced at another clipping.

CIRCUS FLYER CROSS SENT TO MENTAL INSTITUTION!

This time, the newspaper page contained a smaller picture, of Jenny sat in a courtroom, dressed in a business suit.

Blakelock deftly re-read the article again. Then, he inhaled deeply on his cigarette and gazed absently at the desk lamp.

He was sat in a small dome of light, the rest of the tiny room virtually pitch dark at this late hour.

He liked to work this way. And he was proud of what he had come up with. Picking up another clipping, his eyes twinkled. This one he had worked especially hard for. He had found the story, and its all-important picture, after noticing a name in Jenny's diary. A name familiar to readers of the New York Post's arts pages.

The headline screamed: TOP DEALER GRIFFIN OPENS NEW MANHATTAN GALLERY.

The story told how New York art dealer Lloyd Griffin had entertained the city's high society at his new gallery, which had finally opened at a swanky gala evening.

The picture showed a middle-aged man in a shiny tuxedo, clutching an over-sized novelty pair of scissors as he cut a ribbon at the new gallery. Standing next to him was a beautiful woman in a long, sleek cocktail dress, clapping happily and looking proud and regal.

There was no mistake. It was her, alright.

And the gala, the dates and the names involved all tied in with her diary entries from earlier that year. It was beautiful.

Griffin had been some kind of temporary meal ticket. Sandwiched conveniently between Thornton, her saviour from Wrangways, and then Generoso, who represented a portal into a new life. It was all so simple for a woman like Cross. Convenient, and simple.

Blakelock found it all so surreal. It seemed inconceivable…just three years ago, right here in Vegas, Jenny had been involved in a shocking moment in the circus at the Golden Dune casino, almost killing Shapiro, and then herself. Now, she walked easily among the city's power elite, dining at its finest restaurants and attending VIP parties, her true identity unknown to seemingly all who bowed before her. Her only cover was a false name, yet she remained one of the privileged few, living a fabulous lifestyle in the same city that had almost destroyed her.

For the umpteenth time, Blakelock shook his head. He dragged on his cigarette. It was all going to end. Right here, in that same city.

And he was playing the trump card in this dangerous game.

Suddenly working with haste, he began putting the file together at the small motel desk.

He thought it all through in his mind. Again.

Blakelock knew Jenny was staying at the Delano Rossiter Health Spa for the following two nights. A short break, she had told the receptionist at the front desk – if his lip-reading had been correct.

Just as well, he thought. It gave him time to concentrate on Generoso. And the next stage of his carefully constructed plan.

With care, Blakelock filed the last piece of paper into its cellophane covering.

Then, in an almost symbolic gesture, he held the black leather display file before him. He studied it and smiled softly. Finally, he said just one word.

"Bingo."

Suite 1888.

Blakelock had been tipped off by a gaming floor employee at the Xanadu. A 50 dollar pay-off had given him a wealth of information. Generoso used this upper floor suite in the sprawling Xanadu complex as a private business office and general second home.

Flanked at all times by two heavies, the Mob's gaming manager was untouchable at the Xanadu… and, indeed, every casino in the desert.

Now, Blakelock strolled casually along the gaudy green carpeting, as if attending a Sunday social. The corridor was long, but looked immaculate, as if seldom used.

Finally, he reached 1888. Double door. The place must be really something, he thought to himself.

He was dressed in an expensive black and silver business suit, an enormous gold medallion hanging over the front of his shirt and tie. He held the black file firmly in his hand.

Standing outside the suite entrance, he took a deep breath.

Then, he knocked.

There was a long wait. He heard voices. Then, without warning, one of the doors sprung open and a huge, musclebound figure in polo shirt and slacks hovered before him, his immense frame filling the entire doorway. He held a half-eaten sandwich in one hand, and wore a look of disgust.

"You lost or something?" the man snorted.

Blakelock looked at him earnestly. "I'm here to see Ray Generoso."

"Yeah right," the man at the door grunted. "You think you're gunna just walk in here and see the boss!" He took a bite from the sandwich. Pastrami. Then he shook his head. "Get the hell outta here. I'm eating!"

Blakelock remained impassive. "The name's Balzini."

"That the whole thing?"

"I work for Vincent Falconi. Over at the Atlantis. Paradise Valley. He sent me here. We recently came upon some information that Mr Generoso would want to see. Urgent and confidential. The Falconi family said he needs to see this. It's an emergency…" he held the file aloft.

The man stared at the file. "Hey! What you got there?" He made to grab it.

"It concerns Miss Carson."

That did it. The heavy's eyes widened. He looked behind him momentarily. The wheels were turning in his head.

"Alright, get in here."

With that, he grabbed Blakelock's blazer lapels and hauled him in roughly. Once inside, he slammed the door shut.

Blakelock showed no resistance. Once inside, he looked around at the enormous, deluxe suite. It was more like an apartment than a hotel room.

A huge lounging area sat before them, featuring matching leather couches, coffee tables and footrests. An alcove led to a peculiar little room that featured a giant television set and a row of seats, as if transported from a cinema. At the back of the lounge, a spiral staircase led up to the first floor. Beyond that was a bench seat and a giant, floor to ceiling window, that offered an impressive, panoramic view of the Strip.

As Blakelock took in his new surroundings, he was suddenly spun around by the doorman. "Hands on the wall, spread your legs."

He placed the file on a dresser next to the door and did as he was told. The man expertly frisked him, running his hands roughly all over his body, and paying particular attention to his arms and lower legs.

Finally satisfied, the heavy stood back and picked up the last of his sandwich.

"Wait here," he barked.

As the man wandered slowly to the back of the lounge and began climbing the spiral staircase, another heavy appeared from the television room. This man was older, lighter A grizzled veteran, Blakelock surmised. In his experience, heavies and goons came in two forms. The musclebound ape, and the older head. Generoso appeared to have both prototypes within his employ.

The new man wandered casually around the suite, eyeing Blakelock suspiciously. Then, he slumped down on to one of the couches, and began drinking from a bottle of water.

Blakelock continued looking around the huge room. He spotted a large, old-fashioned steel safe in one corner. A money counting machine sat atop a coffee table. Another small table contained the remnants of an abandoned poker game. Large stacks of dollar bills were sat to the side of the cards and chips.

Then, there was movement at the top of the stairs. Blakelock looked up. His eyes narrowed.

Ray Generoso padded down slowly. A large, bull of a man, with a strong-looking neck and receding hair, dressed in a shirt and tie, he resembled a retired wrestler, with an intimidating air and build.

Finally, Generoso reached the bottom and paced slowly across the lounge to Blakelock. The musclebound ape followed him, two steps behind. The grizzled veteran remained on the couch.

"Alright, start talking," Generoso spat out as he stood before Blakelock, looking ready to pounce.

"Thank you for seeing me," Blakelock said in a dour tone. "I work for the Falconi crew over at the Atlantis, in Paradise Valley. As you know, sir, we do a lot of business with the Panuccis here at the Xanadu, and the other casinos the brothers own. One of your board members, Nicky Caprice, is our general manager."

Generoso looked bored, as if he didn't understand. "What about it?"

Blakelock looked deadly serious. "We're all making green together. Your success helps our success. However…" he paused for effect. "Recently, one of our boys brought something to our attention. It concerns you, Mr Generoso. And your personal life. A potential threat. To you and your reputation."

Generoso gave him a look that could only be described as murderous. "What the hell is this?" he roared. His eyes bulged. "If you're looking to take a lifelong bath in Lake Tahoe, keep talking sucker. You don't start making sense soon, you're gunna stop breathing."

Blakelock nodded. "It's your partner. Miss Carson. One of the boys recognised her. From the news. Mr Falconi wanted to bring this to your attention. He did what he always does, and got his private detective to do a file on her. Purely for your attention, sir."

By now, Generoso was riled beyond reason. "You've got a file on Julia?" he cried incredulously. "What the hell is this? You looking to get your head blown off, sucker?" With those words, both of the bodyguards moved to the boss's side, flanking him like guardians. All three men scowled at the newcomer. All looked ready to pounce at any second.

But Blakelock was impassive. His breathing normal. Moving a slow hand, he held up the black file. With seemingly magnetic force, Generoso's eyes followed the item as it was held high.

"Her name isn't Julia," Blakelock whispered. "It's Jenny. Jenny Cross."

Then, as Generoso stared at him insanely, he boldly pushed the file into the boss's chest. Generoso grabbed at it dumbly, and stared at it, as if it held some unknown alien power source.

Without wasting another second, Blakelock turned for the door. He had them surprised, on the hop. He didn't intend to hang around.

"So long," he said over his shoulder as he moved. He made it to the door, opening it quickly and stepping deftly into the plush corridor. He turned.

There was nothing to worry about. Entranced, Generoso had already opened up the file and was studying the first entry, eyes slowly widening. His two goons were eagerly looking over his shoulder, all semblance of order and rank suddenly forgotten after the unexpected revelation.

Blakelock suppressed a satisfied smile. Then, like a departing ghost, he silently closed the suite door and paced rapidly away, down the corridor towards the elevators.

And an escape from this cesspit.

CHAPTER 25

One of the most geographically fascinating cities in the world, San Diego had always been a utopia within itself, with a charm matched by few metropolises anywhere in the US.

The burgeoning city was built upon canyons, hillsides and mesas – with the flat mesas used for commercial development and properties, and the steep, urban canyons left wild and untouched. The result was a curious hybrid of a bustling municipality mixed with eye-catching parks, ridges and red rock peaks, which all blended together and formed this unusual community.

Often referred to as the birthplace of California, it was the first site visited and settled by Spanish explorers, and the area's Hispanic heritage is obvious in just about everything projected throughout the city. From shops and cafes to churches and office blocks, most of the architecture resembled Spanish colonial housing and missions, giving much of the city a vintage, European feel.

The jewel in the crown of the Hispanic city was undoubtedly Balboa Park. A 1,200-acre complex, it is surrounded by a beautiful urban forest containing rare trees and groves, while more than 20 different gardens can be found inside

The park hosts various museums, theatres, restaurants, and a zoo.

Its wide promenades and boulevards were filled with buildings in the Spanish colonial revival architecture style.

Much acclaim had been showered upon Balboa Park down the years, but the one commendation most often put forward concerned its supreme levels of cleanliness, leading many media observers to describe the grounds as "sparkling".

Descending upon this urban utopia of immaculate gardens and red rock ridges came an enormous convoy of trailers, camper vans, flatbed trucks and transport vans, totalling more than 40 vehicles.

The almighty caravan of motors rolled slowly down the main San Diego highway, passing through the city limits at a leisurely pace, as if trying to keep perfect formation.

The trailers featured a glittering array of colours, with many covered in banners that read: DOUBLE G CIRCUS!

At the head of the brightly coloured convoy was a large silver camper van featuring a huge metal circus sign on its side.

At the wheel, Heavy Brown smiled with pure glee as he looked around, wide-eyed, at the memorable sights and scenes of San Diego.

Beside him in the cab of the great trailer, Klondike also stared at the passing scenery, spellbound as always by the environment down here at the southern-most tip of California.

"All roads lead to San Diego…" Heavy mused as he deftly steered them down a main road, past the renowned San Diego harbour. The waterfront looked more like a Mediterranean port, with its whitestone beach houses and cantinas.

"A famous circus man once said that," Heavy continued as the trailer passed the harbour area and both men stared in awe. "Before a big show here."

Klondike nodded as he watched the waterfront whizz past. "Billy Robinson. 1952. He pitched up at Balboa Park too. For the show of his life."

Heavy grinned, hands firm on the immense wheel. "Just a perfect spot for a circus, man. That park is a beautiful, beautiful sight."

Klondike tried to smile. "Especially for our sore eyes."

The trailer continued through the city suburbs, leading the massive convoy of trucks and vans.

City residents stopped and stared as the colourful procession lurched past. Many pointed, a sight the circus troupe glimpsed in every town and city they played in, anywhere in the country. Excited children became a touch animated by the new arrivals, and young and old alike took note of the banners and boards on the vehicles, trying to catch the name of the troupe – and the names of any performers advertised.

However, any well-versed city resident knew exactly where the convoy was heading. There was only one place any circus performed at when in San Diego.

Finally, the vehicle caravan arrived at the main entranceway to Balboa Park, a large and heavily wooded gateway at the foot of Cabrillo Bridge.

Once inside, the convoy rumbled through a pleasant clearing and on to the famed El Prado, a long and wide promenade that runs directly through the park's centre and upon which most of the main featured attractions can be found.

El Prado lead the procession all the way to its latest home, the sprawling Cortez Garden.

With its immaculate, peppermint green grass and surrounding forestland, the spot felt like a rural outpost located within luscious countryside, not a wide open space sat right in the middle of a big city.

As the trailers and camper vans slowly drove into the Cortez Garden, heading for the far side, where they would all park up, the troupe members felt like they were entering a secret garden, a hidden world from a dream, all nature and beauty, a real-time Garden of Eden.

Klondike and Heavy were the first to park up on the far edge of the green. Climbing out of the trailer, stiff from the 10-hour drive from Phoenix, they waded out onto the carpet-like grass.

"Beautiful, just beautiful," Heavy muttered as he looked around, gaping.

"All roads lead to San Diego," Klondike repeated with a sly grin. "Let's hope our road is a path to redemption. A glory trail."

Heavy held out his arms. "This is the perfect setting for something special."

Klondike watched as the never-ending conveyor belt of vans and trucks manoeuvred their way into parking spots at the end of the massive garden. He squinted into the sun-kissed forestland all around.

"This has been a happy hunting ground for us in the past. Why not again?"

He chuckled slightly at his own musings. "Why indeed…"

Within six hours of arrival at Balboa Park, the Double G Circus encampment was up and running.

The pristine Cortez Garden had been hastily transformed into a giant circus midway, with the troupe's stalls and booths erected across the immaculate peppermint grass, forming the usual shanty village that visitors would enjoy. The sea of trailers – homes to every man and woman involved in the circus – was conveniently settled behind the midway, largely out of sight.

As always, at the head of the makeshift community was the enormous white and gold big top, which had been raised in seemingly record time in the late morning sun.

The tent was up, and now the roustabouts, all bare-chested and wearing stetsons and neckerchiefs, were placing the chairs and arena barriers inside. Not to mention the countless sacks of sawdust.

Inside the great tent, Klondike was instructing several of the roustabouts with specific orders. This show was to be attended by a string of well-known media commentators, people Klondike had known for years. He was determined to construct a press area for the esteemed reporters. Their presence here could actually spell a disaster for the Double G, he told himself. However, they deserved something special as they were making the effort to visit.

Klondike watched as the team of men placed several leather-backed chairs in a vague square formation, clustered around four smart tables. The area was separated from the general seating by a run of gold bunting.

As Klondike watched, he sensed Heavy ease up alongside him.

"Almost like the old days," his old friend grunted. "Press zones. Dignitaries. Prestige." He watched as a roustabout dusted off one of the fancy leather chairs. "I can't help feeling this is the wrong show for all this, old buddy."

"I dunno," Klondike murmured. "The people love their circuses down here. This could be our salvation."

Heavy eyed him mischievously. "Care to put your faith to the test, Kal?" With that, he whipped out a pack of cards, seemingly from nowhere.

Klondike could not help chuckling. Their old ritual. Cut the pack, and the cut card acts as some kind of metaphor or omen for the season.

"I thought we'd stopped all this after pulling out that damn joker on the ship to Europe!" Klondike rasped. "Hell, that card sure told the story of that tour." He frowned. "Besides, we already did this year's cut. Back at Sidewinder. Seems like an age ago. Everything is different now, man."

Heavy raised an enquiring eyebrow, shuffling the deck. "All the more reason to cut for this season again. Why, it's about time."

With that, the big man deftly placed the red and blue deck of cards upon a storage box lying beside them. "Go ahead, Kal. Put your weight on it."

Klondike grinned. With a playful sigh, he approached the tall box and slowly moved his hand to the cards. He paused, closed his eyes, and grabbed at the cards, raising up about a third of the pile in his grip. Opening his eyes, he showed Heavy his bottom card.

"Well?"

Heavy's eyes widened. "Well, we sure as hell haven't cut that one before."

Klondike frowned and turned his hand around.

There it was. The queen of diamonds.

"Well now," he said softly. "What in the world could-"

His thoughts were suddenly interrupted by a high-pitched whining coming from the tent's flap.

"Mr Klondike! Mr Klondike!"

Klondike and Heavy turned. It was Betsy. She raced into the big top, holding up her long blue dress slightly to allow her legs to move faster.

Heavy moved towards her. Klondike frowned, placing the cut deck back on the box and following. The two men broke into a jog as an alarmed Betsy ran towards them. They all met directly in the arena's centre.

"Betsy! What happened?" Heavy roared as they came together. He held the youngster in his meaty hands. Klondike caught up to them and noticed the tears in her eyes. He was about to speak when he noticed another figure lurching towards them.

It was Hondo Cloud. And there was a problem. He spotted it immediately. His right hand was covered in a white hand towel. White… with red swathes all over it.

Klondike left Heavy as he calmed Betsy and immediately strode towards the Native American.

"Hondo! What the hell happened? Tell me that hand ain't injured?"

Cloud looked genuinely crestfallen. Defeated. His left hand held the towel over the right. He winced as he spoke.

"Damndest thing I ever saw," the burly figure rasped through gritted teeth.

"What happened, dammit?"

Cloud shook his head. "I was practising that knife juggling act. You know, the spectacular version, what you showed me, Kal."

Klondike grimaced, and shuddered internally.

"Anyway, I, ah, well, I musta misjudged the fall, or the pressure, or the weight, or something…" Cloud stammered uncontrollably. "And, well, the blade came down like a rocket and damn near sawed my hand off."

Klondike placed a hand on the thrower's good arm. He raised his head and bellowed towards the roustabouts carrying the chairs. "Medic! This man needs medical attention. Someone fetch the designated medic. Now!"

One of the cowboys left the chair assembling detail and raced for the flap.

"Here, look at what happened…" Cloud mumbled, fiddling with the hand towel, now coloured a deep crimson.

"No!" Klondike barked. "Keep it covered, and tight! The boys will bandage it up and get the pressure on it. We'll get you a doctor right away."

Betsy and Heavy had now joined them. Betsy was breathing deeply, her eyes locked on the injured hand. Heavy stared at the mass of blood, then looked knowingly at Klondike.

"Nasty injury, Hondo," he said dumbly.

Cloud looked up at Klondike in despair. "I'm so sorry, Kal." He thought rapidly, eyes maddening slightly. "But, don't worry, brother, I'll be alright for the show. We have a week to prepare. I'll rest the hand, and it will heal just fine."

Klondike was already shaking his head. "Even if it does, you're still out, Hondo."

The thrower seemed incensed. "But we have plenty of time, man! It will heal by Saturday."

Klondike was angry now. "God damn it, Hondo. We're talking about throwing knives here. At your woman! Not spinning plates and twirling batons. This is serious! You've cut your hand open! You're not gunna be on the sawdust any time soon."

Cloud took a step forward, still holding the hand tightly. "But this is too important a show! We need-"

Klondike held up a hand. His dark eyes seemed inflamed. "I said you're out, man. Now, you got that?"

Both men stared at each other in sheer defiance. Each had eyes like coal, deep and cold.

Then, a middle-aged man in a large stetson and plaid shirt raced over, carrying a green medical bag.

"Alright, son," the newcomer blurted, "now just you let me take a look at that."

Klondike stood with Heavy and a sobbing Betsy as the apparent circus medic looked over the hand, holding it tenderly. He quickly wrapped a fresh cloth around it, tight. Then, he put a hand around the hulking Cloud's waist and made to heave him away. "Come, let's get you in my trailer."

He turned to Klondike. "We'll stitch him up real good, Kal. There's a call in to a local doctor. Won't be long getting down here, I'm sure."

Klondike nodded. He didn't even know the man. "My thanks."

The two men slowly wandered back towards the flap. Betsy tapped both Heavy and Klondike on the shoulder. "Thank you, boys," she whispered before hurrying over towards her stricken boyfriend.

Then, as they all departed, Cloud turned slowly towards the two authority figures in the centre of the arena. He was almost at the flap now, and called back a final message.

"I'm sorry, Kal."

Then, the three of them were gone, back into Cortez Garden.

Klondike and Heavy stared vacantly at the flap the trio had just passed through. Both were silent for several moments.

Finally, Heavy broke the eerie silence in the vast, empty tent.

"God damn it. They're dropping like flies."

Klondike removed his hat, ran a hand through his thick black hair, and gazed around, as if in some kind of trance.

Heavy looked at him, studying his oldest friend. He suddenly felt sad. Dejected.

Before the start of this spring, Heavy had never seen Klondike look as dispirited and frustrated as he did now. Sadly, this year, he had glimpsed this very look on multiple occasions. Throughout the tour of Europe, and, most emphatically, on the bridge of their boat, the Floating Top, when it had suddenly and unexpectedly exploded beneath them.

Now, that look was back again. And it was one of utter despair.

Klondike almost staggered as he walked, lurching through the sawdust, his feet seemingly stuck in treacle-like ooze.

He wandered absently back towards the seating area he had been supervising just moments earlier. Concerned, Heavy followed obediently, rubbing at his hands.

Then, Klondike fell heavily into one of the audience folding chairs, that had been simply left lying around for now, like many others.

He rubbed at his eyes viciously. Heavy moved slowly, standing next to him, over him. "We've been blessed, got lucky, so many times down the years, Kal," he whispered gently, placing a hand on his shoulder. "This year… well, maybe this year it's the house's turn. To win some of that credit back."

Klondike's eyes were still closed. "You mean, this year we're cursed? All these damn mishaps? Walsh, Peerless and now Cloud." The eyes finally opened. He looked drained. "This year… this time we suffer! Somehow… it just ain't gunna happen for us?"

Heavy looked down sadly. "Sure feels that way, Kal."

Klondike shook his head irritably. "No. I can't accept that, Heav. That forces greater than man are somehow conspiring against us. Making us fail."

Heavy patted his great friend on the back as he sat sprawled in the chair, on the edge of the sawdust. "We always find a way."

The big top was completely empty now, save for the two of them. The roustabouts erecting the makeshift press area had headed back outside to unload more equipment. Klondike and Heavy were completely alone within the tent. All felt suddenly quiet and crypt-like.

"There's always a way," Klondike said softly. Then, curiously, his eyes shifted to the storage box sat next to him, and the deck of cards he had just cut. With a frown, he picked up that queen of diamonds, studying it with seeming interest.

The immaculate Dobie Shears illustration of the queen stared back at him.

Then, in a queer, subconscious, dream-like moment, he thought he heard cheers outside. Some applause. Shouting. He shook his head.

Then, his eyes studied the queen. With a huff, he threw the card back down upon the box.

But the vision of the queen of diamonds directly before him was replaced with the sight of a similar figure, decked out all in yellow.

A woman, appearing silhouetted in the bright sunlight at the flap.

She was walking towards them now. She wore a yellow blazer, pencil skirt and high heels, and seemed to glide across the sawdust.

Klondike smiled to himself. His mind was obviously over-animated and playing tricks on him. Playing out now was one of the happiest memories of his life. The first time he had ever laid eyes on Lacey Tanner. Back at their old circus camp in Santa Cruz, northern California. Four years ago. She had rolled up to their dirty, dusty headquarters in a fancy yellow Corvette, dressed all in yellow, looking like a European Countessa.

"Er, Kal..." Heavy mumbled dumbly beside him.

Klondike shook his head. Then, he rubbed at his eyes again.

This was no daydream. No figment of his imagination. It was real. It was happening.

There was a woman. Right there in his tent. Walking towards him. And dressed all in yellow. Black sunglasses covered her eyes. And there was a beautiful smile beneath them, which warmed him even from that distance.

Klondike involuntarily shuddered in his chair, pushing himself back. He blinked multiple times, rubbed yet again at his eyes.

"Wh… what the…" he murmured absently. His head was spinning, and he felt like he was hallucinating. He stared entranced at the graceful figure in yellow, coming closer to him with each step.

That walk. Those clothes. That elegance. All had featured in his happiest memory from Santa Cruz all those years ago. And they were all back… back, right here and now. And they were here to form what was undoubtedly, inexplicably his new favourite memory – of all time.

He sat bolt upright in the chair, transfixed and gaping.

Finally, the woman decked out in shining yellow was upon them. She stood, five yards before him, like a royal embracing her court. Hands on hips, she looked up at the tent's summit, across at the chairs encircling them. And then, at last, the huge black sunglasses dropped, and the beguiling eyes fixed upon the seated Klondike. The smile was ever present.

"Hello, tiger."

It was as if someone had pressed a button. Klondike sprung out of the seat like a jack in the box. He stood there, gaping like a zoo animal.

"Lacey? Lacey? Oh my god! Is it really you?"

She held her head back, and used one of his favourite expressions. "Damnnnn straight!"

Then, she removed the shiny black sunglasses, and he felt himself fall hypnotically, truly lost, into her beautiful violet eyes. They seemed to sparkle like never before.

"And it looks like I'm just in time, baby," she purred. "It would appear we've got a lot of work to do."

Unashamedly, he had fallen into her arms like a lost child reunited with his mama. He couldn't help it. What he felt at that moment was truly overpowering.

Lacey held him tight, despite the size difference. It was like a kitten holding up a Rottweiler, but she managed it. She closed her eyes, smiling warmly and nodding to herself. After several seconds, a tear rolled down her cheek.

Then, she moved an arm and motioned for Heavy to join them. Not one accustomed to such scenes, Heavy nevertheless threw himself into the mix, happy to be part of a three-way hug.

The trio held each other for several seconds. All alone in the centre of the empty big top.

Then, Klondike finally pulled himself away. He looked dumbstruck.

"Lacey, you're here!" he kept blurting.

Heavy held her by the arms. "It's really you," he said mischievously. "Oh my god, it's so great to see you again. And what a surprise!"

"Great to see you, Henry," she panted, trying to remain calm. As she addressed Heavy, her eyes were on Kal. "I thought I'd surprise you boys down here."

Klondike seemed to take a step back to study her. "God damn, it's good to see you, Lacey. And, well, I feel like I'm dreaming. This is the exact same outfit you wore…"

"The time we first met." She finished for him. "I know. It's all for effect, tiger. Like everything with public relations." She gave him a beautiful, wanting look. "You once said the greatest thing that ever happened to your circus was the day I, er, 'waltzed' in." She laughed dizzyingly. "Well, now I'm waltzing in again, boss man. And trying to make a similar impact."

Klondike's head was spinning. "What are you saying, Lacey? And, damn it all to hell, what are you doing here? Where did you come from?"

She stared at him directly, all business suddenly, despite the high emotion. "What I'm saying, Kalvin, is that your new circus is a shambles." She held up a firm hand as he made to protest. "I've seen the reviews, heard the talk. You're lurching from one crisis to the next. So there is only one conclusion." She moved a step closer, and then suddenly lost the seriousness and smiled deliciously. "You need me!"

Klondike stared at Heavy. Then back at her. "I can't find no argument, Lacey."

She began pacing around before them, her eyes dissecting all aspects of the big top. "So I am here to save your circus, kitty cat." With a theatrical flourish, she removed her blazer. The two men stared at her beautiful, off the shoulder frock. She threw her hair back in a fiery gesture. "I've been working for a LA PR firm these past months. It's all very well, the pay is good, but... well..."

Heavy, eyes wide with wonder, stepped toward her. "But it's not the circus, right?" He laughed spasmodically. "You miss this, don't ya Lacey?"

She tried to maintain a straight face. She wanted to scream with joy. "Of course!" She turned again to Klondike, looking full of exuberance. "I've been following the Double G Circus, ever since I read you had joined up here. And I've been in pain reading about all the misfortunate you've suffered, Kal." She shook her head in defiance. "But now... now, the tables are going to turn, baby. I have a beautiful plan. The wheels are already in motion. We're going to make this show in San Diego one of the greatest nights in circus history." She began breathing heavily, almost hyperventilating. "It's time... it's time to save the Double G, boys! And that... that is why I am here!"

Klondike and Heavy stared at her, as if facing a crazed revivalist promising the Second Coming.

"Er, Lacey," Klondike muttered, trying to remain calm. He rubbed at his stubbly jaw. "Maybe you don't know what has happened in our outfit down here. We are losing talent, fast, as well as losing face with the fans. Ticket sales are weak, and we don't even know what kind of show we're gunna be putting out on Saturday."

Lacey surprised them once again by smiling knowingly, as if at some unknown, internal joke. She made a magician-like flourish with her hand. "Did I neglect to mention..." she whispered sweetly. "That I didn't come alone?"

Klondike felt an electrical pulse buzz through him, like a bolt of lightning. Heavy experienced a similar sensation.

"Er, what's that?" Klondike prompted, eyes wide.

Lacey grinned like a Cheshire cat. As if on cue, another round of cheers erupted from outside the tent. More applause.

"What the hell *is* that?" Heavy blurted.

"Let's see, shall we boys..." Lacey murmured in a tantalising tone as she turned and paced towards the flap.

Klondike and Heavy followed like lapdogs, hungry for a treat. The trio marched rapidly across the sawdust, their collective pace quickening as they neared the exit.

Lacey reached the flap first, and in another grand gesture, held her arm wide, motioning for the two men to go ahead.

Klondike led the way, wading through the short exit tunnel in an apprehensive state, as if awaiting an ambush. Squinting as he came under the edge of the domed polyester ceiling, he felt the mid-afternoon heat smother his frame instantly.

But what greeted him in Cortez Garden took his breath away.

Directly before him was an almighty throng of humanity. People were everywhere. It was the roustabouts, all congregated together in a big circle. There were others, too. Members of the public, he guessed. Day trippers to Balboa Park.

Everyone seemed excited, enlightened, bubbling.

Klondike frowned, exasperated. What were the work teams playing at? Everyone was smiling as if they'd been given the rest of the day off.

Then he saw it. What all the commotion was about.

With another tingle that ran through his body, he noticed three figures in the centre of the gathering. Everyone's attention was directed towards them. The trio were shaking hands, signing autographs and posing for pictures with the army of excited well wishers. They were celebrities. Not just here, but anywhere.

No, Klondike thought, his mind racing. Again. It can't be!

He recognised the three newcomers, staring at them through the crowd. And he felt as if he was gazing at stardust itself. They were here. It seemed inconceivable. But they were here.

Gino Shapiro.

Decked out in a caramel tracksuit, wearing aviator shades, the superstar trapeze ace looked, as ever, like a million bucks. He was posing for pictures with several teenage girls, while exchanging banter with the roustabouts. His hair and skin looked like they had been sculpted from wax. Every part of his being seemed to shine.

Roddy Olsen.

In a Hawaiian shirt with white pants, the youngster with the thick blonde hair was performing voice tricks for a pair of young girls, while men in stetsons watched, roaring with laughter.

Corky the Clown.

Dressed in his trademark yellow and brown polka dot suit and bowler hat, the beloved funnyman was high-fiving a seemingly endless line of roustabouts, who all seemed to have frozen in shock.

Klondike felt Heavy move beside him. The duo quickly stared at each other, then back at the miracle-like scene before them.

"OK, now I think I really am dreaming," Heavy whispered in awe.

Klondike could not stop smiling into the sun-lit parade. "I thought that inside when Lacey appeared. Now… well, we must be hallucinating in the sun, old buddy."

Then, Lacey stood between them both. She seemed ecstatic, and put her arms through each of theirs, linking herself in the middle.

"I thought your circus could use some help, boys," she purred. "And I knew where to find the best in the business."

"Oh my good lord, Lacey," Klondike wheezed.

Then, the three performers in the middle of the excited hubbub simultaneously noticed the arrival of Klondike outside the big top.

All three gently eased themselves away from the fans, and made their way over. Like mythical spirits in a heavenly vision, the trio floated across the gardens, as more clapping and excited chit chat echoed around the park.

Then, they were stood majestically before Klondike, Heavy and Lacey. All together again.

Shapiro took a step forward. He somehow looked younger, fitter, more agile. What had happened to him?

"Chairman!" he roared. "They tell me you need some guys for Saturday night." He looked around airily. "It just so happens I'm available."

"Gino!" Klondike barked. His face exploded into a delighted smirk. "You're here! I don't believe this!"

Shapiro shook hands warmly with Klondike and Heavy. "I was in the neighbourhood," he said, before patting Lacey's shoulder. "And madam publicist here tracked me down."

Klondike was shaking his head incredulously. His gaze moved on to Olsen, who was grinning at him like a mischievous juvenile.

"Roddy," he whispered in a dream-like tone. "This is unbelievable. I thought you'd be in the movies by now. Or locked down to a Vegas gig."

Olsen came forward, and shook hands with everyone. "Kal. It's a long story. But..." he gazed up at the imposing white and gold tent towering directly above them. "I'm hoping it will have a happy ending."

Klondike cackled wildly and slapped the youngster on the back.

Then, in a wonderful scene, Corky ran up to him and the two hugged like reunited wartime brothers.

"Ah Kal, I can't tell ya how good it is to see ya again," Corky bellowed.

"Believe me," Klondike said happily, "the feeling is mutual."

As Corky gave Heavy a similar bearhug and they all stared at one another, Klondike looked out dumbly at the mass of roustabouts and passers-by, who now all stared at the reunion with awe.

It was a surreal scene, and the circus boss simply did not know what to say or do.

He stared at each of the performers again, as if checking it was really them, here and now in San Diego.

Heavy put his arms around Olsen and Shapiro in an unusual show of deep affection. He nodded at Klondike. "Looks like we're putting the band together again, Kal!"

For the umpteenth time that hour, Klondike shook his head in utter disbelief. Then, his gaze fell upon Lacey. She had been stood to the side, watching him, proudly, a strange paternal glow emanating from her angelic presence.

"You did this, Lacey," he said in a dreamlike tone. "You did all this. You rounded these guys up, didn't you? Brought them here? The biggest stars in the circus world... all here, at the Double G! It seems impossible."

Lacey folded her arms gaily. "Like I said, tiger. I came here to save your circus. With a few, ah, blockbuster signings."

Klondike kept shaking his head. Now, he gazed queerly at Shapiro, Olsen and Corky. They all looked happy. Content.

"You came back," he blabbered, standing before them. "You all came back. But why? Why?"

Shapiro stepped forward. "Sometimes, amigo, a man does things because it seemed a good idea at the time. This…" he gestured to Klondike, the assembled group, and then the almighty tent. "This seemed like the best idea of all time."

Klondike laughed in a wild fit. Then, Lacey strode towards him in a curious manner. She magically pulled a cigar from her person and held it before him. "Here!"

He opened his mouth on her command, and she firmly wedged the cigar in the corner of his gums. Then, she produced a match, again from out of nowhere, and lit it on the side of a gatepost. She held the flame before his mouth, and he lit up, a great cloud of purple smoke quickly enveloping them both.

Klondike held the cigar happily before him, surveying the people all around them.

"Lacey," he barked, "let's go to work."

CHAPTER 26

Colonel Griff Garrison had the look of a long-serving inmate glimpsing his first sunset after busting out of jail.

Dressed in a spotless beige suit with chestnut shirt, he wandered around giddily inside the big top, staring at the assembled group before him with utter glee.

Klondike had introduced Lacey and his three former star performers earlier, bringing everyone across to the owner's trailer for a big welcome. The circus owner had almost passed out in shock at the extraordinary revelations put forward by his manager. Lacey, taking charge of affairs, had suggested a meeting in the tent an hour later.

Now, inside the vast, empty big top, it appeared the Colonel's aura of shock and disbelief had not worn off. Far from it. The veteran stared at Shapiro, Olsen and Corky like a boyhood baseball fan meeting his idols before a match. His wife Karen was also present, having entered moments ago with a cup of coffee for her over-excited husband.

Klondike and the others all sat in the comfy leather chairs in the hastily prepared press area, looking up at the Colonel in a form of wonder, waiting for the man to finally say something legitimate.

"This is all so completely fantastic," Garrison finally blabbered. "We were down and out, practically. Stars injured. Another one expelled. People laughing at us. A schedule in ruins. And now… now this!"

He suddenly paced hot-footed over to the press zone and stared in triumph at the gathering. "Three of the greatest names in world circus. Here… here! At my show. Ready to perform for us. To star for the Double G!" His animated grey eyes locked on to each performer, then floated across to Lacey, sat next to Klondike at the front. "And you, Miss Lacey. From what Kal and Heavy have told me about you, well, they made you sound like some kind of angel. Well, now I can begin to understand what they were talking about. You've flown in here… and, just like that, changed everything."

Lacey nodded, lighting a cigarette. "Kal and I have a long and rich history, Colonel Garrison. I heard he was in trouble, and acted accordingly." She blew smoke sweetly into the air like a teen hep cat. "He needed me."

Garrison nodded eagerly. Karen spoke from behind him. "We thank you, Miss Tanner. For all that you have done. Which is plentiful."

Lacey smiled. "Me and the boys are delighted to be here."

Garrison's wild-eyed gaze shifted to Klondike. "I knew it!" he stammered. "Bringing you here, Kal. You're a magnet for stars. I knew only good things would happen. This is why we wanted you here, dammit. First, Doc Irwin. Now… oh my, now your old Klondike's Circus stars. All here!"

Klondike frowned. "With respect, Colonel… this season has been a disappointment, both commercially and critically. I appreciate your kind words, sir, but I have hardly worked any magic for you. After that last show in Phoenix, we'll be lucky if they ever allow us back in town again."

Garrison stepped towards him eagerly. "But now…"

A new voice broke the animated exchange.

"But now… it's a different ball game. The commercial appeal is going to skyrocket."

Everyone turned towards the flap, where the high-pitched tone had emanated from. Klondike could not help but cackle.

Richie Plum had wandered into the tent, dressed in shirt and tie and with the obligatory leather file under his arm.

They had all reunited with the finance whizz earlier outside the big top. As always seemed to be the way, Plum had gone unnoticed as everyone swanned around Lacey and the three performers she had recruited.

Klondike leapt out of his chair and paced over to Plum, putting an arm around him and nudging him gently to the front of the assembly.

"Colonel," he barked, "meet Richie Plum. My old finance manager. He'll be going through the books and, well, I guess he'll be the one to say whether or not we've been a commercial hit."

Garrison and Karen both approached and shook hands with the newcomer. "Mr Plum," said Garrison, "an honour, I'm sure."

Then he grinned at Klondike. "Hell, you're bringing an A-list team out here, Kal. I don't know how to thank you. How to thank all of you!"

The assembled group all looked up at him, a sea of faces displaying hope, tinged with concern.

"My Colonel," Shapiro said loudly from the press desk he was seated at, legs folded on the table. "I will need to see your trapeze rig pronto. I understand it has been stuck in a van all summer."

Garrison gazed at the flyer dreamily. "Yes, of course." He held his arms out. "Anything you guys want, just tell me or one of my crew. We'll make sure you're as comfortable as possible."

Corky spoke up. "You're very accommodating, sir. We are all happy to be here."

Garrison stared at him. He was still gazing around in a dreamlike manner. "All these years of running a circus… we never actually had a clown. Not even one! Now, we have Corky!"

"Don't start welling up on me, Colonel," Corky called. He pulled one of his customary pink handkerchiefs from his sleeve. "Here, dry those eyes."

Everybody laughed.

Then, Karen stepped forward, staring at Olsen. "I've got to ask you, Roddy," she said in an almost frightened tone. "Have you brought Rusty Fox?"

"Of course," Olsen replied. Then, he made a curious cupping gesture with his hands over his mouth.

A gruff, Brooklyn accent suddenly boomed across the tent, seemingly coming from the park outside. "Will you guys knock it off? A fox needs his sleep."

More laughter.

Then, holding a hand up, Lacey finally rose and stood alongside Klondike and Plum to the side of the group.

"And so it begins," she announced airily. Her face turned serious, businesslike. "Alright, folks. We have one week. One week… to prepare, publicise and then execute a circus show like no other. Ladies and gentlemen… I give you the Double G Circus Comeback Special!"

An almighty cheer went up. Garrison was practically beside himself by now, eyeing Lacey like a child watching a light show.

She continued in a sharp tone. "Time is short. We have to reach out far and wide. But, ultimately, everything is here that we need." She began pacing in front of the gathering, incessantly eyeing the great circle of chairs that filled the edge of the arena, as if the sight troubled her.

"One week. Saturday night will be the biggest show in the history of the Double G. The biggest circus show in America this summer, if I have anything to do with it. But, for that to happen, our publicity has to be perfect. Overpowering. I have already drafted up a new press release, advertising the star power of Gino, Roddy and Corky, together with the great Doc Irwin of course. They will go out tomorrow morning to every outlet in California, and some beyond. There will then be a press conference on Wednesday morning, three days before showtime. The Pizarro Hotel, on the waterfront. A pristine, prime location. I have reserved the conference room. Payment is on arrival. Then, interviews with Kal, with you, Colonel, and with the talent in the afternoon. If all goes to plan, the local TV crews will want to come here to Balboa Park and run features on what is happening."

She paused for breath, trying not to smile at the sea of astonished faces staring at her. "Tomorrow is meet the public day. Every one will be in San Diego, getting out and about, having photo ops. The Rollergirls will be skating around town, handing out flyers and arousing interest in the show.

"The box office is opening tomorrow morning, no matter what. People will want tickets right away, and we've got to ensure they have them. And then…" she waved her hand around in a circle, indicating the perimeter of the tent. "We need more chairs in here. We've got to get grandstands set up, like we had at Klondike's Circus. The more paying public we get in this tent, the better it is for everyone. More profit, more acclaim, more word of mouth, more commercial viability. I'll, er, see what I can do on that score."

She finally stopped talking, still eyeing the rows of spectator seats around them. Then, she looked up suddenly. Everyone seemed to be nodding in agreement. Klondike kept his arm planted around Plum, a knowing smile on his lips. "My oh my, how I have missed that," he said happily.

Garrison was staring dumbly at Lacey. Klondike was trying not to laugh at how animated the Colonel had become.

"Miss Lacey," the older man stammered, "that is sensational. You've managed to arrange all that in one day?"

She sat back down again, reaching for her bag. "One morning, actually, Colonel."

Garrison clapped his hands with delight. "God damn…"

Klondike spoke up. "Our Lacey is the best in the business, Colonel. A publicity whirlwind, alright."

Heavy had taken it all in, arms folded, at the front of the gathering. "And she's got some very exciting ideas for the actual show, too."

Lacey was pulling some papers from her bag. "Some special set pieces for our, ah, night of stars."

Heavy turned to face Shapiro, Olsen and Corky. "You boys have got one week to practise for this. You're in a whole new troupe… new tent, new equipment. Hell, a new crowd."

Shapiro looked across at Olsen, then nodded. "And a whole new roster, amigo. When do we meet our new team-mates?"

There was a sudden silence in the great tent. It was Karen who finally spoke.

"Well, dinner is served in the canteen in one hour. Seems as good a time as any."

And that was the truth.

Everyone gathered in the chow tent as the sun began to set, casting a beautiful brownish orange glow across the stunning Balboa Park.

The spacious grey marque was full of neatly arranged tables and chairs, with a long buffet station full of mixing bowls of vegetables and chilli, and platters of hamburgers and sandwiches. Pitchers of milk and lemonade were everywhere.

All of the Double G troupe found themselves drawn to the three celebrity newcomers, who were currently standing around the temporary bar area at the far side of the marque.

The big canteen was soon full of excited chatter as the talent all made for the small mahogany bar set-up.

Shapiro, Olsen and Corky all shook hands and exchanged pleasantries with Arletta LaRue, the Riders of the Double G, the mighty Soolaimon and several show stewards. Then, the Rollergirls all approached, led by a beaming Pamela Hotch. The skating team were dressed in flamboyant purple vest tops, with the Rollergirls logo splashed across the front, and beige shorts, and all looked tanned and lean.

Despite the fact both Rawley Walsh and Hondo McCloud, who up until now had been the undisputed stars of the Double G Circus, were both still in hospital, the atmosphere was jovial in the camp.

The trio of newcomers were treated like saviours in the canteen, praised and celebrated by their wide-eyed brethren.

Shapiro had just kissed the hands of each of the Rollergirls as they lined up to meet him, when a new voice broke the camaraderie.

"Gino! I almost didn't recognise you."

Shapiro glanced up in alarm. His glistening black eyes narrowed slightly at the sight of the small, bald, older man, dressed in an American flag-inspired tracksuit.

The newcomer continued. "Until, that is, I saw you around the ladies! Now, I know it's really you!"

Shapiro smiled tightly. "Doc Irwin." He seemed to forget the five women stood around him and turned to the older man, extending his hand. "Been a long time."

Irwin smiled genially. "Not since I performed for Ribbeck back in the day." They shook hands. Irwin looked skywards. "Funny to think, we were on the same card back then. Now, all these years later, here we are… together again, with Kal. Out here!"

Shapiro nodded. "I heard you had hooked up with Kal a few weeks back. I must confess amigo, I was shocked. I thought you were performing for the president, or some such thing…"

Irwin chuckled. "I was getting disillusioned with the A-list, let's say. Fancied a new challenge. And, boy, did I find it!"

Shapiro smiled. He turned to Olsen and Corky standing at the bar beside him. "You'll remember our clown here from the old days, Doc. This here is Roddy Olsen, our resident doll man."

Irwin laughed and shook hands with the others. "Corky. Great to see you again. A true pleasure." He eyed the youngster with the beautiful blond hair. "And Olsen… boy, have I heard a lot about you, young man."

"Mr Irwin," Olsen cried enthusiastically, pumping his hand, "it is a true honour, sir. I can't believe I'm going to be on the same card as you. I saw you perform as a kid."

Corky chimed in. "Old Doc here has been around longer than cotton candy. And he's still the best there is."

"You're too kind. All of you," Irwin boomed. He stood up straight. "Well, boys. I'd like to buy you all a drink. To toast your joining us. And us performing together. What'll it be?"

Shapiro grinned. "Sarsaparilla."

Olsen looked embarrassed. "Orange soda."

Corky roared with laughter. "Hell, I'll have a real drink. Scotch, please!"

Irwin was laughing as he nodded at the barman. "Well, I'm having milk. Cheapest round I ever bought!"

At that moment, two newcomers wandered over to the group and hovered besides Shapiro. A musclebound African American and a teenager with reddish blond har. Gino nodded as they joined him.

"Ok folks, say hello to Andros Murphy and Tommy Rogers. Murph here is my support man. Tommy is, well, an apprentice, let's say."

They all shook hands.

"Glad to have you onboard," Corky said. He studied the tough-looking Murph. "Well, Mr Murphy, you're not as pretty as Gino's last support, I'll say that!"

Murph grimaced playfully. "Or the last 10, from what I've heard."

They all laughed.

As the talent all mingled happily, many finally serving themselves some dinner, another group had already filled their plates and were now seated in the opposite corner of the marque, eagerly watching the performers mingle before them.

Klondike, Heavy, Lacey and Plum all sat around a large oval table, transfixed as they watched Irwin shake hands with the three old favourites.

It was as if the past three months had never happened for the four of them as they sat there, together again, eating and drinking and discussing business. Nothing felt unusual, despite the time apart, and their own individual ventures in different spheres of existence.

Now, they were back together as one, and that was all that mattered right now.

Klondike could not have felt more at ease. He had his three closest lieutenants back around him again. As if by magic. The cooling effect it had upon his conscience was overwhelming. A true blessing.

"Would you look at that," Heavy was muttering as he held a hamburger before him. They all studied the performers at the bar. "All back slapping, hand shaking, laughing and joking. Like they's old pals."

Lacey watched with animated eyes. "That has gone down exactly as we hoped. They are all friends. It's perfect." She scooped a big spoonful of chilli from her bowl, smelling the mixture with glee.

Klondike was watching everything with a wisened glare. "Shapiro and Irwin will get along fine. They respect each other. And they have worked together before, which always helps. Olsen seems to be in awe of Irwin, and Doc likes the kid's act. No one ever has a problem with Corky. So, all in all, it's a good mix."

Plum was chewing thoughtfully on a breadstick. "Gino…" he mused, "something has changed with that guy over the summer. He seems to be more relaxed. Affable."

Klondike nodded. "He's seen the other side of celebrity. The dark side. Both in Europe and now out in Hollywood. It's no doubt made him appreciate everything he has, or had, back here."

"He'd do anything for you, Kal," Lacey murmured. "I just know it."

Heavy finished his hamburger, and reached for a glass of beer. "Well, it's just as well they're all getting along real nice." He looked up blankly. "If they are going to do what we've got in mind for this show on Saturday, they're gunna need to work like blood brothers, man."

Plum shook his head. "I'm still nervous about all this, guys."

"Just relax," Klondike said softly. "We've done this type of gig before, most recently in Rome. And look at how that went down. The only real difference here is we're putting Doc in the middle of it."

"That's kinda why I'm nervous," Plum whispered.

"Don't be," Klondike replied, still eyeing the group in the opposite corner of the canteen. All of the troupe members were now sitting down at the assembled tables with drinks and trays of dinner. "Doc Irwin is the best wire walker in the world. Hell, he's more comfortable up there than he is on the ground. You can throw any change of routine at him, any alteration in his act, even at the last minute, before he goes on… and it won't make one god damn bit of difference to him. He is purely at ease on his high wire, no matter what."

A curious silence engulfed the table. Lacey, drinking from a tall glass of wine, finally spoke. "Well, hopefully they will all get it perfected in rehearsals." She watched each of the assembled performers with her giant eyes, which probed around the table. "This is our grand finale, boys. The showstopper. For our big show. We can't afford any foul-ups. This is going to send the Double G Circus into super-stardom, if I have anything to do with it."

Plum stared into nothingness. "And we all have one week to make this show great. One week!"

Heavy nodded, munching on another hamburger. "That's some tight odds."

Klondike glanced across at Lacey. They locked eyes. An unseen, mutual pulse seemed to pass between them.

"That's how we like it," Klondike said.

Lacey smiled playfully at him. "Damnnn straight!"

An avalanche of public relations activities and communications seemed to erupt from the encampment in Cortez Gardens over the following two days.

Fresh press releases, photographs and newspaper packs were mailed and couriered to news outlets across the west coast.

The Double G Circus's talent set forth through the streets of San Diego, meeting the public and posing for pictures. The tourist-heavy waterfront area seemed a very happy hunting ground, where the performers were recognised and swamped by amazed passers-by.

As planned, the Rollergirls skated around the historic city with gusto, handing out circus flyers, talking to locals and stopping for pictures. The team also spent a great deal of time playfully batting away the attentions of excited male teens, who seemed to follow the ladies in purple everywhere.

Corky the Clown was also a ubiquitous presence across San Diego, wandering around the waterfront and the park, putting together balloon animals for children and performing hand magic. Like the Rollergirls, he soon had a crowd of youngsters following his every step.

Lacey's other big order of new A3 size posters also arrived at the camp. Klondike and Lacey had long argued for the value of show posters, which seemed to work as well, if not better, than word of mouth, advertising and press coverage.

Lacey had somehow rapidly designed and ordered a whole new range of posters, at her own expense, seemingly before she had even arrived at the camp.

Now, there was an all new Double G Circus poster, that looked more like a Las Vegas show bill. The background consisted of a cactus-filled desert, with a snap of the white and gold tent at the top, and then miniature shots of all the talent exploding across the page. Superimposed pictures of Shapiro, Irwin and Olsen were dominant in the centre of the piece. Each were dressed in their trademark costume – Shapiro in his fireball orange singlet, Irwin in his stars and stripes tracksuit, Olsen in that silver waistcoat.

The Rollergirls were pictured skating away at the bottom, as if about to burst straight out of the poster. Cowboys dressed in silver filled every corner, each firing his pistol straight ahead.

The large heading at the bottom was in a gold, wild west-style font, and screamed: THE ALL NEW DOUBLE G CIRCUS PRESENTS… THE SAN DIEGO SPECTACULAR!

Before long, crisp new Double G posters were appearing all over San Diego. Aside from the main show bill, there were single posters of Gino, Roddy, Doc, Corky, the Rollergirls and the

Riders of the Double G, all stuck to bus shelters, news stands, shop doorways and waterfront walls.

Lacey had sent half of the roustabout detail off on poster sticking duty over the course of one morning. The results were emphatic; leaving no one in any doubt that the Double G was in town.

Her publicity machine had hit top gear, and the effect was astonishing. Klondike, Garrison and Heavy simply could not understand how she did it.

Designing so many posters, having them printed and ready to go so quickly, not to mention the creation and distribution of a plethora of press releases and media packs… the whirlwind of work was otherworldly. And it had all come together in barely two days.

Before long, an excited throng of spectators had gathered around the perimeter of Cortez Garden, all eager to catch a glimpse of the big top, the midway and, if they were lucky, one of the performers. The assembled group seemed to hold a non-stop vigil outside the circus camp, seemingly present at all times.

The hastily assembled box office cabin at the entrance to the midway entertained a conveyor belt of humanity, with a long queue forming outside.

When a convoy of giant flatbed trucks arrived, all carrying temporary grandstands, it was like a missing piece in a puzzle had arrived for Lacey.

Her grand scheme had seemed outrageous to many when she had first outlined it two nights ago in the tent. An impossible dream perhaps, the fantastical claims of a Hollywood big shot far from home.

The delivery of those grandstands proved that this remarkable publicist had delivered on every scheme she had foretold. This was like watching her grand prophecy slowly unfold.

And whenever anyone asked her how she did it, she always had the same response.

"I know a guy," she would say mischievously.

CHAPTER 27

ALL SET FOR THE SAN DIEGO SPECTACULAR!

By George Merrill, San Diego Citizen

Balboa Park is abuzz with talk of the superstar circus playing out in our fair city this Saturday night.

And, in a remarkable twist of fate, this show is threatening to become one of the greatest big top attractions ever to hit San Diego.

The troupe is called the Double G Circus, and is led by none other than Kal Klondike, who we all remember from those TV specials a few years back.

However, in an incredible coup for the former knife thrower, his big top and all circus lovers in the city and beyond, Mr Klondike has managed to reunite several of his old stars for a highly anticipated night of action.

Most will recall that his former troupe, Klondike's Circus, folded earlier this year after an ocean liner transporting them back from Europe sunk off the coast of New York, killing a team of horses and causing untold carnage.

Since that fateful day, the evergreen Klondike has been running the low-key, Sierra Nevada-based Double G, traditionally a wild west show.

However, this Saturday, Klondike and Co have somehow recruited an all-star trio synonymous with his old show – in the form of trapeze flyer Gino Shapiro, ventriloquist Roddy Olsen and all-round entertainer Corky the Clown. Now, add all that to the show's recently acquired signing of legendary wire walker Doc Irwin and you have quite the line-up.

Klondike's team haven't wasted a second publicising the appearances of these all-stars, with posters showing their faces covering almost every wall in the city centre.

Now, all eyes are upon Balboa Park this Saturday as circus fans young and old gather at the Double G's glorious white and gold big top for the stage spectacular.

The assembled media gathered in the grand lounge of The Pizarro Hotel, nestled at the heart of the beautiful San Diego waterfront.

Within the gaudy, green-carpeted room, several neat rows of chairs had been arranged directly in front of a long rectangular table that sat at the front of the lounge.

A beautiful red tablecloth had been draped over it, with several microphones connected to a sound system sat in place on the surface. Behind the great table an enlarged Double G Circus poster sat mounted on the wall.

There were between 20 and 30 reporters in all, professionals from press, magazines, TV, radio and a smattering of freelancers and stringers. They all sat expectantly as the big clock at the rear neared 10am.

Finally, the circus people all entered from a side room, with the assorted press gang offering hearty applause at the arrival.

Klondike sat at the very centre of the table, with Gino Shapiro and Doc Irwin on either side of his frame. Corky the Clown and Roddy Olsen sat at the two ends, with Lacey stood to the side, dressed in an immaculate white trouser suit. At the side door beyond, Colonel Griff Garrison hovered excitedly, the lines in his rawhide brown suit sharp as razor blades.

As the gathered crowd offered their welcomes, Lacey held up a hand and uttered a loud introduction.

"Ladies and gentlemen of the press," she squawked, "thank you for attending our press call. Please state your name, outlet and question for the panel, one at a time. There are press packs on your seats, which include free passes to the show right here in fabulous San Diego. If you require more information at the end, please see me. I will do all I can to help. My name, for those of you who don't know, is Lacey Tanner, head of publicity for the Double G Circus. My business card is in the packs."

She came up for air, looking about excitedly. The turnout was better than she had hoped for. "And now," she announced, "I give you the stars of the Double G!"

A second fainter round of applause followed. Klondike held up a hand in thanks. He was wearing his standard attire of brown leather jacket and fedora, and the press gang were lapping it up. He looked more like an adventurer than a businessman.

"Thank you," he began." I'd like to thank all you people for coming out here today, to the wonderful Pizarro Hotel, here in this beautiful city." He paused, eyeing the sea of expectant, longing faces, all staring right at him. A cascade of camera lights flashed, suddenly forcing him to close his eyes in shock. He quickly got back on track. "The Double G is aiming to create history on Saturday night. With the greatest show in the company's long and illustrious timeline. We hope it will be remembered as one of the greatest circus shows in San Diego history too." He stopped, then hesitated. "OK, we will happily take your questions now, folks."

A sea of hands shot up from the press pack. Lacey pointed and orchestrated the questioning.

A suited man with white hair opened the proceedings. "Alan Becker, California Today. This must feel like some kind of fairy tale for you, Mr Klondike. Back with all your old superstars again, after the death of Klondike's Circus back in April."

Klondike baulked slightly. "Er, yes, well… it has taken a bit of magic, a little luck but… well, we are back together again now. Getting Gino, Roddy and Corky onboard here at the Double G is a real blessing, and we are all eternally grateful and very excited."

Becker titled his head. "And how did it all come about?"

Klondike smiled. There was no other way around it. He turned, still smiling, to Lacey at the side of the gathering. "It is all thanks to Lacey Tanner here, folks. After we all went our separate ways earlier this year… well, we all experienced different outcomes. Lacey here wanted to come back and help me. And she persuaded these three to join her. It was a wonderful moment."

Lacey looked at him from her standing position. There was no beaming, no blushing. The consummate professional, she offered him a curt nod.

Then, Becker inexplicably fired a question at her. "What made you rejoin Klondike, Miss Tanner?"

Lacey stared at the reporter with a cool gaze. "Kal Klondike and his circus gave me the greatest time of my professional life. When the chance to work with him again presented itself, I did not hesitate." She fired off the response as if she had memorised it earlier. "Now, next question, please."

She pointed at a young, feisty-looking woman.

"Joan Abbott, Entertainment USA." The reporter glared across at Klondike up front. Lacey suddenly regretted choosing her. "This has all worked out quite well for you, hasn't it Klondike?" She stood, clutching her notepad loosely. "Four months ago, you were at rock bottom. That ship of yours on the seabed of the Atlantic. Branded a horse killer… as well as a dream killer. And now…" she raised her hands theatrically. "And now all this. The so-called San Diego Spectacular. All these big-name stars. All this prestige. It would seem you've done alright for yourself… out of a disaster."

Klondike glared back at her. He and Lacey had prepared for a response such as this. They just hadn't expected it so early on.

"Is there a question attached to all that?" he rasped.

Abbott looked around the room airily. "I suppose my question is… do you deserve all this acclaim?"

Klondike tried to remain calm at the table. His performers all looked across at him with concern.

"Listen, lady," he barked, "in this business, you get what you deserve. Four months ago, I *was* at rock bottom. Devastated. Closing down my own circus, my pride and joy, the bedrock of my existence. I had offers, sure, but I chose to join Colonel Garrison, and make a go of the Double G. We've had some tough times along the way, but we've made the best of it. These people have chosen to perform for me, for my show, because they know that I'm honest and fair. That the public will come to see a circus with my name attached to it. They know I'm a man they can trust."

Abbott opened her mouth to speak again, but Lacey was having none of it. "Next question. You, sir!"

She pointed at a jovial-looking man in a red suit.

"Chuck Hayes, West Coast Weekly. My question is for Doc Irwin. Doc, you've performed for some of the biggest circuses in the world. What made you decide to join the Double G?"

Irwin, resplendent as ever in his stars and stripes tracksuit, leant back in his chair. "Well, son, I've known Kal Klondike for more than 20 years. We worked together in our youth... well, his youth! And I always kept an eye out for what he was up to. I'd been working for the Sherman Brothers, out of Chicago. Big time troupe. You could say I became disillusioned with how those boys ran their outfit and, well, ultimately, I longed for the honesty and integrity of a guy like Kal here. That's about the whole of it."

Hayes raised an enquiring eyebrow. "There's a rumour, sir, that you walked out on Sherman because he stopped your All-American Association passes for vulnerable children."

Irwin stared back impassively. "I have no comment."

Another young man jumped up on Lacey's mark. "Jim Corrigon, San Diego Citizen. This one's for you, Gino. Is it true you were getting more fan mail than Richard Lewis when you were working in the movies earlier this year?"

Shapiro burst out laughing, and stood up, showing off his immaculate grey fur coat and huge golden belt buckle. He held his arms out wide. "But of course, señor. More fan mail than anyone in the movies! And that was just as a stunt man!"

"Then why did you leave Hollywood?" A new female voice boomed across the lounge. Shapiro squinted across the assembled press corps. Then he sighed. Janet Mulverhill, who he had last seen at the charity ball in Bakersfield last week, stood up at the very back.

"Well, Miss Mulverhill, it is a long story."

She looked across the room knowingly. "Did Lewis have you booted out because you were more popular than him?"

Shapiro chuckled. "That would make a good scoop, no?"

Lacey had pointed at another reporter.

"Bill Carson, LA Tribune. I have a question for Roddy. Rod, what happened with Miles Courtland and the Courtland and Co Circus? That was a massive story for us all a few months back. He pulled the plug just a week before the launch date!"

Olsen nodded vaguely, a little disconcerted. He tried to look confused. "You probably know about as much as I do, friend. Mr

Courtland told me in a meeting it was all over, just as we were about to head out for the first tour. It was a great disappointment. Mr Courtland was, well, devastated."

Carson leaned forward hungrily. "Isn't it true that the show was pulled due to interference from one Eric Ribbeck?"

Olsen looked downwards. "Well, you'll have to ask Ribbeck about that."

"What are you doing here, Roddy?"

The sudden enquiry came from Alan Becker in the front row. He was gazing at Olsen with a queer, desperate look on his ageing features. "You could have gone to Hollywood, Las Vegas, the big networks. But you chose the Double G! You chose San Diego!"

Olsen looked almost sad. "Alright. I came here because I believe in the project. I believe in Kal Klondike. And I believe in his management and way of conducting business. Buddy, that is more beautiful than all the stars in Hollywood, and all the neon lights in Vegas."

Becker grinned like a cherub as he hastily noted down the words. The quotes made for fantastic copy for his magazine. This was gold dust.

Then, another male voice boomed across the lounge. "Tom Peterson, Sacramento Journal. Corky the Clown, how does it feel to be reunited with Kal again?"

Ever the entertainer, Corky took his cue. "Just so beautiful. You know, it makes me want to sit right down and cry…" With that, he produced one of his custom polka dot handkerchiefs and dabbed his eyes before blowing his nose, emitting a deafening roar akin to a fog horn that reverberated around the press room. Everyone laughed.

But the laughter soon died out at the next question.

"What do you say to people who call you a horse murderer, Mr Klondike?"

It was her. Joan Abbott. She had called out the question uninvited while the others chuckled merrily.

Klondike stared over at her, as she sat back, almost hidden in the direct centre of the press pack, toking on a cigarette.

Lacey was flapping on the sidelines. She held up a hand angrily. "That is a completely inappropriate question for-"

"I say they don't know what they are talking about!" Klondike rasped. The press gang seemed to hush as one. Lacey shot him an icy, irritated stare. In the corner of his eye, he saw her shake her head imperceptibly.

"And how is that?" Abbott asked sternly.

Klondike cooled significantly. "What happened on that ship was an accident, pure and simple. How could I have anything to do with an explosion like that? It was..." he hesitated, and seemed to crumble slightly.

The assembled reporters watched him with rapt fascination. The lights on him suddenly felt brighter.

"It was what?" Abbott mused, seemingly enjoying the exchange. She raised that enquiring eyebrow again. "There are rumours of sabotage. An attack. Foul play. Would you, ah, care to comment on any of these claims, Klondike?"

Klondike took a deep breath. He avoided looking at the feisty reporter. "All I can tell you, Miss..." he let the words hang tantalisingly in the air. He thought of the Floating Top. Of Mike Blakelock. And of Jenny Cross. That wave goodbye she had given him. The one he still saw in his nightmares.

His face remained impassive – a craggy, grizzled rock, like the edge of a dynamited granite quarry.

"All I can tell you," he continued, "is that it's all being taken care of."

The words were uttered with chilling finality. A cold air of disbelief and disenchantment spread across the assembled journalists. They all stared at Klondike, and no one seemed keen to challenge or question his assertion. It was a somewhat unsettling silence.

Lacey had watched Klondike with mild distress, and had suddenly found herself lost in the moment.

She quickly came back on track, raising her hands.

"Alright, are there any more questions?"

Several hours later, they walked leisurely along the waterfront, seemingly carefree and without haste.

It was a beautiful spot, with an enormous, mile-long asphalt promenade running parallel to the Pacific beyond, alongside marinas, bars, cafes and tourist shops. Piers offering up bowling alleys and carnival games jutted out into the mighty ocean, while pleasure craft were tied up to awnings along the promenade's stone walkway.

"I still can't believe you came back."

He said the words softly, as if in a dream, as he gazed out at the endless tide to their left.

Lacey smiled tightly. She tucked her hand under his arm, as she always used to. My god, my god, Klondike thought. How he had missed that feeling. All of this. Just her presence, knowing she was close.

"Of course I came back," she breathed quietly. "I never wanted it to end. Never even knew it had ended. Don't you remember, tiger? Back at Rio Cristo? You told us all to leave. The next day was like a Biblical exodus."

Klondike shook his head as he studied the mighty Pacific. "Argh, I don't know what I said. It was like a nightmare come to life."

She threw him a haughty sideways gaze. "You were drunk."

He rolled his eyes. "So were you!"

Now, she giggled. "Who could blame us? That day…" her mind flashed back through time, to when all the assembled performers had turned away from the stage. The grim finality of it all. "That day was something I hoped I would never experience. It was like watching our… our castle, that we had built together, like watching it all come crumbling down. In our hands."

They walked on, past a small pavilion and a length of green wooden decking, where fortune tellers, caricature artists and street dancers gathered daily, out to make a living. Klondike looked at them all as they haggled with big city tourists, the exchanges polite and affable.

The promenade walkway soon became narrower, with canning plants and factories now running alongside the path.

"It's been a whirlwind of a year," Klondike muttered. "I just hope it ends on a high with our show on Saturday."

Lacey's voice became very quiet, almost a whisper. "We haven't even talked about Daryl."

Klondike closed his eyes. "I'm sorry. I should have told you, and offered to take you to the funeral."

"I heard about it after I'd already moved to LA. Saw the news in an out of date trade journal." Her huge violet eyes fell on him. "My first thought was of you, Kalvin."

"The funeral was a terrible day," he muttered icily. "What made it worse was learning I'd been blackballed out of his organisation by his money-counting cronies, damn them all to hell."

She patted his arm soothingly. "He'd be proud of you, Kalvin."

Klondike nodded vaguely. Then, his eyes caught sight of one of the many Double G Circus posters that were littered across the waterfront. It was stuck to the side of a small beach hut.

Absently, he mouthed out the words emblazoned across the jazzy show poster.

Then, he looked down at Lacey alongside him.

"Let's just do the old man proud on Saturday."

Gino Shapiro picked up the tray of drinks from the bar and slowly ambled across the crowded tavern to the corner table he had picked out earlier.

As he sidestepped bar patrons and moved around groups of revellers, many gaped at him and offered greetings. It was hardly a surprise – his face was plastered across posters covering half the city.

He finally reached his table and grinned at Murph and Rogers, who were sat in the booth watching all the comings and goings.

Shapiro placed the tray on the mahogany table top. One Sarsaparilla, one beer and one coke.

As he settled down, Gino held his tall glass high. "Well, boys, here's to our latest venture, and the big show on Saturday!"

Murph grasped the beer and clinked glasses. "Well, I guess I owe you one, Gino. You got us a gig… and what a gig! This show on Saturday made the local news, I saw it on the common room TV this morning."

Shapiro chuckled. "Does your Gino ever disappoint, eh? Though we really are indebted to Lacey. Madame Publicist. Without her intervention, I would never have known about any of this."

Murph nodded as he sipped his beer. "She is quite a dame, that one." He eyed a group of rowdy youths as they nosily passed their table. "And what of Klondike? Your 'chairman'? You think he'll take us on after this? Permanent?"

Shapiro studied his old friend, who looked wired, ready to pounce. "But of course."

Murph's big buggy eyes narrowed. "And do we want to stay on? Ain't there a bigger gig out there somewhere…"

Shapiro shook his head. "There is nothing bigger than Kal's shows."

Rogers had watched them with wide eyes as he nursed his coke. Finally, he joined the conversation. "Listen guys, I sure appreciate you all taking me along and all, but… well, I still don't see how I fit in with your act. With any of this. I mean… what the hell am I doing here?"

The other two scowled at him. Then, Shapiro patted his hand. "Is ok. My dear Tommy, you are here to learn. To watch, to listen, to remember. And to train with us. Consider yourself our training partner. You, ah, will help keep me in tip-top shape, eh?"

The youngster stared at him. "You mean, like a coach?"

Shapiro frowned. "More of an understudy."

"Understudy." Rogers went slightly glassy eyed. "Now that I like." He sipped his coke, still looking at them awkwardly. "But I still feel bad taking wages from Mr Klondike when I'm not really doing anything."

"You'll work, kid, don't you worry. An extra pair of hands will be a blessing. You can help carry equipment, bags, you get the idea."

Rogers looked at him glumly. "Bags…"

Murph roared with laughter, slapping him heavily on the shoulder. "Come on, kid. Look at it like this. You're the future." He put an arm around him and pointed at Shapiro. "You're learning from the best in the business. What could be better?"

Rogers smiled again and raised his glass. "Here's to you, Gino. The debonair king of the air."

Shapiro held his Sarsaparilla high. "Here's to all of us. What an adventure we have had. And long may it continue."

She had been skating around town for hours. But she felt like she could do this forever.

Pamela Hotch glided slowly around Balboa Park on her roller-skates, not needing to concentrate on her legs and feet in the slightest. She could do this blindfolded and with her hands bound behind her back.

Her grandfather had handed her a homemade pair of skates when she was seven. That had been the start. She quickly got the hang of it. Then, she started rollerskating to school every day.

While at high school, she began entering regional, and then national, competitions, and soon became a star athlete in the burgeoning world of rollerskating tournaments.

When she was offered money to perform skating tricks by a carnival owner, she had a vision of a superstar team of performers, as radiant as they were spectacular. Pamela then spent the next three months travelling the country, scouting other performance skaters and cutting deals, eventually forming the Rollergirls.

Now, as the sun began to set across the fabulous Balboa Park, she slowly winded her way along a circular cement path and into Cortez Gardens.

The sight still made her tremble slightly, seeing all the trailers and midway stalls assembled within the shadow of the mighty big top at the head of the clearing.

As was her new custom, Pamela swung in and out of the various pathways between the trailers and cabins, skating at barely a crawling pace as she slalomed along, gazing at all the activity around her. Roustabouts were still busy carrying boxes and chairs… it never seemed to end.

Bending slightly, she swung between two of the larger, executive trailers in the packed-out setting. It was like visiting a holiday camp site, even down to the smell of fresh hamburgers cooking on a hotplate.

Pamela found herself at the perimeter of the camp now. With a faint smile, she slowed right down to a stop at a most peculiar sight.

There before her stood the unmistakable American flag-coloured trailer. And outside the vehicle was its owner's practice wire. A mini-contraption, consisting of two 10-foot steel platforms and a thin plastic cord running the 16 feet between them.

And sat upon the practice wire was its owner, Doc Irwin. The rubbery, plastic tubing was barely an inch thick and hung high off the ground. Yet old Doc sat there as comfortable as a junior high schooler on a swing. Arms folded, lost in thought, he was perched up there in shorts and vest, content and complete.

"Hello up there," Pamela called. She had stopped skating and walked slowly over to the wire, the skates making her stride look ungainly.

Irwin shook himself out of his reverie, and glanced at her. "Hello... down there."

She lurched across to the bottom of one of the platforms supporting his wire, and grinned up at him.

"Your balance is just incredible. Have you, like, ever fallen off one of these things? Ever?"

Irwin chuckled as he remained perfectly still. "A few times, back when I was starting out. Long before you were born, lady." He cocked his head, eyeing the camp as it spread out before him from his lofty perch. "Balance is all in the mind. If you think you're gunna fall, that's just what's gunna happen. If you convince yourself that the wire is no different to the earth, and you just have to walk, and move, as if you're on the ground... well, eventually it becomes normal to you. To your mind and your body."

Pamela smiled up at him, leaning on the platform rigging. "You make it all sound so easy. You're the only man in the world who can do this."

Irwin shook his head, rocking slightly as he sat on the slender wire just above her. "Well, there are a few of us still around. But wire walking peaked in the 1930s." He glanced across to the glorious gold and white big top, dominating the skyline before them. "These days, folks prefer the daredevil trapeze acts, right in the summit. The jumps and the vaults. All of the high-flying derring do put on by Gino and his contemporaries."

"Gino..." she breathed, letting the name hang in the air. Her hazelnut eyes slid upwards to study him. "Does it bother you that he's here? The great king of the air?"

Irwin looked up at the reddening sky above them. "Shapiro is one of the greatest acts in trapeze today. No doubt. Having him here, at the Double G, is a remarkable coup. It will truly benefit the circus, and the fans. The box office receipts, the publicity, the clamour… all will be heightened by having him on our bill." Now, he looked back down at Pamela. "And, Miss Hotch, when you have been around as long as I have, you come to realise that enhancing the show, and not yourself, is the most critical factor in any circus production. Gino feels the same way. He is a true industry man. As am I. I am glad he's here. And he feels the same about me. I know it."

Pamela shook her head in a kind of awe. She ran a hand through her light brown hair. "Such respect, such professionalism. It's wonderful to see. It really is."

Irwin looked down at her wistfully. "On Saturday night, we're aiming to put on one of the greatest shows in the country this year. Possibly *the* greatest. We're all invested in this, Miss Hotch. The show's success is our success. It's a collective effort."

She nodded. "I'm just happy to be onboard. Me and my girls. This will be our most incredible performance yet."

Suddenly, Irwin slipped over backwards from his wire. His legs went upwards and his head and shoulders down, his arms still folded. As Pamela gasped in shock, Irwin landed on his feet directly in front of her, barely a yard away. Arms still folded.

She placed a hand on her chest in shock and laughed. He did too.

As she stared at him, he placed a hand on her shoulder. "We're all counting on you guys," he said simply. "On Saturday night, this magnificent stage is your theatre, your domain. You and your girls just have to own it. Show everyone out there why the Rollergirls are the most extraordinary act on the road today."

They both looked into each others' eyes for a moment.

Then, he patted her arm. "You can do it, Miss Hotch. And, most important of all… enjoy it."

Then, he grabbed a thin white towel, draped it across his shoulders, and headed for his trailer.

Pamela watched him slowly ebb away, like a mystical vision. People often said Doc Irwin was not just a name, but a legend. She was beginning to see why.

She whispered to herself as he opened his trailer door. "Thank you."

The empty circus tent felt like a great, dormant beast, bereft of its lifeblood – a raucous audience of cheering spectators.

The towering new grandstands had all been fitted within, forming a new ring of seats akin to a sports stadium – and raising the big top's capacity crowd by a whole two thousand people.

The scaffolding supporting the stands ensured there was less room around the tent's perimeter for anything. A small gap had been arranged where the flap was, allowing the performers to enter and exit as before.

At this late hour, the dormant tent felt eerie and surreal, like all empty big tops. Just a few floodlights spaced around the edge of the arena offered a glimpse of the stands that now formed a wall around the sawdust floor.

Roddy Olsen was pacing slowly along the edge of the stage, lost in his memories of years of performing in circuses.

It felt like an eternity since he had last entered a big top. He missed the feel of the sawdust at his feet, and could barely wait to see the grandstands full of delighted families. Again.

"I thought I might find you in here…"

He turned at the familiar sharp voice behind him, and smiled widely as he saw Lacey wandering across the floor towards him. She wore a fashionable turquoise shawl over her flowery dress.

Olsen nodded. "It's amazing how you miss it… being in one of these things every day."

Lacey's grin dominated her face as she approached him. "You remember the old line? To know the circus is to love it. You'll have sawdust in your shoes…"

He cocked his head. "And sawdust in your heart."

She finally joined him. In a maternal gesture, she grabbed both of his hands and rubbed them slightly with her own. It was a nice, sensual feeling.

"So, how are you feeling, champ?" she purred.

He rolled his eyes. "Well, better now…"

Lacey had to laugh. "Well, I'll feel better this time on Saturday night. After I've seen you perform live again. My god, how I've missed it. Your genius, your talent…"

Olsen looked around, up at the seats and across to the flap. "Hard to believe how this has all come together so quickly. Look at us all… we're back in the same outfit again, after all we've been through."

"The papers are calling it the 'Klondike comeback'."

Olsen's face dropped. "It's a shame not everybody came back."

Lacey took a deep breath. She had not heard him mention Suzi Dando's name since the day the Floating Top went down.

"I tried, Roddy," she whispered. "I tried to locate her. Ran a few channels. No one knows where she is. I'm sure she is singing at a club or in a production somewhere. Somewhere out there…"

Olsen nodded absently. "Yeah."

She rubbed his back, feeling suddenly lost. "It's alright, Roddy. If she knew what you were doing, she would be proud of you. Of all of us. And, who knows, maybe one day she will come back as well."

"I sure hope so," Olsen muttered, feeling like a child again. He often felt this way around Lacey.

He gave her a long look, his baby blue eyes locking on to her scintillating violets. Then, he threw himself into her and hugged her tight, almost painfully so.

Lacey closed her eyes happily and allowed herself to be gripped. It was a wonderful feeling, one of warmth, love and respect.

As they embraced, she too looked up at the new grandstands, their fresh surroundings. Then, she whispered softly into his ear.

"Everything has changed… but it still all looks the same." Then, she grinned. "We're back, Roddy. We're back."

CHAPTER 28

Eric Ribbeck cackled wildly as the cork exploded out of the champagne bottle, disappearing into the grassy knoll behind him as the bubbly fizz sprayed out over his hands.

He was standing with Veronica Hunslett and Tip Enqvist next to an outdoor bar, hidden away within the vast circus village that surrounded his mighty green and purple big top. The Ribbeck World Circus encampment was a truly sprawling metropolis of trailers and cabins, all spewing across the parkland of Quarry Heights, Seattle.

Ribbeck filled three glasses and handed them all out. Then, he held his one aloft, grinning like a hyena.

"Here's to us," he rasped. "That's 15 consecutive sell-outs after last night. And all four shows here in Seattle will be the same. Capacity crowds!"

Each had a long sip, cherishing the sweet taste as they stood in the midday sun.

Enqvist looked unrecognisable in a plaid shirt with fashionable slacks. He seemed to have de-aged. "I gotta hand it to you, Eric. Your circus is like a juggernaut. Truly, the greatest big top in the world. I have never seen fans so wild for our act. The adulation is overwhelming. For all of us."

The old man purred like a contented bobcat. "What I tell ya? Sign with me and the heavens are yours."

Enqvist grinned broadly, toasting the boss again before idly sitting at a nearby picnic table, which was covered in Ribbeck World Circus merchandise.

"I just can't stop looking at all this stuff," Enqvist murmured as he sat down. He idly held up a small pennant, that featured a jazzy yellow and black logo for The Daredevils. "It's like what baseball teams have."

Ribbeck nodded. "There's more where that came from, boy."

Veronica looked around slyly, glass in hand. "By next season, we'll have our own merchandising and souvenirs division. Right here, on the train, setting up at each town."

Ribbeck emptied the contents of the flute down his throat, and hungrily reached for the bottle on the bar top. "Just you watch, doll. The circus industry will be *our* industry. We are going to own it. I can practically taste it!"

With that, he held his head back and roared with laughter, a curious, high-pitched sound that unnerved the others.

Then, seemingly from nowhere, Luca Marconi appeared at the bar, having ambled across from the trailers. He had a newspaper in his hand, and a look of shock on his face.

Ribbeck had been chortling to himself, then caught sight of his bodyguard and chief aide. His face fell slightly.

"What the hell's the matter with you, boy?"

Marconi said nothing. Instead, he casually flipped the newspaper on to the bar top. The front page headline screamed up at Ribbeck as he glared down at it beneath him.

"That's this morning's San Diego Citizen," Marconi blurted.

Ribbeck stared in shock at the bold banner headline.

KLONDIKE COMEBACK IS ON!

Then, he began reading the front page article beneath. As his eyes consumed the words, his face paled. Marconi noticed a vein in his boss's forehead throbbing intently.

As if in a trance, Ribbeck picked up the paper and stared at it, disbelieving what he saw.

"No!" he rasped. "No! It can't be…"

Veronica was beside him now, concern clouding her plain features. "Eric, what…"

He slammed the newspaper into her shoulder. Flustered, she held it before her and read rapidly.

Then, she looked at Ribbeck in alarm. "What the? How is this so? Klondike and his old crew? All back together again! But… but I thought they'd all dispersed. Started new lives. New gigs."

Veronica's cold blue eyes took in the front page splash picture, of all the performers standing outside the circus tent.

"Oh my god," she hissed. "Shapiro. Olsen. Doc Irwin. Corky the Clown. All together."

Ribbeck glared at her, shuddering slightly. "All for this so-called 'Klondike Comeback Special'. And the press are loving it. He's put the band back together. And they've turned it into the story of the year!"

Veronica was incredulous. "How the hell did this happen?"

Marconi spoke up. "You can bet your life that fancy talking broad was behind it. Look, she is in that picture on the front page."

Ribbeck rubbed at his leathery face. "This will be a media sensation. That paper is calling it the show of the year." Then, suddenly, in a shocking outburst, the old man seemed to explode. "God damn it! I thought Klondike was dead and buried! Out of my hair forever! The stage was set for us to have all the limelight…finally! And what happens? The god damn, good for nothing, yellow yahoo drums up a comeback! His circus was a swamp for drunks and deadbeats, they said. And now look!"

Veronica was still staring at the photograph. "They all came back."

Then, Ribbeck grabbed the newspaper from her grip and hurled it angrily into a hedgerow running alongside them. She shrieked.

"No!" he cried angrily. "No, no, no! This is not how this is supposed to work. We are in the stratosphere, dammit. In our greatest triumph. We are on top. For good! No god damn cowboy punk with a loyal band of bums is gunna ruin this for me!" He seemed strained, his eyes bulging, as he roared at them all. "He can't stop me! No one can stop me, dammit!"

He slumped on to the bar. Marconi and Veronica stared at him in rapt fascination and fear.

Then, suddenly, he came up again, a look of wild frenzy in his green eyes. He surprised them all by focusing on Enqvist at the table beyond.

"You!" he snarled savagely, pointing at the stunt rider.

Enqvist looked up in shock, gulping. He said nothing.

"You! You, Enqvist. You are going to stop this. Stop it all."

Enqvist baulked at him, stunned. "Er, what?"

Ribbeck smiled insanely, still pointing, as he slowly approached the picnic table.

"It's perfect. Get down there, to San Diego. Say you're joining this reunion of his. This comeback. But that you were delayed. Then, no matter what it takes, bring the whole thing down. Ruin the show. Take that son of a bitch Klondike down!"

Enqvist found himself leaning backward on his bench seat as the boss hovered ever closer. "Eric!" he rasped. "Are you insane? What the hell am I going to do down there? I haven't even been invited to this show. They know I work for you now!"

"Put a sock in it, sonny." Ribbeck stood over him, like a teacher admonishing an unruly pupil. His eyes looked vengeful, wild. "You're the only one who can get in there and pull the plug on this. You can get in there. Klondike's people all know you."

"This is crazy!" Enqvist leapt up, and paced around the clearing in a frenzy. "I don't want no part in any of this, man."

Ribbeck glared at him with a cruel, sadistic look. "You ain't got no choice, boy."

Enqvist stopped pacing. "What's that?"

Ribbeck smiled smugly. "You either get down to San Diego and ruin that show of Klondike's... or you're finished here, Enqvist. You hear me? Your contract will be ripped up. You and all your boys."

Veronica and Marconi were watching on at the bar, frozen to the spot. Neither dared speak. They had never seen the old man quite so deranged.

Now, Enqvist was mad. He paced across to Ribbeck and glared at him, nose to nose. "You can't do that, dammit. That contract is for five seasons."

"The small print says everything is at the owner's discretion. You follow orders, Enqvist, or so help me god I'll blackball you out of this entire business. You follow?"

Enqvist made a fist, and looked like he was about to attack. Thinking better of it, he looked around in desperation. Marconi sensed trouble and positioned himself on his boss's arm.

"You god damn snake!" Enqvist hissed, glaring at the circus boss.

Ribbeck seemed to alter his stance. "It's your fault, Enqvist. All of this. You were supposed to recruit Shapiro and Olsen to my outfit. They were supposed to join you."

"How the hell am I responsible for their decisions?"

"You screwed it up, way I see it. Now... now, you have a chance to rectify your failure. By wrecking this show in San Diego."

Enqvist looked him over bitterly. "You're deluded."

"Alright," Ribbeck said quickly, his mind racing. "I'll tell you what, son. I'll make it all worth your while. You take down Klondike, and I'll pay you double your salary for the season. Just you. Not your boys. Now, how do you like that?"

Enqvist's head was spinning. It was a surreal, mind-blowing exchange. "You're actually serious?"

"You'll get the second instalment on your return… as long as Klondike is out of the picture."

Veronica finally, bravely spoke up. "Er, Eric, do you really think this is wise? I mean you-"

"Quiet!" he snarled.

Enqvist was beyond incredulous. He ran a hand through his blondish white hair, his eyes vacant. "You really mean all this, don't you?"

Ribbeck was impassive, his face hard as stone. "You're god damn right I do."

"What do you want me to do, dammit? Kill him, for Christ's sakes?"

"You do whatever the hell it takes to wreck that show, boy. Put that son of a bitch out of the picture for the rest of the season, and you'll get extra."

The two figures stared at each other. Enqvist tonged the inside of his mouth. Marconi simply stared at his boss in disbelief, unable to comprehend any of what he was hearing. He remained silent.

Veronica crept up to the trio, and lightly touched Ribbeck's shoulder.

"Eric! For Christ's sakes! Think about what you're saying here!"

He shrugged her off. His cold green eyes were locked on Enqvist's rugged, hardened features.

Veronica shuddered. It seemed inconceivable such a bizarre and vile conversation could take place amidst a backdrop of carnival attractions and cotton candy stalls. A children's world of wonder.

"So, whatya say, hot shot?" Ribbeck spat out.

Enqvist looked around moodily. "San Diego is more than a day's ride from here, man. I'd have to leave right now."

Ribbeck gave him a look that made the others' blood run cold. "Then what the hell are you waiting for, greaseball? You better get moving!"

Still, the biker was torn, hesitating as he stood in the park clearing. "And you think Klondike and his team are gunna just open up the door to me? Let me waltz in?"

"If they don't, run it down. Along with his entire tent."

Finally, Enqvist made to turn and walk away. He offered a stern look at each of them. Then, he snarled to the boss: "You're crazy, man."

Then he was gone, wandering in a daze towards his motor pool.

Ribbeck watched him, a maddening look of hate embedded on his craggy features. Then, he stumbled absent-mindedly towards the small outdoor bar. With a smirk, he reached behind and grabbed at a full bottle of bourbon. Pulling the cork out with his teeth, he took a long pull.

Marconi slowly followed him, as Veronica stood there in shock.

"You really want to play it like this, boss?" said Marconi quietly.

Ribbeck shook his head bitterly, holding the bottle before him. "This thing has got out of hand, dammit. The bull has gotten into the hog pen. We have to act."

"But... but this? That crazy biker could do anything down there, boss."

Ribbeck turned and glared at Marconi. "Don't you see, boy? Kal Klondike and his crew of deadbeats have been a thorn in my side for too long. I'll do whatever it takes to come out on top."

He took a long, slow, deliberate pull on the bottle. Then, he smiled devilishly.

"No matter what..."

CHAPTER 29

As the bright, indigo brown rays of dawn filtered across the luscious green domain of Balboa Park, the sprawling enclosure slowly came to life.

Park rangers slowly appeared, doing their rounds. Maintenance and garbage trucks began circling the gardens. Early morning joggers were out in force, pounding across the pathways and tracks.

Kal Klondike had been conducting his own rounds, wandering around the Double G midway, checking the stalls and equipment, and generally ticking off boxes in his head.

It was the morning of the big show.

In his head, he imagined the thousands of fans scattered all around the midway later that night. Children, families, devoted fans of the big top.

Shaking his head, he followed a timber ash path that led past the remaining games stalls and straight up to the mighty circus tent.

With a deep breath, he stopped right outside the behemoth, about 10 yards before the main customer entrance, where spectators would file past later to take their seats in the newly erected grandstands.

As he simply stood there in awe, taking in the magnificent white and gold fabric of the great tent, he slowly visualised his old Klondike's Circus big top. The red and blue stripes. His colours. Instantly identifiable with his outfit. He smiled ruefully in the early morning sunrise.

"It's finally show day."

Klondike turned slowly, and saw Griff Garrison creeping up next to him. As always, the Colonel looked resplendent, this time dressed in a rawhide beige suit with a Nashville boot tie at his throat. He wore a white Tom Mix stetson.

"Seems like an eternity since we landed in San Diego," Garrison continued, his boots crunching the gravel as he approached. "And now here we are, just hours away… from the extravaganza you've created."

He finally joined Klondike. The two shook hands warmly. Garrison patted his back.

"You're up early," Klondike muttered.

Garrison looked offended. "Are you kidding? I've already been out riding. Took Rising Sun, my favourite mount from the remada. It was beautiful. I saw the sun rise at Isabella Point, at the far edge of the park. We trotted back along the south side."

Klondike had to hand it to the Colonel. He looked downwards. For most of his life, he had sold and promoted himself as a cowboy. A wild west star. Yet, one born and raised in Hell's Kitchen, New York. Taught all his life skills by a street gang.

Then there was the Colonel. A proud son of the High Sierras. A rancher, horse trainer, cattle breeder. A son of the soil. A true cow man. And the real deal.

He finally spoke. "Your horses are the best I've had the pleasure of working with, Colonel. And I've worked with a whole lot of remadas."

Garrison nodded vaguely. He looked immaculate. His white moustache had been closely clipped. His blazer and shirt crisp and tight, seemingly brand new. He smiled thinly.

"I still can't believe all this, Kal. This show. The talent you've put together for this circus card. It's... well, it's beyond my wildest imagination. And I just can't believe it's all going down at the Double G Circus. My circus!"

Klondike nodded. "What can I tell ya, sir? We were due a change of luck after everything that happened on the road. Well, this... this influx of performers is just the answer to our prayers."

Garrison paced around in a daze, his eyes enlarging as he studied a circus poster stuck to a cabin wall nearby, one of the hundreds pasted across the camp.

"I've dreamed of this moment, Kal. All of my life. Promoting a top circus show. One full of household names. Seeing the Double G on TV, having the newspapers scrambling to get us in their pages." His gaze went back to the entrance of the tent, spread out just before them like a portal into another dimension. "And now we have an all-star line-up. Shapiro, Doc Irwin, Olsen, Corky. The Rollergirls. All performing for the Double G." He removed his hat and ran a hand through his shiny silver hair. "I just can't get over it."

Klondike smiled over at him. "You've got some star sluggers in your bullpen, Colonel. And I should know."

"That's right." Garrison looked at him knowingly. "It was you, Kal. All you. You put this together. It's just like I said before, the talent came because of you. And none of us will ever forget it."

Klondike stepped towards him. "All of the credit belongs to Lacey. She was behind all this."

The Colonel nodded vaguely. "That's just it, Kal. Not only have you assembled a top team of talent, but you've got yourself a first class management group. You, Lacey, that Richie with all of his files. I can't tell you how impressed I am. And it all goes back to when I first called you, all those months ago. Why I wanted you here as my manager. You're a circus man, god damn it. You know top people, you attract them. They, ah, want to be around you, in your outfit."

Klondike shifted uncomfortably on the spot. "That's all great to hear, Colonel. But, with all due respect, nothing has happened yet. Sure, a lot of publicity, a lot of heat. But it all comes down to tonight... and what happens in there, our beloved colosseum..." he pointed inside the big top.

Garrison thought it over, and placed himself next to Klondike again on the gravel. They both looked inside the tent, at the sawdust floor and the mighty grandstands surrounding it. The whole domain had been transformed, all thanks to those new seating blocks.

"No matter what happens tonight," Garrison whispered in a gravelly tone. "I'm proud as hell to be putting this show on. I just want you to know that, Kal. This...this kind of circus, this whole environment, is something I've dreamed of for years. Something I thought had eluded me. Until now. And I owe all that to you, Kal. And, well, er, like I say... I just want you to know that." He breathed in deeply, and seemed to inflate. "This is the one I've been waiting for, my boy. All my life."

The Colonel held out his hand again. Klondike took it with a grin.

"In many ways, this is all down to you, Colonel. You've made all this possible. You and your outfit. You gave us an outlet... a platform, on which to put on our show. You gave me an opportunity, a chance, to run a circus again. After my own operation got ripped apart. Way I see it, Colonel, I owe you just as much."

The two men stood there, in the shadow of the big top, staring into its heart. Both cut from the same cloth, and bound by the same unshakable code of honour towards the industry, and all within it.

They stood there for some time, lost in the moment. Silently recalling the many travails the season had brought them; the long and arduous path that had led them to this moment. It was truly overwhelming.

Then, their reverie was broken by the booming call of a roustabout, ready to begin his morning shift. "Alright. Tent detail, let's go!"

Garrison patted Klondike on the back as they both turned around.

"Well," he said cheerfully, "let's get to work."

The immaculate, gleaming bright yellow Gran Torino glided almost silently down the entrance lane of the mansion house, pulling into the huge gravel driveway and slowing to a gradual stop.

Jenny Cross climbed out of the driver's seat, her designer sunglasses protecting her eyes from the piercing midday sun. She looked all around at the Red Rock Canyon mountain range that seemed to encompass her current, temporary home.

Then, with a relaxed smile, she looked up at the magnificent whitestone mansion, nestled within a beautiful, tropical garden, where palm trees and tall grass sprung up seemingly at will.

She walked towards the front door, stumbling slightly as she moved. Her bags remained in the car. A servant could collect them later.

Less than 100 yards away, a black Sedan pulled up outside the line of fur trees that encircled the gardens.

Mike Blakelock let the vehicle roll silently for several feet, until the nose of the bumper peeked out past the final tree. He had a clear view of the lane leading up to the house.

Leaning back in the leather driver's seat, he watched. His face twisted into that look again, one of dismay mixed with regret, as he watched the swaying, unsteady figure of Jenny Cross staggering across the driveway into the millionaire's row mansion.

He killed the engine. And still he watched.

Once inside the colossal home, Jenny paced slowly through the marbled porch, past the lounge, and towards the grand staircase.

She could still taste the alcohol in her throat, and felt like she was walking on air, like an astronaut in outer space. It was a pleasant sensation.

At the top of the stairs, she stumbled slightly and ducked into the upstairs dining room. Just as she had expected, breakfast was laid out. Everything was ready. She had called Grace from the health spa with specific instructions. All had been followed to the letter.

Now, still wearing her tennis attire of white skirt and yellow polo shirt, she collapsed wearily into a chair at the head of the long dining table, positioned by a giant window that offered an impressive view of the gardens.

With a hungry grin, she poured coffee into a white porcelain cup, all the way to the top. She took a long sip, then fished a tiny bottle of brown liquid out of her handbag, and poured it into the coffee.

Another sip, and she felt her pulse slow and her limbs relax.

Contented, Jenny reached for the assorted treats laid out before her and pulled a croissant and a hot roll onto her plate, followed by several lashings of ham and a fried egg.

With another sip of the modified coffee, she licked her lips and eyed the other dishes Grace had expertly prepared that morning.

After devouring the contents of an over-filled breakfast plate in an unceremonious manner, akin to a starving hobo, Jenny emptied the remains of the cup down her throat.

With a satisfied gurgle, she dabbed at her mouth with a napkin, before reaching for the copy of that morning's Las Vegas Sun, nestled neatly beside one of the plates.

She lit a cigarette, crossed her legs, and idly scanned the pages, taking little note of anything but the headlines and pictures.

As she rifled casually through the paper, she thought she detected a creaking floorboard out on the landing.

She looked up. Nothing but silence. Even Grace and her housemaids were busy somewhere else in the sprawling complex.

Dragging on her smoke, her pale blue eyes returned to the newspaper. She turned the page.

Then, she froze all over. The cigarette fell from her fingers to the tiled floor. Those beautiful, intoxicating eyes widened in alarm. And the whitish lips twisted.

The banner headline screamed up at her:

KLONDIKE CIRCUS COMEBACK SPECIAL SOLD OUT…SHOW OF THE YEAR EXPECTED TONIGHT!

Then, the eyes took in the enormous picture above the headline. It showed Kal with a colourful crew of circus performers, all standing in front of a white and gold big top. Her eyes narrowed and her nostrils flared as she recognised Gino Shapiro. That accursed prima donna. She recognised too Roddy Olsen. Corky. The Tanner woman. All smiling widely. It looked like a snap from a top Las Vegas show. A spectacular.

Feeling like she was slipping into a dreamy abyss, she began to read the article. After skimming through the first six paragraphs, she dropped the newspaper to the floor, absently standing on the burning cigarette butt.

"No!" she hissed, staring into nothingness. She made to stand, but instead slipped forwards, landing flat on her face on the dining room floor. She angrily slapped her hand against the tiles, and rose unsteadily, slumping into the table. An almighty crash shattered the relative tranquility of the dining lounge as a selection of china plates and cups smashed to the floor.

Her mind racing, Jenny pushed herself away from the breakfast banquet and rushed towards the doorway.

Moving out on to the landing at the top of the grand stairwell, she pushed her hands through her hair and thought rapidly. She moved to the ornate iron railing that ran along the edge of the landing and looked down. The marbled porchway below was still deserted, the house still silent.

Jenny cursed wildly to herself. Then, she turned and made for the stairs.

"Going somewhere… sweetheart?"

She froze again. Rooted to the spot, she quivered all over.

Then, forcing a wide smile and taking a deep breath, she turned around with a flourish.

Ray Generoso stood at the far end of the landing. But something was wrong. He looked livid. Ferocious. He was in his short sleeves, but with no tie. So he'd been in the building for some time. But it was the look on his wide, fat face that terrified Jenny. His eyes bulged, and his lips were curled in a nasty, intimidating sneer.

He slowly waded over, hands curled into fists at his side.

"Darling!" Jenny cried happily. But there were cracks, and she knew it. "I didn't know you were in. Had no idea at all. Why, I've just this minute returned from the health spa, and was tucking into some breakfast. I'm famished! After all that tennis!" She rolled her head back and laughed. "You know, those few days away up there in the mountains did me the world of good. I feel so refreshed. Must be the mountain air. And this breakfast spread that Grace laid out was so-"

"Enough!" Generoso wailed. He was walking ever so slowly, staring at her almost hypnotically. His voice was an anguished whisper. "You almost got away with it…"

Jenny took a step backwards. A stabbing pain hit her chest, and she felt icy cold pin pricks across her back. He knows! she thought. The revelation hit her like a juggernaut. But how? She tried to remain clam, nonchalant.

"My goodness, honey. What are you talking about?"

He now hovered before her, his chest heaving as if he was under some immense pressure. Then, he said the words she had long dreaded. The onslaught of fear and paranoia that plagued her nightmares unfolded like a tidal wave.

"I know who you are!"

"W-what?"

Generoso's eyes looked murderous. "That's right! I know! I know all about you! The real you. Miss… Jenny Cross!"

The sound of the name, her real name, made her shudder convulsively. She tried to think of a way out, another line. But her mind was beyond rationality. The booze and the news about Klondike had sent her into a meltdown.

He smirked at her, seemingly enjoying it. "Jenny Cross!" he roared.

She began hyperventilating. Then, she screamed.

Generoso didn't seem to care. "I know everything, dammit. I know who you are." He moved even closer, looking vengeful and incensed. "You've been playing me all this time, you dirty little slut! You tramp! Bleeding every dollar outta me you can! And I'm not the first! Well, mark my words, *Julia*, I'll sure as hell be the last! Cos you ain't gunna live long enough to pull this scam off again. I'm gunna break you apart with my bare hands!"

Then, in a lightning fast move she never even saw, he thrashed out a meaty hand and slapped her across the cheek. The impact sent her flying across the landing to the far wall. Stunned, she held her jawline and stared at him with wild, crazy eyes.

He looked her over in absolute disgust. Then he turned his hand into a fist, pulled it back and approached in a threatening pose.

"No!" She let out a bloodcurdling scream.

Then, summoning all of her poise and coordination, she leapt forward and threw a lunging kick straight into the older man's groin.

Generoso let out an awful, animal-like cry, his hands shooting between his legs. His face seemed to distort in agony, his eyes crossing over.

Jenny hovered over him as he tiptoed backwards, his head bowed low as he breathed wildly in ugly grunts. His legs touched against the railing as he struggled to stay upright.

Jenny felt like her actions were being controlled by some unworldly spirit, guiding her through the madness, keeping her alive. She steadied herself before him.

Then, with a wild cry, she grabbed his bull-like neck and rammed her bare knee straight into his face, feeling his nose shatter as she slammed her leg into his flesh.

With a deranged howl, Generoso threw his hands to his face and leant away from her, stumbling backwards.

What happened next felt like it transpired in slow motion. The big man's momentum sent him crashing into the iron railing. He seemed to sit on the smooth bannister for a second, then tumbled straight over backwards, into thin air.

As he went over, Jenny saw a horrified, petrified look on the mobster's face. Then, with a primal scream, he was over the railing, his feet slipping from view. A horrendous smattering sound then emanated from the unseen domain below.

Jenny's hand flew to her mouth. Quivering slightly, she crept to the rail and glanced down at the porch way below.

Ray Generoso's body was lying directly below her, his dead eyes seemingly glaring up at his killer. A bright pool of thick crimson blood was forming behind his skull, widening with each passing second on the white marble flooring.

Jenny stood there for several seconds, staring down at the body. Her breathing came in short, spasmodic gasps.

Then, she rushed into the master bedroom, heading straight for a mini bar in the corner. Without hesitation, she grabbed wildly at a bottle of scotch, pulled the top out with her teeth, and began guzzling noisily. Standing there in her country club tennis kit, she gulped for several moments, draining a third of the bottle.

Finally, she came up for breath. Then, she caught her reflection in a giant, floor to ceiling dressing mirror.

At that moment, Jenny Cross looked hopelessly and emphatically insane. Drunk, delusional and lost. Standing, drinking whiskey, in tennis ware, within an opulent mansion fit for a countess. She had achieved everything she had ever dreamed of... and yet she had fallen further than she ever could have imagined.

She studied her reflection. Then, something very queer and disturbing happened. She nodded to herself. She knew what now needed to be done.

Jenny moved smoothly now, more steady on her feet, somehow. With cool, deliberate movements, she made for a desk at the far side of the room, by a window seat. As she walked, she grabbed at a small, chic handbag made of alligator skin.

Placing her bag on the desk, she threw open the second of three drawers at the front of the desk. She pulled something out, and then stared at it as it rested in her hand. Her eyes were wide, a mixture of fear and desire dominating her beautiful features. She looked down at her possession.

A Colt 45 revolver.

It felt good in her grip. Powerful, and pleasurable. Her breathing steadied. She studied the gun silently.

Then, with a grunt, she thrust the Colt into her handbag and turned.

She stormed out of the master bedroom. As she raced down the landing and headed for the stairs, she shrieked once again.

It was an unsettling, disturbing sound. And it echoed across the wide hallways.

Blakelock was stood beside his car just beyond the path that led to the mansion house. He had his camera in one hand and stood poised, ready to take a shot of whatever might unfold.

It had been two days since he had handed Generoso his file on Jenny. The mobster had been at home for most of that time, as far as he knew. Waiting for the woman he had known as his girlfriend to return after her stay at the health spa.

Blakelock could only imagine what kind of scene was unfolding within the sprawling home. His gaze drifted from the dining room balcony to the master bedroom window. He was sensing something. An instinct. Something had gone wrong.

Suddenly, his dark eyes flew to the front door.

There she was. Jenny Cross. Still in her tennis outfit. Running wildly, like a drunken sailor, she flew across the gravel driveway and straight into the Gran Torino. In seconds, the beautiful car had spun around in the drive, and was tearing down the entrance lane towards the feeder road that led to the highway.

Blakelock ducked in desperation behind his Sedan. He need not have bothered. Jenny did not seem to notice the black car at the head of her manor lane, and simply sped off down the road. It had all happened in seconds. Now, she was off.

Blakelock leapt into action, opening the driver's door and diving behind the wheel. Revving up the motor, he took off, eyeing the road ahead as he made to tail her.

For the umpteenth time in recent weeks, he thanked the heavens that her bright yellow car was so distinctive and impossible to miss.

By the time Jenny had pulled on to the highway, Blakelock was right behind her. He meant to keep his usual distance, but Jenny was accelerating dangerously, clearing the speed limit by far.

Mystified, Blakelock followed in desperation. He couldn't match the speed of the Gran Torino, but managed to keep the yellow flyer in his sights.

However, dumbfounded as he was over her speed and dangerous driving, he was far more concerned by another question whirling through his over-active mind.

Where was she going?

An almighty roar of exhaust permeated the desert air as the fancy-looking yellow and black motorbike tore off the freeway and headed down a slip road towards Highway 91.

Tip Enqvist wore grey garage coveralls over his regular clothes, and had biker goggles pulled over his eyes to protect them from the desert dust.

As he gently guided his bike down the small slip road, he felt as if he was riding into hell. On a mission he didn't understand. Could not comprehend. He was merely following orders. As he had for much of his life.

What lay ahead? It was hard to understand. All Enqvist really felt at that moment were two emotions. The chance for riches, and great acclaim, courtesy of the famous Eric Ribbeck. And the opportunity for revenge against Klondike, who had almost killed him and destroyed his act forever after that shipping disaster. That was how he saw it.

With another loud roar, the bike ploughed onto Highway 91, floating among the cars and vans, like a mule passing cows on a cattle drive.

Enqvist accelerated, sending the bike surging across the asphalt. He had been riding non-stop for hours since yesterday afternoon. And there were many more still to come.

As he raced down the highway, he noticed a sign up ahead and seemed to nod to himself. The words were most welcome.

You are now entering Southern California.

Blakelock had never seen anything quite like it.

He battled to keep the flying, supercharged Gran Torino in his sights as it zigzagged wildly across the lanes of the freeway.

Like a bright yellow bolt of lightning, the jazzy sports car blazed down the asphalt, seemingly not content with remaining in a single lane.

Horns blared across the busy freeway, as cars skidded out of the way and wheels screeched. Somehow, the flying yellow juggernaut avoided any collision.

Blakelock just about kept the Torino in view as he struggled to keep up, while staying at 70 mph. He kept his foot on the gas pedal, sending the old Sedan lurching along at a pace it was not accustomed to. He manoeuvred his vehicle through the traffic, all the while trying to keep his fix on the yellow blur far ahead.

As he battled to maintain control of his rampaging motor, Blakelock's mind was racing along at a similar speed.

What was she up to? And why?

As he watched the Torino surge recklessly from lane to lane, looking for all the world like it would roll over at any point, he shuddered at the thought of a multi-car wreck.

She was obviously drunk. But there was something else. Why the speed and haste? The recklessness. Idly as he clung to the steering wheel and manoeuvred the Sedan along, he wondered if Jenny Cross had succumbed to a form of madness.

Then, it suddenly hit him.

Inexplicably, the Gran Torino slowed and peeled off the main freeway onto a slip road.

Blakelock turned slightly to join the feeder lane on the busy interchange. Then, he too joined the slip, finally getting a clear sight of the Torino as it rumbled along towards a local highway.

As Blakelock followed, mystified, he looked up and read the overhanging signpost.

Pacific Highway. San Diego - 80 miles.

San Diego! The words hit him like a thunderclap.

He knew Klondike's schedule and, even if he didn't, he had read the papers and seen the news. The big show was going down tonight at Balboa Park.

Blakelock looked ahead as the yellow supercar suddenly raced out onto the Pacific Highway and accelerated wildly once again. It quickly became a dot ahead of him.

With a snarl of anguish, he pushed the pedal to the floor and gripped the wheel with whitened knuckles. It was time to get everything he could out of the trusty Sedan.

Eyes like stone, his face ashen, Blakelock grimly followed in the wake of the yellow flash.

CHAPTER 30

Five o'clock. A full two hours before showtime.

And Cortez Gardens was awash with excited spectators milling around the Double G Circus midway, and the entrance to the encampment.

Fans were everywhere, thousands of them. Convoys of humanity swarmed down the paths and tracks that zig-zagged across Balboa Park. An enchanted atmosphere gripped the enclosure around the midway.

The great white and gold big top sat like a beacon at the head of the gardens. Its immensity could be glimpsed from far around, and the growing crowds flocked towards it from all corners of the park.

Within the midway, people snapped up programmes, posters and pictures of the circus stars. The shooting galleries and pitching pits were packed with enthusiastic customers, and fans gobbled up cotton candy, hot dogs and popcorn.

In many ways, it was an idyllic picture for any circus promoter eyeing a major score, a big-time take.

And it set the scene for what everyone connected with the Double G hoped would be an unforgettable, record-breaking night.

At the front of the encampment, by the gates to this magical kingdom, a TV newsman blabbered excitedly into a camera, ensuring the big top was behind him as he made his grand proclamation: "And so the big night is finally here, at glorious Balboa Park, San Diego. The biggest circus show this city has ever seen. And it all gets under way in less than two hours…

"An almighty gamble from cattleman and circus owner Colonel Griff Garrison, redemption for the disgraced Kal Klondike, and a night of stars unlike anything this city has ever seen. It all adds up to a Hollywood blockbuster under those bright lights, right here in our fair city…"

Inside the big top, the atmosphere was fervent, creating an unrecognisable, almost frightening environment for the stewards and roustabouts, none of whom had ever seen or envisioned anything quite like this.

The newly erected grandstands seemed to rise into the tent's ceiling, the great walls of spectators a dizzying sensation to look upon.

The circus's maximum capacity attendance had more than doubled with the innovation of the stands. The tent had an electric feel, like a sports stadium at kick-off.

Standing proudly at the flap, Kal Klondike was gaping up at the patrons all around, engulfing his arena. He was trying to put his finger on what exactly had gripped all these spectators. They had all come, in their thousands, for this San Diego show. This latest date in the Double G's schedule.

As he gazed into the grandstands around him, he saw goggles of schoolboys dressed as cowboys, with tiny stetsons and holsters carrying plastic pistols. Many youngsters in the audience were dressed in replicas of Gino's trademark fireball orange jumpsuit.

The media had dubbed this the "Klondike Comeback Special". He decided that was the spark that had set off the explosion of interest. Circus fans wanted to see the Klondike stars back together again, and in this new troupe. That in itself was something of a spectacle, it would seem.

As he looked up at the spectators, Lacey slowly nestled herself alongside him, barely five feet away from the edge of the sawdust floor, by the side of the grandstand scaffolding.

"Just like old times, tiger," she whispered delicately in his ear.

He smiled in awe. "Everything seems the same. Even the fans in their replica costumes. They've still come out… after all that's happened."

Lacey grinned wolfishly. "I think half of the great and the good of Southern California are here. I lost count of the dignitaries in our VIP area."

They both glanced up at a roped-off square of leather padded seats in the very centre of the main grandstand to their left. The block of seats was bustling with men in business suits and women in cocktail dresses.

There was the mayor of San Diego, Jesus Mendosa, scores of local councillors, the head of the chamber of commerce, and a number of prominent California businessmen.

Colonel Griff Garrison and his wife Karen were seated in the very centre of the amassed dignitaries, both smiling grandly as they hob-nobbed with the esteemed guests, gesturing at the tent and answering questions happily.

Klondike nodded. "The Colonel's dream has come true. This is his night as much as anyone's."

Lacey's gaze went from the VIP area to the circus's own press box, also located in the same central grandstand. And similarly filled.

"His stock is rising with each passing minute," she purred.

Klondike grunted. "He can buy you your own Broadway theatre as a show of thanks."

At that moment, Richie Plum wandered through the entrance tunnel into the flap enclosure. He joined Klondike and Lacey.

"Never seen anything like it, guys," he muttered. "Last available seat for tonight went five hours ago. We were sold out long before the gates opened, 90% of sales were advance. Not on the day."

Klondike patted him cheerfully on the back. "The hottest ticket in town, Richie my boy."

Plum stared at him. "In the country…"

Klondike and Lacey both looked down at the smaller man.

Then, before anyone could say another word, the arena was filled with the sound of dramatic opera music flooding through the tannoy.

Then, right on cue, the resplendent Heavy Brown walked out of the tunnel, the ringmaster's ringmaster in his scarlet blazer and black top hat. Microphone in hand, he marched into the centre of the stage and waved at the cheering fans.

Klondike winked at Lacey. "This is it!"

"Ladies and gentlemen…"

Heavy stood in the centre of the arena, his free hand raised in the air. The applause slowly died down, and the opera score grew quieter until it faded out. Then, every set of eyes under the big top locked on to the man in red. He roared into the mic.

"Welcome to the fastest-growing circus spectacular in America today. The grandest, the wildest, the most incredible blend of action and excitement on offer anywhere in the world. Where cowboys roam… and rollergirls whirl. The wild west brought to life, and where superstars are given flight! Presenting our very special San Diego Spectacular tonight here in Balboa Park, just for you… ladies and gentlemen, I give you the sensational, show-stopping Double G Circus!"

He pumped his fist into the air as the audience applauded wildly.

"And now," Heavy continued, practically screaming into his mic, "please welcome our opening act. The wild riding, sharp shooting, kings among cowboys! Give it up for the Riders of the Double G!"

A big cheer seemed to sweep around the arena as the cowboy team erupted from the flap on their magnificent golden palominos, and began their customary laps of the circus floor.

The riders looked sublime in shiny new silver and red western outfits, and all wore white hats.

The riding tricks began, as the cowboys performed saddle headstands, swapped mounts and leapt from their stirrups, diving from horse to horse, as the palominos ran in mighty circles over and over again.

And the audience lapped it up with wonder, cheering and clapping enthusiastically.

As the riders continued their laps, the applause grew louder, causing the riders to gaze up in awe at the noise, a sensation none of them had ever experienced in all their years of performing.

Klondike felt himself exhale mighty breaths. It was all a far cry from their first few shows in Tennessee and Texas. This kind of ovation was what they all lived for. This was the circus.

"They're digging it," Heavy murmured to Kal as he joined him at the flap.

"As if the last few weeks have been a sorry nightmare," Klondike said. He could not stop looking up at the wall of cheering fans beside him. "Looks like we've found us a circus crowd again."

The cowboys executed their plate shooting act next, wowing the spectators with their usual stunning accuracy, as the noise of blasting caps and smashing china reverberated throughout the tent. The sight of real-life cowboys drawing their pistols and blasting the fast-moving plates was a surreal treat for many in attendance.

Then came the high-speed, mid-air saddle swap routine. With Rawley Walsh still in hospital recovering from his fractured arm, two of his fellow team riders had been perfecting the bold and daring act.

The two selected cowboys completed the difficult manoeuvre with panache and great velocity, performing the swap with faultless ease and grace as a drumroll thundered across the speakers.

More hearty applause followed as the Riders of the Double G performed a routine, final lap of honour, waving to the adoring audience as they slowly headed for the flap.

Next up was Corky's act.

"And now," bellowed Heavy from the entrance area, "it gives me great pleasure to introduce to you all, one of the greatest performers in circus history. A showman and a hero, beloved by all who see him in action. Ladies and gentlemen, please welcome the world's greatest clown, Corky!"

The beloved clown entered the big top to hearty applause. Several roustabouts followed in his wake, clapping also. Corky was dressed in his famous stage attire of yellow chequered suit, crooked tie and brown bowler hat.

He began his act by riding a six-foot tall unicycle, catching various items as the roustabouts gently threw them up at him. An iron, stool, imitation ham and basketball were all dispatched, with Corky catching each one. He then threw each piece back at one of the others, before hoisting himself up, twisting in midair, and riding the cycle with his hands while balancing himself vertically in a surreal handstand. The crowd whistled and cheered as he did a lap of the floor.

Then, as the cycle was led away by the helpers, he was handed an opening set of six juggling pins.

As another hearty drumroll sounded on the PA system, the clown began juggling, gaining more momentum, going faster and faster until the red pins were a blur of motion. Corky moved them around expertly, never pausing or even blinking.

Finally, he rounded up all the pins in his customary manner, catching them in the front of his pants. Bowing gamely to the applause, he handed over the pins and then began one of his customary tricks. Holding an imitation bowling ball, that was really made of soft rubber, he juggled the black ball, a tennis ball and a marble. As he kept the items floating through the air, he allowed the heavy-looking bowling ball to land flat on his head, pretending to be dizzy.

Next, he juggled four small rubber balls in the "high juggle", sending the items up to 12 feet in the air. As he kept going, he mounted a roustabout's shoulders and was paraded around the floor.

His juggling finale was a stunning sight. A backstage helper set alight four pins with a gasoline feeder and a lighter. Corky again jumped up on to the unicycle. The lit pins were handed to him and, as another drumroll sounded, he juggled the flaming pins while riding the cycle. From any kind of distance, it looked as if the clown was juggling fire.

The audience screamed as one as Corky finally dismounted the unicycle, handing the fire sticks to a steward dressed in a fireman's outfit.

"And now," came Heavy's voice, as the ringmaster moved towards the star clown, "we come to the piece de resistance. Corky will now perform for you his most daring feat of all… the human cannonball!"

A giant, old-fashioned cannon was wheeled out from the back into the near side of the big top. The clowns pointed it at a huge net that had been set up on the far side of the arena, that was tilted at about 45 degrees.

The cannon was in fact a giant catapult, with a huge spring inside that could fire a human 50 yards through the air. Corky donned a pair of airman's goggles and a pilot's cap and climbed into the cannon via a ladder.

As the drum roll returned, a roustabout lit an imitation fuse at the rear of the cannon. This was done purely for effect. The coiled spring was activated by a switch underneath that the same man now pressed with his foot once the flame reached the end of the fuse.

With a bang, Corky shot out of the canon's mouth and flew across the circus floor, shaping his body like a dart, arms crossed over his chest for safety. His body slammed into the tilted net, and the clown bounced several times in the lining before manoeuvring himself on to the ground.

"There he is, Corky the Clown," Heavy roared as Corky and his assistants offered a bow, gave a wave and headed for the entranceway again. As he neared the flap, Corky delighted in producing a bouquet of flowers from within his jacket sleeve, which he threw to an elderly woman in the third row.

Klondike shook hands with the clown as he sauntered towards the tunnel. "You look better than ever, old buddy," he drawled.

Corky grinned as he exited the stage floor, still waving at the cheers. "Feels like an age since I've been on." He eyed Kal knowingly. "I guess I needed a purpose... something to believe in."

Klondike slapped his back. "Believe in me, man. I'll take you back to the top."

As the applause gradually died down, Heavy waded out on to the sawdust again.

Klondike returned to the edge of the floor and whispered to Lacey and Plum. "Now, we go from the sublime to the macabre."

Plum frowned. "She can't be that dark."

Lacey rolled her eyes. "You haven't seen her perform, Richie dear."

Heavy made the introduction, as an eerie, classical tune emanated from the speakers.

"And now, ladies and gentlemen, prepare to be left spellbound by the enchantress of the west. The snake charmer extraordinaire... Arletta LaRue."

Two stewards ambled to the centre of the arena, carrying the large black coffin between them.

As the haunting tune grew in depth, there was a mighty cry from within and then there she was, Arletta LaRue, climbing out of the coffin and standing tall. She looked different from the previous shows. In a frilly black dress, shiny high heels and a silver tiara, Arletta resembled more an actress from an expensive horror film than a demon of the occult.

This time, the reaction from the audience was different, too. Klondike noticed it immediately. There were gasps. But also laughs, cheers and a fair share of whistles from excited teenage boys.

Then, the diminutive, mercurial Arletta began her beguiling, almost hypnotic dance, while deftly lifting her squad of snakes out of the coffin, one at a time.

The climax of her act, as she hoisted up all five snakes onto her shoulders, was met with screams – a mix of alarm and excitement. Many watching were disturbed by what they witnessed, others vaguely inspired. What every single spectator watching that night could agree on was one factor – none had ever seen anything so unusual, and original.

There were more gasps and exaggerated laughs as Arletta then winked at the main grandstand, before clutching her array of snakes and simply sitting in the coffin again.

She led down, pulling the lid closed over her.

As the stewards collected the black casket and hefted it back to the flap, a swelling, somewhat disjointed ovation reverberated around the dome of stands.

As the two stewards wandered into the flap enclosure, hoards of fans raced to the edges of the bleachers to gaze down upon the coffin as it left the arena. Many pointed and gestured at the strange sight, as the casket was taken down the small tunnel, and out of sight.

The reaction was one of stunned excitement, Klondike decided. The fans were intrigued, mystified. And that was a unique selling point in his book. He knew it immediately. From this moment on, he would promote Arletta LaRue as a woman of mystery, a master of the mystic arts, one who nobody knows anything about. An enigma.

He smiled smugly to himself. Finally, he knew what to do with her. After the shocked, disturbed reactions at the beginning of the tour, now a game plan had emerged.

"You've got something there," Lacey purred in his ear, as if to confirm his inner thoughts.

"Damn straight," he drawled. He smiled thinly. "And to think I used to hate snakes."

Their rapport was shattered by Heavy's next booming announcement.

"Behold, ladies and gentlemen, as the Double G Circus presents to you… the world's strongest man! It's the Mongolian Giant…Soolaimon!"

As the old-fashioned horror movie theme sounded, the circus giant came striding out menacingly, trying his best to resemble an otherworldly monster, snarling and flexing his enormous muscles in his Genghis Khan attire.

For this performance, Klondike had drawn on his knowledge of professional wrestling folklore. As Soolaimon strode out on to the sawdust, a team of four roustabouts pretended to attack him, with the giant effortlessly hoisting them up and carrying them on his shoulders, or lifting them clean above his head in the gorilla press position, even performing push-ups with their bodies.

He dropped each delicately to the floor, as the group played out the spectacle of an unstoppable monster repelling attacks from the ordinary folk.

After the roustabouts gave up and ran away, Soolaimon raged and over-acted as he went through his spinning barbell routine. He executed his latest trick with nonchalance, hurling the weight high into the air before catching it one-handed.

Then, as the giant prepared to repeat the feat, one of the roustabouts suddenly reappeared, riding a bicycle – and heading straight for the strong man.

As the bike flew towards him, the rider ringing the bell in a comic fashion, Soolaimon crouched low and braced himself, concentrating.

What followed almost defied belief. The bicycle collided into the giant, who allowed the front wheel to roll on to his shoulder before miraculously gripping the bottom bracket, holding it steady, and then hauling the bike – with the rider still in the saddle – high above his head.

Soolaimon then settled the bicycle, hilariously, on to his hulking right shoulder, as the roustabout on top looked about in shock.

With another roar, the strong man simply walked back to the flap – with both bike and cyclist sitting upon his shoulder.

It was another surreal sight, and garnered a hearty applause from the amazed audience.

As Soolaimon wandered into the flap enclosure, deftly hauling his huge load, Heavy slapped him on the back, and headed out on to the sawdust again.

"And now, ladies and gentlemen, please give a warm San Diego welcome for the new sensation of the ages. They've been whizzing through town all week, and now they're here to amaze you. It's America's stunning speeding superstars... The Rollergirls!"

Klondike, Lacey and Plum all clapped boisterously as the rollerskating team exploded out of the flap to the sounds of fervent rock n roll music on the tannoy. They sped past the trio, and raced onto the stage floor at an impossible velocity, dazzling in their purple leotards and sparkling silver skates.

As the Rollergirls blazed around the arena floor, and the rockabilly tunes roared across the big top, the watching crowd began clapping in rhythm, like teenyboppers at a pop concert.

When the skaters zoomed up onto the small wooden wall separating the audience from the sawdust, the cheers were wild and ecstatic.

The Rollergirls' balancing acts and somersaults were an awesome spectacle, and the repertoire of tricks and vaults had everyone on their feet applauding.

Then, Pamela Hotch and her training partner Sharon performed their daring, high-speed spinning routine in the small metal half-dome.

The spinning duo were little more than a blur as they completed their ultra-fast turns, Pamela gripping Sharon's ankles with a seeming ironclad grip as she expertly, incredibly manoeuvred herself around and around. Sharon's body was like an arrow, her arms tucked in, her skull exposed. Her frame led at roughly a 40 degree angle as she let herself be hurled around like lightning.

It made for a frightening, dangerous spectacle as the duo went round and round, faster and faster, a whirl of blurred purple.

Pamela and Sharon held the move for a full 30 seconds longer than in any previous performance. And the crowd went wild, shouting out their delight and whooping aloud in a deafening mix.

When the high-speed spin act finished, the Rollergirls performed two laps of honour, skating slowly and waving to an audience that was on its feet in amazement.

As the team glided through the exit area, Klondike and Lacey hugged each skater joyously. Plum was stuck to the spot, still incredulous at the high-speed spinning gig.

At the rear was Pamela, who halted her skates at the flap and waded, on somewhat shaky legs, into the tunnel. Lacey helped her, supporting her arm and walking with her.

"Have you ever had an ovation like that, Pam?" she cried over the cheers reverberating around the tent.

"Hell no," Pamela replied, laughing in a kind of awe-inspired joy. "This is insane. All these people. Watching us! Cheering for us! It doesn't feel real."

Lacey patted her back as she led her down the tunnel to the gardens outside. "These people will never forget The Rollergirls. And, what's more, this is just the beginning!"

Pamela laughed, a gushing, spasmodic sound. "I better take these skates off. I feel dizzy!"

Lacey gave her a wave as she trudged off in that peculiar manner of hers, walking on the heavy skates.

Now, Lacey was exactly where she wanted to be. Outside. And she quickly saw the reason why.

Walking confidently towards the tunnel in front of her, there he was... her favourite performer of all. In many ways, her favourite person.

Roddy Olsen looked like a Hollywood teen idol as he approached her. Lacey felt her mind drift back through the years as she glimpsed him once again in his silver waistcoat and purple pants, carrying his great leather suitcase.

Placing an arm around his shoulder, she walked him through the tunnel.

"Here we go again, champ," she said softly. "Another massive crowd. Another adoring audience."

Olsen stared through the flap into the big top, seeing and sensing the fans. They were cheering loudly.

"Them's the best kind ma'am," he said simply, re-quoting an old line he had told her years earlier.

"Good luck, Roddy. And, well, I guess I should say… welcome back!"

He looked at her. Then, he gave her a quick hug. She squeezed him tight. He saw Heavy belting out his introduction inside the tent.

"It's magic time."

He strode forward, past Klondike and Plum, and out on to the sawdust.

"Ladies and gentlemen, it is time to welcome one of the superstars of our show. He has conquered Las Vegas and Hollywood, and now tonight he is here just for you. Please give a warm welcome to the wizard of ventriloquism! The man who can make anything talk! It's the legendary Puppet Master himself… Roddy Olsen!"

The audience erupted at the mention of the name. The applause and screaming was overwhelming.

Then, Olsen walked out, lugging his suitcase with one hand and waving happily with the other. His shining waistcoat looked like something from a futuristic space age as it sparkled in the bright lights.

Olsen placed the case on the floor and grabbed the mic.

"Thank you. Thank you all so much. What a wonderful ovation." He grinned at the immense wall of spectators lined up all around him.

"Now," Olsen began with a grin, "some of you are probably wondering just who I am. You've seen all those posters, seen my name up in lights, and you're thinking, 'What's the big deal?' This guy don't look too special. Well, I'm here to tell you that–"

"Let me out!"

The deep Brooklyn drawl sounded like it was coming from underground, a light, muffled growl. Many watching laughed. Others watched on, spellbound.

Olsen smiled. "I'm sorry, folks. I was about to introduce you to my good friend. But the little guy is very impatient and–"

"Get me out of here Roddy! Now!" said the mystery voice.

"Ok," said Olsen, moving to the suitcase, "but you've got to promise to be good."

He bent down and reached into the suitcase.

"Now let's see here," he murmured.

"No, no," sounded the new voice, clearer now. "Not the hand! Not the hand! Yeow!"

Olsen emerged carrying the comedic-looking Rusty Fox, who looked like a child's cuddly toy that had somehow come to life.

"That's better," the puppet said. The fox puppet was wearing his trademark black leather jacket and jeans.

The audience cheered at the appearance of the beloved character.

"Man," the little fox continued, "it sure is uncomfortable in that case. And it really stinks."

"Now, Rusty," Olsen told the puppet. "Why don't you introduce yourself to our friends."

The fox stared at the audience and laughed. "Good evening, folks. My name is Rusty Fox, and I am a rock n roll star. A teen idol."

"And what do you do, Rusty?"

"I sing, man," replied the puppet. He then broke into a chorus of Amazing Grace. More cheers rained down from the seats around them.

"That's great, Rusty. What else do you do?"

"Impressions. Here's my impression of President John F Kennedy…" the puppet began mumbling a presidential address in a perfect impersonation.

"And John Wayne." The fox leaned back in a peculiar stance. Then he spoke in a perfect send-up of the legendary actor. "Hey there, pilgrims. Get off your horse, and drink your milk."

The audience were laughing and cheering with glee.

"Tell us a joke, Rusty." Olsen prompted to the puppet on his arm.

"Hell, I should work in politics."

"Why's that?"

"The White House is full of dummies."

"Are you going to sing then, Rusty?"

"I sure am, Rod." The fox cleared its throat. "I'm going to perform Bobby Darin's hit Rock Island Line…"

At that, the audience suddenly broke into wild cheering. It was his most famous skit, and in many ways had helped launch his path to stardom.

Olsen held up a hand in thanks. "Bobby Darin, eh?"

"Yeah. Just don't tell him. He's still mad at me after I ate his budgie."

Rusty Fox cleared his throat. But suddenly another voice erupted from the suitcase.

"Attention! Stop that singing." This voice sounded like an old man, and was harsher.

"Uh-oh," said Olsen. He dipped into the suitcase and miraculously emerged with a second puppet – the grey-haired Napoleon, dressed in his army fatigues. The new puppet scowled.

"Don't let that good for nothing punk kid sing! I've told him his singing days are over. No more juvenile delinquency. It's time for this kid to join the US Army. And that's an order!"

Olsen spoke next. "Ladies and gentlemen, please meet my dear old friend, Napoleon."

The new puppet saluted. "US Army. Retired."

Rusty spoke next. "I'm not joining no army. I've got to conquer the music charts. And Hollywood. I'll be famous. Then I'll get all the chicks. To eat by myself!"

"You need to learn respect and discipline first, you slimy little maggot." Suddenly, the Napoleon puppet stared into the crowd. "Any army veterans out there tonight?"

Several cheers broke out. "Hell, that's enough for a platoon," Napoleon said. "We need to take this damn maggot out!"

Rusty cried: "I'm not a maggot. I'm a fox!"

Olsen, a puppet on each arm, spoke again. "There's only one solution, guys," he said, smiling. "We're all going to sing. Come on, Napoleon, it'll be fun."

The army man puppet shook its head, but Rusty had already begun singing Rock Island Line, the legendary track known for its speeded-up chorus.

And then the magic began.

Like a mini choir, Roddy and his two creations took it in turns to belt out the tune, a few lines each, getting faster and faster.

As the song reached its climax, the astonishing, three-way singing reached a crescendo. It was hard for many watching to believe what they were actually seeing. Olsen blurted out the lines at an impossible pace, in three different voices – including his own – while also moving the puppets' mouths in time.

Then, the Rock Island Line marathon reached its conclusion, and everyone in attendance was on their feet.

More banter between Olsen and his puppets, Rusty Fox and Napoleon, then followed – and the fans lapped it up, many cat whistling at the young man.

Finally, he moved towards the climax of his performance. Another perennial crowd pleaser, debuted two years earlier.

"Ladies and gentlemen," he began, gently putting Rusty and Napoleon down on a pre-placed bench.

"It has been my sincere pleasure to perform for you all. Just like it has been my pleasure to perform in towns and cities all across America. In every state. In front of all Americans, no matter who they are, or where they come from. And now, in recognition of my years of travelling America, performing from sea to shining sea, I would like to perform a very special song, just for you. The song is called… America The Beautiful. And it goes something like this…"

With that, the sound of soft piano music grew over the tannoy. The audience applauded in approval.

Olsen held the microphone before him like a seasoned crooner.

Then, he began singing the patriotic classic. His voice sounded as beautiful as that of an accomplished tenor. Punching his fist with each dramatic line, he looked every inch the accomplished star.

Just as he reached the opening chorus, belting out the lyrics with gusto, he was somehow drowned out by another voice.

"Hold it! Hold it! What the hell are you doing, son? I sing the big numbers round here. Remember?"

Olsen stopped singing and looked around in shock. The whole big top went quiet, many fans looking confused by the sudden interruption.

"Who is that?" Olsen roared into the mic, still looking around in alarm.

"You know damn well who it is! Me! The greatest crooner in America today. I just got in from Vegas, man. Now… help me down!"

Olsen looked upwards, towards the tent ceiling, and smiled. "Ladies and gentlemen, there he is! The king of the Las Vegas Strip, Tony Tan!"

Every head in the big top darted upwards, and every pair of eyes widened at the sight above them.

The Tony Tan puppet was being lowered from the trapeze rigging at the tent's summit to the sawdust by an abseil rope, with the figure slowly descending to join Olsen. Despite being suspended far above, he was still talking aloud as if being operated by the ventriloquist. And Olsen was somehow projecting his voice to sound like it was coming from the ceiling.

No one could believe it. Tony was dressed in his usual tuxedo.

As he came down from above, he landed perfectly upon Olsen's outstretched arm, like a pet falcon, and suddenly he was alive with his master.

A kind of stunned applause broke out, as every pair of eyes followed the tuxedo-clad puppet as he floated down to the sawdust.

Then, the music stirred again, and Tony and Olsen began singing together, one line at a time.

And, for the rousing finale of the song, both man and puppet somehow sung together, with Olsen creating an effect where it sounded as though they were holding notes in unison.

As America The Beautiful finished, both held their arms aloft, cherishing the applause.

Olsen had performed this show-stealer during a TV special two years earlier, and it seemed a fitting finale for the San Diego Spectacular tonight.

As the spectators cheered wildly all around, Klondike, Lacey and Plum joined them at the flap, all smiling with pride at the sight of the "kid from Fresno" performing for them again.

"There he is, folks, the Puppetmaster, Roddy Olsen!" Heavy roared into his mic as Olsen jogged off the stage floor with his suitcase. The two shook hands as the ringmaster returned to the centre of the arena.

Olsen was embraced by everyone watching at the flap, even an awe-struck roustabout, before Lacey took his arm and accompanied him down the tunnel and outside into the night.

"Oh, Roddy," she gushed, emotional and joyous. "That was just the best. You get better as you get older!"

He laughed. "I loved every minute. Being out there." He turned and looked at her, sending her weak all over with his giant baby blue eyes and quirky smile. "And performing for you, Lacey. For you and Kal. In your big top."

She put a hand over her mouth, shaking slightly as they reached the gardens beyond. "This cannot be a one-off, Roddy. It has to be a new beginning."

He looked out at the beautiful, reddish-brown sunset falling across the woodland. Then back at her. "Well, that sure sounds sweet."

Lacey turned back to the flap as she heard Heavy's next announcement. "I'll see you later, champ."

She kissed his cheek rapidly and rushed back inside.

Within the cauldron of the big top, the audience was reaching fever pitch.

"And now, ladies and gentlemen," the big man in the top hat roared, "the Double G Circus is proud to present to you a legend of American entertainment. One of the greatest living performers in the circus world today. Please welcome the wonder of the high wire, the All American… Doc Irwin!"

At the mention of the name, the stands burst into rich applause.

Doc Irwin came jogging out on to the sawdust, in his stars and stripes singlet, and with his usual American flag tied around his neck. As was tradition, he high-fived several patrons in the front row, before donating the flag to an elderly man in a wheelchair, whose blazer was adorned with medals.

Then, he jogged across to the gleaming high wire stage that had just been wheeled in by the roustabouts

As the usual patriotic marching band score began playing on the sound system, Irwin ascended one of the two tall wooden platforms that held the wire. Then, he stood braced on its roof, 20 yards in the air, ready to begin.

Irwin performed his standard routines. He began by walking across the wire, walking backwards, and then performing the splits in the middle of the tightrope, followed by a star jump.

He then jogged along the ultra-thin wire, before launching himself into a set of cartwheels, rolling effortlessly along the plastic cord, around and around, arriving at the far platform with a flourish.

The fans were on their feet, clapping hungrily at the amazing feats on display.

Next, Irwin removed a four-metre walker's pole from a chest within the platform. Then, he opened a duffel bag and pulled out a pile of white dinner plates which, of course, he then balanced upon his head.

The "plate walk" was met with another rousing ovation, as he crept across the wire, the pole lying horizontal across his midriff.

Next up was the equally stunning skipping rope crossing, before a delighted chatter swept across the big top as Irwin disappeared into a trapdoor in one of the platform bases – and re-emerged with his bicycle.

The stands were full of excitement as every pair of eyes followed the veteran performer's every move.

Below, at the flap, Klondike was grinning like a hyena, sensing the anticipation and delight in the air. He grinned at Lacey, Heavy and Plum alongside him.

"Here comes the money," he said, nodding at the wire stage.

Then, up on the high wire, Irwin mounted his bicycle and rode across slowly, beeping his horn when he got to the far edge. True to form, he then rode the bike backwards across the wire.

Then, when he reached his platform, he dismounted.

As cries of wonder emanated from the stands, Irwin led on top of the bike, so that his chest was firm on the saddle. Then, lining up his arms, he placed his hands into the pedals and pushed down hard. With a sudden jerking motion, he expertly lifted his legs into the air and pushed his chest off the saddle… and began peddling with his hands, driving the bike across the high wire while maintaining the handstand.

And, once across, the small, agile figure in the stars and stripes began riding backwards, until he reached his starting platform.

When he finally got to the side podium, Irwin expertly allowed his chest to fall to the saddle before flipping himself up into a standing position again.

The ovation that followed was otherworldly – stirring and monumental.

Irwin grinned and waved to the fans, bowing grandly and holding his arms aloft.

Then, Heavy's voice was booming across the PA system again. "Have you ever seen anything like it in your entire lives, folks? The wonder of the wire, Doc Irwin. Let's hear it for the Double G Circus's own superstar! The All American! Our death-defying, dynamic Doc!"

Klondike turned and allowed himself a glance at the VIP area above. He couldn't help but grin. All the suits were standing and cheering, like ecstatic football fans after a touchdown.

Garrison was in the thick of it, punching the air jubilantly. He caught sight of Klondike on the floor and the two locked eyes.

Klondike nodded up at the Colonel, who removed his stetson and bowed his head.

On the sawdust, Irwin had dismounted the apparatus and was jogging around the edge of the arena, high-fiving just about everyone seated in the front row. He stopped by a large group of small children, clustered together close to the flap enclosure at the very front. These youngsters were all from local orphanages, and were the recipients of this show's All American Association passes.

Irwin hugged them all and addressed each one sincerely, giving them his time. The veteran acrobat seemed content to remain with the group, as he chatted gently while rubbing his bald head with a towel.

Klondike and Lacey watched the curious get-together beside them, lost for words, before Heavy marched out on to the floor again, for his most famous introduction.

Klondike turned slowly, and felt an overwhelming sense of nostalgia and wonder as he glimpsed his champion of so many years, hovering impeccably at the flap, ready for action.

Gino Shapiro stood like a regal warrior, surveying his battlefield, his posture rigid but his eyes cool and relaxed.

His fireball orange singlet was covered in a Roman-like feathered cape, as he stood there proudly.

To his right, the musclebound figure of Andros Murphy jumped lightly on the spot, decked out in a red singlet with the same style of cape. Superheroes, ready to pounce.

Behind them, the kid Tommy Rogers stood in an orange tracksuit, his eyes wide in wonder at the sight of the packed grandstands engulfing them.

Klondike paced over to Shapiro, patting his back. "Gino… words fail me. It's like the last few months never happened. And, somehow, we're back together… and stronger than ever."

Shapiro allowed himself a grin, though his dark eyes remained fixed on the summit above.

"Si, chairman, is true." He finally eyed the circus boss. "I did not envision this… this kind of show. This reunion. I salute you and madam publicist for putting it all together."

"Thank you… for coming back."

Shapiro winked at him. "Thank *you*, chairman. For giving us this fantastic stage to perform on."

Klondike looked at the intimidating Murph, who then smiled at him like a baby. "Great to have you on board, Andros. Knock it outta the park."

Murph nodded. "You bet, man."

Then, any attempt at conversation was drowned out by Heavy's grand introduction.

"And now, ladies and gentlemen, behold one of the premier attractions in world circus today. Appearing live with handler and long-time partner, Andros Murphy. Direct from Hollywood, California, the Double G Circus proudly presents the daredevil sensation… one of the greatest trapeze artists that ever lived. Love him, cheer him, never forget him. It's the debonair king of the air… the one and only Gino Shapiro!"

With that, another thunderous cheer whipped around the arc of grandstands, rolling through the tent like a tornado.

Shapiro and Murph strode out grandly, waving at the cheers. Rogers followed behind deftly, tentatively, in awe of the scene.

As the flyers released their capes, the young apprentice quickly grabbed them and watched as the two partners began climbing the tall ropes, that led all the way up top.

As Shapiro leapt up on to his thick support rope, he looked down. "Just you watch this, Tommy!"

Then, he was gone, ascending his rope with astounding velocity, his arms spinning like wheels as they churned over repeatedly, eating up the rope. In seconds, he was halfway towards the top.

Rogers retreated dumbly, until he joined the others at the flap.

"You're learning from the best, kid," Plum said as Tommy stood beside him.

Rogers was watching the two figures in red and orange as they flew up their ropes. "I can't thank you guys enough for letting me be a part of this," he mumbled simply.

Klondike slapped him on the back. "Relax, kid. You're part of the circus now!"

Then, all eyes were on the trapeze rigging high above.

As a dramatic, orchestral tune blared out across the tannoy, Murph set himself up on the centre ring at the summit, while Shapiro stood poised at the far platform, which rested like a diving board attached to a tall scaffolding base at the far side of the tent.

Then, the beautiful trapeze artistry began.

Shapiro dived from his base, and caught ahold of the first ring. Without pause, he swung round twice, head over heels, to build momentum, before releasing his grip and flying through the air towards the centre.

Murph, hanging over backwards on his ring, his massive legs supporting him as he led suspended upside down, held out his arms and caught Gino's hands. He swung him back and forth twice, before releasing the grip, with Shapiro sent soaring up toward the ceiling, where he performed a textbook double somersault and then landed, in a sitting position, on ring three.

The applause began… and hardly died down.

The great Shapiro performed his full repertoire of vaults and trapeze leaps. There were several double spins, a triple, and a mesmerising quadruple turtle roll, where he was sent high into the air before tucking his knees into his chest and becoming a ball.

He also executed a rarely seen helicopter fall, coming down with a straight body, arms in a T shape, while spinning on the spot.

Both flyers then performed synchronised house whirls, spinning around in unison on their rings, before then maintaining handstands with perfect stability as the rings swung back and forth.

Then, while Murph held his handstand, coiling his feet in the ring ropes for a little extra support, Shapiro then stood up, swung back and forth several times, and vaulted across to the centre ring – landing almost on top of his partner, his feet somehow finding space on the base next to the upside-down Murph's hands.

As the ring continued swinging back and forth, Shapiro climbed upwards, until he was standing tall, his feet directly on top of Murph's, sole to sole, creating a bizarre-looking pose of two men standing – one on his hands, one on his feet – on the same ring.

As the cheers erupted, every pair of eyes in the tent staring up in horror and amazement, Shapiro then inexplicably placed his hands on the bottom of Murph's upturned, stockinged feet – and performed a handstand of his own.

This was all too much for just about everyone in attendance. There, high above in the tent's summit, two men performing handstands – on top of each other – on a single circus ring, as it swung rapidly back and forth.

As the cheers rang out, Shapiro manoeuvred himself around, this time standing on Murph's upturned feet again. Then, as they swung out towards the far side, Gino bent his knees and dived into thin air once more.

As the thousands of terrified fans held their collective breaths, the lithe figure in orange performed a quick-fire somersault and seemed to whizz through the air, arms outstretched.

Ring one swung towards him, its momentum now all but gone, and Shapiro grabbed at its base as it reached the height of its swing.

He made it.

Holding on to the ring base with all his might, Shapiro let his body dangle vertically and be propelled slowly along as he clung on.

When he eventually pulled himself up into a sitting position, he merely sat there for several moments, panting with the effort and sheer exhilaration of the wild stunt.

Every member of the capacity crowd was on their feet cheering, staring up at the daredevil above. As he sat swinging lightly, Gino waved and blew kisses at the fans. He also massaged his right shoulder, which felt ready to explode.

As the applause continued, Heavy's voice suddenly blurted out of the speakers, diverting everyone's attention.

"And now, the debonair king of the air will perform his traditional closer, on the high wire. But wait..." Heavy's voice became a curious, high-pitched whine. "Someone is already there! It's Doc Irwin again! How about that?"

Now, the circus crowd was alive with curiosity and wonder. All eyes shot back down to the wire stage, where Irwin was indeed back on the tightrope, riding his bicycle slowly, back and forth.

In an instant, high above, Shapiro had leapt across to his tall rope, and descended rapidly down to the sawdust. He seemed to slither and glide down in seconds.

As fans cheered and called his name, he jogged over to the wire platform and scrambled up, until he reached the top of the apparatus.

Standing erect at the roof of the wooden base, he eyed Irwin with mock bravado. A drumroll then sounded on the PA system.

Suddenly, the spectators turned deathly silent. For many, particularly veteran circus fans and big top aficionados, this was an historic moment.

Here stood Gino Shapiro and Doc Irwin, two legends of the circus, together now, at opposite ends of a high wire. A once in a lifetime happening.

The two figures stared each other down, like rival gunslingers in the old west, ready to draw and see who was the fastest gun.

At the flap, Klondike drew in a deep breath, his eyes wild and bulging. Lacey rested her chin on his shoulder. Plum put an arm around young Tommy, who looked ready to spontaneously combust.

Then, it began.

Irwin had been hovering on his bicycle, remaining steady on the spot. A perfect picture of expert balance.

Slowly, he began turning the pedals. Then, he was suddenly rolling along the wire.

Taking this as his cue, Shapiro made his move, walking rapidly across the wire. The two legends were headed straight for one another, and disaster looked imminent.

Several patrons watching in the stands screamed at the frightening sight.

Then, as Irwin cycled at the man in orange, seemingly intent on mowing him down, Shapiro took a quick few steps and leapt at the cyclist, placing his hands atop the bald head and inexplicably leapfrogging over the top of him. He landed on the other side of the bike, and merely continued walking along the wire to the opposite end.

Another wild, earth-shattering ovation shook the big top all over, like a shock wave rippling through the fabric and grandstands. No one could believe what they had witnessed – an unfathomable display of balance and death defiance.

Then, as Shapiro stood on the far platform, breathing heavily, a trapdoor near his feet popped open and out came Roddy Olsen, with Rusty Fox on his shoulders.

The plan had been to partially recreate the scene-stealing climax from the troupe's famous Rome performance earlier that year.

The routine had never been seen in America before, and this was the perfect night for such an act.

Olsen waved at the surprised cheers, then slowly mounted the wire, Rusty blabbering away in exaggerated excitement on his shoulders.

The ventriloquist expertly walked across the 30-yard tightrope, in conversation with his puppet passenger the whole time.

When he reached the other side, Irwin embraced him warmly, holding his arm aloft in a show of respect.

Then, in a fitting finale, all three performers mounted the wire, walking across with ease and meeting in the centre.

With Irwin in the middle, flanked by Olsen and Shapiro, all three men held hands and raised their arms in celebration. Balancing expertly on the plastic cord, they stood with their arms raised, and savoured the standing ovation bestowed upon them.

This was it... a wonderful moment for all the fans to remember. And quite a sight, as the three performers maintained their balance perfectly with their arms aloft, standing on the tiny tightrope.

At the flap, Lacey wiped away tears while Klondike joined everyone else in saluting the trio, clapping his hands like a man possessed.

The applause lasted more than a minute. It felt like the sound of euphoria...the ultimate expression of human emotion. Appreciation and admiration from a crowd that was beyond impressed, in many ways beyond exhilarated.

For the thousands watching, it was an unforgettable image, seeing the three greats together on the wire. The sight would stay with everyone who glimpsed it for some time. It was just one of those moments.

In the VIP section of the main grandstand, Garrison felt a mighty wave of pride and passion, and hugged Karen overwhelmingly. The plaudits and praise rained down on him from dignitaries all around.

The Colonel still could not believe what he had seen...and simply found it hard to accept that this was *his* show. The wild action that had gripped these thousands of spectators had gone down in his old tent. It was all just too much.

As the applause continued, Heavy strode out once again into the centre of the stage floor.

"And now, ladies and gentlemen, please show your respect for the stars of the Double G Circus. Your beloved San Diego superstars! Here they come!"

With that, all of the performers appeared at the flap. Rock n roll music began oozing from the speakers.

As Shapiro, Irwin and Olsen remained on the high wire, waving at the cheers, Corky and his helpers appeared, and began lightly jogging around the perimeter.

The Rollergirls followed, skating slowly behind them. Then came the Riders of the Double G, all on horseback and trotting around the floor, doffing their stetsons to the fans.

Arletta LaRue was perched upon Soolaimon's mighty shoulders as they too came out to more applause. The strong man carried her around for her entire lap of honour, jogging slowly.

Shapiro, Murph and Rogers joined the procession. Olsen followed with all three puppets – Rusty Fox, Napoleon and Tony Tan – in his grip. And bringing up the rear was Doc Irwin, who had invited his special pass holders on to the sawdust. The children all ran alongside him in wonder, waving happily at the cheers all around.

Eventually, the entire troupe of performers, along with all the roustabout helpers, gathered in the centre of the floor, in the shadow of the high wire stage, and waved at the thousands of fans.

The pop tune finally ended, and the San Diego Spectacular had reached its glorious conclusion.

As the entire troupe stood in a mighty throng in the centre of the big top, Klondike looked across at Lacey, Heavy and Plum, then nodded at the group in the middle.

"Come on," he drawled. "Let's join our all-stars."

He led the way as the management team began strolling across the sawdust, all looking up in sheer awe at the still-clapping spectators. Many were now beginning to leave the bleachers, but many more stood staring down at the stage floor, as if wanting this moment to last forever.

As Klondike wandered happily over the sawdust, he felt the wave of wondrous energy pulsing through the big top. His big top.

Nearing his all-conquering band of heroes, he looked them all over with pride and said one word, quietly to himself.

"Dynamite."

CHAPTER 31

"Alright guys, let's have a picture!"

"Come on… everyone get in there by the high wire. This will be rich!"

"Mr Klondike! Over here! Can you get all the guys in with you?"

A platoon of press photographers had swarmed wildly, racing across to where Klondike, his management team and all the performers had gathered in the centre of the stage floor, in the shadow of the high wire stands.

Like ants clamouring around a sugar pile, the snappers jostled and shoved as they aimed their cameras. A bunch of reporters had also scrambled down from the press box in the main grandstand, and they too were trying to get close to the troupe.

Within minutes, an almighty melee had broken out in the centre of the tent, everyone wanting a piece of Klondike and his team.

As the media representatives made their move, the thousands of spectators emptied the big top at a leisurely pace, many staring down in fascination at the scenes on the stage floor.

As the performers all embraced each other while smiling for the flashing cameras, Heavy attempted to restore a semblance of order.

"Alright folks," he bawled, "the circus stars will all pose for pictures. You'll get all the shots you want. I promise. There's no rush, now. Can you just…" he unceremoniously pushed an overexcited photographer out of his way. "Can you just remain calm and give us all a few moments. Please!"

The thunderous tone of the ringmaster seemed to have the desired effect. The snappers all took up positions in a semi-circle formation around the troupe and took their shots. The reporters waited patiently behind, watching the proceedings with glee.

As Klondike wandered through the group, congratulating everyone, he suddenly felt a hand wallop against his shoulder. He turned and saw an exuberant Griff Garrison grinning at him. In an unexpected show of emotion, the Colonel bear-hugged him with utter delight. Klondike could not believe the strength.

"Kal! Kal!" the older man croaked. "You did it! What a show! I can't believe it!"

He released his grip. "No," Klondike replied. "*We* did it. None of this would've happened without you, sir. You gave us this platform. And we'll never forget it."

Garrison slapped him on the back. "I'll never forget this night." He turned and clapped his hands as Lacey approached, picking the ace publicist up in another hug. She wailed in mock surprise.

"You guys are incredible," the Colonel cried. He raised his arms next, gesturing to the entire big top, the immense grandstands all around. "What a night!"

Klondike and Lacey joined him in looking around, soaking up the rich celebratory air that was intoxicating.

"Hey folks," a photographer suddenly cried from amidst the mass of bodies before them. He held an old-fashioned press camera with a giant flashlight. "How about a shot of you two, Mr Klondike and Miss Tanner, with Colonel Garrison, and the three high wire stars – Shapiro, Olsen and Irwin? Right under the wire?"

Everyone mentioned nodded happily, and a clearing slowly formed within the mighty throng of bodies.

Klondike once again embraced Gino, then threw his arms around Roddy and Doc. He stood between the three stars, with Garrison, Lacey and Heavy on the sides. They all stood there, arm in arm, linked together, as they posed in a neat line under the high wire.

The camera bulbs began flashing as the photographers snapped away. Many envisioned this prized shot gracing front pages and centre spreads in tomorrow's papers.

Klondike and his team all smiled widely, lost in the sheer euphoria of the moment.

Then, a youthful photographer leapt to the front of the media pool and took a snap, the resultant flash hitting the line-up's eyes like an explosive laser.

Klondike looked away, blinking several times as his vision faded momentarily. His arms remained linked with the others.

"Jesus! You trying to blind us all, son?"

Everyone laughed.

Then, Klondike frowned. His face took on a puzzled look, one of curiosity… but also recognition. It was a sound. Somewhere beyond the big top. A whirring. A buzzing. A roar.

He cocked his head slightly, trying to listen amidst the jovial banter of the press team and his group.

He shook his head, as if trying to shake off the magical feeling that had gripped him tightly. No one else seemed to notice the noise as the cameras clicked endlessly.

But he did. Then, it hit him. Exhaust. It was a motorbike. And it was coming closer.

Then, the whirring noise seemed to lessen slightly. Klondike frowned, squinting into the sea of bleachers beyond them. Then his eyes deftly fell to the flap. And then they froze in shock.

Breezing gently through the entrance way was a motorcycle, ridden by a tall-looking man in coveralls.

Now, Klondike felt like he was hallucinating. Nothing of that nature would be a surprise after this crazy night. But this was no mirage. A rider had entered their colosseum.

As he watched the bike creep inside the tent, still seemingly unnoticed by the others, he suddenly felt a queer sensation all over. He recognised the yellow and black motorcycle instantly. He should do. It had been a part of his troupe for two years.

Finally, he snapped out of his trance and pointed to the flap.

"Look!" he cried. "It's… it's Enqvist. Tip Enqvist. He… he's here! He's here!"

The others posing for photographs all looked up. Each pair of eyes widened at the sight of the mysterious rider who had suddenly appeared between the grandstands. The media pool all stopped and stared also. A surreal silence suddenly filled the tent.

The motorbike slowly glided onto the sawdust, drawing closer and closer.

"What the hell!" Heavy stammered. "Is he trying to join our reunion?"

"He's a bit late," Plum said in shock.

"And," Lacey breathed as she stood, still arm in arm with the others, "he was never invited. Nor, for that matter-"

She was cut off as the bike suddenly roared into life. Having crept gently onto the stage floor, its wheels suddenly spun with unexpected fury, sending the machine flying forwards at breakneck speed. And it was heading straight for them!

A woman screamed and several photographers cried out aloud at the realisation that the bike was racing straight at the group. As if activated by an unknown mechanism, the press pool spread wildly, everyone running desperately in a different direction.

Klondike and the others were still stood in their line, arm in arm, as they looked on in dumbstruck horror at the crazy scene.

The roar of the engine was deafening as Tip Enqvist drove straight at them across the sawdust.

Klondike was momentarily glued to the spot. He recognised the grizzled Norwegian stunt rider now. Tip was wearing pilot-style goggles and grey coveralls, but there was no mistaking the man's gait and distinctive silver/black hair.

Finally, the line-up beneath the high wire dispersed in a wild flurry as Enqvist arrowed his bike straight into its epicentre.

Klondike and Irwin dived to their left, taking Lacey and a still animated Garrison down with them. They all crashed to the floor in an ungainly heap.

Olsen and Shapiro both leapt aside with astonishing grace and speed, both slamming into a bewildered Heavy and throwing him to the ground.

As the line broke up with bodies falling either side, Enqvist roared straight down the middle, soaring into the spot Klondike had vacated a half second earlier and missing him by inches.

Instead, he rode into thin air as everyone dived clear, storming directly underneath the high wire and heading straight for the barrier in front of the facing grandstand.

Enqvist applied the brake frantically, and the bike skidded along the sawdust, spraying wooden chips everywhere in a mighty shower. He somehow remained in the saddle as the bike slid across the floor.

Pandemonium reigned. Suddenly, the great scene of celebration and joy became a hornet's nest of panic. Bodies scrambled everywhere to be clear of the stage floor after the surprise attack.

Reporters and photographers dropped their notebooks and cameras and bolted for the safety of the stands.

The few remaining spectators in the grandstands watched in horror as the unexpected turn of proceedings played out below them.

Klondike sprang to his feet, his head reeling. He watched Enqvist struggle to regain control of his bike as it skidded across the sawdust.

As he looked on in shock, he saw the deranged rider glance up. The two men locked eyes for a second. Enqvist let out a demonic snarl.

"Move!" Klondike barked, quickly pushing Lacey and Garrison towards the wooden high wire platform towers, which housed the internal ladders. "Get inside the wire tower and stay in there."

Irwin grabbed Lacey's hand and tugged her to the tall wooden structure, with Garrison following. Shapiro, Olsen and Heavy were all taking cover behind the opposite platform. Cries and screams seemed to rain down from every angle.

Then, the exhaust roared again. Klondike seemed to freeze on the spot. He watched in terror as Enqvist pointed his killer bike straight at him. He felt like a matador, facing an enraged and merciless Ronda bull.

The bike charged towards him, possibly 30 yards away.

In the corner of his eye, he noticed Heavy suddenly leap out from his hiding place and drop to one knee, as if about to fire a rifle.

The big man had something in his grip, and hurled it suddenly towards the rampaging bike.

Klondike recognised the flying object as a wrench, that had been hidden in the wire tower for repairs.

The spanner flew through the air like an Apache's tomahawk, spinning over and over. It slammed loudly into the bike's rear wheel, and immediately sent the machine sprawling into a slide.

Enqvist crashed down like a fallen racehorse, erupting into a cloud of wood chips.

The motorbike's roar finally ceased. Everyone stared across at the fallen rider.

Klondike had tensed all over, but now sprinted over to the ugly mangled mess of man and machine. Incensed, still overwhelmed after everything that had happened, he lunged over at Enqvist, who was sprawled on the floor, dazed and dumbfounded.

With a snarl, Klondike grabbed the rider's coveralls and hauled him up onto his feet.

"You crazy son of a bitch! You could've killed me!" he cried.

Klondike was beyond reason. In shock and operating on high emotion. He hammered his fist into Enqvist's solar plexus, making him double over. Enraged, he held up his closed hand for another blow, as Enqvist grabbed at his shoulder to remain upright.

Klondike was about to launch a right hook into the man's skull when another deafening sound thundered through the tent. This time a cry of alarm, emanating from the flap.

"Kal! Look out!"

Holding Enqvist before him like a giant dummy, Klondike turned and looked up in confusion. The whole episode was turning into a surreal, unreal dream. A true nightmare.

He squinted at the flap. A man was running into the big top, waving his arms in panic.

Klondike gasped in amazement. It was Mike Blakelock. Here! But that could mean only one thing. It meant that…

Then, he froze all over. A shock wave rippled through his body, like an electrical charge.

He saw what Blakelock was signalling. Too late.

Amidst a cluster of reporters, roustabouts and performers all scurrying away from the high wire, a sole figure was drifting towards him. A ghostly entity, bizarrely dressed in a tennis skirt and tracksuit top, with a pale white face and long blonde hair plastered to her skull with sweat. She was walking purposefully, like a robot, straight for him, oblivious to the throng of people panicking all around. She looked like she'd been hypnotised. It was a truly unnerving sight.

"Kal!" Blakelock screamed as he raced into the big top. "Get out of there!"

Irwin emerged from the nearest platform tower, then froze when he saw the woman walking in a trance. On the other side of the apparatus, Shapiro and Olsen both stared in shock, while Heavy froze, eyes widening in horror.

Klondike was spellbound. Standing like a statue, he softened his grip on the wincing Enqvist. Finally, he spoke.

"Jenny!" His voice came out in a gnarled growl. It was just the second time he had seen her in the flesh since that night in Las Vegas in 1958. And the other time had been in New York harbour. When she had waved goodbye… before the explosion.

Now, she walked straight at him, her eyes wild and frozen, the face a mask of concentration and eerie fascination. She was possibly 10 yards from him now.

"Jenny… what the…"

Then, her hand slipped into a light bag she wore on her shoulder. And came out holding a black and shiny revolver. Still showing no emotion, she stopped walking and held the gun before her, pointing it straight at her former lover.

A mutual gasp of shock reverberated around the onlookers. Everyone seemed to be rooted to the spot for the surreal episode.

Klondike stared at the gun in sheer horror, then up at the stone cold features of Jenny Cross. She had the face of a killer.

"No…" Klondike blurted.

She seemed to stare straight through him. "Goodbye Kal."

Then the muzzle exploded.

There was a bright flash and everyone jumped.

Klondike closed his eyes. He felt the bullet whizz under his arm and tear into Enqvist beside him, slamming into his chest and sending him flying over backwards, going down like a rag doll.

The vicious recoil of the gun made Jenny stumble, and she swayed drunkenly, making another step forwards.

Finally broken from his trance by the sound of gunfire, Klondike lowered his body and sprinted towards the shooter, before throwing himself towards her in a desperate dive.

Regaining her footing as she staggered over, Jenny clattered into him and they both sprawled on the floor, rolling over in an unseemly bundle.

Klondike scrambled to his feet rapidly, pulling her up by her wrists. The revolver was locked into her right hand, as if glued there. He grabbed hold of her wrist with both hands and desperately tried to prise the weapon free.

They stood nose to nose, grappling like wild dogs. He stared at her face, just inches away. She had a possessed, insane look, panting in crazy gasps. He had her wrist with both hands, the gun swinging around, as she fought to keep ahold of it. He shouted like a madman, and let one of his hands fall away, before thrusting it at her neck in an ugly stranglehold. He wanted to squeeze the life out of her. In response, she raised a foot and slammed it down on to his toes. He cried out in agony, and the entangled pair stumbled across the sawdust as if joined together as one.

Blakelock finally made it to the struggle, but immediately leapt backwards as he saw the gun muzzle swing towards him in the grip of the grappling duo.

Everyone from the circus had emerged from cover and was now staring, entranced, at the almighty struggle between Klondike and Jenny. It had been mere seconds since the gun had fired, but everything seemed to freeze in time.

Lacey emerged from the wire tower she had hidden in and, immediately recognising Jenny Cross, watched in utter incredulity as she and Kal wrestled for control of the gun.

As he maintained his hold around her throat, Klondike suddenly realised his other hand had lost its grip on the revolver. He stared into her cold blue eyes, inches from his own. She looked back sullenly, and seemed to smile.

A gunshot rang out.

Everybody froze, staring at the wrestling duo before them. Time seemed to stand still as all eyes focused on the man and woman grappling over the gun.

Both stood still, leaning into each other. Man and woman. Joined as one. There was a deathly silence.

Klondike and Jenny stared into each others' eyes. Neither moved for several seconds. The onlookers all held their collective breaths.

Then, as they held each other in a desperate last embrace, Klondike felt Jenny crumble in his arms. She slipped slowly through him towards the ground. As he stared at her, Jenny's eyes rolled into the back of her skull.

She had fired the gun. And the bullet was lodged in her spleen.

As Klondike watched in rapt fascination while Jenny slowly collapsed at his feet, he knelt down, hovering over her frame, lowering himself with her.

In a second, Blakelock was beside him, squatting down and leaning over her. He placed two fingers to the side of her neck. After a few moments, he glanced across at Klondike. He shook his head.

Then, as if activated by a master switch, everyone was upon them. A crowd rounded on the fallen duo in one big swoop. A sea of faces stared down at Klondike, many pale and fraught.

Then, everyone seemed to speak at once, spewing out exclamations of alarm.

Lacey was on him immediately, kneeling beside him and throwing her arms around his shaken frame.

"Oh Kal, my god! Are you alright?" She sobbed spasmodically as she clung to him.

Heavy knelt with them. He patted Kal's back. "Jesus Christ! Jenny Cross! Where in hell did she come from?"

Klondike merely knelt there, staring in shock at her dead body, lying before him.

They all gathered round. The performers. The roustabouts. The press.

Shapiro knelt down and hovered over the body of his former apprentice and partner. "Santamaria…" he said softly.

Klondike looked at each of his team. His stars. Then, his eyes followed Blakelock, who had stood and wandered over to where Enqvist lay sprawled on the floor 10 yards away.

Again, Blakelock felt the neck. And again, he stood and caught Klondike's eye, shaking his head sadly.

"Oh my god…" Klondike finally said, his voice coming in a strained, faltering whisper.

"What has happened here?"

It was the unmistakable voice of Garrison, who was standing just behind them all, his eyes wide in fright and shock.

Klondike still knelt over the body. Finally, with Lacey's help, he rose unsteadily to his feet. He clung to her like an unstable toddler. Heavy also placed a hand on his shoulder.

Irwin slowly began attempting to usher everybody away from the two bodies, and was joined by the roustabouts and the welcome might of Soolaimon. Olsen was trying to comfort the Rollergirls, who were tearful and traumatised, except for Pamela, who was trying to push an over-animated photographer away from the scene.

Garrison looked around at all the commotion, the aftermath of a night of elation… and disaster. It was all too much.

He stared at Klondike, who was standing arm in arm with Lacey and Heavy.

"Who the hell was that crazy broad?" Garrison snapped.

Klondike closed his eyes and shook his head, as if trying to vanquish an unwanted memory. He was standing in his big top, with his closest friends, after the greatest night of his life. And the worst nightmare imaginable. The two had somehow merged, euphoria and dysphoria, on this night.

"What is this, Kal? What happened? Kal!" Garrison cried.

Klondike finally opened his eyes. His vision was blurred, his heart still thundering like a jackhammer.

He took a look back at Jenny's fallen body. Shapiro had placed a jacket over the face, and was now kneeling, bowing his head.

"The end of a long road," Klondike finally muttered. He eyed Garrison, who looked completely bewildered.

Outside, an ambulance siren wailed, getting louder each second.

"A road to hell and back," Klondike continued, his voice a low growl. "But it's over now. It's all over."

CHAPTER 32

GUNSHOT TERROR AT THE BIG TOP!
By Jim Hunslett, San Diego Chronicle

Violence and horror erupted at the San Diego Spectacular last night, as the biggest circus show in the city's history ended in mystery and bloodshed.

Two seemingly unwanted intruders were shot after the final act, a horrific and frightening conclusion to what was supposed to be a night of magic.

The Double G Circus show had been an unprecedented success, an advance sell-out and an incredible, star-studded line-up of top talent, roared on by a massive audience of an estimated 5,000 fans.

But mayhem and disaster followed as the circus came to an end, after its incredible high wire grand finale.

As reporters and photographers rightly rained down praise upon the performers and management at a curtain call-style media gathering, just minutes after the show had ended, the great tent was thrown into chaos.

First, an uninvited motorbike roared into the arena, its rider intent on mowing down legendary circus manager Kal Klondike, who was posing for pictures.

After just missing his target and thus murdering the boss man, the biker was then gunned down by a mysterious woman, who had appeared out of nowhere, firing a revolver.

After a struggle, the female was herself shot, apparently a suicide.

Later in the night, a circus official revealed that the killed biker was in fact Tip Enqvist, a former superstar stunt rider for Klondike who had defected to rival outfit Ribbeck World Circus.

What exactly he was doing at the big top, and his motivations for trying to run people over, were last night still unclear.

As for the mysterious woman, speculation was rife late last night that the gun-toting blonde was none other than Jenny Cross, the former trapeze flyer who infamously tried to kill superstar Gino Shapiro at a Las Vegas show in 1958. Miss Cross had been institutionalised, but her whereabouts over the past two years are now being investigated.

All in all, the surreal night in Balboa Park represents yet another frontline nightmare for the great Klondike.

Just months ago, the former knife thrower hit the headlines when his circus ship sunk in New York Harbour on its return from a tour of Europe. He lost his fortune... and his circus.

Now, after mounting a spectacular comeback with this star-studded show in San Diego, it would seem his world has fallen on its head once again.

Attempted murder. People getting shot. Blood on the sawdust.

Not what your average circus-goer expects to see on a night under the big top.

The following days represented a surreal nightmare for the men and women of the Double G Circus.

And it should not have been that way. After the most spectacular night of the company's history, its horrendous conclusion and aftermath had quashed every idea of glory and success.

The box office take had been astronomical, both in the tent and on the midway. The show had been a seamless delight, despite the rapid pooling together of talent and resources barely a week before the big night.

And the fans had been wild with joy at what they had seen.

It was only an act of heavenly fortune that meant just a handful had witnessed the horror that had befallen the troupe after the show had finished.

Just how much of an impact the shootings and bloodshed would truly have on the Double G and its success was a giant unknown factor. Only time would tell. But the press coverage had rightly panned the entire atrocity – despite all media outlets praising the show that preceded it.

A strange, indescribable air hung over the circus camp in Cortez Gardens. The rush of such a spectacular success, nullified by the horror that followed.

For many, it felt as if the greatest night of their lives had been robbed from them. By those enslaved by power, vengeance… and madness.

The Double G had delayed their departure to Los Angeles by several days as a result of the shootings.

The circus encampment remained largely in place, with just the big top brought down and folded up and the grandstands placed on the flatbed trucks for transportation.

Elsewhere, everything remained the same. The midway stalls and attractions, the trailers, the ticket booths. There was just one element missing… the magic in the air.

Police and various investigators had made the camp a second home in the immediate few days after the San Diego Spectacular.

Circus members were all interviewed, statements were taken and photographs and crime scenes were put together… and dismantled.

Detectives were, predictably, dumbstruck by the entire episode.

Ultimately, they had a murder on their hands. And the murderer had killed herself. The San Diego PD requested that the Double G team remain in Balboa Park until the end of the week, as they continued their on-site investigations.

Beyond that, nobody seemed to know what to expect.

The troupe merely mulled around Cortez Gardens, lost in their thoughts – and perplexed by their futures.

Klondike had known that the only person alive who knew all, or even some, of the answers was Mike Blakelock.

So, as soon as the police left the camp, their snooping at a conclusion, it was time for internal action.

Klondike had arranged for a grand staff meeting in the canteen. Everyone – performers, roustabouts and management – gathered in the white marquee, which was jam-packed as all on the payroll filled the tables usually reserved for mealtimes.

Klondike sat at a 'top table' at the very front of the gathering, along with Garrison, Heavy, Lacey and Plum.

Before them, everybody associated with the Double G filled dining tables in great bunches.

After a brief welcome and greeting, Klondike introduced Blakelock to the entire troupe. His old army buddy had stayed on since the night of the show, enjoying temporary quarters in a vacant trailer.

Klondike had explained his history with Blakelock, before the private investigator had offered an in-depth explanation of everything he had learned.

An enraptured audience hung on his every word, finding it hard to comprehend that anything so sensational and far-reaching could affect their travelling circus.

When Blakelock concluded his piece, explaining how he had chased Jenny all the way from Las Vegas, he was faced with a sea of confused faces.

Colonel Garrison, still as bewildered as he had been on the night of the show, spoke first.

"None of this makes any sense, dammit," he said from the front. "This Cross woman should've been locked up all this time. Not cavorting around with all these rich men. Planning to destroy Kal's circus. Then us!"

Blakelock, standing at the front, looked across at him. "The psychiatrist who fell for her has a lot of explaining to do. None of this would've happened if he'd played by the rules."

"God damn it all to hell," Heavy blurted, chewing on an old cigar. He looked exhausted. "The mess… the carnage that woman has caused. It's… it's…"

"Immeasurable." Lacey finished for him. She was seated next to Klondike, resembling a guardian angel. "That accursed woman has tried to ruin us repeatedly. And she destroyed Kal's reputation in New York."

"Well," Blakelock said quickly, turning to look at her, "one good bit of news there is… the New York Harbour Police are now re-investigating the sinking of The Floating Top. After what she did on Saturday. So, let us hope, Kal will finally be cleared of any wrongdoing."

Klondike remained impassive as he sat at the long table. He could not get the image of a lifeless Jenny Cross crumbling before him out of his mind.

He cocked an eyebrow as a low sigh drifted from the nearest table to the front. He looked up.

Gino Shapiro. Sat facing them. A large towel covering his shoulders. Murph and Rogers sat either side of him.

"That crazy, mixed-up dame," Shapiro muttered quietly. He looked deflated. "She could have been the greatest star in all of circus. With that face, that flair… ah, is mesto."

Klondike eyed him. "We gave her everything, Gino. Our knowledge. Our wisdom. Our centre ring. And… and she tried to destroy us."

Doc Irwin was sat just behind the flyers, arms folded, nursing a glass of milk. "All those people out there… children, families… none of them should ever have seen anything like that."

"You don't need to tell us!" Garrison snapped from the front. The older man rubbed at his eyes. "Why, oh why, did she have to choose that show? On Saturday? The biggest night of our lives…"

Blakelock sighed as he stood hovering over them all. "The publicity was huge. She heard about it and figured she'd failed. It sent her over the edge, I guess. So, off she went, drunk and crazy… off to San Diego with a gun in her handbag."

Plum was seated at the side of the top table, his briefcase on his lap. He was riled. "How was all of this even possible? She tried to kill Gino. Yet was allowed to walk around free in Las Vegas all that time!"

Blakelock nodded at the small financier. "She was with Generoso. The Mob. Nobody looked at her, or into her. Everyone just looked the other way."

A grim silence engulfed the canteen tent.

Pamela Hotch was seated with the rest of the Rollergirls next to Gino's table. The group looked almost unrecognisable dressed in plaid shirts and jeans. The leader of the skaters spoke up.

"And what was the story with that other guy?"

Klondike rubbed at his stubbly jaw. "Enqvist. Another madman. God knows where he came from." He shook his head. "The no-good son of a bitch."

Blakelock looked at Pamela. "It would seem, Miss Hotch, he was on some kind of mission as well. The same one as Jenny. To kill Kal… and his circus."

"He was sent here," Klondike growled. "By Ribbeck."

"Damn straight," Heavy murmured.

Garrison was incredulous beside them. He stared at Klondike. "For a man running a circus, bringing magic to children and families… you sure have a long list of enemies. I mean, what the hell is all this? People trying to kill ya! On every damn tour!”

Lacey placed a protective, comforting hand on top of Kal’s. She answered. “Kalvin’s success has been unprecedented. He went from running a backwoods show with next to no capital or backing, and turned it into a million dollar enterprise, with merchandising and television exposure. And…” she added dryly, “an international market.”

She continued with a haughty gaze around the tent. “Now, that kind of success, that growth, generates jealousy, bitterness and even hatred. Kal has rivals everywhere. They are irked by his rise. His fame. Now, throw all of those elements together, and you have a pretty dangerous junction, in my opinion. To say nothing of an insane, unstable ex-lover, with access to guns.”

Garrison nodded slowly. “You make a good case, Lacey. I just can’t believe all this madness can stem from running a circus.”

Lacey stared at him, her hypnotic violet eyes piercing. “Jenny Cross was beyond reason. And Eric Ribbeck… well, he is more than just a rival. He has proven in the past he will go to extraordinary lengths to hurt us. Destroy us, even.”

Again, a stony silence fell over the marquee. Everyone seemed to stare into nothingness. At the rear of the canteen, the roustabouts and stewards were seemingly pretending they had not heard a word, unwilling to be involved in anything so radical. None of this seemed real.

Finally, the quiet was broken by Roddy Olsen, who was sat alone in a chair behind the Rollergirls.

“I guess the big question is… what happens now?”

Klondike squinted across at him. “Now? Simple. We roll. On to Los Angeles and the conclusion of the tour.”

Then, he studied Olsen and caught sight of Corky, sat at the far side with the cowboys.

“Listen,” he mumbled uneasily. “We are eternally grateful to you guys, Roddy and Corky, for showing up and making this show a blockbuster. A barn burner.” His eyes fell to the table directly before him. “And to you Gino, and your friends, Murph and Tommy. You guys saved us, and made that show the greatest. You gave the Double G the best night of its existence. We thank you forever. But, now, well…” he looked down, and rubbed that jaw again. "I am sure you'll want to move on, and get back to your old lives. You're not signed up here, you're in free agency. You can go and be attractions anywhere."

This time, the following silence felt genuinely poignant. Finally, Shapiro stood. "Chairman," he said, in an uncharacteristic low tone. "I think I speak for all of us – my boys, the dollmaker, the clown – when I say… we have gone back to our old lives, being here with you."

Corky let off an air horn. Finally, there were a few laughs and smiles. "The king has spoken. And he speaks the truth," he cried.

Olsen looked up and addressed the top table. "Absolutely. We are here because we want to be here, Kal." He chuckled. "And the hell with anywhere else!"

Corky let off the horn again. He added: "And besides, no matter what went down on Saturday… the actual show was a smash. Right now, the Double G is without a doubt the hottest circus around."

Garrison seemed to explode. "How can you say that, dammit? Two people were shot and killed on our sawdust. Killed! We're lucky we haven't been shut down by the federal government. Blackballed outta the business for good."

"With respect, Colonel Garrison," Lacey said quietly, "your circus is the talk of the showbusiness world. And not just because of the notoriety of the shootings. But the show itself." She looked down at the tabletop in front of her and ruffled through several newspaper clippings. "The LA Tribune called it, 'One of the greatest circus spectaculars of our time, or any time.' American World called Gino and Andros's act, 'The most incredible display of trapeze seen in years.' And…" she flashed her eyes at the Colonel in her devastating fashion. "Spotlight described your show as, 'Quite simply, one of the greatest nights in recent circus history.'"

She sat back, her hand still on Klondike's. "Such praise is not dished out with regularity by those outlets."

Garrison watched her thoughtfully, chewing on a half-smoked cigar he held before him. He nodded. His wrinkled, leathery skin was covered in lines, which seemed to enhance the more he mulled it all over. "I'll be damned if I know how to process all this. Saturday was the greatest night of my life, and also the worst. How do you like that?"

Plum, looking down at some files in his briefcase, piped up. "We made over ten thousand dollars on Saturday… through merchandising. Merchandising!"

The Colonel looked at him. "Jesus Christ." Then, he seemed to address the room. "What the hell do I do now?"

They all stared at him, helpless and mystified. It really was all too much for everyone to digest.

Then, as if on cue, Karen Garrison breezed into the marque through the small flap door behind the top table. She smiled cheerfully as everyone watched her. She approached her husband from behind, put a hand on his shoulder and then showed him an envelope.

"You need to see this, hon. Just came in the mail, special delivery from Western Union."

Garrison glanced at her, then stared at the envelope. Opening it up, he produced a sheet of paper, frowning as he read it.

The frown slowly transformed into a look of amazement, the wrinkled, leathery skin somehow seeming to straighten up.

"I'll be damned," he said for the umpteenth time that week.

Another silence. Everyone was curious. Plum sensed something, and leant forward. "What is it, Colonel?"

Garrison made a strange, snapping laugh-like sound, a gasp of incredulity. He looked straight at Klondike alongside him.

"You won't believe this!"

Kal straightened up. "Tell me."

"It's a telegram from the Cow Palace, San Francisco. They are… er, requesting that the Double G plays there this year. They've asked if they can book us! If they can join… join our tour." He stared dumbly at the piece of paper in his grip. "I've never had anything like that before. An offer!"

Klondike offered a wry smile. "Frisco is right up the coast from LA. Can they do two weeks from now?"

Lacey could not help smiling. "You see?" she purred. "The hottest ticket in town. The Palace knows we're going to be in the region. They want us. Just like that."

Garrison looked at the telegram, then at Lacey, Klondike and Heavy, then up at Karen. Then, he stood and gave his wife a big hug.

"God damn!" he cried, suddenly elated again. "This is unbelievable. Even two people getting killed in our big top can't stop us! I can't get my head around it!"

As he embraced Karen, his steely grey eyes were locked onto Klondike and Lacey beside him. The eyes had an enthralled, almost frightened look, as if he were glimpsing aliens from another world. A land of far superior beings.

Klondike stood now, patting Lacey on the shoulder. Everyone in the marquee stared as the circus boss and the Colonel faced each other at the top table.

"Looks like business is booming," Klondike drawled.

He held out his hand. Garrison took it gladly and the two men had a long handshake.

"You're something else, Kal Klondike," he wheezed, looking ready to faint. "You and your team, you've transformed the Double G. And, you know what, you've lived up to every promise you made back at the Sidewinder. You've given it your all... and you've made us a success. Despite all this madness. Everything you've had to deal with."

Then, Garrison removed his stetson and held it aloft. "Kal Klondike, I salute you. We all do!"

At that, the inhabitants of the canteen burst into a hearty, spontaneous applause.

The performers at the front all smiled wisely, while the roustabouts were simply delighted their employment was safe... and possibly long-term.

Klondike turned to face everyone as he stood at the front. Heavy stood and shook his hand. Lacey rose and kissed him on the cheek. The circus boss held up a hand in thanks.

Then, he grinned across at the Colonel.

"Thank you all. I appreciate it. But there's something you all need to know." He let the sentence hang in the air, building suspense before delivering the pay-off.

"I'm just getting started!"

The next morning, the entire picture around the circus camp in Cortez Gardens seemed rosey, healthier in every way.

Roustabouts went about their work with renewed vigour, slowly deconstructing the midway stalls and cabins. The talent all pottered around their trailers, engaging in excited small talk.

The reporters and cops were all gone now, and the only outsiders descending upon the site were excited passersby and autograph hunters. They were not disappointed.

Klondike and Blakelock were wandering slowly around Balboa Park, heading up the main promenade towards the entrance gates.

"So, you're heading back to Hollywood, huh?" Klondike asked, puffing lightly on a giant cigar.

Blakelock, hands in his leather jacket pockets as they walked, could not stop looking all around at the park's natural beauty. "Of course. I dropped everything to help you out, old buddy. I have to get back and catch up." He chuckled to himself. "Hell, those fight scenes won't choreograph themselves. Someone needs to show those fancy-looking dudes how to throw a punch. And, alas, someone needs to take the falls. And the bruises."

"The life of a stuntman…" Klondike mused.

"Fight co-ordinator, pal. Besides, the pay is good and the work is easy. And they love me up there."

Klondike stopped walking, and stood still, leaning his mighty frame against a fence that overlooked a reservoir. "I can't thank you enough for what you did, Mike. I know it was hard, and a big mess. And then you had to see all that on Saturday. It was just too bad."

Blakelock nodded vaguely, watching the waterline. His eyes seemed to darken. "Never seen anything like it. The Cross woman. That guy Generoso. Now… they're both dead. That, er, that was one strange assignment, Kal."

Klondike looked down. "I'm sorry, man."

"No. No, it was my debt to you, old buddy. For that minefield in Gastrade. For what you did in that terrible place. We always said the day would come when you'd call on me. Calling in that IOU for saving my life. Well, Jenny Cross was that IOU. That's all there is to it."

Klondike tried to smile. "Like I said before. You're the best in the business. The only man I'd have trusted with all this."

Blakelock nodded, lighting a cigarette. "Your LA show is a week Saturday, right?"

"Right."

"I'll be there, old buddy. Front row."

"Come and see me beforehand. At camp. I'll get you a VIP pass."

Blakelock smiled, looking around them. "I'm gunna put that one comment right back at ya, pal."

"What's that?"

He made to walk away, looking back at Klondike with a grin. "It's you who's the best in the business, Kal. The circus business!"

Then, he turned and slowly walked towards the parking lot. And his trusty black Sedan.

Klondike watched him go. Sadly. He kept his eyes on the tough guy in the black leather jacket. An enigma in every sense of the word. But one he was glad he had looked up and called upon.

As his eyes followed the departing Mike Blakelock, they were filled with admiration. But also something else.

Regret.

Back at the camp, Klondike found Lacey waiting for him outside his trailer. She wore a bright red trouser suit with a massive brown trenchcoat over her shoulders, a steaming coffee mug between her hands. She seemed to be pacing around absently.

He wandered down the path. "Are you anxiously awaiting my return, Lady Guinevere?"

She grinned. "No such luck, Sir Knight. I am a mere messenger."

"My, my. They employ glamorous messengers in corporate trouser suits these days?"

She rolled her eyes, tossing her hair back. "Well, I have many talents, as you well know, kitty cat."

He reached his trailer, pulling the dead cigar stump out of his mouth and examining it. "And isn't that just the truth. I think for our traditional end of season date this year I want to fly you out to Hawaii for an exotic island cruise."

She giggled. "Well, as luscious as that sounds, I have a feeling there won't be much time for vacations. It would appear we have a lot to plan… for next season!"

Klondike raised an eyebrow. "Oh? Who said anything about next season?"

She slowly meandered over to where he stood at the trailer door, and gazed into his eyes playfully. He had to look away, the gaze was so mesmerising, overpowering almost.

"The Colonel wants to see you in his executive trailer. Well, us actually."

He smiled. "Our Colonel is smashing it out of the ballpark right now. Trying to broker deals with anyone who will listen. Like a true circus boss."

"He likes you, Kal."

"Correction, Guinevere. He likes *us*."

He made a bridge with his arm. "Shall we?"

She happily placed her arm through his and the duo walked slowly to the far side of the accommodation enclosure, zigzagging through a maze of camper vans and trucks.

The massive executive trailer wasn't hard to miss, and the silver exterior looked like it had just been polished by a car wash crew, such was its shiny gleam.

Klondike rapped on the door. One second later, Griff Garrison pulled it open, looking like a proud elder statesmen greeting his favourite grandkids.

"Well, there's my top team. Come on in!"

He led them inside the vast confines of his portable home. Lacey, making her debut in the executive lodge, felt her eyes enlarge as she took in the opulence of the trailer. They both entered the lounge, with Garrison happily handing them small, camping-style cups of black coffee.

"Thanks for coming over," Garrison was saying, looking animated and on edge, a far cry from his bewilderment of the past days.

"It was worth it to see this moving mansion of yours," Lacey quipped. She flopped into an old-fashioned arm chair, crossed her legs and lit a cigarette, still eyeing the fancy furnishings.

Klondike perched on a leather couch, looking over a host of paperwork that covered the rectangular coffee table. A heavy-looking parcel sat amongst the papers.

"You seem, ah, suddenly elated, Colonel," Klondike mused, sipping his coffee. "That offer from Frisco has transformed your mood after the shootings, I imagine?"

Garrison kept on smiling as he paced the lounge, seemingly gripped by anticipation. It was like he was in on some joke the others were unaware of.

"There's more to it than that," Garrison stammered. "That telegram from Cow Palace was just the start. I had two more this morning. Offers for next season. From Cleveland and... and Chicago!"

Klondike stared at him in disbelief. "Chicago! You cannot be serious!"

Still, Garrison grinned like a wisened owl. "It's all there, son," he pointed vaguely at the coffee table. "The Western Union man dropped by earlier."

Klondike rummaged through the paperwork, but could not process what he was seeing. "Chicago. America's favourite circus town!" He glanced up at the Colonel, a mesmeric gaze illuminating his rugged features. "And Cleveland. Hell, big cities. And well off your traditional deep south and west route. This is beginning to sound like the dawn of a nationwide tour!"

The Colonel laughed, gurgling wildly. "I know! I dared to think it myself! The big boys are calling, Kal. Just like I always dreamed."

Lacey had watched the proceedings coolly. "I don't mean to burst any bubbles, boys, but let's not get too carried away, shall we? This isn't a nationwide tour yet. But..."

"It sure as hell is a good start!" Garrison blurted excitedly.

She looked him over. "It is indeed, sir."

Klondike grinned. "Seems like we need to start making some plans for the off-season, Colonel. Things are moving."

Garrison looked down at him with a queer look as he stood at the head of the trailer lounge. Pride, mixed with admiration.

"They sure are, Kal. At every level. And… faster than you think."

Klondike glanced at Lacey in alarm, then back at their host.

"I'm not sure I follow, Colonel."

Garrison nodded to himself, happy and content. "What has happened here these past few weeks, in my circus, is the stuff of dreams, beyond my wildest imagination. Me, a proud, small-time circus owner, who ran a big top just for the love of it. Just because it was something I always wanted. A hobby, in many ways…" he paused at the mantelpiece, looking tenderly at one of the many framed pictures of himself and Karen. This particular one had them standing amidst their horses at Sidewinder Ranch.

The Colonel continued: "What you have done here is transformed my circus from a cowboy outfit into…into a superstar outfit. Kal, you've somehow pushed my circus to become a major troupe. A big-time player in the industry. And it's all thanks to you and Lacey, and your incredible, and loyal, performers. Hell, even now I still cannot believe that Gino Shapiro, Doc Irwin, Roddy Olsen, Corky the Clown and the Rollergirls have all committed to perform for us. For my circus! They want to stay with us! And it fills my heart with joy, I tell ya!"

Klondike nodded happily. "They want to sign with the Double G."

Garrison stared at him. "That's what I wanted to talk to you about, Kal."

He frowned. "What?"

The Colonel paced to the end of the long coffee table. "The Double G was my baby. Our cowboy show, out of the Sierras, featuring a team of guys I'd found down the years – and folks seemed to like them." He eyed Klondike with a look of steel now. "This…this is something different. This is box office gold, Kal. Dynamite. We all know it. And the people and the press sure as hell know it. We've got critical and commercial acclaim now." He shook his head. "No, this is no longer the Double G Circus. The Double G was a foundation block for this project of ours. A springboard, or some such thing. But the show I created has been left behind now. After Saturday night. That… that on Saturday night was the future. That is the gold standard now. A new show."

Klondike and Lacey looked mystified as they glared up at him.

"What are you saying, Colonel?" Lacey whispered.

Garrison took a deep breath. "I'm saying we're rebranding. The Double G Circus is changing its name. From this day forward, we will now be known as…" ever the showman, he paused for effect, enjoying the dumbfounded gazes of his visitors. "From this day forward, we will be known as Klondike's Circus! The new Klondike's Circus. It's back… and it's better than ever. An all new extravaganza!"

On the couch, Klondike looked enraptured. He shook his head wildly. Lacey watched with more than a hint of admiration.

"Woh there, Colonel," Klondike stammered. He stood up, removing his fedora and running a hand through his hair. "Listen, I appreciate it. Really, I do. But you can't do that. The Double G is everything to you. It's your lifeblood. I know that more than most. It ain't right, dammit."

Garrison chuckled. "After all I heard at that meeting last night, it sounds like we're going to become a juggernaut in the circus world. With all that talent signed up. And, Kal my boy, that was all your doing. It was all you. Hell, even Doc Irwin came on board to try and help you out. It was nothing to do with me."

He bent slightly and picked up a newspaper clipping lying amidst the raft of papers on the table. "Besides, the name Klondike's Circus is a major draw. It's an industry titan. Famous across the nation. Seen on TV screens everywhere, and a staple of Las Vegas. It's a draw. And that is why we are changing our name to Klondike's Circus. It is known everywhere as the best in the business."

Klondike shook his head as he stared at the Colonel. "A lot of folks will tell you Klondike's Circus is a national disgrace."

"That won't stop the people coming out to see us," Garrison shot back defiantly. He held his hands aloft. "Think about it, Kal. The return of Klondike's Circus. After this crazy year you've had. Next season will be immense. Everyone will want to come and see our show." He turned and locked his grey eyes onto Lacey, who was sat spellbound in the old armchair. "And just think of the public relations opportunities, Lacey. The name

Klondike's Circus will be on billboards again. You'll be promoting Klondike's Circus again. A brand everyone knows."

Lacey stubbed out her cigarette in a horseshoe ashtray. She glanced at Kal. "He's right. This will generate real heat. Especially after all we've been through this year. The fans will go wild for our roster. Just like before."

Klondike studied her, then looked back at their host. "Just don't seem right, is all. This is your circus, Colonel. I'm just the manager."

Garrison shrugged. "Nothing really changes, son. I'm still the owner and principal investor. The backer. But you, my boy, are the commercial banker. It makes sense from a business point of view."

With that, his eyes drifted down to the mysterious brown parcel sat on the coffee table. Klondike caught his gaze.

"Don't tell me," he drawled. "That is full of more offers?"

'No, no," Garrison laughed. He bent down again and delicately peeled open the parcel. A package of flyers was inside. He lifted one out and prepared to reveal it to the others.

"We had these printed in town last night. Me and Karen had a grand idea. And, well, we just went with it. This… this is our new logo."

With a theatrical flourish, he turned the piece of glossy paper over.

Klondike and Lacey stared, and both had a look of awe.

The flyer showed an illustration of a small heap of gold nuggets, with a white circus tent emerging from the centre of the pile. In dramatic gold lettering underneath, the words KLONDIKE'S CIRCUS were printed.

"Oh my god!" Klondike cried. "Colonel, that is fantastic."

"Perfect," Lacey whispered in shock. She was eyeing the logo like an archeologist surveying a prized historical artefact. "Where…how did you come up with that?"

Garrison smiled with deep pride. "Me and Karen came up with it yesterday. It seemed right. Klondike… the gold rush. Gold being mined. It all just fell into place, so we went ahead and got these printouts."

Klondike had taken one from the parcel. He laughed, exasperated. "You were right," he drawled. "Things are moving fast!"

Lacey had also taken one of the glossy flyers. She held it up triumphantly. "You get ten out of ten for this, Colonel. PR gold, you might say!"

Garrison nodded, sipping his coffee, now calm as can be. "Glad you like em. So, the plan will be to have that logo on everything. Trucks, trailers, flatbeds. Not to mention the big top itself, and all the billboards, posters, programmes, press releases…everything!"

"I don't know what to say," Klondike blabbered. He paced over to Garrison and they shook hands once again. Kal slapped him on the back. "All I can think of is to repeat what I've said since day one, Colonel. Thank you. Thank you for believing in me."

Garrison placed a hand tenderly on his shoulder. "Way I see it, Kal… you chose us. And we are eternally grateful."

Lacey clapped her hands with joy. "A match made in heaven."

No one could argue with her apt assessment.

After Colonel Garrison's dramatic announcement, Klondike and Lacey wandered slowly and quietly around the circus camp – dumbstruck, excited and with a renewed sense of optimism.

Both had felt their minds become reactivated at the prospect of a blockbuster 1962 season. The thought of a potential nationwide tour was thrilling, and already motions were going through their collective consciousness – thoughts on schedules, TV dates, new show material, and so much more.

The duo had walked almost in silence through the trailers and what was left of the midway as the roustabouts rapidly disassembled everything in sight. They made their way on a steady lap of Cortez Gardens, taking one last look at the scene of what had been a truly unforgettable night, in so many ways. A night that would stay with all associated with the circus for ever.

As they completed a perimeter of the now dwindling circus camp, Klondike and Lacey arrived back at the garden entrance.

There before them was an excited goggle of youngsters, teenagers with their parents, all taking pictures and pointing excitedly towards a giant flatbed truck that contained two colourful midway stalls as its load, the shooting gallery and the pitching parade.

And there before the truck, a host of performers were all stood in a line, happily posing for photographs.

Shapiro, Irwin, Olsen and Corky were in the centre of the group, flanked by the Rollergirls, Arletta LaRue, the Riders of the Double G, the mighty Soolaimon and, standing on the edge of the gathering in full ringmaster attire, the inimitable presence of Heavy Brown.

The whole group suddenly gave a big cheer as a host of fans snapped their pictures.

Klondike and Lacey stopped by the camp entrance and watched with pride.

"Like the Colonel said," Lacey purred as they watched the scene. "Everybody loves our guys."

Klondike nodded solemnly. "It's been the honour of a lifetime to work with so much top talent."

Lacey rubbed at his arm. "They all came back. To perform for you, Kal."

"Right." He studied the group assembled before them, happily interacting with the fans. He looked at the faces, then closed his eyes, envisioning the many different circus posters his team had produced down the years. For so many shows.

"It's just like Corky always used to say," he proclaimed. "We are all stars. But, together, we are the heavens."

Lacey wiped her eyes at the reference. It was an oft-repeated line, quoted down the years by many within the troupe. "They are all stars, baby. Superstars. And they are all here for you."

He nodded. His eyes seemed to sparkle as he looked around the camp, and then back at his performers. The words practically burst from his mouth.

"I'm a lucky man. To have all the stars. All the stars in heaven."

EPILOGUE

A silver flash sliced through the clouds. Fast, sleek and impossible to detect from the ground.

The Learjet 23 multi-cabin, high-speed luxury craft had rolled off the assembly line just weeks earlier. Its curved, bulky design was like nothing ever seen up to that point. To anyone lucky enough to glimpse the ultra-modern jet, the plane would have resembled a space age contraption fresh from the realms of science fiction.

If the exterior of the jet was unusual in appearance, the interior confines were truly mind-blowing – an impossible display of opulence, high technology and exaggerated decor, unknown and unimaginable to the public.

The main cabin of the jet was actually a converted office. And it resembled the backstage area of a film studio.

Along one wall stood an enormous bank of television screens, eight in total. A desktop control panel alongside contained buttons and switches.

The set-up was part of a massive mahogany work desk, that curved around in a semi-circle.

To the side sat bookcases and filing cabinets, all lined up on plush burgundy carpeting. Padded walls ensured the roar of the jet engines was completely silenced inside.

A large, military-style door opened at the far side of the great, cavernous office.

A woman wearing a grey business suit walked in, carrying a large file and a roll of film.

"All set, sir?"

She was addressing a figure seated in a throne-like leather chair placed before the mighty desk, and the bank of screens.

Dressed in an all-white suit, with a turquoise tie, the man was middle-aged, tanned and had oily, styled blackish grey hair. Curiously, he wore designer sunglasses, despite the gloomy interior of the cabin.

"Let's have it, Jean."

The woman handed him a large manilla file, full of pages and black and white photographs, all neatly fixed onto a ring binder.

As he began examining the contents of the file, Jean placed the roll of film into what looked like a giant record player, set within a polished oak cabinet. She wound the film around its reel and fed it into a slot, then pressed a green button on a small control panel.

Suddenly, all of the television screens came to life, somehow joined together to project one big picture, like in a cinema.

Indistinguishable fuzzy nothingness filled the screen for several moments.

Then, the massive display burst into life. The film showed a tall man in a fedora and leather jacket walking inside a circus tent, carrying a gold-topped cane.

The figure wandered around inside, looking up at an empty grandstand, speaking to an unseen figure.

The seated man watched, then his cool blue eyes dropped to the file in his lap, and a photograph. It looked like an old studio portrait, and showed a man dressed as a cowboy, holding a knife in a throwing position. He turned the page. Another picture. This one showed the knife thrower a few years older, now wearing a suit and standing behind a podium full of microphones, seemingly a press conference.

The man looked back at the screen, and the fellow in the circus tent. The man on the TV was the man in the file.

"Kal Klondike," the figure said, seemingly in awe.

At that moment, another fuzzy blur burst onto the screens. When the picture returned, it showed a trapeze artist, leaping between circus rings, propelling himself through the air, while high above a watching audience of thousands. The picture changed abruptly to show the same figure performing a handstand on a circus ring, as it flew back and forth near the ceiling of a big top.

At the desk, the man flipped through a few pages in the file until he came to a full-size photograph showing the guy in the film. Hispanic looking, with slicked back, jet black hair, the man looked like a Hollywood film star from the golden age, his effortless smile enigmatic and dashing.

"Gino Shapiro…" the seated man whispered. He rubbed at his jaw as he watched Shapiro perform an incredible stunt on the film, launching himself high into the air and catching hold of a metal bar joined to the tent's roofing, before allowing himself to drop again, and landing on the swinging ring.

The man in the white suit turned the page in the file, and looked down at a picture of a bald, older man dressed in what looked like an Olympic wrestling singlet. A few minutes later, the film before him cut to grainy footage of the same bald man, riding a bicycle along a high wire – between two buildings in a busy city centre.

This time, the man in white gasped in awe.

"And Doc Irwin," he murmured. "This is incredible."

Jean had stood obediently next to the giant chair, watching the footage with widened eyes.

"What do you think, Mr McCready? Are they suitable for the project?"

The man called McCready continued watching the screens, as if in a trance. He answered without looking at her.

"No." He smiled, the eyes behind the sunglasses alive and enraptured. Something was stirring within him. A queer, almost hypnotic sensation. It gripped him, and he sat back with satisfaction as the hi-tech jet coasted on through the skies.

"They are perfect."